D0996827

Stage Fright

Stage Fright

Alan Dunn

PIATKUS

Visit the Piatkus website!

Piatkus publishes a wide range of bestselling fiction and non-fiction, including books on health, mind, body & spirit, sex, self-help, cookery, biography and the paranormal.

If you want to:

• read descriptions of our popular titles
• buy our books over the internet
• take advantage of our special offers
• enter our monthly competition
• learn more about your favourite Piatkus authors

VISIT OUR WEBSITE AT: www.piatkus.co.uk

First published in Great Britain in 2006 by
Judy Piatkus (Publishers) Ltd of
5 Windmill Street, London W1T 2JA
email: info@piatkus.co.uk

The moral right of the author has been asserted

A catalogue record for this book is available from the British Library

ISBN 0 7499 0806 8

Set in Times by
Action Publishing Technology Ltd, Gloucester

Printed and bound in Great Britain by
William Clowes Ltd, Beccles, Suffolk

Chapter One

It's a week short of midsummer. I'm sitting on a warm wooden bench in the lawned, shrubbed and flower-bedded sandstone cloisters of what was once an abbey, but is now the oldest part of a sprawling, modern university. The cloisters are friendly and intimate; I only wish that the City Metropolitan University shared those qualities. I'd hoped that Kirsty would choose to study further away to bolster her independence, but I suppose CMU is near enough for her to run home if she needs to. It's not, for the most part, a pretty place. It squats just outside the city centre in the shade of chemical works and cooling towers. Its buildings are the bastardised children of concrete polytechnic and red-brick teacher-training establishment, the city's art and technical colleges completing the unholy *ménage à quatre*. Like any unloved, unruly child it has outgrown itself, lost its way; it's a juvenile delinquent of a university, uncultured and rootless. If it has a redeeming feature, the car parks are extensive and free. And despite being only an hour's drive away from my own familiar home town, it is, to me, an alien place. I can only be glad my daughter arranged to meet me here, in the cloisters.

I'm waiting for Kirsty. As usual I'm early and, in the true family tradition, she's late. She's like her mother. If there was ever an important event that demanded us being in a certain place at a certain time, I'd always tell Sara we had to leave half an hour before the actual cut-off time. Eventually, of course, she learned to anticipate my deception and took some of my cushion time to get ready. It would infuriate me, anger would wash over me and our enjoyment would be spoiled before we even left home. But today I feel calm, tranquil. I feel content.

My eyes are half-closed, my head raised to feel the sun's warmth, and sound is suddenly important. I turn my head, focus on what I can hear. Two young people are watching their child take its first stuttering steps, launching itself from one pair of safe arms to the next. With each faltering footfall there's a high-pitched trill of happiness, a murmur of encouragement, an almost silent yell of pride.

A girl is sitting cross-legged in the shade of a cherry tree, reading to her boyfriend lying beside her. It's a poem, I can't hear the words but I recognise the cadence, the rise and fall, the rhythm of poetry. She slows as she nears the end, her voice falters; without opening his eyes the boy completes the poem and reaches up to wipe a tear from her cheek. She bends to kiss him.

Words wander past as if they have an existence of their own. Some are sad, alone; others have companions and form phrases or whole sentences. Where do they go after they've been spoken? Do they set off on adventures, braving new and unforeseen worlds? Do they recognise, once heard by their intended audience, that their task has been fulfilled? Do they then creep away to die in some hidden corner? Or do they linger through ages to tease and tantalise those willing to listen? If so, they're speaking to me now. The Latin chimes of some long dead monk preach with cool, sonorous syllables. A stonemason chisels a block of sandstone with some distant, hard-edged memory and complains at the weariness of life. A gardener croons to his roses. Two choristers argue over the correct notes of a psalm; disharmonies prevail.

The cloisters have all but lost their religious significance, but there's still an air of peace in the place. Even students, normally a boisterous, vociferous breed, are hushed in their passage. No phones bray, traffic noise is somehow abated; someone has put up a sign saying 'only pleasant sounds are permitted'.

I open my eyes. The rich, red stones in the walls are rounded by years, here pierced by sharp sunlight, there decorated with stalks of heavy-blossomed buddleia and vertiginous ivy. House martins dive from their haunts high in the crannied remains of the nave. The cloisters themselves are a dark shadow, re-roofed to provide shelter for those passing from one part of the university to another, hung with honeysuckle, clematis and wisteria. The square of grass they encompass is lush and green, its angular nature softened with beds of flowers and shrubs. The university has sent its undergraduates home for the summer, perhaps that's why it's so quiet. But why do I feel so content?

A familiar perfume reaches out from behind me. 'Kirsty?' I ask.

'Shh,' comes the reply. I feel her glide into place beside me on the bench, a faint touch of her thigh against mine, a butterfly kiss on the cheek. We sit together in silence, absorbed in being. The feeling I described earlier, the essential completeness and control of oneself for a brief moment, is there again. I begin to smile, turn my head to find Kirsty looking at me, her expression a mirror of mine. She sighs.

'Hold onto it,' I whisper, 'it doesn't get much better than this.'

The toddler falls and begins to cry. A jet rumbles overhead, the two young people turn on a radio. A cloud obscures the sun, a cat climbs onto the roof of the cloisters in pursuit of a mocking blackbird.

'And it doesn't last long,' I add. We turn to look at each other. If the jewel of the moment is transitory, then at least we can remember its setting. Eventually I break the silence. 'How are you, love?'

'Absolutely great, Dad.' Kirsty's happiness is tangible and infectious; she can barely keep still as she speaks, and her words are a torrent. 'I'm so pleased you can help out, we'd really be stuck without you.' She glances around her. 'And it's such a wonderful place to perform, we were down here the other night rehearsing and the moon was coming up, you've no idea how beautiful it was, and it felt like ... Oh, I don't know, I can't even begin to describe it.'

'It felt like you belonged,' I suggest, 'right there; right place, right time, exactly the right people. The rehearsal went well and afterwards you couldn't sleep, it was hard to come down from the high.'

She seems astonished that I should guess her feelings; not surprising, really, understanding women has never been my forte. But she quickly manages to hide her surprise. 'Dad, it was perfect. We'll never get it any better in performance.'

'You will,' I tell her. 'Just wait 'til you've got an audience in front of you. Lights ...'

'... camera, action!' She laughs aloud. 'Yes, I suppose you're right, an audience will get the adrenaline flowing. And you've got your part to play as well, isn't it great, the two of us working together! Do you want to see the set-up?'

I rise to my feet. 'Yeah. Come on then, tell me what I've let myself in for.'

Kirsty's excited, she's behaving like a little girl. She takes my hand and drags me across the grass. I glance back at my bag, it contains my work clothes, T-shirts and underwear, several pairs of socks. It was only after I'd volunteered to help that Kirsty told me the work would probably take a few days. When she said she'd find me a bed somewhere, I had visions of sleeping on the floor in her room, but she assured me that wouldn't be the case. 'We're all moving into a hall next to the cloisters, we'll need to be all together to set things up and some of us have to be out of our own rooms anyway.' I told her I didn't mind, as long as I didn't have to share sleeping space with

4

lots of good-looking young women. She promised me a room of my own.

She takes my arm, leads me forward. 'There'll be banked seats over there, at the back half of the cloisters,' she explains with a wave of her hand, 'except they'll be at an angle. You see, the stage is in this corner.' She points to the junction of two sides of the square where the abbey wall is at its highest. 'No curtains, of course, but we'll have some black cloths hung in the cloisters themselves, so the audience can't see the actors going backwards and forwards to the changing rooms.' She runs away from me into the corner, turns to face me and stretches out her arms. 'Ta-da! "This green spot shall be our stage,"' she bows and points at a tall shrub, '"this hawthorn brake our tiring house, and we will do it in action as we will do it before the Duke."'

I have to point out her mistake. 'That's not a hawthorn, it's a flowering cherry. And what do you mean, "do it before the Duke"? Is someone important coming to see you?'

Kirsty drops her arms to her sides, stares upwards, either in exasperation or searching for divine inspiration. 'It's a quotation, Dad. From a play. *A Midsummer Night's Dream.* You know? Shakespeare?'

'I thought you were meant to be doing *Twelfth Night.*'

'We are, Dad. But there aren't any appropriate quotations I could use from *Twelfth Night.*'

I wish I could contradict her. I wish I could find a quotation from any play at all to impress her, but I know only two; somehow neither 'When shall we three meet again' nor 'He's behind you' seems right for this occasion. I didn't like English lessons when I was at school. Oh, I could remember the action bits all right, I could – what did Mrs Lynch say I was doing? – re-tell the story of the play. But I couldn't remember any of the lines. I failed English Lit, got through the Language paper because I was good at analysing non-fiction and could use my imagination to write stories. But I've always felt I was missing something. I don't know Shakespeare's plays, I've never read Dickens or Austen or any of the Brontës. That's one of the reasons I said I'd help Kirsty. I thought at the very least I'd get to know a little more about one of Shakespeare's plays.

'So how far does the stage extend?' I'm returning the conversation to more solid ground.

'About here, I think.' Kirsty's walking a boundary line determined by a radius of about six metres, its centre the corner of the cloisters. 'Except it's not a curve, it's got three straight edges to it.'

'So how ...'

'And it's actually a wooden platform, on three levels, about twenty centimetres off the ground at the front.'

'Where ...'

'And some of the entrances and exits are from the side, or through the audience, so we'll have a scaffold at the back with someone working a super-trouper.'

I wait to make sure she's finished. 'Why not just call it a roving spot?'

'More romantic, probably. And I think it's a trade name.'

I look around. This shouldn't be too difficult. There are several places high on the abbey walls where it should be possible to fix lighting racks, and the cloisters roof is also high in places. I may not know much about the theatre, but I do know about outdoor lighting and its associated electrics. It would have been better, of course, to have a rig above the audience, but that's obviously out of the question. Some scaffolding either side of the stage should, however, do the job just as well, and it might even be possible to get some lightweight battens across, hang floods from them.

'What do you think, Dad? Can you do it? Is it possible?'

'When's the performance?'

'Wednesday to Saturday.' She's beginning to sound worried. 'This coming week.'

6

'I don't see why not. I'll need to talk to . . .' I can't finish the sentence, Kirsty's hanging round my neck. 'Hold on, young lady, hold on,' I gasp, disentangling myself from her grasp, 'what will people say?'

Kirsty looks around. 'What people? And even if there were any, they'd assume we were . . .' She breaks off, unsure how she might compliment me.

'They'd wonder how such a short, fat, bald man,' I go on, determined to finish, 'could have such a tall, attractive daughter. I'm just glad you inherited . . .'

'. . . Mum's looks *and* her brains? Don't be so modest, Dad, I've got GCSEs in Maths and Science, and I didn't inherit my logical thinking from Mum. *And* I can read a map the right way up, even when I'm travelling south. So don't put yourself down.' She stops and looks at me quizzically. 'Gosh, I'm beginning to sound like you as well.'

I decide to change the subject. 'So what happens next?'

'Well,' Kirsty glances at her watch, 'Vicky should be down here in, let me see, minus ten minutes . . .'

'You mean she's already late?'

'Yeah, she's far worse than me. And she's the producer, she has to organise everything. But she knows what Belle wants – Belle's the director, by the way – and somehow she manages to get everything done.'

'Is it an all-girl performace?'

'Good God, no! Too bitchy by far. No, there are some lads as well, you'll meet everyone tonight. And Jonathan Taylor – he's our tutor, this was all his idea – said he would come down to see you as well.'

I'm trying to work my way through the excesses of Kirsty's enthusiasm to some basic facts. 'So this Taylor person is the one who's really in charge?'

'No, Dad, it's a cooperative, we're all in charge. At least . . .' She realises she'll have to tell me quite a long story and decides it will be easiest to proceed at great pace and let me interrupt if I lose track. 'Look, it was Jonathan's idea in the first place, he suggested that his Theatre Studies

7

group raise funds for a permanent stage by putting on some outdoor performances this summer. Yes, I know cynics might say it's good for him as well, not to mention making sure his course gets full in future, but it's also good for the third-year students who want to be professionals, gives them an extra showcase. So we all agreed to do it, *then* he said we should do it as a cooperative. So we did, we elected a producer and a director . . .'

'Ah, democracy! Did you vote for the programme seller as well? And did the group decide which actors should take which roles?'

'Dad, stop it.' Kirsty can read me too well, she knows when I'm not being serious. 'Everyone auditioned for parts, except those on the technical side. Of course, the major roles mostly went to the third years, after all, that's what you'd expect. They've had more time to get really good.' She sounds as if she doesn't mean what she's saying, and I suspect there's a touch of jealousy there. Kirsty was always good at drama at school, she played lead roles in all the plays they did. I saw her perform once, not the whole thing, just the end when I finished a shift early. She was good, but I'm not sure how good; parents are either hyper-critical or over-indulgent when it comes to appraising their children's talents. But now it's clear that she's finding others better than her. I'm about to console her when she rushes on, talking as much to herself as to me.

'Still, Anna got a part, and she's just a year older than me. She's mad, though, mad enough to make it. I mean, I know my own limitations, I'm strictly amateur; I'm doing this to help me get a teaching job. But Anna's the biz.' She pauses, both to reflect and to gather breath. 'She'll make it, if she doesn't burn herself out first. And if she gets the grades for her written work, she's good at acting but has problems with essays. She's got a bit too much attitude.' She stops again, considering whether this brief portrait of a woman I don't know is fair. 'But she definitely has talent. In fact, there's quite a few who've got talent. I'm going to

8

keep in with them, one day I might need friends in high places.'

I'm beginning to forget what she was originally talking about, then it comes back to me. 'So why am I seeing this Taylor person? He seems to be strictly hands-off the whole project.'

'Jonathan, Dad, his name's Jonathan. And he's not hands-off. Quite the opposite really, most of the time his hands are on everything and everyone within groping distance.' She notices my eyebrows rise. 'It's all right, I can deal with him, he's harmless. It's only what the other girls say, and even one or two of the lads. He's a bit of a creep, he touches people. Not over the top, mind.' She drops into role, squints at me. Her fingers begin to dance in mid-air in front of me. Her voice is soft and breathy. 'Oh, my dear, you do look beautiful today.' She pats my forearm. 'Perhaps you ought to come and see me about that essay you submitted. There are some, uh, passages, yes, some passages require a little, how shall I say, exploration?' My distaste must show, she becomes Kirsty again. 'That wasn't very good, like I said, I'm not really an actess. Jonathan's nothing like that. He understands a put-down when it hits him between the eyes.'

'Something like "Keep your filthy paws off my silky drawers"?'

'Dad, I do believe that was a quotation.'

'Mm, I can cope with *Grease*.'

'Anway, JT's okay. And he does help out, he's just not the type to take credit. Doesn't want his name up in lights. That's my opinion, at least, though I don't know him well.' She bends close to me as if I'm a fellow conspirator. 'I'm not used to these theatre people.'

'Luvvies?'

'No, not that, that's a stereotype, Dad. No, I think it's that some of them are preoccupied. It's only university after all, but it's their whole life. And JT's like that.' She looks straight at me. 'You know, a bit like you were when you

9

were in the force. And afterwards. Before you met Jen.'

It's difficult being told by your daughter, even if she manages to do it politely, that you had little time for her when she was young. It wasn't that I was a career man, just that I was in love with the job. I wasn't in it because I had a burning desire to help the victims of crime, or because I wanted to bring criminals to justice. The justice was the least interesting part, it was the destination and I was more interested in the journey. No, solving crimes gave me the buzz I needed. I was always first to volunteer for extra shifts, I told myself it was to earn more money for my family, to keep them in a lifestyle they deserved. But that was a lie. I was simply being selfish, I was desperate to do what I loved doing. And Kirsty is right to remind me of that. There's a silence between us now, an awkwardness that threatens to cloud the day that, a few minutes before, seemed almost perfect; I'd warned Kirsty that such moments were fleeting, temporary, but I hadn't believed this one would begin to dissolve so thoroughly, so swiftly, in my own acid-bath of guilt.

'Kirsty!' The rescuing yell is loud, shrill, piercing, Glaswegian. 'Kirsty! Oh, there y'are. I'm so sorry I'm late. Or I'm sorry I'm so late.' The figure rolling across the lawn towards us appears to be a beach-ball with arms and legs. Its top half is a bright red shirt with a yellow tie; its bottom half comprises equally vibrant blue trousers, below which large polka-dot clown shoes beat an unsteady rhythm. The pink-faced woman wearing the garish outfit is conducting her monologue as if she were already on the stage. Her volume is impressive, not unlike that of a football manager issuing team instructions from the touchline. Her gestures are equally exaggerated, hands waving, head shaking. 'And you must be Mr Oliphant,' she shouts, 'Kirsty's father. Words cannot express my apologies. But then,' she changes her voice again to an ecclesiastical warning, '"words are grown so false, I am loath to prove reason with them."'

10

'Shakespeare?' I whisper to Kirsty.

'*Twelfth Night* this time,' she confirms.

The beach-ball won't be silenced. 'No, words just won't do. Instead,' she halts before me, her voice merely loud now, 'I shall abase myself.' She lowers herself to her knees, placing a bulging plastic bag on the ground before she does so, then stretches out in front of me, arms spread wide. 'Please forgive me,' she hisses, 'for my lack of punctuality.'

'Vicky,' Kirsty says, embarrassed, 'please get up.'

'Only if you and your father forgive me,' the muffled voice replies.

'I certainly forgive you,' I say, 'so please get up. I'm not used to having women prostrate in front of me.'

Vicky rolls to one side and squints up at me. She grins and her voice changes, it stops booming. 'I bet you say that to all the girls.' She rolls back again, pushes herself to her knees and then to her feet. She dusts at her trousers, takes a deep breath, holds out her hand. 'I'm Vicky Ellis, producer of *Twelfth Night* which is, of course, Shakespeare's answer to *Priscilla, Queen of the Desert*.' As I reach out my hand in turn, she takes hers away, raises her hand to stroke a non-existent beard, then offers her hand again. 'I'm very pleased to meet you.'

I shake her hand quickly, before she can remove it again. 'I'm Billy Oliphant.'

Although I'm aware that Vicky's outfit was designed to make her appear as wide as she was tall, Vicky's slim hands and face confirm that she's remarkably slight. I'm trying to figure out how such clothing might prepare her for a part in a Shakespeare play, and she catches my air of bewilderment.

'Kirsty hasn't told you, then, that I'd be coming straight from the day job?'

I shake my head, look at Kirsty who opens her mouth to speak, but Vicky shakes her head. 'No, it's okay, I'll explain.' She pulls her arms into the foam-rubber outfit and

11

adjusts something within, the costume slips a little and it becomes clear she's slipped some braces from her shoulders. 'Extra money at holiday time,' Vicky explains, pulls at some Velcro and the top half of the outfit splits open, 'I'm doing some street theatre as,' she pulls down the trousers with more difficulty, 'a very fat clown.' When she stands upright she seems to be no more than twelve years old, she's wearing a cropped shirt and baggy shorts that hang on her. 'I had time to take off the make-up but not the costume. Let me tell you, it's bloody uncomfortable trying to run with this on. And very hot.' She grins and laughs loudly. 'And I'm sorry I was so loud and silly, sometimes it's really difficult to get out of role. But I *am* pleased to meet you. You've come to our rescue, no doubt about that.'

I don't like being told that I'm rescuing someone. It makes me feel like a professional philanthropist, a primary-coloured, skin-tight-spandexed superhero. It makes me feel embarrassed because I know that my apparent altruism is driven by the selfish gene, the one that demands action only to promote the benefits of family. In short, if anyone but Kirsty had asked me to help, I would have said no. I'm not helping them, I'm helping her. But it would be churlish to point that out, so I smile self-consciously and say, 'It's not a problem, I'm pleased I can help.' That's when I realise how little I know about what I'm meant to be doing, about the form my 'help' will take. Yes, I'll be rigging up lighting for an outdoor performance. But I don't know what resources I have – there must be some equipment some-where in the university – and, more importantly, how much money I can spend on simple stuff like cabling, ducting and scaffolding. If Vicky's the producer, however, she might be able to help me.

'Kirsty's shown me the rough layout,' I tell her, 'but I need to know exactly what you've got already, where it's to go, what I can spend on ...'

'Ah,' Vicky interrupts, 'you need to talk to Belle about that.'

12

'That'll be Belle the director?'

'Yeah, ding dong. She's got some weird ideas of how she wants things doing, I'm sure they'll look great, but ...' Her words disappear into a foggy thoughtfulness, Vicky clearly doesn't believe that Belle's ideas will look great at all.

'So when can I meet Belle?'

'Um ... Don't know. She'll be here tonight, there's a rehearsal scheduled. Trouble is, she'll be rushing about being dictatorial.' She twists her face into a question mark. 'No, wrong word. Directorial, that's what I meant. It might be better if you talk to Kenny, he's the set designer.' She stops again, nods to herself. 'Now that *is* a good idea. Kenny could show you his model of the stage and the scenery. I don't think there've been too many changes.'

Kirsty interrupts, sounds almost apologetic. 'I don't want to anticipate problems, but I heard Belle and Kenny arguing yesterday about whether everything would work properly. She wanted some changes and he said he couldn't change at this late stage, she said his design wasn't workable, he told her ... Well, he wasn't very polite.'

'Oh, that's the way they are,' says Vicky, 'they're not happy unless they're arguing.'

I'm becoming worried. 'So when I meet them and Belle says she wants one thing, then this Kenny says he wants something different, whose instructions do I follow?'

'Kenny's,' suggests Vicky. 'Belle's,' Kirsty says at the same time. They glower at each other.

A deep, resonant voice prevents either of them confusing me further. 'If you are, as I assume, Mr Oliphant, then I think the best thing would be for you and I to discuss the production. You say what you can do with the limited resources we can offer, I'll tell you what we'd like, and we should manage to meet somewhere in the middle. I'm Jonathan Taylor, by the way.' The voice is everything. It's warm and dry and assuring, a doctor's handshake for the ears. It's in charge without controlling, it suggests rather

13

than commands, but at the same time it's aware that its suggestions are the only logical way to proceed. It's strong coffee and dark chocolate, velvet and old whisky. It's liberal and authoritarian at the same time. Turn the volume up and God's speaking to you; turn it down and it's your lover.

Even as he's speaking, as I turn to face him, I'm expecting someone old, someone whose face has been lined by time and experience. He should be bluff, red-faced and fat, or tall and stooping with an unruly thatch of grey hair. His appearance should command attention or even devotion, just as his voice does. But reality disappoints. To begin with, although he looks physically strong (his white T-shirt is tight and does little to hide a well-developed torso and muscled arms), he's shorter than me by two or three inches. It's as if some cruel deity has decided that he should be small to compensate for his large voice; Taylor has fought against this by working out, but this hasn't made him big, just small and brawny. I glance at his feet; they're encased in discreetly platformed shoes.

'I'm pleased to meet you, Mr Taylor.' I shake his hand.

'Everyone calls me Jonathan, or JT,' he says, 'although I know of at least one literary nickname circulating at the moment. Eh, Victoria?'

If Vicky is embarrassed she doesn't show it. 'Only one, Jonathan? I'll draw up a list of the others when I've a spare day or two. And I do prefer to be called Vicky.'

While Vicky's speaking, Kirsty mouths 'Curly' at me. I don't understand. Jonathan Taylor's hair is cropped, shaved to stubble. Is this an example of students' inverse humour? Or should I be linking words? Does 'short and curly' make the joke complete?

'Anyway, I'll have to go,' Vicky continues, 'I've another two sessions of clowning before I can come to tonight's rehearsal.' She throws her costume over her insubstantial shoulders. 'See you all later. Nice to meet you, Mr Oliphant. I'm sure you'll be, uh, quite safe. In Jonathan's

14

hands, that is.' She flaps a goodbye and waddles away across the lawn, towing the empty husk of her fat clown behind her and leaving me to puzzle whether she meant that last remark at anything more than surface value. Kirsty is ignoring me, taking great care to look away, finding much to examine in the antics of the young child's adventures in walking.

Taylor steps towards me, shakes his head. 'It's been a bugger getting everyone together for this production,' he says in an aside, 'so much enthusiasm at the beginning, but everyone's so involved in other things. Still, that's what they say, isn't it? "If you want something doing, ask a busy man."'

'Yes, I suppose that's true.'

'So thank you for agreeing to help us.' He reaches up, puts an inappropriate arm round my shoulder. 'I'd hoped, when I first suggested this project – a semi-permanent outdoor theatre – that we'd secure funding from the vice-chancellor. I proposed that we make it a regular occurrence. We could expand it, have other groups come in all the way through the summer. For example, the Open University uses the place for its summer schools. Now if we could agree with them to perform some of their set texts – Shakespeare, Beckett, Aphra Behn, Brecht – we could make a small fortune at the same time as providing our students with a valuable learning experience. But he said no. "Show me you can do it first on a small scale, show me you can make a profit, then I'll give you some additional finance." That's why I've had to get the kids – not that they're kids really, just that they're so young in comparison to you and me – to do so much.' He lowers his voice to a conspirator's stage whisper. 'And, between you and me, some of them aren't up to organising the prover-bial piss-up. But I've diverted a little money from here, borrowed some equipment from there, and the result will be a bloody good production. First night is Wednesday, today's Friday, all we have to do is build the stage, put up

15

the lighting and sound rigs, have a technical rehearsal, a couple of dress rehearsals, make sure everything's up to scratch and . . .let them bask in the glory.'

As he leads me across the lawn, Kirsty a subordinate pace behind, I try to ask a question. 'So what do you want me . . .?'

'Now then, this is the schedule so far. Later on this afternoon the stage will be arriving, portable blocks for the most part, some extensions to be added, that should be done this evening.' As he speaks, his hands are pointing at the extremities of the area where the stage will be situated. 'I've already had the lighting taken down from our studio, there isn't a lot but it should be adequate for the high floods and spots, we can run a scaffold pipe across the angle from there,' he thrusts to left and right with dagger fingers, 'to there. I've borrowed some extra stuff from the local amateur dramatic club – to be returned intact on pain of death – and we can wall-mount that, though only on the new timber parts of the cloisters. English Heritage won't let us touch their sandstone walls, even though the damn things are already falling down. Oh, and there are some freestanding modules as well.'

'So you want me . . .'

'Mr Oliphant! In due course, please. "I would be loath to cast away my speech, for besides that it is excellently well penned, I have taken great pains to con it."' He holds his hands out as if waiting for applause; when there is none he continues unabashed. 'Act One, Scene Five,' he explains, in case I haven't realised that he's quoting from a play. 'Now where was I? Oh yes, the set-up. The problem lies in making some sort of unity from this ragbag of equipment. There'll be a tower at the rear with a twenty-four channel lighting controller and a twelve input sound mixing desk. This is where you come in. What we need, Mr Oliphant, is the cabling to allow us control over our system. When Kayleigh told me . . .'

My daughter beats me to the interruption. 'My name's

16

Kirsty,' she announces haughtily.

'Oh, I'm sorry, Kirsty, you know how bad I am with names. And of course, your name's a word, "and to dally with that word might make you wanton," Act Three, Scene One, I believe. And, even with the paraphrasing, I'm sure your father wouldn't want that.' He returns his attention to me, my incomprehension sliding smooth from his oily popinjay feathers. 'Anyway, when Kirsty said you'd be willing to help us out with this ...Well, putting it simply, you've saved us, Mr Oliphant.'

Taylor pauses for breath. I'm already aware that this doesn't happen very often, so I take the opportunity to begin listing my questions, rather than waiting for each to be answered before beginning the next. 'I need to know where the nearest mains power source is, and the fuse box or boxes, I don't want to overload the system. Then I need the exact positions and wattage of each light. If you have cabling already I'll need to see that, it's too easy to get interference between lighting and sound systems if you're not careful. Access for fixing may be a problem, I'd rather not work from ladders, a mini-tower would be best. I can provide that, together with fixings.' It looks as if Taylor is going to begin again so I speak more loudly, a little faster. 'I can't do this alone, I'll need help over – let me see – the next two days, if we're to have it finished for Monday. Two bodies if they're inexperienced. Of course, you won't be able to rehearse properly on the stage if we're hanging lights. I'll have to work late, Kirsty said there'd be somewhere to sleep ...'

'Accommodation's no problem,' Taylor says confidently. 'I've requisitioned the ground floor of a hall of residence for the duration, two minutes' walk away. But as for the rest ...' He reaches into his pocket, brings out a dictaphone. 'Could you go over it again? I can't quite remember ...'

'Here you go, JT,' Kirsty says, flourishing a piece of paper in front of him, 'I've noted it all down.' She passes it to me first for scrutiny. I can read the invisible ink which says, 'You may not be able to remember my name, but at least I'm more efficient than you.' I check it, hand it to Taylor.

'One more thing, Mr Taylor. Have you thought about security? This place is open to the public, at least when the university's open. You'll have a lot of valuable stuff scattered around. Temptation for some.'

'Fear not, Mr Oliphant.' Taylor's back on familiar territory. 'It's past the end of term, so as soon as we move equipment in, all the internal doors will be locked. Security is the least of our worries.' He turns his eyes heavenwards, puts his hands together in an attitude of prayer and shakes his head. It's too dramatic to mean anything to me, but I know he wants me to ask what his main worry is. I don't want to put him out of his misery, so I remain silent. He strings out the moment. Still shaking his head, he glances downwards, clenches his teeth and inhales. He sighs. He lowers his hands, places his fingertips together and taps them against each other; the rhythm is first a solid beat, then a rippling arpeggio.

Kirsty looks at her watch. 'I'm sorry, Dad,' she says, 'I'm meeting someone at four. Rachel, she's in charge of costume. And I need a word with you before I go, so ...' Her voice is suddenly louder, she intends releasing Taylor from his spell. 'JT, surely nothing else can be worrying you.'

'Now? Now I've spoken to your father there's far less troubling me. The only major problem is with the cast.' He bends closer, he smells of mint and expensive perfume. 'Speaking in confidence, I do wonder if it was a mistake to give the kids quite so much autonomy. I'm all for them learning as they go along, but from what I've seen so far, they'll have to work very hard to get it up to performance standard. Still, *mea culpa, mea maxima culpa.*'

'It'll work out,' Kirsty says cheerfully, 'it always does. It'll be a rush but we've got you to lead us, JT. We'll just

18

follow your example. Now I just need a quick word with Dad.' She ushers me to one side. 'See what I meant? He's a good lecturer, good on the theoretical side, but in practical terms he's a ham. I'm a better actor than he is, and I'm assistant stage manager.' She can see I don't understand. 'Lowest of the low, Dad, general dogsbody. And don't believe what he said: Vicky's a bit of an airhead but she's got all the seats, programmes, posters and tickets sorted out. And Belle's good, really good. I just wanted to tell you, in case you thought you were getting involved with a bunch of amateurs.'

'But you *are* amateurs,' I point out with relish.

She shakes her head. 'Oh no, we're getting paid for this. Not a lot, but we get to keep a few pounds of the gate money if there's enough to cover costs. Which there will be, because you're working for free.' She kisses me on the cheek, pats me on the head. 'Who's the amateur?'

'You're a cheeky young madam, your father should put you over his knee and spank you.'

Kirsty puts on her I'd-like-to-see-you-try look. She sticks out her tongue at me. 'I'm sure JT would really like that,' she says, 'but I'll have to go. JT will sort you out. I asked him to give you a quiet room. I'll see you later. Okay?'

'Oh, one more thing. Do you call him Curly because he's cropped his hair, or because there's something pubic about him?'

She giggles. 'It could be either, probably is. But the real reason is that Belle said he reminded her of a character called Curley – in a John Steinbeck novel, *Of Mice and Men* – who's short and bad-tempered, always picking fights with big guys. That way, if he beats them, people say how strong he is. On the other hand, if he loses, people say he didn't really stand a chance. So really, he *can't* lose.'

'You mean Taylor attacks tall people?'

'No, Dad, we're speaking metaphorically.' She considers further explanation but decides I'm a lost cause. 'Don't worry, it's all to do with literary analysis. I'll see you later.' Then she's off, waving a backwards goodbye like Liza Minnelli in *Cabaret*. I may not know much about the theatre, but I can tell a good film when I see one.

Chapter Two

I turn my attention once again to Jonathan Taylor. He's taken the opportunity to collect my bag from the bench, he's swinging it gently in his right hand. He smiles at me, he seems pleased to welcome his audience's return. 'Kirsty's a nice girl,' he says, 'and I'm sorry I got her name wrong.' He does actually seem sincere, until I remember he's an actor. 'Do you ever call people by the wrong name?' he asks me.

'Sometimes,' I reply. Once – and only once – I called my wife by a former girlfriend's name. I was telling her I loved her. I decide that Taylor doesn't need to know that, and he's more interested in telling me about him than requesting further detail.

'I do it all the time, I really am hopeless with names. I have these techniques, for trying to remember names. When I meet them for the first time, I get my students to introduce themselves to the class and I do some word association. You know the type of thing. Someone says "I'm Sandy from Liverpool and I like football," so I try to imagine that person running down a sand dune in a red football shirt. I'd link a name like Peter to a rock, imagine him sitting on one. I told the students, I thought it might help them remember information for exams. But they started deliberately confusing me. Sandy would come in wearing a blue football shirt. Dave would come in and offer me a piece of seaside rock or mention he'd been rock-climbing. I used to insist on them wearing badges with their names on, but they swapped them around.' He shakes his head in wonderment. 'Always up to some type of mischief.'

I wish the young people I'd had to deal with when I was on the beat restricted themselves to such evils. Any Pete I met was more likely to throw a rock than sit on one, Sandy would kick grit in your eye to prove she could live up to her name.

'You'll find this little group really quite pleasant. But first things first. Would you like me to show you to your room?'

'That would be great, Mr Taylor. And I could do with somewhere close at hand, somewhere secure, to leave my van. It has valuable tools inside, and I can store cables and other equipment in there. And I need to know where to go to buy materials if I need them.'

'Let's do all that then. Room first – I'll show you the kitchens as well, we've agreed a food rota – then I'll get you a permit for your van. There's a space just outside the external entrance to the halls, the doorway leads through and into the cloisters, that would be a good place to leave it. Secure as well. Should we go?' He leads me across the grass to what will be the stage area. 'And then, let me see, what happens after that? Oh yes, everyone else should be arriving. I've arranged for us all to meet to discuss the way forward, at six of the clock. Then there's a rehearsal, you can meet the technical crew, sort out your schedule for the weekend. Now what else do I need do?' He pats his pockets with his spare hand, either for reassurance or because he's feeling for something. 'Oh yes, I remember.' He takes out his dictaphone and speaks into it, 'Remember to buy alcohol.' He realises he should explain. 'It's not for me, I assure you, Mr Oliphant. No, it's the start of the weekend and I promised everyone we could have a party. You're invited, of course. I'm providing the starter punch, a few cans and bottles, after that it's each to his own poison. Can

22

I get you a tipple of your preference?'

'I don't drink, Mr Taylor. But a few bottles of peach-flavoured still water would be welcome.' I reach into my pocket for some money but he's too quick, his hand grabs my wrist. His grip is strong.

'My treat,' he says, 'I'm sure the department's resources can stretch that far.'

In the corner of the cloisters there's a break in the wall. Taylor doesn't bother with that, he vaults the wall (my bag still in his hand) at its nearest point to a glass door. I head for the gap, I know my limitations. Before I can get there, however, he's blocking the way. 'Not superstitious, are you?' He points at a ladder leaning against the wall, above a door through which, I guess, we must pass.

I shake my head, 'No, I'm not superstitious. Why, are you?'

'No need to be,' he says ebulliently, 'I'm the seventh son of a seventh son.'

'Another quotation from a play?'

He puts his head on one side, almost like a dog. 'I don't think so. It might be a song. But seven is my lucky number. Not that I'm superstitious, I bring my own luck with me. Though I won't say the name of Shakespeare's Scottish play. But I'm definitely not superstitious.' He grins at me, waltzes twice around the ladder, then reaches out to touch the handrail beside the door. 'Touch wood.'

I'm not sure how to take him. Every time he says something he does it as if he's in role, as if he can't be himself. He waits beside the door. 'Through here,' he says, 'are the halls. They were originally the monks' cells or the refectory, something like that. Destroyed by Henry VIII – well, he managed to leave the foundations – the shell restored by some mad Victorian with more money than sense, converted into halls three years ago.' He punches a code into the pad beside the door, I can't help but watch and – with a guilty ease and almost criminal pleasure – remember the six digit code he uses, 1-1-2-3-5-8. I have no need to do this, I'm sure that if I were to ask him for the code, he'd tell me; after all I'll be using the door regularly to go into and out of the halls during my stay there. But I do it because I can, to keep in practice. The need to be devious will certainly arise again.

'Oh,' he says as he pushes the door open, 'the code is 112358, you'll probably need to get in and out this way quite a lot over the next few days.'

'Is that all you need to get in,' I ask as I step into a long, newly painted corridor, 'a six-figure code?'

'Good Lord no,' he chortles, a deep, bubbling old man's snigger he must have found discarded in an archive of lost laughter. He points at a card reader on the wall beside the door. 'Normally the card is essential as well, but security let me change the code while we're using the building and they don't want to issue new cards for such a short period of time.' He taps the side of his nose, a caricature of a retired major from an old black-and-white film. 'Too expensive, they tell me. So they've switched the card-reader off. They'll switch it on after we leave, change the code again. They're very security conscious.' He laughs again, twists his face into a leering grin and sucks, Lecter-like, at his bottom lip. 'Don't want just anyone to gain access to the sacred temples of our undergraduates' virginal bodies,' he whispers, 'that's a perk reserved for lecturers and professors.'

I can understand why Kirsty felt Taylor was creepy. He seems to change his personality without warning, but the characters he chooses are clichés. Perhaps he feels that, if his creations weren't instantly recognisable as creations, the people he's trying to impress wouldn't know he was acting. They might assume he really was as strange as he appeared; or they might think he was a lunatic with a multiple personality disorder.

'Now then, the keys are in the doors, they'll be taken as everyone arrives so I'd advise you to make your choice pretty quickly.' He opens the door to the nearest room.

24

'Not quite basic, there's a bed – big enough for one, two can fit if stacked vertically – wardrobe, toilet and shower. Rooms on the left catch the sun in the morning. There are two kitchens halfway down to left and right, a common living area at the bottom. If I were you, I'd pick a room as far away from the common room as possible, these youngsters do tend to be a little noisy late at night. I've claimed this one.' He points at the door nearest to the entrance.

'I'll take the one opposite, then.'

'Excellent!' He puts my bag on the floor inside the door. 'And now I'll hurry you quickly through the tour, if you don't mind. I've essays to mark and grade and paperwork to burn. Or is it the other way round?' He opens the door again, takes the key and hands it to me. 'Preciouss hass it now,' he lisps, bending forward, trying to lengthen his arms. Then he's back to what passes for his normal self, so quickly I'm not even sure he's aware of his momentary change. 'Now then, I need to show you where to park your van.' His passage further along the corridor begins but is interrupted by the arrival of two young people, arms locked around each other. 'Ah, Tom and Angie, how fortuitous,' Taylor declaims, hands together in an attitude of prayer. The couple half turn to face him; each has a hand tightly wedged in the hip pocket of the other's jeans, and they seem unwilling to withdraw. 'Hiya, JT,' they nod at him.

'Tom is our sound engineer,' Taylor goes on. 'Tom, this is Mr Oliphant, Kirsty's father. He's volunteered to install the cabling for the performances.'

The couple rotates again to face me. I can see their faces more clearly now. The girl, Angie, is round-faced with a beatific smile and golden hair to match her name. The boy appears to be exactly that, nothing more than a boy. He seems no more than sixteen, with unfashionably long curls of black hair and a downy moustache struggling unsuccessfully to add years to his youthfulness. He holds out his

25

spare hand with the embarrassment of someone who knows that this is the gesture normally used to greet a stranger, but who hasn't had a great deal of practice in its application. It's his left hand, but I shake it anyway.

'It's great you're helping out,' he says with what sounds like real enthusiasm. 'I mean, I can do the balancing and setting up, I've done quite a bit in studios, but I thought I might have to actually do the hard wiring as well and ... Well, I just couldn't have done it.'

'Yeah,' Angie adds, 'he was really beginning to get worried. Tom'll be a great help, as long as you tell him what to do.' Tom nods his head vigorously, Angie does too. Film them in slow-motion and they'd be walking adverts for hair-care products.

'Angie's in the play as well,' Taylor adds.

'But only a small part,' she hastens to explain, 'I'm Curio.' She must sense my lack of knowledge and hurries on, 'He's one of the lords at Count Orsino's court. And I'm a maidservant to Lady Olivia. And there's quite a bit of music in the play, so they get me to join in that because I can play the violin.'

'Angie's a very useful person to have around,' Taylor announces. 'I can see her being a great asset to the company in years to come.' He pats her on the shoulder; the couple step gingerly away, a small step, but noticeable both to me and to Taylor. 'Yes,' he goes on, 'I can imagine her in many, many positions. But Tom, can you do me a favour? I was going to show Mr Oliphant where he can park his van, just outside the other entrance. Would you mind guiding him? The two of you can discuss what he needs to get set up. And Angie, I'm in a little bit of a hurry, but I really do need to take you through your movements in the opening scene. I can probably spare a few minutes now, but ...'

'Angie was just going to get her stuff,' Tom interjects, turns to face her. 'Weren't you?'

Angie nods her relief.

'But we can show him where to put his van, it's on the way.'

'Very well. Another time. Perhaps I'll have the chance to get you alone this evening.' Taylor doesn't seem disconcerted by what even I can tell is a snub. He leans closer to me as the couple head down the corridor. 'Now don't forget, Billy, anything you need, let me know. I'll be in my office for the rest of the afternoon, everyone knows the number. When you know exactly what you need to buy, please let me know.'

'Come on, Mr Oliphant,' Tom yells. 'We'll show you where to go.'

'Ah, the impetuosity of youth.' Taylor waves me after them.

I follow Tom and Angie. Halfway along the corridor, just past the kitchen, there's a branch off to the right and an exit. They shuffle sideways and hold the door open for me. We step outside into the sun.

'Phew,' says Angie, 'that was close.' She reaches up to peck Tom on the cheek. 'Thanks, lover-boy. I'd better hurry, you know what Simon's like.'

Tom winks in reply. 'Tell him I enjoyed feeling your bum. See you later.'

'Yeah. Bye, Mr Oliphant.' She hurries away and I can't help feeling I'm missing something.

Tom can see the perplexed look on my face. 'Simon's her boyfriend,' he explains, 'he's one of my mates, we share a house.'

'So why the glued together routine?'

'Taylor protection.' Tom looks worried. He's said something controversial and he's not sure how I'll react. He goes on anyway. 'You heard him in there. He can be a real nuisance sometimes, always offering "hands-on experience" or individual coaching. It's all talk, and it's suggestive rather than in-your-face. But Angie's really keen on drama, she was desperate to be in this play even though she knew about Taylor's reputation. So I'm her

27

insurance policy. I look after her.'

I'm beginning to get worried; despite Taylor's protestations that he's misunderstood, he's my daughter's tutor. 'But you can't be around all the time.'

'No, that's why the girls stick together. They never go to see him alone, yet even then there's innuendo. More double entendres than in a *Carry On* movie. And he touches them, never rudely, just on the shoulder or on the hand.' He shrugs. 'I think he's harmless really, but it's better not to take risks.'

'Has no one complained?'

Tom shakes his head. 'I don't think so. The post-grads get to the freshers first and warn them, so they're well prepared. And, so far as I know, he doesn't do anything beyond being suggestive.'

'It still doesn't sound too good to me.'

'I agree entirely Mr O. But the thing is, he's good. He's not much of an actor, but he's a pretty good director and producer. And he has contacts. There'll be five or six casting agents come to see this performance over the four days it's on, his track record for getting people work is excellent. Not only actors, sound and lighting as well. So we put up with him. And we take precautions. We all help each other.' Having told me all he knows, he now sees me as a fellow conspirator. He can also recognise my concerns. 'There's no need to worry about Kirsty, she's got an old head on her shoulders. She can look after herself.' He beams into the afternoon sun, holds his hand up to his face. 'So where's your van?'

I find my bearings quickly. The van's in the visitors' car park, it's not too far but the short walk across the hot tarmac has me looking forward to the evening cool still four or more hours away. I find myself wishing I'd brought a hat. I wind down the windows before climbing in, but I still break into a sweat as soon as I sit down. Although the university term has finished, the car park is full. Even the dullest, dustiest metallic sheen reflects the jagged sun. The

28

heat dances like a thousand migraines. I see Tom in the distance, guiding me down to a safe landing in the fore-shortened shadow of the building.

'It's going to be pretty warm setting up in there,' I tell him.

'Yeah. There's never much of a breeze in the cloisters. So what do we do first?'

'Get the kit in, I think. Ladders, I've a scaffold tower in the back, drills and extension cables. Then we measure up, find out what we've got and what we need.'

'Sounds okay to me.' Tom reaches into a pocket and finds a hair-band, pulls his curls through it away from his face. 'Just tell me what to do, what to carry and where to go.'

Despite his youthful appearance and thin frame, Tom proves to be a capable worker. He doesn't complain when I ask him to carry the other end of a family of heavy scaffold battens, nor does he object when I ask him to pause because I need a rest. He also knows his subject. I'm pretty good at security systems, the live and passive electrics of sound and video, different types of lighting. I'm confident I can wire up a workable system; after all, the end hardware, the lights themselves and the micro-phones, are already known, even if they aren't yet in place; all I need do is make sure the cables are in place to provide electricity and information. But Tom fills in the gaps. He knows where individual lights and micro-phones are to be hung, he knows the positions of the auxiliary lighting tripods, he decides where the control box will be situated. He also shows me his pet project, his video camera. 'It's state of the art, digital, zoom mike as well as a zoom lens. I'm going to set it up in three different places on the first three nights, then move it around on the last two nights, I'll even get on the stage during rehearsals. Then I can edit it into a marketable form, might even make some money.'

I manage to calm him down without affecting his

enthusiasm and together we trawl the resources of the drama studio; within a few sweaty hours, we know what we're going to need to make everything work.

I've already gleaned a list of potential suppliers from the yellow pages, both electrical wholesalers and specialist sound and lighting companies. It's the work of a few minutes to pass on details of what we want, to extract promises of keen prices and swift replies. By six o'clock we're ready to hand over our costings to Taylor. We head for the common room where, in one of his visitations, he's promised there'll be a supply of cool drinks and food. He didn't mention that there would also be a large number of young people draped over every available piece of furniture. Taylor's hard at work, unpacking bottles and cans from a pile of cardboard boxes. Two tables are spread with plates of sandwiches and other food, and there's a large bucket of ice resting on a towel, its sides wet with welcoming condensation. Despite his duties, Taylor notices me as I enter the room. He waves me over, silences the room with a loud 'Shut up, rabble!' and hands me a very cold bottle of peach-flavoured water.

'Ladies and gentlemen,' he announces grandly, 'it is my proud privilege, honour, and delight to present to you, this very evening, at – thank God – virtually no expense, on and around a stage very near to you and your hearts: the pulchritudinous, peripatetic, pugnacious purveyor of provocative pieces (he'll have you all a-tremble with his tenacious terpsichorean tendencies), our very own wizard of the wattages, father of the gorgeous Kirsty for which reason alone he ought to be praised to the skies, I give you your own, your very own, Mr Billy Oliphant!' His pace and volume have increased as his introduction has progressed; his arms have begun to wave around; his performance has certainly captured the attention of his audience, most of whom appear to be regarding him with great embarrassment. Dress him in green and he could be Kermit the frog.

It's my turn to be embarrassed when the students – led,

I suspect, by Kirsty – begin a round of applause. I don't like being the centre of attention, unlike my daughter; I've never been a performer. I nod, acknowledgement and thanks together.

'I'll let the group introduce themselves to you in due course,' Taylor continues, increases his volume again as he speaks to the room at large, 'and can I remind you all that we have a rehearsal at seven. But for the moment – please do have something to eat, ladies and gentlemen.'

The move to the tables is slow and courteous. There are two recognisable faces – Angie and Tom – but most of the group is unfamiliar. Taylor materialises at my side with a tea-towel draped over his arm. 'Is everything to your satisfaction, sir?' he enquires unctuously.

'All under control,' I tell him, fish some battered sheets of paper from my back pocket, hold them in front of him. 'This is a list of what we need.' I point at the individual items in case he can't recognise a list when he sees one. 'I've already rung round to find the best local prices. This is the total. If you give me the go-ahead now I can get the cables and clips, the live electrical stuff, tonight.'

Taylor glances at the total. 'Okay,' he says, 'I'd actually thought it would come to about ten per cent more, then I built in a five per cent contingency. So if you need anything extra up to that limit, just get it, no need to check with me. Now then, payment. We don't have an account with those firms, but I can give you some cheques ...'

'I'll pay,' I tell him. His eyebrows rise, his forehead furrows. 'You can give me a cheque before I finish.'

'That's very kind of you, Mr Oliphant. There's really no need ...'

'If I need anything else I'll get it, but it'll be easier if I just bill you for the total. I'll keep the receipts, of course.'

'Excellent.' He likes the taste and the sound of the word, he splits it into syllables and rolls it round his mouth. It makes him sound like a villain in a James Bond movie. 'By the time you get back from your shopping trip the stage should be in place and the lighting gantry erected. You should be able to start putting everything together tomorrow . . .'

'Tonight. I've brought some floodlights, I'll be able to start tonight. I'd rather put the work in at the beginning and finish early than be pushed for time later on. So I'll get started tonight.'

'I'm impressed, Mr Oliphant. No wonder Kirsty's so diligent in her studies.' For once his words seem genuine, his own creation. But his voice is neutral, anonymous even, lacking in personality. Perhaps he only comes to life through his stereotypical characterisations, clichéd though they are. He nods to himself, genuflects, then moves away. Even as he goes he's assuming another personality, I can tell by the way he moves, the way he carries himself. I'm still trying to figure out which Taylor I prefer when Kirsty appears by my side. In her hand is a plate loaded with sandwiches. She links her arm in mine.

'You need to eat,' she tells me, guiding me away to a sofa. Taylor's in the midst of a crowd of young people, moving, touching, provoking a wave of antipathy wherever he goes. He's like a negatively charged pole, repelling others around him; indeed, negativity hangs over him, cloud-like, depressing.

'Bunk up,' Kirsty says to a girl I haven't met before, 'old man in need of somewhere to rest his arse.' She's obviously been drinking, just enough to allow her the licence to make fun of me. I don't mind. I believe that fathers have three main roles in life: the first is to be a source of money, and my bank balance reminds me every month that I'm certainly in command of that role; the second is to embarrass their children at inappropriate (usually when the greatest possible number of the youth's friends are present) and irregular times (that adds to the element of surprise) throughout their lives; and the third is to allow their children to make fun of them as a sign

32

of maturity. Kirsty is enjoying role number three. At some time in the weekend I shall return the compliment in role number two.

On the low table in front of me is a plate of sandwiches and salad, sausage rolls and vol-au-vents. 'I got those for you,' Kirsty announces generously, 'before the hordes descended.' She grins amiably, a little too readily; perhaps she's had more to drink than I first thought. She reaches for a bottle of lager and drains it quickly.

'Thanks, supergirl.'

'You're welcome. How did you get on with JT?'

I think back to his confession earlier that afternoon. 'He seems to want the best for everyone. But he is a little strange.'

'Yeah. But we all know about him, and I think he knows that we know. I think he's sometimes outrageous simply because we expect him to be. And he comes up with the goods for his students, finding them jobs and so on.'

'You're the second person to say that,' I tell her. She raises her eyebrows in a question and so I go on. 'Tom – I assume you know him, sound engineer – said exactly the same thing.'

Kirsty smiles again, a deeper smile, an undirected smile which – I suspect – has not been generated by the coincidence of two people thinking the same thing, but by thoughts of the other person. I decide to push the investigation. 'He helped me with my measuring, he's going to help with the wiring as well. He seems a very pleasant young man.'

'He is,' she nods, 'very pleasant.' Her smile is reaching from one ear to another, her expression is dreamily vacant. Her thoughts aren't with me.

'You been going out with him for long?'

The direct question brings her attention back to me. 'Dad!'

'Yes?'

She seems suddenly incapable of finishing her sentences.

33

'We're not . . .' She decides against a direct lie. 'We're just
. . .' She knows that would be embroidering the truth a little
too much. 'How did you . . ?' That's when she realises she
might as well tell me everything. 'About six weeks.' She
juts out her chin defiantly, threatening me to make any
further comment, ask any further question.

'I'm off sausage rolls at the moment. Trying to lose a
little weight.' I pat myself on the stomach. 'Would you like
mine?'

She relaxes. 'Yes please.'

I hand a plate to her, place two sausage rolls on it. I add
a sandwich resting on its crust as a nose, a samosa is a
triangular mouth. 'Is he kind to you?'

She smiles again. It isn't because of the face. 'Yes. He's
lovely.'

'Good. Nothing less than you deserve.'

She sighs in relief.

I missed a large part of her childhood, the change from
girl to young woman caught me by surprise and caused
some problems between us. She'll be wondering whether
I'm assuming they're sleeping together. I am. It doesn't
trouble me as much as I feel it ought to. Perhaps, like
Kirsty, I'm growing up as well.

'Ready for the guided tour?' she asks, breaking my
reverie.

'Taylor's already shown me round. I've even bagsed my
room.'

'No, Dad, not the place. The people. I thought you might
like to know who's who. I mean, I know you'll forget, but
I'll keep on reminding you. I make allowances for your
senility, you know.'

'You're so kind. Remind me to cut you out of my will.'

'You mean I'm in it at the moment? Okay, I'll remind
you. But you'll forget again. Besides, I'm such a loveable
character you won't be able to resist showering me with
money when you're rich and famous.'

'It's clear I should have beaten you soundly when you

34

were young and you wouldn't have turned into such a calculating young lady. Enough, tell me who your reprobate friends are, or I'll tell Tom the secrets of your youth.'

She's about to keep the repartee going, but she's not sure if I'm joking or not. She scowls at me; I try to look innocent. She opens her mouth as if she's going to argue, but my finger on her lips succeeds in silencing her. 'Your friends,' I remind her.

'Okay.' Someone has handed her another bottle without me noticing, or she has a secret supply hidden on the floor. 'Now then, who do you know already? JT of course. And Tom.' She smiles but doesn't blush. 'And Vicky's just arrived, late as usual.'

'And without her clown outfit. She looks almost normal.'

Kirsty seems almost affronted. 'Dad, this is a drama group. Don't assume that anyone here's normal. In comparison to this lot, even you're normal. And we all know how un-normal you are.'

'Abnormal,' I correct her.

'It was ab-necessary of you to remind me of that,' she declaims. 'Now then, anyone else you recognise?'

'Angie? The cute blonde girl over there? I met her before, she was with Tom. He was doing his protective big brother act with her.'

'Oh? Really?'

The jealousy isn't difficult to detect. Tom said Angie was going out with his flatmate, but Kirsty's reaction suggests the relationship might not always have been so semi-detached. I hurry on, I don't want to get involved any further. My shoulder's Kirsty's, crying on for the use of, but I value my life too much to take any pro-active role, objective or subjective, in my daughter's love life. 'Everyone else is a stranger,' I tell her, 'so fill me in. Not that I'll remember who's who. But you can give me a test later on this evening.'

'These students, they all look the same. Especially

35

through a haze of alcohol.' She thinks about what she's said. 'Sorry, Dad, not that you'll have any problem in that area.'

Vicky's heading towards us now, threading her way past bodies thrown randomly into her path. She reverses neatly onto the arm of the sofa then slides down beside me, pushing me over towards Kisty. 'My feet 're killing me,' she announces, 'and I never want to see another child again in my entire life. D'you realise how unpleasant they are, Mr O? I've had ice-cream thrown at me, sweets dropped down my cleavage and my bottom groped.'

Kirsty's quicker than me. 'And that's just the fathers.'

'Ha ha ha. Y'know that juggling trick I do, where I get somebody to throw a fourth ball in? Well, I chose someone trustworthy, least that's what I thought, and the little bugger swapped my ball for a raw egg! And he didn't just throw it for me, he threw it at me!'

'I expect it got a laugh, Vicks.'

'Not as much as when I chased him to give him his reward.'

I'm not quite working at the same speed as the girls. Kirsty's trying to keep her mouthful of beer in her mouth and Vicky's doubling up with laughter. 'Tell me,' I whimper, 'what's the joke?'

'It's Vicks' reward trick for people she doesn't like,' Kirsty giggles, red-faced. 'Go on, Vicks, show him.'

Vicky holds her hands in front of her. 'Well,' she says, 'it's like this. One hand holds the reward, chocolate or something like that, but ice-cream is best. As long as it's soft and squidgy. Then the other sort of encourages, like this.' Her left hand is hovering in front of my nose, and I can feel her right rest gently on my shoulder. I try to pull away, but it merely brings my nose closer to her left hand. 'See,' she continues, 'you're stuck. And that's when I do this.' She quickly nips me on the back of the neck and, as my head jerks forward, lightly taps me on the nose. 'I can usually get three or four painful nips in before the kid

36

bursts into tears, and the audience thinks it's just because the kid's overwhelmed by the occasion. Works every time.' She wriggles back down into her seat.

'And I thought you were a pleasant young lady,' I tell her.

'Oh no. Appearances can be deceptive, Mr O. Especially round here, remember, we're all actors. What you see is definitely what you don't get.'

'So this is Vicks, child torturer,' Kirsty continues. 'And over there, by the window, see the couple talking to each other? The girl's Belle, she's the director. She's destined for great things.'

'As an actor?'

'No, though she could be if she wanted. World dictator's more her career path. I'd love to know what she's doing here instead of Oxbridge but I'm too frightened to ask her. She's clever. She talks about Shakespeare and I don't understand a word she's saying.'

'Y'know,' Vicky adds through a mouthful of chicken, 'she knows the whole play.'

'Well she should, shouldn't she? She *is* the director.' I can't help thinking I've missed something again, but Vicky painstakingly explains.

'No, Mr O, y' misunderstand. She knows the whole play by heart. Every line. Every word. She only has to hear it two or three times and she remembers it. Y'know how, when you're little and you go in the car, your parents play you tapes to stop you whining. Kids' songs, "The Wheels on the Bus" and so on. Well apparently her parents – both of them English teachers – used to play tapes of Shakespeare plays. And that's when she found she had a photographic memory.'

'It's only photographic if you remember things you see,' I point out pedantically, 'if you remember things you hear it must be, well, a phonographic memory, I suppose.'

'Yeah, whatever. But she remembers.'

Belle is, interestingly enough, the type of person who

37

doesn't stick in the memory at all. She has no striking features. Her hair is shoulder length, nondescript brown. It frames a round, worried-looking face, though I can't see why I should think this because her eyes are hiding beneath a pair of glasses too large for her small nose. Eyes are the character, the personality, and if I can't see them, why should I imagine she's worried? I move on to look at the rest of her and realise why I made that assumption. She's dressed in a medium-length skirt, a blouse and cardigan, and her shoulders are hunched. She's tense, her empty hands are fists by her side. She's escaped from a 1950s costume drama where she's been cast as the brainy grammar-school girl with no interests except books. I wonder, without the urge to find out if I'm right, whether she'll become wild and liberated if someone removes her glasses from her demure face.

'The guy she's talking to,' Vicky continues, 'is Kenny. He's the set designer. He's probably arguing with Belle right now, complaining that he can't get things done the way she wants them, or there isn't enough money, or there isn't enough time.'

'Yeah, he's miserable,' Kirsty agrees, 'never happy unless he's picking faults. And he's got appalling taste in girlfriends.'

'Watch it, shit-for-brains, you're talking to a Glasgee lass here. I'll have you!'

'I take it,' I say, feeling a little happier with an antagonism obviously built on friendship, 'that you're stepping out with Kenny?'

Vicky leans forward, puts her chin in her hands and gazes across the room. 'Yeah. Isn't he gorgeous.'

Kenny's sharp-nosed and eager-eyed, his hair shaved close to his thin head. His hands move rapidly when he speaks and are thrust into his pockets when he listens. It's as if he fears that, like a hyperactive child, they might escape unless they're locked safely away.

'Are they really arguing?' I ask.

Vicky sighs. 'It's amazing how often Kenny's discussions turn into arguments. And he and Belle don't get on that well. So ... Yes, I suppose they are.' She looks at Kirsty. 'D'you think I should rescue them from each other?'

Kirsty nods. 'Use Dad as an excuse. Say he needs to talk to Kenny.'

'Oh no,' I tell them firmly, 'I'm no arbitration service. And anyway, I'll have to go soon, I've stuff to pick up.'

'Coward,' Kirsty hisses. 'Okay, I'll tell you who everyone else is in two minutes flat. Rachel over there, the stunning redhead, she's lovely and I hate her cos she's so good-looking. She's in charge of costume. See the handsome guy by the table, the one looking at the girl's tits?'

'Kirsty! They'll hear you.'

'Dad, it's true. He's George, our Count Orsino, looks of a God, brains of a pea. The object of his attention is Lorna, she plays Olivia. Orsino fancies her in the play but she doesn't fancy him. Bit like real life. Now, who else is there? Yes, see over by the door, fag in hand, the girl with blue hair standing by herself? That's Anna, I mentioned her earlier, natural actor, bit of a goth, I don't really know her that well. Bit strange. She plays Viola, the play sort of hinges on her performance.'

Anna looks unusual. Her hair is the bright, fluorescent blue of the perfumed ink in teenagers' pens. When she moves there's a metallic glint of piercings in nose and ears, eyelid and lower lip. Her face is asymmetrical, at some time her nose has been broken and it's slightly off centre with a small bump at its bridge. Even when she isn't talking or moving she's the opposite of Belle, flamboyant and confident, loud and extrovert.

'The boy with the spiky hair is Rad, he's funny.'

'Ha-ha or peculiar?'

'Both. He's an ace musician – you name it and he can play it. He tells the rudest jokes. And he's a great mimic, he can do anyone, any voice at all. And he's great at street theatre, he juggles and rides a unicycle, he breathes fire. Look at his eyes, they're wild. He's Feste, the jester.'

'You mean a clown? Like Vicky?'

'No, Dad,' Kirsty sighs, 'clowns and jesters in Shakespeare's plays were allowed to do things other people weren't, like being cheeky to their betters.'

'Oh, you mean it's the same as with daughters these days. But go on, there are lots more people waiting to have their characters assassinated.'

Kirsty sticks out her tongue, the last refuge of someone with no defence against logic. 'Okay, Father dear, let's see who's left. Oh yes, the tubby guy with the pint in his hand, the one with the goatee. That's John. He's not doing drama, not even doing Arts, he's a chemist or a physicist or something, so I don't see that much of him. But he's sweet. He's playing Sir Toby Belch, Olivia's drunkard uncle.'

John sees us looking at him and waves genially. He's made up of concentric and overlapping circles, an exercise in how to draw; his round beard and moustache offset from the centre of a round face set in a round mass of black curls, all this above a round body. He nudges the boy he's talking to, a tall, pale, scowling stick-insect of a youth who looks as if he'd snap in two if a light breeze caught him. He peers owlishly at us, then performs a deep bow.

'Louis,' Kirsty explains disdainfully, 'engineer.' It's as if the one word explains a whole catalogue of personal shortcomings. 'Plays Sir Andrew Aguecheek. Typecast.'

It's clear I'm going to receive no further explanation. Two girls are escaping from a conversation with Jonathan Taylor, they mouth their relief as they come towards us.

'Siobhann, Natalie, this is my Dad.'

'Hello, my Dad, I'm Siobhann.' A tall young lady with a red, vacuum-cleaner mouth and wide-spaced eyes shakes my hand. Her hair cascades almost to her waist.

'I suppose I must be Natalie, then,' the second observes. 'Hiya Mr Oliphant.' She's delicate, almost elfin in comparison to her friend. 'What do you think of this bunch of lunatics?'

'They seem quite pleasant to me.' This is clearly the beginning of one of those meaningless conversations from which escape is almost impossible, and I'm already looking for a way out when Taylor's voice foghorns through the chatter.

'Ladies, gentlemen and any others present. I realise it's not yet seven, our scheduled rehearsal time, but all of you have been here for long enough to eat a little and drink too much, so I think we ought to get started in – now what would be reasonable – five minutes' time?' He ignores a chorus of groans. 'There's a lot to do and little time to do it. However, we'll finish at ten and I assure you there will be further copious supplies of alcohol available.' The groans turn to cheers. 'Now then, Belle, you'll find, in a box under the table, a large number of small digital cameras borrowed from the philistines of the media studies department.' Belle dutifully brings out a cardboard box and displays its contents to the crowd.

Taylor holds up his hands to bring comparative quiet again. 'I'd like you to use them to photograph anything and everything you see that could be of interest. Do not—' the volume increases to counter the swell of laughter that has begun '—do not photograph anything which may be construed as pornography. At least, not without checking with me first. Seriously, people, this will allow me to put together an exhibition showing how we've managed to create our show. I want everyone to see how good you really are!'

There's a round of applause and cheers. Taylor lets it subside before he begins again. 'This is, however, your last opportunity to indulge your excesses for a week. Tonight, the bacchanalia commences! But from tomorrow you'll only have time for eating, sleeping, performing and shitting yourself with nerves. Now go to it!'

Taylor's rather unique method of inspiring his troops

41

may not succeed in motivating them, but it certainly moves them from the room. I join the flow, keen that I shouldn't be left behind with only Taylor for company. I find Tom waiting for me, squatting on the grass beside my van.

'Hello, Tom, what can I do for you?' I'm tempted to ask him if he's come to request the hand of my daughter in marriage, just to see what his reaction would be. I curb my warped sense of humour.

'I thought you might need some help. There's nothing much I can do with my mixing desks until everything's set up, so I can come with you if you want, help carry stuff. Or I can start putting up scaffolding and ladders, if you tell me where you want them.'

'That's kind of you. There's not really much to carry that's heavy, so if you're happy to get to work on the scaffolding . . .'

'No problem, Mr O. Do you want to work towards or away from the stage?'

'Towards. That way we won't interfere too much with the rehearsals.'

'Okay. See you later.' He shoots me with his index finger then shuffles away in that strange, rolling, ape-like manner beloved of young men, perhaps prompted by the low-slungness of his jeans.

I open the doors of the van; it's hot inside despite the shade in which the vehicle has been sheltering. I wait for a while. It's a pleasure to be alone again, if only for a few minutes. It's not that I'm nervous in a crowd, but I do normally avoid them. I prefer to be with one or two people, to listen to everything everyone says; in a crowd conversation becomes a mumble of inconsequential, unconnected words. I can't recall many of the names Kirsty mentioned, and the faces have become a series of homogeneous clones; even male and female have become difficult to differentiate. It doesn't matter a great deal to me, my contact with them will be limited. I'll be too busy working to talk to anyone except Tom; I'll show

42

face for a few minutes at the party, then mention how tired I am; and with having the room at the far end of the corridor, I might even be able to get some sleep. If the noise should prove too great, I have the option of taking the mattress and quilt from the bed and spending the night in the back of the van, safely moved to some distant, more quiet spot; tidiness won't be a problem.

When I get moving, I find that driving with the windows down is pleasant. The day's latent heat is still shimmering on the mirror-like roads, pedestrians are clad in shorts and T-shirts or less. They walk slowly, sipping from bottles and cans. In contrast to snakes and lizards which absorb the sun's rays and increase their metabolic rates, people are slowed by the heat. Fractious children demand ice-creams and receive only pleas for quiet in return; boys are too hot to raise a whistle at halter-clad girls undulating their bodies in slow motion. There's a smell of spice and diesel, perfume and sweat, sublimated lust. Even the flowers in the municipal beds, shaped and planted in heraldic lions and unicorns, are wilting, desperate for the evening visit from the water truck. Old women are sitting on doorsteps, men clad in vests and pensioned suntans waft the air with the late final. Dogs in bad-tempered yards curse the unremitting brightness, cats slink from shadow to hard shadow, paws dancing over scorched pavements. The heat is unnatural. Overhead a weft of parrots sails over fabric jungles of tall green; small invisible monkeys screech the arrival of tropical weather; elephants and gazelles remain hidden in distant garages and bus-shelters, waiting for dusk before venturing to the nearest water-hole. The air is filled with the immobility of impending madness. And, after a short drive, I find that the electrical wholesaler where I intend buying my cables and clips has no air-conditioning.

The evening passes in a curious rush of activity. Tom and I, working from our vantage points up ladders and hanging from scaffolding, can see most of what's going on around us. Although we're working hard, concentrating on what we're doing with me yelling instructions along the length of the cloisters, the busyness of the rest of the group sometimes intrudes. Almost all of those who'd gathered earlier to eat and drink and talk are now carrying on their interaction in the stage area. The platform itself is being put together around them by four men of my age who I assume are porters or site managers from the university. Belle, one of the few individuals whose face and name I can recognise and match, is trying to direct actors, stagehands, workers and any others who wander into her sphere of influence. Like Taylor, she possesses a voice which seems at odds with her appearance. From the depths of her round-shouldered frame she can summon a volume and pitch to halt those around her in their tracks. It has a physical presence; people move around it, change direction to avoid its sharp edges. I would hesitate to attempt controlling such a diversity of tasks and individuals, but she seems able to do so with a formidable ease. And the auditorium is taking shape.

Taylor motions to one of his charges, the girl with the blue hair, Anna. He's carrying a roll of fabric, it looks as if he's going to discuss costume with her (and her attitude demonstrates her lack of enthusiasm for the task) until he rolls it onto the floor with a flourish. Within are four or five swords and a selection of daggers. He selects one of each, she does the same, and they move through a clearly choreographed set of movements. There's no malevolence in their swordplay; quite the opposite, both seem bored with their roles, secure in their knowledge of what the other intends doing.

Kirsty waves and smiles as she hurries past me, does the same to Tom. She can see us looking at the swordfight. 'Anna plays Viola who disguises herself as a man, Cesario, so she can go and work for Count Orsino. She's in love with Orsino, of course, but he can't love her back because she's a man and anyway, he's in love with Countess Olivia. Orsino sends Cesario to woo Olivia, but Olivia falls in love with Cesario, who is, of course, really a woman. With me so far?'

'No,' I answer honestly, 'and you still haven't explained the swordfight.'

'Ah, that's because Olivia's Uncle Toby has a friend, Sir Andrew, and Toby wants Andrew to marry Olivia. Toby has Andrew challenge Cesario to a duel because Cesario's in the way. The trouble is, Andrew's a bit of a coward, and Cesario's really Viola and she doesn't have much experience at swordfighting. So their duel's a bit of a non-affair.'

'But Anna looks pretty good with swords.'

'That's the whole point, she is. That's why JT's taking her through the fight.' She comes closer, speaks more softly. 'Louis, he plays Andrew, is pretty hopeless in the swordfight. He's not a good actor, in fact he plays himself, but that's the type of person we need. In effect, Anna has to act for both of them in the swordfight, she has to control the whole thing. She has to act as if she isn't very good, she's got to unlearn her swordfighting. Does that make sense?'

'Sort of.'

'Don't worry,' Tom adds, 'I've been to rehearsals *and* I've read a summary of the plot, and I still get confused.'

It seems more difficult for Anna and Jonathan to fight badly. There's a lot of slowed down action, deliberate misses, wild swipes.

'I take it they aren't real swords and daggers,' I say. 'That would be really dangerous.'

'Well,' Kirsty says, 'they're real in so far as they handle like a real sword, they've got good balance. But the blades aren't sharp, the points are blunt and they have little plastic buttons on the end.' She sneaks forward to the open bundle, brings a dagger away with her. 'These are great, they're spring loaded.' She holds it in front of her chest then thrusts; it appears as if the blade penetrates to the hilt. 'And if you want to cut someone's throat, you just put red dye in the little chamber here,' she holds the knife up to me, there is indeed a small hollow in the handle, 'and squeeze. It's like a pen, you just draw the cut on the flesh and it oozes blood. Smart, eh?'

Anna has evidently been losing patience with her instructor. He spins her around and smacks her on the backside with his sword in what may be part of the play. It's obvious that she doesn't think so, she turns swiftly and aims an overhead blow at Taylor's head. He defends himself but doesn't counter-attack, he gives way to Anna's onslaught until his sword is sent spinning from his hand. She takes her own sword and thrusts it into the ground between his feet before stalking off.

'I wouldn't like to be in a fight with her,' I tell Tom. He nods in agreement.

'Jonathan knows her well enough to let her win,' Kirsty tells us with a certainty that demands agreement. 'I've seen him before, he's really good. See, Anna's gone to join the others. If he'd won she'd have started sulking and left altogether. Anyway, I'd better go myself, don't want to get on the wrong side of our glorious leader.'

Three of the actors are speaking their lines, hiding behind a large plastic plant-pot containing a very small shrub. Their performance is, to me, pantomime; I can't hear clearly what they're saying, but their actions tell me enough for me to distinguish their individual characters. I find myself watching them instead of working. One of them, a girl, carries a letter. She places it on the ground, she and two others (the tubby young man and his tall emaciated companion) wait for a fourth person to enter, to find the letter and – it seems to me from my viewpoint of height and ignorance – to express feelings of love and desire, unaware that he's being watched. Only when I look around and see Tom watching, see the stagehands watching, see each person in the cloisters focused on the still incomplete stage, do I sense the atmosphere of excitement. Everyone is contributing in some way. Everyone feels part of the magic. Everyone feels part of the team.

46

I return to my task. It's late on a Friday evening, I should be at home enjoying the cool end of a long day. I should be watching Jen, waiting for her to look up from her reading, glance at me with bedroom eyes. Instead I'm up a ladder trying to fix cables to a wooden batten half hidden by centuries of ivy. I'm hot and dirty, my shirt is stained dark by sweat, small insects are exploring bodily crevices I've never seen except in a mirror. I'm not being paid for this work, but I can feel a sense of pride, I can feel a smile on my face. I'm enjoying myself.

Chapter Three

Everyone is replete with the success of the evening. The stage is in position, its separate levels and easy access providing the actors with a springboard for their performance. They seem amazed that Kenny's stage plan and set design (until now existing only as a chalk outline on a rehearsal room floor) actually work; people don't bump into each other, entrances and exits are smooth. The lighting gantries are in position, with the first lights already hung and tested – my cables and wiring stand up to the test. Racks of seats have arrived and are stacked along the side of the cloisters, waiting for the lawn levels to be checked, timbered and boarded. My halogen work-lights have been useful, they (and the late evening sun) have allowed us to work on; Taylor has had to order people to stop, it's clear he's worried about us being too tired to do anything at all tomorrow. Even then, it's only when I switch off the current to the cloisters and the lights dim that shadows drift away to the halls, preparing for the next bout of hard work.

I can hear from my room that the party's begun; there's a high-pitched beat and a melody that the walls are able to muffle, but the bass drum echoes through the walls, the ceiling, the floor and my chest cavity.

I decide to shower before joining the young people. It did occur to me that I wouldn't be missed, that if I waited long enough I might be able to avoid going along to the lounge to see the type of debauchery for which students have become famous. But even as I'm drying myself, Kirsty's knocking on the door, arranging to meet me in a few minutes. I can't avoid spending some time with my new and temporary colleagues. But first ...

It's later than I thought, and when the phone is picked up Jen sounds sleepy.

'Sorry, did I wake you?'

'No,' she yawns, 'not quite. I was reading and watching the TV at the same time, and next thing I knew the phone was ringing. So I'm pleased you rang. Actually I'm double pleased because it's good to hear from you. How are things going?'

I tell her, briefly, about the day so far. She asks questions in all the right places. Her day, in comparison, has been quiet. She's doing ad hoc locum work for several GPs, as well as helping out two days a week as a surgical registrar and one afternoon at a GUM clinic. That's meant a lot of extra reading, catching up with best practice in several different fields. That's why I haven't felt too guilty about coming away this weekend, Jen has encouraged me to do so. We chat about Kirsty, I tell Jen about Tom and she asks questions about his looks and personality that I can't answer because, according to her, I just haven't been paying attention to the important things.

'But I don't look at young people's backsides,' I protest, 'how do I know if he's got a "nice arse"? And anyway, I don't like this concentrating on physical appearance. What's more important, what he looks like or whether he's kind to Kirsty?'

'Both,' Jen answers too quickly. 'After all, I often comment on your furry little Hobbit bum.'

'But it's not the most important part of me.'

'But it is *an* important part of you. Like most other parts of you, come to think of it. Take any one of them away and life would be far less enjoyable. Take some away and life would be less enjoyable for both of us.' She pauses to let me think what she might be referring to. 'And take some parts away and I'd murder you.'

I ignore the threat. 'But they're complementary. They add up to less than the whole. You can't consider them in isolation.'

Jen reconciles herself to a detailed discussion, what some people might call an argument. 'Come on, Billy, that's not true. Yes, they're less than the whole, but that doesn't stop you looking at, or talking about, the different bits that go to make up the whole person. I mean, how often have you heard somebody saying "Look at the tits on that!" and you agree with them. Bodies are important, believe me, I'm an expert. Both professionally and personally.'

'Are you feeling more awake now?'

'Don't change the subject because you're losing the argument, Billy Oliphant!'

'Why not? Can you think of a better reason for changing the subject?' I let the statement sink in. She'll be wondering now whether she's persuaded me to her point of view, or whether I can't be bothered to argue any more. Then, because she's intelligent, because she knows me well, she'll realise that there's little point in arguing over the phone anyway. Whenever we argue at home we resolve the dispute in bed. We can't do that now.

'How's your room?' she asks. 'Is the bed comfortable?' It's another change of subject. It's a sign that we're thinking together.

'The room's small, the bed's small. But it's still too big without you.'

'I know. I'm used to you, Billy. I don't think I'll sleep well tonight.'

I deliberately misunderstand her. 'Yes, too hot. Just sleep with a sheet.'

'Are you fishing for compliments, Oliphant?'

'Yes. Have you got any on offer?'

'You know exactly what I mean. I'll miss having you in my bed. Our bed. I'll miss hearing you snuffling in your

50

sleep. I'll miss the way you pull the bedclothes off me. I'll miss the feel of you next to me. I'll miss the way you wake me up on Saturday mornings.'

'Keep this up, Jen, and I'll be on my way home now.'

'Really? You mean it turns you on?'

'*You* turn me on.'

'I should damn well hope so.' She yawns again. 'I think I'll have to go to bed now. How about you?'

'I've been summoned to a party.'

'A party? Who'll be there?'

'Oh, Kirsty and her friends. The kids helping out with the production. It's just down the hall. I won't stay long.'

'I bet. All those young, good-looking girls. You just save yourself for me, Oliphant. When do you think you'll be getting back?'

'Probably Sunday. Saturday night late if we really get a move on. But I don't think this lot will be able to make an early start tomorrow, and some of the things, like positioning lights, will need the director and most of the cast on stage. I'll ring you to let you know.'

'Well make sure you do! I might want to have a little surprise waiting for you when you get in.'

Being away from Jen for a year when she was in Canada was difficult for both of us. Regular face-to-face communication was awkward to arrange, emails were perfunctory, unsatisfactory. At first we spoke briefly every other day, then once a week; we wrote less often and in less detail. There was a time when I wondered if she would return and, if she did, whether she would want to come back to me. She may have felt as unconfident as I did, but when she came back, when we met again at the airport, there was no need to even mention my worries. Simply being together solved all problems, at least in the short term. No, that's not true. There's no need for a qualification. I'm never happier than when I'm with Jen. Just thinking of her makes me happy.

'Go on, then,' I ask her, 'what's the surprise?'

'If I told you, it wouldn't be a surprise. And I need time to think. After all, I want you to be impressed.'

'So give me a clue.'

I hear her yawn again. 'No, I'm too tired to think. I'm going to bed. Want to come with me?'

'Love to.'

'Come on then. I'm getting up, switching off the lights and the television. The curtains aren't closed, I can see the streetlights outside. And the sky's still light.'

'Sunset and sunrise are close together at this time of year.'

'It's a beautiful pale blue colour. Now I'm closing the door, heading upstairs. Mm, I'm tired. Now I'm at the bedroom door. I'm opening it. It's really warm in here. I don't think I'll put the light on, I'll leave the curtains open. I'm sitting on the bed now, it's so soft. I've no socks or shoes on, I had a shower before so I'm wearing those baggy multi-coloured trousers of yours and one of your T-shirts.'

'No wonder I can never find any of my clothes.'

'You know you like me in them. And anyway, you're welcome to wear mine any time you want.'

'Thanks, but no thanks.'

'Spoilsport. It really is warm in here, Billy, it's no good. I'll have to take my top off.' There's a rustling noise, as if some fabric has slid across the phone mouthpiece. 'That's better. And now the trousers. Down they come. I think I'll just lie on the bed now. It's so hot, Billy, you should feel how warm my skin is. Mmm, it feels so good, just to run my hands over my skin. Can you tell how good it feels by the sound of my voice?'

'I can tell,' I reply, but the words are almost a croak. Jen can imagine the effect she's having on me as easily as I can imagine what she's doing.

'I'm using my fingers now, just pushing at the muscles beneath my skin, feeling the flesh. My belly feels so soft, but if I move up just a little way I can feel my ribs. I could move up a little higher if you want me to. Do you want me

52

to, Billy? Or I could go back down, down, a little further down and . . .'

There's a bang on the door. 'Dad, you haven't fallen asleep, have you?'

I pull the phone away from my mouth. 'No, love, I'm just coming.'

'You might well have been,' whispers Jen's soft voice, 'but I can tell you're a popular man. Give my love to Kirsty, lover boy. And don't forget to let me know what time you'll be back.'

'No, Jen, don't go . . .'

'Dad, come on, you're the only one not there. You don't have to stay long.'

'Ring me tomorrow, Billy. Bye.' The line clicks dead in one long, timeless echo. I close my eyes. Sometimes things don't go quite the way they should. Or perhaps, I reflect as I open the door, that's the way Jen would have finished our conversation anyway. She knows which strings to pull, which buttons to press. And, I must confess, there are times when I enjoy being her puppet, her toy. I enjoy letting her take control. Sometimes I need someone else to take charge. I open the door.

'Come on, old man,' Kirsty grabs me by the arm, 'things are beginning to swing.'

'Yes, from the ceiling, by a rope. It's called suicide, people are driven to it by the noise.'

'Bollocks. You've just forgotten what it's like to be young.'

'No, Kirsty, I can recall some of it clearly. Remember, I was a teenager in the seventies. That's why I often look miserable.'

My impersonation of a bad-tempered old man is ignored or treated with contempt. I can't tell which because Kirsty's face is hidden from me, she's dancing ahead down the corridor. The door to the lounge area has a square of wired glass in it, through it I can see a glare of red light. I squeeze past a couple leaning against the wall, they're pressing against each other with great force, as if they're both trying to occupy the same physical space. Kirsty waits by the door for me to catch up, opens it quickly and pushes me inside. I decide that this is probably to prevent any of the occupants escaping.

The combination of noise, heat and smell is suffocating. Young bodies seem capable of producing a unique odour, equal parts sweat, perfume and raw hormones dissolved in alcohol. Add to this a stroboscope of red light and a swirling laser beam fighting its way through a miasma of fragrant smoke, add that faster-than-it-should-be heartbeat of drum and bass, and strangers might think they'd arrived in one of the outer regions of hell without even suffering the ignominy of death and refusal of entry at St Peter's gate. All around the room the lesser devils of this temporary purgatory are gorging themselves. Mouths are open to food and drink and each other. Some of those who have tired of gluttony are exploring other vices and each other's bodies wherever the angles of wall and floor provide leaning space, or where cushioned sofas allow more comfortable (though equally leisurely) investigation. Others are jerking their bodies on a makeshift dance floor, as if invisible pitchforks are being thrust into them.

'Come on,' Kirsty yells, 'dance!' We face each other. I try to move in time with the beat, though it's a little too fast for my indolent sense of rhythm. I'm not a natural dancer. Show me the moves and I can use them with a certain amount of skill; I learned to dance when the gorgeous Mrs Lynch, English teacher with long legs, short skirts and no sense of humour, offered to show us how to quickstep in the gym a few weeks before the school dance. Lacking talent, I never attract attention to myself when dancing. My moves are conservative, my hands never stray far from my sides, my feet describe small circles in the vicinity of my centre of gravity.

Kirsty dances wildly, with the abandon that first attracted me to her mother. Yet all her body moves in harmony,

54

she's in control, she knows what she's doing. Even though she's had too much to drink she can still dance beautifully. At first I try to match her, but soon give up. In dancing and dealing with daughters I know when I'm beaten. But there's something troubling me. Why is my daughter so keen to dance with me? Where's Tom? I scan Kirsty's face, but there's no sign that she's upset. It's easy for young people to fall out, for drunk young people (and even those not so drunk and not so old) to fall into the arms of someone other than their partner, but she seems too happy for that. 'Where's Tom?' I mouth at her; she bends her ear close to my mouth to let me bellow the question again. She looks around, points at the source of the flashing lights. Behind the stack of amplifiers, decks and lights a hazy figure is searching through what appears to be a box of CDs.

'He's a DJ?' I yell again.

Kirsty nods, beckons me closer. 'Funny. Good sense of rhythm, but he's worse at dancing than you!'

That's when my role becomes clear. I'm a boyfriend substitute. Tom can't dance because he's deejaying, won't dance because he's bad at it, and I'm a safe alternative. This leads me to wonder about Kirsty's friends. When I was her age I had platonic female friends, girls I'd hung around with at school and then kept in touch with after we left. We'd meet, usually by accident, sometimes by arrangement, at parties and discos or even just in the local pub. Some of them were very attractive, but I never ... I can't go on. A memory has suddenly returned, a memory of a party and a nameless blonde who, like me, had drunk too much. I struggle to remember when this was, before or after I'd started going out with Sara. The girl was certainly engaged, to a friend of mine who was a soldier. We danced, we kissed, there was, I recall, a guilty thrill in sneaking away from the dancing to a dark, fumbling bedroom. We were found out; I think she confessed to her boyfriend. He forgave her, hit me, but didn't tell Sara. Perhaps Kirsty's more sensible than I ever was. Perhaps she's right to dance with me after all.

Nostalgia isn't good for me, it makes me feel old. When I was younger I would get up to dance with the knowledge that a record would segue into the next after three or four minutes, and that would give me an opportunity to leave the dance floor if I was too tired, had drunk too much, or was disenchanted with my partner. But this music goes on and on. The rhythm is relentless, even if the tune (one does surface occasionally) gives way to another. I can feel myself getting hotter, sweat begins to break out all over my body. Even Kirsty, who – given the amount of deodorant, anti-perspirant and perfume she uses – is solely responsible for the well-being of several chemical factories, is developing a damp and shiny glow. Eventually I have to signal to her that I need to stop; she seems relieved.

'I'll get you a drink,' she shouts, 'what do you want?'

'Orange squash with ice,' I shout back. I head for the food table, determined to browse to contentment before making an excuse and retiring for the night. Taylor has, once again, provided a huge amount of good food. It occurs to me that he has an agreement with the campus caterers to take the surplus conference provisions they're contracted to supply, there's certainly a large variety of savoury and sweet appetisers. I pick up a plate and a serviette, use the latter to mop my brow, my pate and all other areas above the neck. Then I choose several exotic sandwiches, two pakoras, some miniature curls of spicy sausage and a spoonful of rice salad. Before I can begin to eat, Kirsty returns with my drink.

'I think I'll go outside,' I mime to Kirsty. She seems to understand, she nods and makes a gesture which suggests she'll follow me.

I go down the corridor and push open the door to the cloisters. It's blissfully cool and almost quiet, though my ears are still buzzing with the music I've left behind. I put my plate and my glass down on the low wall and move my arms around, let the air circulate inside my shirt. That's when I notice something on the stage.

It's dark. Not entirely dark, this is, after all, a summer night in the middle of a large city. Light leaks into the cloisters from outside, from the lights in the passageways at the side of the square. Someone is sitting on the stage, on the stepped section just in front of the grassed area. It takes a while for my eyes to become accustomed to the gloom, and at first it looks like the person is hunched, crying; I can hear a sobbing sound. I'm distracted for a moment as a bat cuts the air overhead, I follow its flight then return to the stage. It looks and sounds as if there's something wrong, I can't ignore it. I'm about to leave my food and drink behind, enter the scene as the white knight on his charger coming to the rescue, when I realise that the sound isn't crying. I look closer. There's not one but two people, one is sitting on the stage apron, the second is sitting astride the first. I look closer, knowing what I'll find. It's a couple making love.

I should leave, or make a noise so they'll know I'm there. I do neither. Instead I watch more closely, letting my night vision develop. I find myself able to resolve the two figures, they appear to be clothed. The one sitting on the other's lap, the one I assume to be female, has her head thrown back. I catch a glimpse of blue; didn't one of the girls Kirsty identified have hair died electric blue? There's a flash of pale flesh, she seems to have her shirt bunched up around her neck, and her partner has his head (again my heterosexuality assigns gender roles to the protagonists) pressed against her breasts. There's a sudden urgent movement, a keen desire expressed in a nuance of motion. I can hear no words.

The door behind me swings open and Kirsty appears.

'Hello, love,' I say, not too loud, as if this is part of normal conversation, 'I've just got here myself. Stopped off to go to the loo.'

'Isn't it gorgeous out here?' Kirsty says, alcohol making her voice louder than mine. 'It was definitely a

bit noisy in there. Good atmosphere, though.' All movement on the stage ceases, the bodies disengage with a
snigger and a giggle I'm sure only I can hear. There is,
of course, only one way out of the cloisters, only one
way back to the party, and that's through the door beside
which Kirsty and I are lounging. The lovers on the stage
can either wait for us to leave, or they can walk past us.
They don't know how long we'll be there, they don't
even know who we are. It doesn't surprise me when they
appear at the end of the long stretch of walkway, holding
each other up in a staggering, four-legged lurch. Although
they've been drinking – their giggling laughter and over-
loud conversation confirm this – the disparity in their
sizes makes their progress towards us almost comical.
The girl is indeed the one with blue-dyed hair, I remember now, Kirsty mentioned her name was Anna. She's
not very tall, while her partner is the tallest of the young
men in the group. He's trying to shorten his stride, she's
lengthening hers, and they can't quite synchronise their
efforts. Every few steps one of them does a little skip;
once they skip together, remaining out of phase with each
other after their mutual adjustment, almost falling over
each other in their delight at their silliness.

Kirsty's eyebrows rise when she sees them clearly
enough to grant each an identity. 'Anna,' she says, 'Louis,
what're you doing out here?'

'Admiring the view,' Anna says with a lop-sided smile.
It looks as if Louis is holding her up. ''S a *lovely* night,
Kirsty. 'Lo Mr Oliphant. Y' all right?'

'Yes thank you.'

'I thought she needed some fresh air,' Louis explains, 'a
quick walk round the cloisters. She's had quite a bit to
drink.' Although his speech is clearer than his partner's,
he's swaying on the spot as he speaks.

'Too true,' Anna confirms, 'fresh air.' She wags a finger
at me. 'But really, really really, why we're here, is 'cos
Louis here, big Louis,' she pulls his head down and licks

58

the end of his nose, 'he wanted to get his hands on me. He did. Isn't that right, big boy?'

'Tha's right,' Louis answers obediently.

'He wanted to get his hand on my bosom, his head on my knee,' she shrieks, 'or was it his head on my bosom and his hand on my knee? Something like that. But I wouldn't let him. Not yet, anyway. We' gonna go back 'n' dance.'

Neither of them looks capable of standing upright, let alone moving in time with music. Indeed, Louis seems to be deteriorating as we watch. His swaying becomes more marked and his face loses its colour, it sheens with a sudden film of sweat.

'Are you okay, Louis?' Kirsty asks. She too has noticed that he appears unwell. He begins to nod his head but that turns swiftly to a shake, a slow shake accompanied by a groan.

'What's the matter? Kirsty asks.

'Feel sick,' he says.

'Keep away from me then,' Anna says, suddenly in control of the basics of speech, 'I hate puke.'

'Somebody should take him back to his room,' Kirsty says. 'Come on Anna, give me a hand.'

Anna shakes her head, slides down the wall to slump at my feet. 'I can hardly hold myself up, let alone him.'

'Dad?'

'Okay. Do you know which room is his?' Kirsty shakes her head. Anna has her eyes closed, it looks as if she's going to sleep. I continue the interrogation. 'Louis, which room is yours? Do you have a key?'

Louis struggles to place his hand in his pocket, but he does eventually manage to produce a key. Kirsty takes it from him.

'You go ahead, hold the doors open,' I tell her, 'I'll help our friend along.' I put Louis's arm over my shoulder, guide him in the direction of the door. We edge through it and Kirsty waves us towards a door right at the end of the corridor, beside the communal room. The music's still playing, loud and strong. Louis groans. I half carry him into the room, allow him to slide gently onto the bed. 'See if you can find a bucket,' I ask Kirsty, 'he's bound to be sick.' I switch off the main light, switch on the light in the small toilet. I want him to be able to find his way there during the night.

Kirsty bustles back with a bucket and a facecloth. She soaks it in cold water and pushes me away from the side of the bed. 'I'll see to him. He'll be okay if he can get to sleep. Could you check on Anna, see if you can persuade her to come back inside?' She's taking on a new role, nurse, carer, confessor, and I'm her assistant. I don't want to spend the rest of the night comforting drunk teenagers, so I'm tempted to slip into my own room and try to sleep. But first, just in case, I open the door and peer out into the cloisters. Anna's where we left her, but she looks up in response to the door's squeaking hinges.

'Hiya, Mr O. Louis okay?'

'I think so. He'll have a hangover tomorrow, and he might be sick tonight, but he'll be okay.'

'Good.'

I'm not sure whether the response shows Anna's pleased her friend will survive or if she wants him to suffer. Perhaps she doesn't actually know herself.

'How about you?' I ask.

'Great. Not quite pissed as a fart. Not yet.' She grins. 'I can cope with the booze. Loads of practice.'

I don't want to argue with her, but I can see that her eyes aren't quite focused on me. 'Don't you think you'd be better off back inside?' I ask.

'Why? In case I black out and choke on my own vomit?'

'No. But I'd hate to think of you feeling unwell, by yourself.'

She puts her head back, eyes closed. 'But I'm not by myself, am I? You're here.' She reaches into a pocket and pulls out a half-bottle of vodka. She unscrews the cap and takes a swig, wipes the lip of the bottle on her sleeve, offers it to me. When I decline she shrugs, takes another drink herself, then puts the bottle away. 'Besides, I'm too drunk to enjoy dancing. Too drunk for dancing, not drunk enough for sleeping. Just drunk enough for sex.' There's a huge amount of effort involved in staring at me. I assume it's to determine whether I react – how I react – to her statement. I do nothing. My face doesn't change. I've been propositioned by too many drunk young women before, women who've made comments about men, men in uniform, policemen, handcuffs and truncheons. I've had women lift skirts and blouses at me, I've had them rub themselves against me, drop to their knees in front of me, paw me and try to undress me. I've had women collapse in my arms, I've had them lose control of stomach, bladder and worse; once I had to clear the vomit from a fourteen year old's mouth and then give her the kiss of life. Nothing Anna can do will shock me. But I don't think she'll realise that.

Anna opens and closes her eyes again. In apparent repose she looks young and innocent. But then, as if aware of this, as if she's determined to negate the image, the tip of her tongue parts her lips, licks its slow, lascivious way from one side to the other and back again. She keeps her eyes closed this time, pretending she doesn't care what I think about her.

'You're such a bore, Mr O. No entertainment value at all.' From somewhere in the city's subdued roar a siren sounds. She turns her head a little to enjoy its interruption, the passage of its echo across the cloisters.

'And you're so quiet,' she continues. 'I like my men to make a little noise.'

I feel like telling her I'm not her man, but if I speak, she wins. I decide I'll go, she's obviously able to exert control over her speech, her behaviour. She'll soon tire of sitting when her audience disappears. That's when her eyes snap open into a horror film stare.

'Would you mind helping me up? I think I'd like to go back into the bedlam.' She holds out her hand to me, rolls her head to show she's still dizzy and can't raise herself to her feet unaided, no matter how hard she tries.

I give her my hand, pull gently, wary that she might catapult herself into my arms. I have no wish to become entangled with a drunk, complicated young woman. My fears, however, appear to be groundless. She struggles to her feet and sways on the spot, trying to focus her eyes and attention on some small, stable part of her immediate environment. She takes a deep breath. 'Phew,' she hisses, 'I didn't realise how ...'

'How drunk?'

'No, how ... How ... I can't remember what I was gonna say!' She begins to laugh again, this time silently, head nodding like a dozing politician not listening to a debate. She stops, takes another breath. 'Oh shit,' she mutters.

I step closer, frightened she might hurt herself if she faints. 'What's the matter?'

'I think ...' She takes a small, staggering step. 'I think ...'

She's already moving when she falls, it isn't the downward crumple of a faint, her momentum and mine cause us to collide. I manage to dip, get my forearms under her armpits, haul her upwards. I pull her backwards, lean her against the sill of one of the stone window frames, shuffle round her so I'm supporting her with one arm round her shoulders.

'I think ...' she mutters again, then opens her eyes. 'I think I love you, Mr O.' Her arms snake quickly around my neck and she moves round in front of me so I'm the one resting against the cool sandstone. I can't retreat. She presses the lower part of her body against me and pulls my head down into a kiss.

My first reaction is to push her away, but the only parts of her body available for such an action are her breasts; I

62

don't want her to misunderstand me. Part of me – clad in red, clutching a pitchfork and sitting on my left shoulder – says don't fight it. How many middle-aged men are propositioned by attractive young women, it asks. Go on, it says as her tongue tries to force open my lips, kiss her back, it's what any red-blooded male would do. And if she wants to take it further, well, she's not a child.

On my right shoulder the angelic me whispers urgently. She's drunk, she wouldn't go near you if she was sober, you can't take advantage of her like this, you'd hate yourself in the morning. He's reading from a list but saving the most important item for the end. What if Jen found out? And the argument's final, unerring thrust, how would you feel if Jen was in your position and gave way because she thought you wouldn't find out?

In the end I don't push Anna away, I simply freeze. I lock my mouth closed, keep my hands immobile by my sides, hold my arms and legs stiff. She can tell I'm not responding. She pushes herself away from me slightly, so she can look into my eyes.

'Don't you fancy me?' she asks.

My reply's a cliché. 'You're a very attractive young woman, Anna. But I'm in a relationship. And you've had too much to drink. Put all that together and it would be wrong of me to ...' I try to think what it is I shouldn't be doing, how I can express it delicately, then realise Anna's already losing interest. I finish lamely, 'It would be wrong of me to do anything.'

'Yeah, I suppose you're right.' She smoothes down her skirt, kisses one finger and presses it briefly against my lips. 'But it would've been fun.' She shakes her head, unable to understand my reluctance to respond to her. 'You would've enjoyed it. I would've enjoyed it. And now all you'll have are fantasies. Ah well, see you later.'

She weaves her way to the door, pulls it though it's clearly labelled 'push', then remembers she has to enter a code. She tries once, tries again, presses the palm of her hands against all the buttons. She looks as if she's about to hit the keypad when someone opens the door from inside. She pushes past Kirsty without saying anything.

'What's wrong with her?' Kirsty asks as she joins me, looking back over her shoulder.

'She was overwhelmed with passion for me, but in the end she was disappointed when I wasn't up for it.'

Kirsty puzzles at the double entendres. Sobriety and appreciating wordplay don't go together. 'Dad, surely you don't mean . . ?

'What?'

'She came on to you? And you couldn't . . ?'

'She did. Her eyesight must be poor. But it wasn't that I couldn't rise to the occasion, it was that I didn't want to. For various reasons.' I refrain from telling her about the demon and the angel, she's always doubted my sanity. But then, so have I.

'Oh dear. She must have been very drunk.'

My daughter knows how to push the sharp pin of reality into the over-inflated balloon of self-esteem. My ego safely burst, I return to the most important matter at hand, eating.

'It's getting a bit quieter in there,' Kirsty mentions between mouthfuls of sandwich. 'I had a word with Tom and he's put something on that's a bit more gentle. Ambient. Soothing. Everybody's drifted off to the sofas.'

'In that case, I think I'll drift off to bed, if you don't mind. I want to get started early tomorrow.'

Kirsty's being helpful. 'Do you want Tom and me to give you a hand?'

'Yeah, that would be great. I'll meet you out here at, oh, let me see, not too early. How does eight thirty suit you?' Kirsty's intake of breath is sufficient reward for me. 'Only kidding, love. No, I can get on by myself. You have a lie-in.'

'Thanks, Dad.' She leans forward and kisses me on the cheek. 'You're the greatest. G'night' She still has the capacity to switch on the current and light me up. She turns and leaves and, when she opens the door, I find that the music has indeed been muted. I might get some sleep after all.

I sip my water and finish my sandwiches. The night is quietening, I find when I check my watch that it's well after midnight. The air is cool, scented with the honeysuckle and jasmine clinging to the cloisters walls. Jen, I decide, would have enjoyed being here. I sometimes feel I'm too old for her. I'm staid and conservative, aged beyond my years; she's extrovert and youthful, a perpetual teenager. Perhaps we complement each other, contribute the yin and yang to our whole. I certainly wouldn't have her change, and she's said she likes me the way I am. But it would have pleased her to be around so many young people, she would have enjoyed their company. With thoughts of Jen in my mind I gather my plate and glass, enter the door code and make my way back inside.

Although the music is quieter than previously, I can still feel the bass through the soles of my feet. I would take my key from my pocket if my hands weren't occupied with plate and glass. I could, of course, take them into my room with me, sneak them back into the lounge in the morning; I'm sure no one will make the effort to clean away the mess before they go to bed. Tidiness is, however, my most sociably acceptable vice, so I decide to take my dishes back now. There is also, I will admit, a certain prurience in my decision; Kirsty's phrase 'everyone's drifting off to the sofas' is still with me. It's not that I want to discover whether she and Tom have joined the same inexorable tectonic movement, but ... Well actually, it is. I want to know what she's up to.

When I open the door I find that the lights are considerably dimmer than they were, redder than they were. It's like walking into a photographer's dark room, and I stand still for a moment to allow my eyes to become accustomed to the gloom. The music has a repetitive melody, the rhythm is almost relaxing. There's a heady atmosphere of cannabis. I can see that some people are still talking, but more – I would say the majority if I could actually count the bodies – are examining each other with an intimacy that would provide the Kinseys and Comfort with a wealth of experimental data. If I had a torch with me I could go around and identify individuals; since I don't (and if I did, wouldn't presume to use it) I decide to refill my glass and leave.

I stumble towards the table in a slow-stepping shuffle, people are sitting on the floor and I don't want to fall over them. Judicious squinting and sniffing identifies my flavoured water; I decide to take the bottle with me, no-one else seems interested in non-alcoholic drinks. Finding my way back is a little easier, a beacon of light shines from the corridor through the glass pane in the exit door. I'm relieved that I can't see Kirsty. That doesn't mean she isn't there, of course, but ignorance is a state in which I'm pleased to find myself.

Beside the door there's a familiar shock of fluorescent blue hair, its owner, for once, not intent on seeking a partner. Indeed, it looks as if she's already been success-ful; she's squeezed into a chair with a male who has one hand fumbling in her blouse, the other pushing her skirt high between her legs. She's moving slowly. I assume this is a sign of enjoyment and I slip past. There's a lull in the music, a coincidence of comparative silence in which I hear distinctly two soft words: 'Please, no.' I stop, but the music begins again before I can tell who spoke them. No amount of turning my head and strain-ing to listen can bring this subliminal message back. I wait a moment, decide it was my imagination, and open the door. The light floods briefly into the room, and as I turn I find Anna's eyes staring at me, glazed in rapture. It's as if she's showing me what I've missed. As I turn to go she opens her mouth and I expect the same lasciv-ious lick of the lips she demonstrated earlier; instead I

66

make out the same sad words I thought I heard a moment before.

There's sometimes little difference between pleasure and pain. The facial paroxysms of agony and orgasm are often indistinguishable. For some, sexual enjoyment can only be gained by inflicting or suffering physical hurt. Anna's whispered words suddenly give her gestures and expression a new meaning, they provide the context to allow me to make a different judgement. She's no longer a sexual predator, she's a drunk young woman being subject to advances she no longer wants. I could haul her attacker from her, but if I'm mistaken about the couple's desires this could prove embarrassing. I decide to take the gentleman's course of action. I stumble, accidentally of course, and the contents of my water bottle are delivered accurately over the back of Anna's over-enthusiastic partner.

He reacts swiftly, pulls himself to his feet. 'What the hell is . . ?' I'm standing with the door open, we can see each other clearly. 'Oh, it's you, Oliphant.' Jonathan Taylor quickly jerks his wet shirt over his head. 'What on earth was that for?'

'I'm sorry,' I reply, aware that we have a small audience, surprised that he might think I'd soaked him deliberately. 'I must have tripped over someone's feet. It's just water.'

He's had too much to drink, his eyes are dancing, he's aware people are watching, he's striking a pose. He has no need to suck in his stomach muscles, his six pack is ample evidence of his daily visits to the gym. 'It's okay,' he says, 'these things happen. But if you don't mind, the door? It's a little bright in here with it wide open.' He gestures back into the room. 'The vampires don't like it.' Bodies are stirring, blinking, trying to see what's happened or trying to ignore the interruption.

'Yes, I can see what you mean. I'll just be on my way, then.' I make as if to close the door, then pretend to see

Anna for the first time. 'Hello, Anna, are you all right? You look a little pale.'

She can muster no more than a groan. I hold the door wider, let in more light. Her skirt is round her waist, tights pulled down around her thighs. Her blouse is pushed almost to her neck, her breasts have red marks on them. I bend down to her level, gently adjust tights, skirt and blouse to preserve her modesty, though I don't think she cares too much. 'I think we'd better get you to bed,' I say, not even allowing her the luxury of treating my words as a question. I stand up again. 'Kirsty? Vicky? Are either of you there?' I call into the room, 'Anna's had a bit too much to drink and needs putting to bed.'

Taylor isn't willing to give in so easily. 'It's okay, I can take her, she's quite light.' He throws what he thinks is a manly wink in my direction, a gesture of knowing complicity. 'Anna and I are a sort of item,' he adds softly, 'we've got a scene going. I'll make sure she's okay.'

I bend down close to Anna again, she's trying to sit up. 'Mr Taylor here has offered to help you to bed,' I tell her. 'Is that all right with you?' She manages to shake her head violently. I look up at Taylor. 'I don't think she wants to go with you,' I say to him.

It's his turn to speak to her. 'Anna,' his hiss opens her eyes, 'it's me, Jonathan. Remember? Jonathan Taylor? Your course tutor? Your friend? We were ... That is, I thought you were going to spend the night with me. We were ... we were going to discuss your dissertation, remember?' He reaches a hand towards her cheek but she flinches, turns away. He gives up, climbs to his feet. 'You'll feel better soon,' he says, his self-confidence still intact. 'You know where I am. I think we need to talk. Come and see me.' He slithers away into the gloom

Anna's eyes close again. Kirsty appears at my side, hair suspiciously rumpled, make-up smudged. Vicky's only a few seconds behind her.

'Sorry to impose,' I say, 'but we've a young lady in

distress here. Would you mind getting her to bed? I'd do it myself but I have a reputation to think of.'

'What happened, babes?' Vicky asks Anna.

'Drunk,' Anna slurs, 'too drunk. Said no but ... He's strong. Bastard!'

'I think Jonathan Taylor was forcing himself on her,' I tell Kirsty while Vicky's getting a series of monosyllabic grunts from Anna. 'You know how drunk she was earlier? I think she kept on drinking and, if my experience was anything to go by, made a play for him.'

'And he wouldn't turn her down,' Kirsty says. 'Everybody knows he's got the hots for her.'

'So she changes her mind but he won't stop, he keeps going.'

'You mean attempted rape?'

'You watch too much television, young lady.' I can feel myself reverting to policeman mode. 'In a room full of people, a young woman – obviously drunk but in control – attempts to seduce a man. I'm a witness to her predatory nature earlier in the evening. No intercourse, so far as I'm aware, has taken place. We'd have difficulty proving attempted rape, even assault. I think we ought to leave things as they are.'

Vicky stands up, adds her evidence. 'She says she felt frightened, he wouldn't stop pawing her. You know the things lads do when you've both had too much to drink.' To my horror Kirsty and Vicky nod together in harmony, as if their own personal experience has helped them sympathise with Anna.

'Can you help her to bed?' I ask them. 'I'll give you a hand.'

I haul Anna to unsteady feet, Kirsty searches through a bag Vicky identifies as Anna's, finds a key. 'Two doors down,' she says, 'next to mine. Can you carry her, Dad? Vicky, you get the door, then come and help me clear the bed. There's bound to be a mess in there.'

I help Anna along to her room. My arm's round her

waist, hers is draped over my shoulder. 'I'm sorry,' she says over and over, 'I'm so sorry.' I tell her not to worry, that I'm becoming quite used to carrying drunk young people to their beds, that I'm thinking of taking it up as a profession. I manage the door to her room with practised ease, lower her onto the bed.

'It's okay now,' Kirsty says soothingly, 'Vicky and I'll look after you. Come on, boots off.' They manage to unlace her DMs and remove them, pull off her laddered tights.

'I hate him,' Anna says to no one in particular, though its obvious who she's talking about.

'Yeah,' says Vicky, 'typical man.'

'Let's have a few less generalities,' I say, 'there are some very pleasant men about.'

'On the surface, maybe, but they're all pervs at heart.'

'I beg to differ.'

'So why,' she says over her shoulder, 'are you still standing there watching us undress Anna?'

I hadn't realised they were going to take all her clothes off, but on being informed of the act I quickly make an exit. In doing so I almost walk into another young woman who's standing close behind me.

'Is Anna all right?' she asks.

I try to pull her identity from my memory but find no face to match hers.

'I'm Belle,' she says helpfully, 'director.' She looks different, no longer the round-shouldered, mousey, over-sincere young woman I now recall from rehearsals. She's tied her hair back and, the main difference, she's smiling at me. She's also sober.

'I think a good night's sleep will do her more good than anything else. And some paracetamol and coffee in the morning.'

'Oh good,' she says, clearly relieved. 'I don't have my glasses on, I couldn't see how ill she was. We've a heavy schedule of rehearsals and, I know this sounds selfish, Mr

Oliphant, but I really don't need people ill or performing under par.' She pauses. 'Well, if everything's under control, I think I'll be going.' She pulls her arms into a light jacket.

'You aren't staying here with the rest of us?'

'My goodness, no. The people staying here are those who live out of town, or who had to leave their own halls for the summer. I share a house across the park, it's not far.' She holds out her hand. 'Thank you for all your help, Mr Oliphant. And not only with the electrical work.' We shake hands formally and she leaves. At last I can head for my room, for bed, for sleep.

I remember that Taylor's room is directly opposite mine and pause outside it for a moment. One weekend, when Kirsty was still at school, she stayed with me because her mother was going away somewhere. She had an essay to do, something about a novel I hadn't read, and she asked for my help. This wasn't a sign that she needed me to provide some knowledge; it was more that I act as a sounding board for her theories. The question was something about characterisation, and she suggested that one of the characters she had to discuss was two-dimensional. We talked about what the phrase meant (I had to refer to films rather than books) and I came to the conclusion that two-dimensional characters were much preferable to their three-dimensional colleagues. Kirsty, of course, disagreed. I had to explain that I found it easier to deal with the predictability of lightly sketched characters, that complexity was just too confusing; it made books and films as complicated as real life.

The memory returns now. When I first met Taylor I considered him a fool. After listening to what I considered was the real him I began to feel sympathy for him. Now I'm beginning to dislike him. The number of dimensions to his character extends beyond the norm, I much prefer those who are good or bad and easily recognisable as such.

I bend close to the door; no sound escapes from Taylor's silent room. Realising I'll never understand him, I head for the refuge of sleep.

Chapter Four

I'd come prepared, as I always do when sleeping away from home, with earplugs and a mask. Even with them I'm aware of lights being switched on and off in the corridor, of footsteps passing my room, of doors opening and closing throughout the night. They interfere only briefly with my sleep before I turn over and resume my frustrating dreams of Jen and falling, being chased and chasing, finding something of far less value than something I'd lost. My dreams are normal.

I decide to get up when Saturday grows too bright (when it penetrates the curtains, my mask and my eyelids) and the sparrows outside my window receive my acknowledgement that they are indeed the noisiest group of birds I have ever heard. I shower and dress, head for the lounge in the vain hope that some good fairy will have tidied up after the bacchanalia, that the table will be laid with fresh country-side produce of the highest quality. What I find lives down to my expectations. The curtains are closed, as are the windows. The light and the smell remind me of the old men's pub on the High Street of my teens, the one they kept deliberately foul to discourage young people from entering with their noise and liveliness. The air is stale and stained, it tastes of cigarette ash mingled with beer slops. The light, filtered through yellow curtains, is the colour of nicotine fingers. Cans and bottles, themselves drunk, lie where they passed out; no chair or table is without some comatose container. The only movement in the room is the faint perturbation of molecules of air, slowly drawn into and out of the snoring mouths of two sofas which, on closer examination, contain the bodies of two young men kept alive only through having been steeped in alcohol.

My delicate nose detects the subtle aromas of sweat and old perfume, socks left unwashed for too long, and the possibility that one of the youths was too drunk to be woken by the urgent calls from his over-stressed bladder.

There's still food around, there's a kettle on the sink in the corner, a fridge probably contains some milk. I could concoct a breakfast. I decide instead to begin work, to get a few hours' labour (rather than food) under my belt, and to find a café later in the day to provide for my nutritional needs.

It's cool and fresh in the cloisters; a distant clock strikes eight. I'm quite pleased no one else is around to disturb me, to take away my morning from me. So when I see a figure sitting on the stage, head in hands, my displeasure at the prospect of company is assuaged by the fact that the person, whoever it is, appears to have a monumental hangover. I could, I tell myself, leave quickly and silently; I don't think I've been seen yet. But where would I go? No, I decide to offer a greeting and get it over with, hope that he or she will feel too ill to take part in any conversation.

'Morning,' I call loudly, 'beautiful day.' I climb over the low cloisters wall and walk towards the figure. As I get closer I can see that the figure is, at the very least, barechested; closer still and it's clear that he's male; then I recognise Jonathan Taylor. 'We should be able to get a lot of work done today,' I tell him, 'might even see me finished by tonight.'

He doesn't respond. He makes no movement whatsoever. He must, I decide, have fallen asleep here, unable to summon the strength or the will to get to his room. I can remember that type of night myself; my shame when Sara found me slumped on doorstep, sofa, kitchen floor or stairs; my stupidity in doing the same thing again and again.

The sun is climbing slowly higher, but the stage is still largely in shadow. To my surprise I see that Taylor's naked. I re-think my opinion; he was in bed and woke up feeling sick, staggered out here and sat down, fell asleep. Even I never ended a binge naked, outdoors.

'Taylor,' I say gently, reconciling myself to assisting drunk number three, 'come on, I think you should lie down in your room for a few hours.'

I touch him on the shoulder. I think that's when I realise he's dead. It isn't the coolness of his flesh, the night has been particularly warm. Nor is it the lack of motion; from the way he's sitting, hunched forward, I can't see whether he's still breathing or not. It's more, I think, the lack of give in his body, as if it's already begun to stiffen.

The morning is, I realise, still mine. I don't have to share it after all. I slide my fingers along to the side of Taylor's neck; there's no pulse. There's no flow of blood through the veins in his wrist either. I should, I tell myself, telephone the police immediately. But he's dead, and a few minutes more will make no difference. I bend down to the ground in front of him and look upwards. He's sitting in what would once have been a pool of blood, but it isn't liquid and flowing. It's thick, dry in places, black, the boards of the stage have absorbed some of it, stemmed its flow. I trace its passage up his body, through the blood-matted hair on his stomach to the dagger buried up to the hilt in his chest. It's very similar to the ones Taylor and Anna were using in their swordfight yesterday, but they, according to Kirsty, were blunt, capped with some sort of shield, and had spring-loaded blades.

I look around his body but there's nothing of note and no sign of his clothes. The stage is scuffed in places, but that could have happened yesterday. The grass at the foot of the stage hasn't been worn away, the earth hasn't been churned up; there's no sign of a fight.

I hardly knew Jonathan Taylor. I found him loud, conceited and – last night at least – unpleasant towards someone, ignoring her requests and needs. But he's been relegated to the past tense. I'm only pleased that someone else will have to find out why. I ring the police.

It shouldn't take long for them to arrive. I decide to use the time wisely. First I write a notice and hang it on the door between the cloisters and the bedrooms, 'STRICTLY NO ENTRY, LIVE ELECTRICITY'. It's a lie, of course, but if anyone wakes up it'll keep them out of the murder scene. Then I try the door to Taylor's room. It's open, the lock held back so that no key is needed. Although the quilt is thrown back untidily from the bed, Taylor's clothes are folded neatly on the chair, his shoes parallel beneath. His travel bag is on the desk. The curtains are closed. Even the waste bin is still empty; there's no sign that this is anything other than temporary accommodation. I bend down, look under the bed as best as I can in the gloom, but see nothing. As I stand again I notice something white inside one of the shoes. I peer closer, it seems to be a piece of crumpled paper.

I should leave it alone. It could be crucial evidence, its position could be important. Anyway, the police will be here soon, if I could find it easily, they'll be able to do the same. I don't need to get involved.

I never could listen to my own advice. I pick the paper up, tease it open. It seems to be a piece of ordinary, unlined photocopying or typing paper, one long side is uneven showing that it's A4 size torn in half. On it there's some untidy writing in blue ink, very small, I have difficulty reading it in the poor light. I open the curtains a little way, that helps, then start to read.

I really want to screw you. I'd like to wrap myself round your _____, put your beautiful _____ in my _____ and we could _____ on the _____ for hours. Come and find me now, you

76

can use the yellow stockings to tie me to the ____! You
fill in the missing words!
    Your True Love (gagging for it!),
    a
                                                                    .

Although lower case, the last initial letter is written large. I read it through again. It makes sense, just about, as a letter of enticement. I don't want to pre-judge matters, but if the large 'a' is someone's initial, it could be Anna's. But the girl who was with Tom before, the one who was good at music, she was called Angie, so it could just as well be her.

It's not really a vital piece of evidence, I tell myself. It proves nothing by itself. It would be interesting to compare the writing with some of Anna's and Angie's and anyone else's whose name begins with 'a'. If I were to do so it would allow me to satisfy my intellectual curiosity and even be of some help to the police. I'm at my most persuasive when I'm talking silently to myself, and that's why I fold the paper carefully, slip back across the corridor to put it in my overnight bag, then go outside to wait for the police.

I feel strangely calm and efficient as I walk out into the sunlight and the first cars arrive. They're pretty quick, two of them screech across the car park at the same time, blue and red and white dazzling in the morning sun. I glance at my watch; four minutes from the end of my call, it must have been a quiet night. Sirens are switched off, lights left flashing; surely no one can be left still asleep in the whole town.

The occupants of the two cars exchange waved greetings as they clamber out, shirts crisp, dignity freshly laundered for the day ahead. I wave to them. Please, I say to myself, let them have brains.

'Hello,' I call, 'I'm Billy Oliphant, it was me reported the incident.'

'That's right,' says the nearest, reading from his note-book, 'Mr Oliphant. Reporting a dead body, suspicious circumstances.'

'The deceased is Jonathan Taylor, a lecturer at the university. I found his body just after eight am – if the church bells are correct – in the cloisters just through here.' I start leading the way, Plod One trying to write and keep up with me at the same time. I know the procedure: tell it like it is to these guys and then do it all over again when the detectives arrive.

Plod Two is close behind, he sniffs the air as we enter the building. 'Someone been having a party?' he asks suspiciously.

'There was a celebration last night. A group of students, they're putting on a play in the cloisters. Most of them are staying here, in the dormitory, halls of residence, whatever they're called. Taylor – the deceased – arranged a party for them, to launch the whole thing. The mess is still there if you want to check.' I point towards the lounge. 'But the body's in the opposite direction.'

'And your role here?' Plod Two asks. He's obviously the more sceptical of the two, older than his colleague, more world-weary, trying to get out of routine duties and onto murder, fraud, something more exciting than crawling the beat.

'My daughter's in the play. They wanted some help with setting up the lighting and the sound.'

'So you're a sound engineer?'

'No, I install security systems. But I know a little bit about electricity.' We reach the door to the cloisters, no one else has – to my surprise – emerged from any of the rooms.

Plod One interrupts, points at my sign on the door. 'This yours, then?'

'Yes, ignore it.' I tear it from the handle. 'Just to keep any of the kids off, if they woke up. Didn't want them disturbing the scene of crime.'

'You're good with the terminology, Mr Oliphant.' It's cynical Plod Two again. 'Watch a lot of crime TV? Read detective novels?'

78

'No. Ex-CID. Been around a bit.'

That gets me the reaction I knew it would, a mixture of wariness and mistrust. There's wariness because an ex-cop knows the ropes, knows what should be done and how it should be done; there can be no shortcuts. And there's mistrust because, when the ex clearly hasn't reached retirement age, the question 'why did he leave?' hangs unasked and unanswered. The police force is a close-knit community, it's unusual for officers to leave unless something goes wrong or they get a far better offer. The plods'll be wondering which of these applies to me.

I open the door, lead them to the wall so they can see Taylor's body beyond. 'I checked pulse and respiration – nothing. He's in a seated position on the stage, no immediate signs of a struggle, he has a knife in his chest, presumably through his heart.'

Plod Two vaults the wall and approaches the body. He does as I did: he checks Taylor's pulse, bends down in front of him, walks around him. He turns to look at the scene around him, the calm and tranquillity. Then he makes his slow, loping way back. 'What you said seems pretty accurate, Mr Oliphant, so I suppose it's out of our hands now.' He seems disappointed.

'And?'

'We put a call in to CID, they arrive to find we've isolated the scene of crime, put up the plastic ribbon, found out who's in the building. You might be able to help us there, Mr Oliphant.'

'I just arrived yesterday, I don't know many of the people here. My daughter, though, she'll be able to give you names.'

'Right, we'll start there. Then we go round waking people up, ask them not to talk to each other.' He looks at his watch. 'I reckon, oh, two hours at the most and we'll be sent on our way.' I can tell by the way he's talking that he's already applied for and been turned down by CID. I feel like telling him to forget it, to think how much he values his wife and family, to get his priorities right. I feel like telling him that jobs can become addictive, harmful. But I don't because he wouldn't listen, just like I didn't listen.

Word spreads quickly amongst the fraternity. By the time we reach the car park again there are four police vehicles; one of the extras is a scene-of-crime van, a large white cabin on wheels; the other is in plain clothes, a drab Mondeo pretending to belong to a sales rep. Its well-upholstered driver is speaking into its radio while the other occupant, on seeing me approaching flanked by my two new best friends, climbs out and heads in my direction.

Policemen annoy me. I know too much about them and the way they work, they're too self-important. They spend too much time solving crimes rather than preventing them, though I suppose the blame for that can be laid at the doors of politicians. The trouble is, most people only see the police on television. Think of the last time you saw a police officer talking to a television reporter. Remember the lapses into police-speak, the air of someone not properly trained for the job they're doing. They need training in talking to people, in listening to people. And, as much as I hate to admit it, they need more people at the top who are trained to detect rather than trained to plod. The good ones appreciate professionalism wherever they find it, but there aren't many of them about. Or perhaps I'm just bitter and twisted because of my own experiences.

'Mr Oliphant?' This one holds out his hand in front of him, his grip is firm. He's older than me, tall and thin, broad forehead tramlined with frowns. 'I'm Detective Inspector Arnison, Harry Arnison. My rotund colleague over there in the car is Detective Sergeant Mike Stephenson.' The familiarity bodes well. 'I've had some details radioed through to me, you found the body, did all the right things. Thank you. You'll need to make a formal statement, of course.' He examines the sheet of paper in his hand. 'You told the officers you were a police officer not too long ago, I believe.' He checks the paperwork in his hand. 'Five years, it says here. I've been in touch with a Chief Inspector Kim Bryden. She tells me you've been helpful to her in the past. "In his own idiosyncratic way," she said.' He looks me in the eyes. 'You're very fortunate, Mr Oliphant. Ms Bryden uses the word "idiosyncratic" and I understand it. Such a high degree of literacy doesn't occur every day in the modern police force.'

I'm impressed that he's done his research, worried that he felt he had to. I suppose I should have expected it, having found Taylor's body and reported the crime, but it's obvious that I was, probably still am, a suspect. I don't like the feeling.

While Arnison's speaking to me, Sergeant Stephenson is giving instructions. Police men and women are heading into the building to wake the occupants. White-overalled forensic officers are pulling on plastic boots. There's an air of calm professionalism. That's why the next question surprises me.

'Any thoughts, Mr Oliphant?'

'Thoughts?'

'Yes. You've only just met the people here, you've seen the security, limited though it is, you were around last night for the party, your room was opposite Mr Taylor's. Have you any thoughts on what might have happened? Suspects? Motivation?'

I'm not used to such courtesy. After I left the force I found myself involved, usually against my wishes, in certain police investigations; it was as if I just couldn't keep myself out of trouble. At first I wanted to help, I found it difficult to accept that I was no longer part of the force. Then, after I'd been told both politely and impolitely where I should put my contributions, I began to keep out of the way. I began to treat my ex-colleagues the same way they treated me, with distaste. The trouble was, sometimes we needed each other. I could do things they couldn't, they could provide information I had no chance of finding

81

myself; we could be of mutual benefit to each other. This could never be a formal arrangement, I am, after all, a businessman and the force is a public body; allegations of favouritism could prove costly to us both. But my relationships with some individual officers warmed a little; at times Kim Bryden and I can spend at least ten minutes in a room together without attacking each other. Her description of me is as cynical as mine would be if I was asked to describe her, and Arnison does at least appear to share that cynicism. And he's asking my opinion; that's a first.

'All I can give you,' I tell Arnison, 'is my opinion, and that's based on very little evidence. Taylor wasn't very popular. He was a good organiser, apparently, his students appreciated that. But he was a little over-familiar. Nothing I would consider grounds for hatred, though.'

'Why do you say "over-familiar"? Any specific occurrence lead you to that conclusion?'

He's quick, he's picked up on the one piece of information I can give him that isn't based on hearsay. 'He was a little over-attentive to one of the girls last night. She'd had too much to drink and was probably leading him on, but ...' Why, I wonder, am I trying to protect him, trying to think of excuses for behaviour that was inexcusable?

'Do you know the girl's name?'

'Anna.'

'And her room? Was she staying here last night?'

'Yes. My daughter helped put her to bed, she really was drunk.'

'Thank you, Mr Oliphant. Anything else you can tell me?'

'Nothing. I mean, I was in the room opposite Taylor but I'm a light sleeper, so I was wearing earplugs. I didn't hear anything specific, just doors opening and closing, footsteps. I assumed it would be students going from one room to another, or just heading for bed. You know the type of thing.'

He nods his head to show that he's aware of what young people get up to.

'The only other thing I can think of is that the weapon, the knife, looks remarkably similar to one he was using earlier. But that was a stage dagger, with a retractable blade, I'm not sure how ...'

'Was Taylor fighting, Mr Oliphant, or did he just have the knife with him?'

'He was fighting. At least, he was coaching someone else in how to do a swordfight. On stage, that is.'

'And who was he coaching?

'It was Anna.'

'I see.' He doesn't, of course, see anything. He hears, then constructs in his mind a sequence of imaginary events. He's heard the same name linked twice with Taylor's and has filled in the gaps. I could have mentioned that Kirsty was annoyed with Taylor because he forgot her name, or that Vicky had expressed several unflattering opinions about her tutor. I could point this out to him. I could also mention the note I found in Taylor's room, but that would mean admitting that I'd been doing things I shouldn't have. It would also mean pointing the finger of suspicion even more firmly in Anna's direction, and I don't want to do that, not yet. Coincidences can often be nothing more than coincidences. Any protestations that Arnison's developing a bias against Anna might result in further questions, perhaps even suspicions, on Arnison's part.

There's a hiss and crackle of the radio hidden inside his jacket. He reaches inside to touch it and listens carefully. 'Okay,' he says, 'thanks. Out.' He turns to me. 'Things fall into place, Mr Oliphant. Your daughter's appeared and is asking for you. Perhaps you'd like to come and explain who we are, she can provide us with a list of who's around, who was staying where. And I think we'll begin by chatting to this young lady Anna.'

I lead him inside.

'Dad! What's happening?' Kirsty's at the far end of the corridor, she hurls herself towards me, throws herself into my arms. She's dressed in a T-shirt and a pair of well-worn, baggy tracksuit bottoms.

'It's all right, love, it's all right.' I stroke the back of her head.

'There's all these police around, but they won't say why they're here. I wanted to go back into my room, to tell Tom, but they wouldn't let me. They said they didn't want us to talk to each other. What's happened?'

Arnison's behind me. I turn my head a little so I can see his face. The shake of his head is definite, I'm not allowed to tell Kirsty what I know. That's understandable; Kirsty is, I suppose, a suspect. My opinion that she'll know nothing about Taylor's murder is based entirely on my being her father. I can't imagine any situation where I'd be able to kill anyone, except in self defence or if someone I loved was being threatened, and so I fix those same conditions on my daughter's behaviour. There's some logic in that, after all, she must have inherited some of my behaviour traits. But if that was the case, then murderers would only kill if their parents were also murderers. So, my argumentative self tells me, my logic is flawed. In that case, the more pliant, reasonable me responds, I have to rely on the subjective; Kirsty's a pleasant, adorable, loved and loving young woman, and there's no way she could have killed Taylor. I can't argue with myself on that, it's a matter of trust and faith. But Arnison has to rely on facts, he doesn't know Kirsty, so she'll be the first to be questioned.

'This is Detective Inspector Arnison,' I say softly, 'he's in charge of investigations. He wants to ask you – and everyone else, of course – some questions. Just tell him the truth, there'll be no problems.'

'But Dad, what's happened? It must be something bad, there's so many police about.'

'DI Arnison will explain everything love, then we can talk.'

'You father's right, Miss Oliphant,' Arnison confirms gently, 'and the first thing I need to know is who's staying here. Do you know who's in which room?'

Kirsty nods. 'I think so. That is, I know who's meant to be there. But ...'

'Yes, Miss Oliphant?'

'Well, there was a party last night. One or two people might not have stayed in the rooms they were meant to.' She looks at me guiltily.

'Such as?' Arnison is pleasantly persistent.

'Well, my boyfriend, Tom. He spent the night with me.' She actually begins to blush.

'It's all right, love, I'm not ...' I want to tell her I'm not annoyed or angry. I've long been aware that she's sexually active, it doesn't worry me as long as she's taking responsibility for contraception and protection, as long as it's something she wants with someone she likes. But as soon as I begin, I realise that would sound patronising, condescending. So I stop. 'I'd better go,' I say, 'I think I have to be interviewed as well.'

'Just a matter of confirming what you've already told us, Mr Oliphant,' he says. 'I've asked one of my officers to do that. We'll need to know how and where we can contact you, of course. But then you can go, if you want.'

'Thanks,' I reply, 'but I think I'll stay, if you don't mind. Just in case I'm needed.'

'Of course.' Arnison's brief nod is understanding. He thinks I'm worried about Kirsty. Though she is in my mind, though I do want to ask her myself what she knows, I must admit that I want to stay for another reason. I'm curious to know what has happened, I want to find out whether Arnison and his squad can find the murderer quickly. Taylor wasn't an easy man to like, that much is certainly true, and everyone knew which room was his. But why would anyone have wanted to kill him? And is Anna's note becoming more important?

'Do you mind if I get dressed first?' Kirsty asks.

'Of course not,' Arnison says. He snaps his fingers, waves his hand and a policewoman steps forward. 'Go with Miss Oliphant please, she needs to get dressed.' He turns his attention again to Kirsty. 'Is your boyfriend, Tom I think you said, still in your room?'

Kirsty nods.

'In that case, please will you get your clothes and bring them out with you, we've an interview room where you can get dressed. Then I'll have a male officer accompany Tom and do the same thing. That's so we can search your room as well. Just routine, of course.' Arnison allows Kirsty, one male and one female police officer to escape his clutches for a moment. 'Drains the manpower,' he explains while we wait, 'but it may be one of those occasions where we can find something important very quickly.'

'Including the murderer?'

'Who knows? But given the locked doors and the security codes that had just been changed, it does seem to suggest that the murderer was an insider. And by your own admission, Taylor wasn't very popular. Somebody drunk, with a grudge, a suitable weapon at hand ... We'll see, Mr Oliphant, we'll see.'

Kirsty reappears clutching her clothes and all of us go out into the sunshine where a small village of police vehicles is now clustered: the interrogation room on wheels has been joined by another, and a third vehicle with the letters MOBILE FORENSIC UNIT on its side is occupying the third side of a square. A large petrol-powered generator is humming to itself, and more people in white coveralls are wandering around purposefully.

Arnison leads us into the nearest room. 'I think I'd like to see Miss Oliphant first,' he tells his sergeant. 'Mike, could you get Mr Oliphant's statement? It shouldn't take long, he's an ex-cop, knows the ropes. I think one of the attending officers has already jotted something down, you can use that to begin with. Then I'll see Miss Oliphant's boyfriend.' He whistles at another plain-clothes officer. 'Trace, give me five minutes and I'll have a list of who should be in which of the rooms in the halls. Work from that, check everyone's there who ought to be there, find out who's there who shouldn't be. Get them dressed, out and interviewed, no one to be left alone, no one to talk to anyone else. Got it?'

'Got it, boss,' the woman replies, starts giving instructions to others around her. An air of activity has descended on the day. Curious onlookers are being turned away by the uniformed officers, down to white shirts in the glare and reflected heat of the car park.

'Oh, and Trace,' Arnison adds, 'send one of the patrol cars off to the nearest supermarket for water, lemonade and so on. It's going to be a hot day.'

It doesn't take long for Mike Stephenson to take a statement. He's friendliness personified, as if I'm part of his team. He treats my information more like evidence from a fellow officer than an account from a witness. I'm clearly not a suspect, though I feel I ought to be; I know I didn't kill Taylor, but there's no way Stephenson can confirm that, not yet. Still, I've no objection if he wants to be my new best friend; docile and gullible policemen are always welcome additions to my notebook of contacts. His attitude, however, doesn't reassure me. Sometimes the elimination of those suspected of committing a crime is easy because that person has a good alibi. Sometimes, I'm ashamed to admit, it's because the investigating officer has a feeling about the person being questioned. That feeling can be wrong, of course, and following a gut reaction can be costly in terms of both time and lives; a murderer who is a pleasant, believable person can commit crimes again before being finally brought to justice. A clever murderer can be interviewed by police yet escape justice entirely. Stephenson's sloppy, I just hope Arnison's more proficient. I don't want a murderer on the loose when my daughter's so close at hand. For the moment, however, I'm free to leave.

To my surprise, Kirsty is sitting outside waiting. 'That was quick,' I tell her.

'I'm not sure if he's finished,' she says, puzzled. 'I told

him who was staying and where, he wrote it all down and gave the list to that policewoman. He asked me if Tom had spent all night with me. He had, and it's a small bed, if one of us had moved the other would have woken up.' Her former embarrassment has disappeared entirely, she's involved in telling her story. 'I told him that we both got up to go to the loo about three o'clock, I can remember looking at the time. Then we woke up about an hour later, it was getting light outside. I looked at the clock again because someone was making a noise and I thought it was a pain, somebody making a noise that late.'

'What type of noise was it?'

'It sounded like a door slamming, then slamming again. And there was laughing and a shushing noise. Tom heard it as well. I wanted him to get up and see what it was, but I was on the outside so I went instead.'

'And did you see anything?'

'Yes. I saw Anna going down the corridor. She was sort of staggering, going from side to side, then she'd laugh and hit her hand against the wall, as if she'd thought of something hilarious. She went as far as Jonathan's room, then she opened the door and went in.'

'Didn't you think to go and help her?'

'Help her do what? If she'd fallen over I would have gone to pick her up, but by the time she'd actually gone into Jonathan's room, it was too late. I was hardly going to burst in and haul her out, was I?' She swallows, shakes her head swiftly as if she can't understand what's going on. 'Anyway, it was late, I'd had a fair bit to drink, I was annoyed at being woken up. So I left it. I went back to bed, it was quiet after that. Next thing I can remember is waking up and hearing another noise outside, when I looked the place was full of policemen.'

'And you told Inspector Arnison all this?'

'Yes. He started asking me about Anna, how long I'd known her, how well she knew Jonathan. Then the policewoman came back, she said Inspector Arnison had better come quickly. He left. The policewoman came back and said the interview was over for the moment, could I wait outside. That was about five minutes ago.'

There are many questions I want to ask, but they remain stillborn. Even as I open my mouth Mike Stephenson hurries down the stairs towards the dormitory. He's wearing no jacket and his shirt has untucked itself from his trousers, as he runs – and his shape suggests he's more familiar with rolling than running – it flaps in his slip-stream. 'Wait there,' I tell Kirsty, run after him.

I expect to be halted by the uniformed officer at the door, but my walk around the scene of the crime with Arnison has given me a semi-official status. Because I'm so close behind Stephenson both of us are allowed to pass. We turn right; a high-pitched wailing is coming from Anna's room and faces are looking out of other doors. The wailing stops when its source needs to breathe, then begins again almost immediately at a higher pitch, a louder volume.

'For Christ's sake, shut up!' Arnison's voice is loud and percussive, it provides a bass accompaniment to the contin-uous keening.

Mike Stephenson announces his presence. 'Boss!'

'Get a cell ready, Mike, we've got something. If only the silly bitch would shut up. I haven't even read her her rights yet.'

I peer round the door. Anna herself is the source of the screaming. She's struggling against the combined grip of three officers, two holding an arm each, the third vainly trying to capture both her legs. She's kicking out, and in such a restricted space having some success. Her bare right foot swings at the policeman holding her left, hits him in the groin. He collapses, and Anna's success causes her to redouble her efforts. She's wearing a long baggy T-shirt, but it rides up and I catch a glimpse of her pubic hair (dyed the same bright blue as that on her head), her stomach, her breasts. Then she twists again and becomes almost decent, all the time screaming loudly.

Arnison sees me, barks out an order, 'Oliphant, out!' I'm conditioned to obey, my back is already turned when the screaming stops and becomes a counter order.

'No!' Anna shouts.

I turn again. Anna's body is suddenly still, limp, the police officers who were fighting her are now holding her up. The third officer, the one still recovering from her kick, crawls towards the door. Anna's gaze is directed at me. She's trying, unsuccessfully, to look confident; her face is defiant, but her eyes are full of fear. 'Let him stay,' she hisses, 'let him stay and I'll be quiet.'

Arnison nods; the slight motion of his head is confirmed by a wave of his hand that dismisses the large policeman hovering at my shoulder. He speaks slowly, clearly. 'Anna Peranski, I'm arresting you on suspicion of murder, you may remain silent but anything you do say may be used as evidence.' He seems relieved to have got his speech out of the way. 'We need to ask you some questions. Before we do this a police doctor will give you a thorough medical examination.' He reaches for a green silk dressing gown hanging on a hook behind the door. 'Will you agree to behave yourself? If so I'll instruct my officers to let go of you.'

Anna inhales, holds the breath in then expels it slowly. She nods. 'Yes,' she confirms, 'I won't do anything silly.'

'Please put this on,' Arnison says, handing her the dressing gown. 'Do you have any slippers?'

'Trainers,' Anna answers, shrugging herself into her gown, 'they'll do.'

Arnison lets her put her feet into the training shoes. She doesn't fasten the laces, but that doesn't matter; before they leave her alone they'll remove the laces and the belt from the dressing gown.

'I didn't kill him,' she says. Her hair is tangled, she's wearing the caked vestiges of last night's make-up.

'Didn't kill who?' Arnison says wearily.

'Jonathan Taylor,' Anna replies, sinking back onto the

90

bed, 'even if the bastard deserved it.'

'I don't recall mentioning that Jonathan Taylor was dead,' Arnison says.

'*You* didn't,' Anna snarls back, 'but your poxy bitch friend did. Why else would I start screaming like that?'

Arnison smiles at her. 'You'll have the chance to say whatever you want when we ask you questions later. But for the moment ...' He gestures towards the door.

'Why her?' I ask.

Arnison's friendliness has deserted him, he now resents my being there. 'Possible evidence,' he says curtly, 'which will be revealed to the appropriate authorities in due course.' I, of course, am not an appropriate authority.

'They found a T-shirt, my T-shirt, in the corner, covered in blood,' Anna announces, throws a glance at a clear plastic bag in one of the policemen's hands; its bright yellow cotton is stained with a dark, sinister red. Anna sniggers to herself. 'And it's not even that time of the month.'

'Why did you ask me to stay?' I ask her gently.

'Mr Oliphant,' Arnison says, 'I won't warn you again, I'll be entirely within my rights to charge you with obstruction if you keep on asking questions. I think it would be best if you left.'

'I didn't ask you to stay,' Anna answers me anyway, 'I just said I'd stop making a noise if you could stay. I was figuring out how far he'd let me go. How much rope I had.' She laughs again. 'Gallows humour, eh?'

'Is there anything I can do?'

'That does it, Oliphant. Out!'

I do as I'm told, I don't want to risk making Arnison more upset than he already is. My decision is aided by the presence of one of his burly plods who's helping my arm out; being attached to it, I follow. Outside in the corridor curious faces are being pushed back into their rooms.

'Is there anything you can do?' Anna yells after me. 'Yeah, you can find out who really did it! Fat bloody chance!'

'You're popular,' says the plod, 'what'd you do to upset her?'

'She can't resist my good looks and vibrant personality.'

'Dickhead! Piss off!' It's not clear whether Anna's yells are directed at me or at one of those unfortunate to be still in the room with her. I don't intend returning to find out. I'm quite happy to be escorted into the sunshine where Kirsty's waiting for me, her face a question mark.

'What's happening?' she asks. 'We heard shouting and screaming.'

'Arnison didn't tell you what happened, did he? He didn't say why you were being questioned?'

'No. But ... I knew it had to be something bad. Somebody killed?'

I pull her towards me. 'Jonathan Taylor was killed in the early hours of this morning.'

'No! Who would . . ?'

I decide to press on. 'Listen to me, Kirsty. It's true, I found his body. And now Arnison thinks he's found his murderer.'

'What? Not Anna?'

'Yeah, 'fraid so.'

'Oh.' That's all Kirsty says. Not 'She wouldn't do that,' or 'That's impossible,' or even 'I don't believe it,' just a plain simple 'Oh.' It's as if she finds nothing surprising in my statement. It's as if Anna killing Jonathan Taylor is a believable act. I take her arm, draw her to one side, to one of the park benches still within the newly formed police compound. We sit down in the heat of the morning.

'Could she have done it?'

Kirsty's still trying to understand, to put everything into perspective. 'Dad, you met Jonathan Taylor. He tried to have sex with her. He wasn't a nice man.'

There's no reply needed, no comment necessary. Kirsty's expecting neither, her pause simply allows her to gather her thoughts.

'He was a lecher. I hated it, watching him leering at

92

some girl. And he'd come up beside them and just stand there, then he'd stand a bit closer and ... He wouldn't touch with his hands, he'd just make sure there was body contact. And if you objected, he'd look all innocent, swear it wasn't intentional, and you'd think you were wrong and he was right. Till it happened again. He tried it once or twice with me, but I spilled some coffee down his trousers, accidentally on purpose. Then, next time, I stood on his toes. It was enough to let him know that I knew he was going too far, and he stopped. In fact, he seemed quite pleased I'd stood up to him. But I'm like you, Dad, and a bit like Mam, I'm not frightened of people like that. Other girls might have put up with it.'

'Anna doesn't seem the type to have put up with anything.'

'Anna's almost as strange as Taylor. I mean, you've seen her hair. And her piercings, let me tell you, Dad, she's got piercings in places other girls haven't got places. She doesn't really have any friends, not that I've seen. She's argumentative, bad-tempered, anti-social. The only reason everyone puts up with her is because she's such a good actor. At first I thought she was practising to be a diva, but she's like that all the time with everybody. She drinks, she does drugs – but not when she's acting, I'll give her that much – and she tries it on with men. Any man, as you know. She made a pass at Tom when I was with him. So ...'

This time the silence is long, it extends into the air and snakes around us.

'So?' I offer the prompt.

'So I don't really know what she's capable of, Dad.' She puts her head in her hands. 'Do you know when they'll be finished with us?' She seems suddenly tired, speaks to the ground beneath her feet.

'Shouldn't be long.' I don't want to go into the details of police procedure, but I need to justify my assumption. 'They'll probably let us go so they can concentrate on questioning Anna, ask us to call in to be interviewed at the police station. As far as I can tell, all they've got so far is a T-shirt with blood on it, but when I heard her Anna wasn't giving some plausible explanation. In fact she wasn't making much sense at all. They'll probably check to see if the blood matches Taylor's; if it does they'll do other tests – DNA , they'll want to find out if there's any of his under her fingernails, hers under his. Not that that'll prove much because they were touching each other last night anyway, there are witnesses to that. There might be other evidence as well, I'm not in the loop and unlikely to be so. But I think they'll let us go soon.'

I put my arm around her shoulder and she aims a smile in my direction, the type of smile that says 'thank you for thinking of me, but I still don't feel any better'. Yet there's nothing else I can say or do to improve matters.

We sit still, lost in our own thoughts. Both of us look up when the door opens. The procession of the accused begins with Mike Stephenson clutching a nest of self-important plastic bags. Behind him a plod keeps the door open to allow a trio to pass through, sideways. Anna's hands are cuffed behind her back, each arm is held by a further plod. Neatly book-ended, she seems small and frail, unlaced trainers flapping on her feet, dressing gown held closed in front of her by a plod's friendly hand. Kirsty tenses under my arm, she doesn't know how to react. Part of her, I imagine, wants to run over and hug Anna; the other wants to turn away, to ignore her. Caught between these extremes, she does nothing but sit and gaze, a look of help-lessness on her face.

Anna turns in our direction, but her eyes are focused on me. She spits forcefully on the ground then avoids my gaze altogether. I can't think why she should feel so angry with me. I'm not hurt by the fact, merely curious; so far as I'm aware I've done nothing to deserve this type of behaviour. If she can remember the previous night then I'm sure she'll also remember that, as well as rejecting her advances, I

94

also helped her when she felt threatened. There's no logic in her behaviour, so she must be taking refuge in the illogical processes of the mind. The word insane doesn't actually come to my mind, but I can taste its cloudy presence.

Arnison brings up the rear, his standard hangdog expression almost betrayed by a smile of triumph lingering at the corner of his lips.

I decide to take advantage of his apparent good mood. 'Inspector Arnison, do you know when we'll be allowed to go home?'

'Mr Oliphant.' He doesn't actually say anything for a while; his look, however, is that of a salmon fisherman who finds a stickleback grinning up at him from his hook, or a single malt *aficionado* with a green-coloured vodka concoction in his glass. Somehow he manages to look down on me from a far greater height than the eight inches that normally separate us. He tilts his head to make sure I can see his face, there's a mixture of disgust that he has to acknowledge my presence, and pleasure that he can demonstrate his power over me.

'I imagine we'll be interviewing your young friend for some time. We'll need to search her room thoroughly, follow up any leads her interview and the search bring up. So we'll take everyone's name and address down, their telephone numbers, and then ... Well, we'll be in touch to arrange further interviews.' He beams his self-satisfaction, allows its lighthouse beam to wash over me.

'I've quite a bit of equipment in the cloisters,' I add, 'tools I'll need to do my work. When can I get them out?'

'Quite a few of the students have got stuff in there as well,' Kirsty chips in, 'can't we just pop in and get the stuff out?'

Arnison reverts to humanity for a moment. 'We've got a sweep going on for evidence, it's a painstaking job and – as you'll remember, Mr Oliphant – can take quite a long time. But I'll see what I can do to speed things up, get a few extra bodies on the job.'

'Thanks,' I say, 'that's really helpful.' I mean it, there's no sarcasm in my voice. Arnison squints at me, he hardly knows me, can't tell whether I'm being genuine or not. He decides to give me the benefit of the doubt.

'Just don't leave until you're told you can do so,' he adds, an exclamation mark of a sentence to warn me that he's still in charge. Then he's off, shepherding his charges to one of the interrogation rooms.

'What are you going to do?' I ask Kirsty. 'This leaves a gap in your timetable, doesn't it? A free week?'

'Christ, yes! Shit, the play, what about the play? Everyone's put so much time and effort into it and . . .' She pushes her hands through her hair. 'Here's me worrying about a play and Jonathan's dead. Doesn't seem right, does it?' She puts her arm round me. 'I don't think I want to stick around here. Tom's got a flat, I could go there. I'll have to talk to him. I might go home, introduce Tom to Mum. Take him to meet Jen, perhaps.'

'She'd like that.' Jen has been absent from my mind all morning, it's refreshing to have her suddenly present again. 'How would Tom feel about that? Isn't it a bit threatening? You know, "Come and meet the folks back home."'

Kirsty pats my knee. 'Don't worry, Dad, we're not at the stage where you'll need to fork out for a wedding reception.'

'That's a relief.'

'Well, not for a few months yet.'

With the threat not yet lodged firmly in my mind I imagine what the wedding would be like. This isn't in specific terms, like dreaming of the venue and the guests. No, it's more of a general panic attack in which faceless morning-suited figures shower me with confetti made from torn-up invoices; people form disorderly queues as they disembark from coach after coach, waiting to enter a marquee the size of a football stadium; and when I stand up to make my speech, I find that all my notes are in Russian

96

or Arabic. I decide that it's worth bribing Kirsty to elope.

'But we are serious about each other,' Kirsty says, blushing.

Any further thoughts I have on the matter are dispersed by Tom's rapid approach. He hurries across the car park towards us, Kirsty rises to greet him with an embrace and a kiss. 'There's gonna be trouble,' he announces.

I ask the obvious question. 'Why, what's happened?'

'You know the police have got the area cordoned off, no one can go in or out without them saying so?'

Kirsty and I both nod.

'Well, we've got a visitor. Belle is at the main entrance, she's acting like a prima donna. She's demanding to be let in, she says she's got a play to direct and if they don't let her through she'll sue them.'

'Didn't you tell her what's happened?' Kirsty asks.

'I don't know what's happened! And anyway, when Belle's in that type of mood you don't say anything at all except how far and what direction.'

I climb to my feet, hoping that both Tom and Kirsty appreciate my weariness and my dedication. 'I'll go and talk to Belle,' I sigh. 'I don't think there'll be any problem letting her know what I know. Kirsty, you'd better do the same for Tom.'

'But Detective Arnison said not to talk . . .'

'Detective Arnison has a prime suspect, love, and I don't think he'll mind you telling everyone the bare bones of what you know. Don't go spreading gossip, but if anyone asks you, tell them.'

I leave Kirsty sitting Tom down, his face curious, her hands compassionate on his shoulders. I weave my way between the parked cars and vans, the mobile rooms and generators. Tall temporary fencing protects the newly formed enclave, and there's only one entrance, guarded by two police officers. I feel sorry for them; even before I can see the gate, the sound of Belle in full haranguing mode is loud and clear.

97

'What do you mean, I can't come in? I've already explained, I've a play to direct. Now would you mind telling me exactly why I can't come in. If you can't, or if you won't, find someone in authority who will. I've already written down your numbers, I'll complain, believe me, I *will* complain.'

'Madam, I've told you as much as I can tell you.' My old friends Plods One and Two have been allocated gate duty. Plod One is taking the brunt of Belle's antagonism. He looks as if he'd love to be back on motor patrol but, given the circumstances, is being extremely polite. 'There's a police investigation. No one may enter or leave the crime-scene unless given permission to do so by the officer in charge. You, I'm afraid, do not have permission.' I'm sure I can trace a degree of satisfaction in his voice as he pronounces each of the last four words carefully, slowly.

'Then bring me the officer in charge.' Belle is unfailingly polite. She's a throwback to those middle-class, matronly women who ruled society between – and during – the wars, certain that God and Britannia were on their side and that nothing could prevent them achieving their aims. The two policemen aren't used to such an approach; they look at each other, each wanting the other to take charge, to grant permission for this worrisome terrier to be allowed in, to get her out of the way.

'The officer in charge is conducting interviews,' Plod Two says, unwillingly assuming charge because of his greater age and experience.

'Then bring his deputy.'

'He's busy interviewing as well.'

'*His* deputy then. Or anyone with authority. Or I will be summoning the Chairman of the Police Authority, who is a friend of my family, and the Chief Constable, whose son is on the same law course as I am, to explain that you two are proving particularly unhelpful.'

'I'm sorry, madam, there's nothing I can do to help at the moment.'

It's not a situation that demands my attention; if I leave now the impasse will merely continue until one of the officers loses his patience and gives Belle something to really complain about. I feel, however, that I should do my best to put all of them out of their misery. 'Hello,' I say brightly to Belle, 'is there anything I can do to help?'

It's pleasant to find that those few words bring a smile to the lips of all three combatants. 'Mr Oliphant,' Plod One begins, 'do you know ...'

'Mr Oliphant,' Belle overlaps and then silences the policeman's voice, 'thank goodness you're here, perhaps you could tell these gentlemen that I have no intention of spoiling their little investigation, all I want is to come in and have a rehearsal.'

'Belle's the director of the play we were putting on,' I tell the policemen. 'She was at the party last night for a little while. I think Inspector Arnison might actually be interested in speaking to her.' That's a lie, of course. Arnison already has enough witnesses to the previous night's events, and he has a prime suspect for Taylor's murder. But the guards probably aren't aware of this, nor do they know that I'm no longer Arnison's bosom friend.

'What exactly has been happening?' Belle asks. 'It must be something serious for all this to be here?'

'Can she come in?' I ask the policemen. They look at each other again. 'Look,' I tell them, 'what's going to happen if you don't let her in? You've seen what a pain she can be. She'll probably go and get a few reporters, they'll come and interview her in front of you, you'll look like pillocks. Your boss'll be annoyed because you let her go and he might have wanted to talk to her. So why not let me look after her, make sure she doesn't do anything she shouldn't. Then, if she does misbehave, it's my fault, and he can come direct to me.'

The two policemen exchange meaningful looks once more. 'What d'you think?' One asks, deferring immediately to the authority of his older colleague.

'God knows,' Two replies. 'But Arnison said we weren't to let anyone in or out.'

Belle picks up the cue. 'I'm sorry, Mr Oliphant, I can't afford to wait any longer. If these two officers aren't willing to take your word and my word then I'm afraid I'll have no alternative but to summon the press.'

One gives in. 'For Christ's sake, come in,' he says, hurling open the gate. He throws a glance over his shoulder, it's aimed at me. 'And if the boss complains, you get the blame.'

'Nothing will happen,' I reassure him. 'What could possibly go wrong?' Before he can answer I usher Belle past him and through the outer arc of police vehicles.

'What on earth has happened?' she asks again.

I lead her towards Kirsty and Tom who, on seeing us coming, rise from the bench they've been occupying. Kirsty opens her arms, folds Belle into them and begins crying. Tom pats Belle gently on the back, sorrow clouding his face. I can't reconcile this Kirsty with the one who was discussing, almost nonchalantly, Taylor's death with me. Perhaps it's a girl thing, this mutual shedding of tears, because Belle too is crying.

'What is it?' she asks again. 'What's happened?'

'Sit down,' I say to her. When she's in her allotted place she looks up at me like an expectant child waiting for some distant uncle to bestow pocket money. I decide the best way of dealing with this is to be honest. If Belle takes it badly I can always leave Kirsty to share her distress and comfort her. 'Last night, or rather, in the early hours of this morning, someone killed Jonathan Taylor.'

'What?'

That's the first stage, questioning. After that comes disbelief. 'Taylor's dead,' I repeat.

'He can't be! I don't believe it!'

Next come requests for further details which, naturally, are sparse at the moment.

'How did it happen?'

100

'He was knifed,' I tell her. 'His body was left on the stage.'

That's when she departs from the script. She should start crying again, hold her head in her hands. She should look helpless, as indeed she is, as we all are. We're reliant on others now, on the investigative powers of boys in blue under the leadership of Chief Inspector Arnison. Belle, in the shadow of this monolithic procedure, should sigh and shake her head, perhaps offer a word or two of sympathy to the memory of Taylor. Instead her brow furrows, her eyes focus on mine, her air of bewilderment is replaced by one of determination.

'The bastard!'

'We don't know who did it yet,' Kirsty says gently, but Belle's words aren't directed towards the murderer.

'No, Taylor! He's the bastard! Just like him to go and get himself killed! The little shit!'

I'm surprised, but I try not to show it. I've had too much practice in hiding my emotions, I'm good at it. Kirsty, however, is too young to have developed this talent (latent in most people but more easily developed, I've found, in women than in men) and expresses her distress immediately. 'Belle,' she speaks the words clearly, 'that's a terrible thing to say! Jonathan's been murdered and you call him names?'

Belle looks as if she's going to fight back. She takes a deep breath; her eyebrows descend as if they want to unite in one. Tom takes a step forward, he too thinks Belle is about to defend herself. But Belle lets the moment last too long, the seconds stretch until she has to breathe out again, and that exhalation seems to reduce her anger. 'Sorry. It was just ... We've been working so hard for this play, and now it's all ruined. I mean, nobody really liked Jonathan. You didn't like him, did you?' She doesn't wait for an answer. 'He was a creep, everyone agreed. But you're right, he didn't deserve to die.' She looks at me and her eyes are misted. 'What happened?'

'I found him. On the stage, sitting down. Naked. Dead. With a knife in his chest.'

'Yes, she says, 'you already said that. But what else happened? Did anybody hear anything? Were there any signs on the stage, of a struggle or anything?' Her questions are like acrobats, tumbling eagerly from her mouth. 'And who would do something like that?'

'There were ... let's just say there were noises. Things were seen.' I don't want to say too much, it's the policeman in me; one individual's evidence shouldn't be made public in case it distorts someone else's. In this instance it shouldn't matter too much, Belle wasn't present last night. But I'm uncommunicative by nature anyway.

'I heard noises during the night,' Kirsty tells her. 'I went out into the corridor to have a look and I saw someone going into Jonathan Taylor's room.'

The pause for breath is natural, but Belle uses it to throw in another question. 'Who did you see?' She leans forward with a teenager's eagerness to know gossip.

Kirsty answers in a similar vein, almost in a whisper. 'It was Anna.'

'No!'

'Yes! She was sort of lurching from side to side, like she was still drunk. And I saw her go into Jonathan's room.'

'But I thought they were fighting earlier.' Belle's words suggest that Anna might have been going to Taylor's room for companionship rather than revenge. Perhaps Taylor's statement the previous night that he and Anna were a 'sort of item' and that they 'had a scene going' reflected the truth.

Kirsty doesn't allow me to ask Belle what she knows. 'They were fighting,' she confirms, 'but that's a motive, isn't it? And Dad said the police found one of Anna's T-shirts in her room, covered with blood.'

'Well.' As a single word sentence it end-stops the conversation nicely. It announces Belle's absorption of the facts, her acceptance of the nuances of Kirsty's joint accusation-information. 'It sounds as if the police have found a suspect, then. Motive and evidence.'

'It's not real proof,' I announce, worried about this over-quick supposition of guilt. 'Yes, Anna had a rather public fight with Taylor last night. But the blood on her shirt need not be his. The police need further forensic evidence, what they have isn't really enough to go on.'

'So what happens next?' Tom has suddenly found a voice.

'They test the blood. Do other tests as well. It'll take them quite a while. I imagine they'll soon let us go home.' That's when I look at the mobile forensic unit, something that didn't exist when I was in the force. Perhaps they're doing those tests now. Perhaps there will be evidence, swift, accurate evidence. Perhaps they'll know sooner than I anticipate.

'I should ring round,' Belle says, 'let everyone know that they shouldn't bother coming in for the rehearsal. Waste of time, really. No lead actor. No theatre. Did someone mention the Scottish play last night?' She takes out her mobile phone and looks at it. 'So many people had so much invested in this. They're going to be so upset. I don't know if I can tell them.'

'Leave it,' Kirsty says. 'Let them turn up. When they see what's happening they'll understand better.'

'Except they won't get in,' Tom says, 'unless Mr O can work his wonders again, with the police on the gate.'

'I think that was a one-off,' I tell him.

'Then we should go and wait by the gate,' Belle announces. 'Us on one side, new arrivals on the other.' The shift into organisational mode is swift and effective. 'Tom, you go and tell anyone still in the halls who isn't in with the police to meet at the gate as soon as possible. Kirsty . . .'

I have to interrupt. 'I don't think the police will like that. They won't want lots of potential witnesses exchanging information before they've been interviewed.'

'Then we won't exchange information. I'll just tell them what's happened, the same way you told me.' She sees me shaking my head. 'Come on, Mr O, they'll know by now that Taylor's been killed. I won't mention the how, I won't mention Anna, all I'll tell them about is the production. You've seen how keen they are, how hard everyone has worked. It's the least they deserve.'

Her voice is very persuasive, it has the gravitas of an airline pilot informing passengers of the plane's height, there's no chance of contradicting it. It isn't hectoring but it has a touch of the teacher or priest about it. What she says is logical as well, it's the way I'd like to be treated if I had to be told tragic news, disappointing news. And, let's face it, the police haven't been overly vigilant in keeping witnesses apart within the boundary of their enclave. They have their suspect, they're not interested – at the moment – in listening to anyone else.

It's suddenly evident that Kirsty, Tom and Belle are waiting for me to say something. It's become my decision; on my say so we (I've begun to include myself in the band of players and associates) will either have a meeting on both sides of the fence or Belle will telephone those already on their journeys. Whatever she does, information and gossip will be passed around; Arnison wouldn't care for either. I don't like making decisions for other people, but this one is made easy by the way Arnison talked to me earlier. Politeness costs nothing, and his lack of civility has cost him my goodwill. 'Well,' I tell my companions, 'I don't think we'll be harming anyone by gathering together, so we might as well head out to the gates now, just in case anyone else gets turned away.'

Three faces grin at me. Tom and Kirsty hurry away to summon their friends, Belle and I stroll towards the gate.

'Do you think Anna did it?' She's the conspirator now, keen to have my personal thoughts, my opinions. She's quiet, almost whispering.

'I don't know.'

'Do you think she could have done it, then?'

There's a subtle difference in the questions that makes me delay answering the second. I honestly don't know if Anna is the murderer. Deciding whether she's innocent or guilty isn't my job, and the decision itself is objective. It's based on facts and evidence. Knowing whether someone *could* do something is, however, making a subjective statement. It's based on supposition, on human traits, on frailties and quirks of character. I've sometimes wondered if I could kill someone. Oh, I know it's part of police training, using force if necessary, and that force can result in death on very rare occasions. But that's official, that's being granted powers by the state, powers which bring responsibilities. What I'm thinking of here is power without responsibility, of being a civilian and taking someone's life. There might be a motive; I've no doubt that if someone placed Kirsty or Jen in danger, threatened to take their lives, and I was in a position to protect them, then I would do so. If that resulted in the death of the individual threatening to harm them, then I would probably make the decision to kill that individual. So, I suppose, I'm capable of murder. But in that case, many other people could do the same, including Anna. The logical answer to Belle's question is that Anna certainly could have killed Taylor. But so could I, Tom, Kirsty, or even Belle herself. I believe we all have the potential to kill buried within each of us; but with some, it's nearer the surface than with others. I give my guarded response. 'She could have done. But so could lots of other people.'

'You don't give much away, do you? What do you think? What's your personal opinion?' She's determined to have me commit myself in some way.

'I don't have enough information to have an opinion. In murder, you can't be subjective. It's not to do with how you feel, it's to do with evidence.'

'Well my opinion,' she says firmly, 'is that she didn't do

it. I don't think she's the type, I don't think she could actually do it, kill somebody.'

I want to tell her that the relationship between Taylor and Anna was more complex than she imagines. I want to tell her about the note, the note that could be a means of entrapment, a way of luring Taylor to his death. I want to tell her that grey-haired old ladies have been known to kill, that innocent-looking children have been known to kill, that anyone under the right type of pressure can kill. But I say nothing. Because if Anna didn't kill Jonathan Taylor, then the person who did is still free and probably making his or her way out to the gate to join us.

Chapter Five

Most of the cast and crew were staying in the university
halls for the night. As Belle and I arrive at the gate they
too are beginning to assemble. They're like the zombies in
a cheap horror film, silent, ambling slowly but purposefully. I can guess how they're feeling. They'll be confused,
their initial inability to understand the horror of the crime
will have been replaced by the opposite, their imaginations
will have taken over and their conception of murder will be
too clear, too personal. This is a standard reaction, police
officers are taught to recognise its stages and deal with
them appropriately. So I know that next will come the need
to talk, to share their experiences, to comfort and be
comforted. There'll be tears, there may even be hysteria. I
almost turn away, I don't want to be involved in this
anymore, I never wanted to be involved in the first place.
That's when I see Kirsty, her hand clutching Tom's,
moving through the crowd and talking to her friends. She
touches one, smiles at another, hugs a third. And because
she's there, because she might need me, I don't really have
the option of leaving.

Beside the gate the two policemen are looking worried.
No one has gone near them, no one has done anything
contrary to their instructions, but they suspect the gathering
wouldn't be welcomed by their superiors. They talk to each
other, then one of them speaks into the microphone of his

radio; he seems to be conversing with a dislocated shoulder.

I sit down on the grass, trying to remember unfamiliar names and attach them to pale, freshly scrubbed faces. Belle and Vicky are straightforward; the razor-haired young man talking to both of them is Kenny, nose like an eagle's beak, set designer. Two of the boys, I think, play a drunkard and his friend; their shapes are complementary, the first round, the second tall and thin. I imagine them together as an exclamation mark, close my eyes, but no names are dredged from my memory. Then the tall one sees me looking at him, looks away in embarrassment, and I realise he's Louis whom I helped to bed last night. Louis who'd been having sex with Anna on the stage until I interrupted them. Louis who might even be wondering whether Taylor's fate might have been his.

'Everyone seems a bit sad,' says a voice at my shoulder.

'Not really surprising, in the circumstances.' I'm pleased Tom's chosen to join me. 'See the couple over there, just sitting down, the two lads? Louis's the tall one, but the other . . .'

'The other one's John. He plays Sir Toby, Louis's Sir Andrew, two comic characters.'

'And Toby's the drunk?'

'That's right. Do you know the play?'

'No. I hated Shakespeare at school. Kirsty's told me a bit about it, though, and I was trying to remember who everyone was. I was introduced last night but . . .'

'They all look alike, these students. I can tell you who they are if you want. But I imagine we'll all be dismissed soon, you probably won't see them again.'

'Yes, you're right. Hardly seems worthwhile. But on the other hand, there isn't a great deal else to do.'

Tom points beyond the fence. 'That's Rad. He plays Feste the jester, he's a bit of a comedian so I suppose that fits. I always had him figured as a computer nerd – that's the course he's on, computing – but he's quite normal

108

really. I think he had a room sorted here but he probably got off with somebody and decided to go back to her place for a quick shag.' Tom seems to have forgotten that he's talking to his girlfriend's father. He looks around. 'I hope the girl, whoever she was, didn't have a good sense of smell, his personal hygiene isn't too good. I wonder who it was? Can't see anyone else missing. Surely he didn't score with the ice-maiden herself?'

'The ice-maiden?'

'Yeah, Belle. I've never fancied her myself, but some of the lads think she could be a bit of a demon when she's roused. They think her glasses and straight hair, and the attitude, they all distract from the real woman within. Anyway, she's the only other one who spent the night outside.'

I'm not sure why, but I feel a need to defend Belle's – and Rad's – reputation. 'He could have just gone to see someone else, someone he already had a date with.'

'With free booze and a handy bed to collapse in here? Come on, Mr O, in the hierarchy of students' needs, sleep is only topped by alcohol, and alcohol's just below sex. No, he sniffed a weakness somewhere and he pounced.' He sniggers to himself. 'I'll have to give him the old cross-examination myself, find out one or two things. I wonder if he was the first?'

'Who else is down there?' I ask him, not because of a thirst for information but because I feel a need to change the topic of conversation. There are some things a father doesn't need to know about his daughter's friends and lifestyle.

'The girl with the red hair, the little one, that's Rachel. She's in charge of the costume and props. The Galadriel look-alike is Natalie, she's stage-manager along with Kirsty. Angie you know, she's our musician, violinist, plays Curio. They're all there. The guy with the glasses cuddling the girl, that's quiet Dave, he plays Malvolio, he's the one the other characters make fun of. His friend is

Lorna the loony. She's not really insane, just a bit of an extrovert, plays Olivia. And George over there, lying down, nicknamed Lennie but not to his face, he's Orsino, the Duke. Do you know *Of Mice and Men*?'

'No. But Kirsty was talking about a character called Curley from the same book.'

'That's right. Well Lennie's another character, he's a bit dim.'

'But this is a university.'

'Yeah, but not a very good one. Anyway, he's a rugby player. Sports scientist. Enough said?'

It isn't, but I nod anyway. Tom's brief portraits have succeeded in filling in time but have added little to my knowledge of the individuals concerned. Nonetheless, I run their names through my head again in an attempt to memorise them: John with the beard is Sir Toby; lanky Louis is Sir Andrew; Angie – could she have written the note I found in Taylor's room? – is the musician; Rachel is in charge of costume and props – where did she keep the knives and swords? Natalie is stage manager; Dave plays someone whose name I can't remember, but the others don't like him; Lorna's Olivia, who's loved by George the plank as Orsino. Surely there are some missing. Yes, Tom hasn't mentioned Vicky's boyfriend Kenny, the set designer. And wasn't there a tall girl with long hair?

I look around again to see where the missing people might be, but my gaze goes no further than the two policemen. They've finished their deliberations, received their instructions. Plod One saunters in my direction. 'What's going on, Mr Oliphant?'

'Nothing to do with me,' I tell him, 'I'm just an innocent spectator. When we were talking earlier you mentioned that no one could come in and no one go out. Belle, she's the girl over there, rather severe looking, she's the director of the play they were going to put on.'

The policeman looks puzzled.

'The play,' I explain slowly, 'on the stage. Remember,

where the body was found?'

He nods, not sure what I'm trying to explain to him.

'Well, she wanted to tell everyone about the play they were doing, how it couldn't go on now. But some of the team are outside and some are inside; out here by the fence is the only place she can talk to them altogether.'

'And what's she going to say?'

I thought I'd already told him this. 'I imagine she'll tell them that Jonathan Taylor has been murdered, Anna Peranski seems to be a prime suspect, and the play's been cancelled.'

The policeman looks worried. 'Tell her not to say anything yet,' he grunts, stalks away already speaking into his radio.

'I'll try,' I tell his retreating back, 'but I'm only the unpaid help.'

Belle is already ushering her team together on both sides of the fence, I stroll across to speak to her. 'Our minders would like you to wait a little while before saying anything,' I tell her. 'They seem to be a little nervous.'

'Why would that be?' she asks imperiously.

I wonder – but keep the thought to myself – if she's modelled herself on Margaret Thatcher; her eyes have the same slight gleam of insanity. I try to explain. 'I think the technical term is "witness collusion". They don't want you saying too much about what happened in case the information colours the statements they'll collect.'

'I won't say too much. The bare details.'

'Really?'

She looks almost affronted. 'Mr Oliphant, don't you trust me?'

'I don't know you well enough to trust you, Belle. And I work by the principle that trust has to be earned, and you haven't had enough time to earn that trust. So I may, at some time in the future, come to trust you. But for the moment, no, I don't trust you.'

She raises a lop-sided grin to her face. 'A wise answer,

111

Mr Oliphant. Not necessarily a wise decision, but certainly a wise answer.' She lifts one shoulder in a half-hearted shrug. 'Does that mean you'll try to stop me if I begin speaking before that policeman comes back?'

It's my turn to grin. 'My police days are long past, I'm not going to stop you doing anything. But if anyone takes offence, you won't be able to say you weren't warned.'

'Thank you for the warning. But I'm not ready to say anything yet anyway; the third estate has still to arrive.'

'The what?'

'The press. You see, Mr Oliphant, I have a little idea about something, and if it all works out ...'

'Yes?'

'Then it all works out. You'll see. I won't say more, I wouldn't want to involve you as an accessory.'

If I ever had any doubts that Belle could organise matters, they're soon dispersed. First of all, just as she glances at her watch, there's a flurry of activity in the car park. An MPV draws up and disgorges a young woman whose face manages to be both tired and attractive at the same time. Before she heads in our direction she checks her hair and make-up in the wing mirror. She leaves behind two technicians who manhandle a camera and tripod from the rear of the vehicle and begin to connect the disparate pieces of equipment together.

I find myself standing close to the comics of the play, doughnut John and skeletal Louis.

'Pray tell me, Sir Andrew,' John says, holding an imaginary microphone towards his colleague's mouth, 'headeth yonder fit television interview damsel in our direction?'

'Verily, Sir Toby, I fear not. A murder committeth is worth two birds in the moss.'

'Surely, my dear coz, thou meaneth a rolling cook gathers no bush?'

'Nay, thou drunkle uncle Toby still in thy cups from yesternight's Stella, speak truthfully for my mind is full of scorpions.'

112

'Wrong play, Louis,' John says.

'Yes, I know, but I'm dazed and confused by the beauty of that woman. She's got beautiful . . .'

'She certainly has. And as for those . . .'

'Truly magnificent! I'd like to . . .'

'After me in the queue. Do you think she'd . . .'

'No, not with you.'

'But I'm very . . .'

'Possibly a little too much, John, you wouldn't want to . . .'

'I might! If she wanted me to.'

I can't bear to listen to the repartee any more. Such flippancy doesn't seem to fit well with the circumstances. 'She'll probably want to interview the detective in charge of the case,' I tell them, 'but it wouldn't surprise me if Belle's got something to do with her arrival.'

'Why would Belle have done that?' The question demands no response. They don't expect me to know the answer, and their eyes don't leave the young woman now almost at the makeshift gate. Her presence gives the duty constables something else to worry about, and the radio is already being consulted even as she arrives. The communication is brief, I can hear none of it, but the woman nods her head vigorously and then steps back, waits for the technicians to arrive. As she motions them into position I see Belle moving nearer to the gate, nearer to the reporter, but neither speaks to the other.

Others are walking slowly to the gate, on both sides of the fence, though I can recall no sign being given that they should do so. It could be that they're simply curious, that they want to hear what's happening; or it could be that Belle has told them beforehand where she wants them, when she wants them. Against my inclination – I too want to hear what's being said – I retreat so that my back is resting against one of the police vehicles. Beside me are the railed steps leading to the door, and Detective Arnison doesn't notice me when he steps out onto them. He's taken

113

off his jacket and rolled up his shirt sleeves, as if he's had to do some manual work; his long, lean face is happier than I've seen it for some time.

'Found your murderer?' I ask quietly.

'Oliphant!' he mutters as he spins round. 'Why is it always you interrupting my thoughts?' He nods at the television camera but doesn't seem overly concerned at its presence. 'I hope this is none of your doing.'

'No, not me.'

He doesn't seem convinced. 'Anytime something awkward happens, your name comes to mind.'

'I'll change my name then, just so you won't be able to blame me.'

'Ah, it would still be you, though, even with a different name. Trouble through and through.' He looks down at me, but there's no real dislike in his face. He's simply going through the motions, telling me what I expect to hear.

'You've charged her then?'

If he's surprised, he hides it well. 'Wait and see, Oliphant, wait and see. There'll be an announcement.'

'So the blood matches?'

He shakes his head, he's not saying I'm wrong, just that he's not going to tell me anything. 'Wait and see.'

On the other side of the vehicle there are people moving; I crouch down to look beneath the chassis, the large forensic unit is being prepared for travel, its steps are being withdrawn, outriders are being wound in. That must mean Arnison has his evidence.

'The blood matches,' I tell him, 'you're getting ready to leave.'

His smile is deliberately enigmatic, he says nothing.

'Is that enough, though? It could have got there in any number of different ways. There must be something else. Fingerprints? Anna's fingerprints on the knife?' I know he's not going to reply, but I go on anyway. 'Trouble is, she was rehearsing earlier yesterday using that knife, fingerprints don't show that she was holding the knife when

114

it killed Taylor. There must be something else.'

'Whoops,' Arnison announces, 'I think it's my cue.' He descends the steps. 'Watch the news, Oliphant, you'll find out what's happened. And if you want the details, well, I'm afraid you'll have to wait for the case to come to court. Unless you happen to be an amateur defence lawyer as well as an amateur investigator.' He strides down towards the gate, trying on different degrees of smile until he finds one most appropriate for the triumphant detective.

'He thinks Anna's guilty, then?' Vicky appears in the shadow at my side.

'I've never seen anyone so sure,' I tell her. 'He's got evidence, motivation, the lot. He must have, if he's making a statement to the press this early. He thinks he's solved the case. He wouldn't be that confident unless the evidence was really solid.'

'So you think she did it as well?'

The note comes to my mind again. If Arnison has sufficient evidence to accuse Anna of the murder, then the scrap of paper is doing nothing but add to my own opinion that she was, at the very least, enticing Taylor. But did she kill him? I answer Vicky's question at the same time as I answer my own; 'I didn't say that.'

'But you implied it.'

'I don't know, and I don't like to guess. All I'm doing is trying to put myself in Arnison's mind.'

'I don't think she did it,' Vicky says. 'I know you'll probably say it's the heart speaking rather than the brain, but I don't think she could do it.'

'Anyone of us has the potential ...' I begin, but I'm not allowed to continue.

'I don't mean she *wouldn't* do it, Mr Oliphant. I mean she *couldn't*. You saw how drunk she was, I had to help her to bed. I've been drunk before, I know how it feels. Christ, I'm a student, I know how uncoordinated drunk people are. Jonathan Taylor may have been small, but he was strong. I don't think it would have been possible for

115

Anna to kill him even if she was sober.'

'The police disagree,' I tell her, 'they must be certain ...' I hear a familiar voice on the other side of the trailer. 'Just wait here,' I tell Vicky, 'I'll see what I can find out.' I head round the front of the vehicle. 'Do me a favour,' I call back, 'go and listen to the interview, just so I know what Arnison says.' She nods and hurries away; I continue to head into the inner sanctum of the police compound.

Sergeant Stephenson is flapping his arms to aid his instructions, but the men under his command don't really appear to be doing as he wants. It's as if he's conducting a Beethoven symphony while his musicians are determined to play an orchestral version of 'Yellow Submarine'. As I walk towards him he seems pleased at the interruption. 'Mr Oliphant,' he says, 'we won't be in your hair much longer.'

At first I'm not sure if he intended poking fun at my baldness (the top of my head is already feeling in need of a hat to protect it from the sun) but I soon decide it's simply a phrase he normally uses; he's incapable of humour that even touches the colour of subtlety.

'Congratulations,' I tell him, 'you must be really pleased at winding the case up so quickly.'

He looks a little suspicious. 'I didn't say we were ...' He looks around him at the activity, the bustle of packing away and making secure. 'That is, we're not making any firm statement yet, not until ...'

'It's all right,' I say, tapping the side of my nose with my finger, a gesture even he can't fail to recognise and understand, 'I've spoken to Mr Arnison. He's just gone down to talk to the press. Seemed in a good mood.'

Stephenson relaxes a little. It's as if I've crossed a line, I'm not a civilian asking awkward questions but a colleague already possessing key information. He preens, swells a little, enjoying the sunshine of praise. 'Well, it's hardly surprising the boss is in a good mood, is it? He'll get promotion for this, case wrapped up in a few hours.'

'She didn't confess, did she?' I try to disguise my

116

statement as a question, then hurry on before it really registers. 'But you hardly need a confession, her T-shirt had Taylor's blood on it. Plus the fingerprints on the murder weapon. I mean, that would be enough to make an arrest by itself. And then there's the other forensic information as well ...' The hook's baited.

'Yes, it all began to build up.' He sniggers. 'It was quite funny, there we were, asking her questions and she's denying everything, then every ten minutes there's something new to say it must have been her.'

'I suppose the DNA's the main thing. There's no arguing with that in court.'

'Yeah, DNA evidence is always impressive. I mean, it's early days yet, we haven't got a full report on that. But we've done outline tests and it looks good. I just hope she keeps on denying it when it gets to court, just so I can hear the evidence stacked up against her.' He looks around to make sure no one's listening or watching. 'Did the boss tell you everything?'

'We talked about it pretty thoroughly. He did have to hurry away, though, before he finished. Said I should pop through and see you. But I can see you're busy, so I'll save it for another day.'

'No, no, it's no bother at all.' He wants his moment of glory, his chance to bask in adulation. 'What it boils down to is this. Like you said, the blood and fingerprints are a match. But we did a medical, stripped her off. At least, one of the female detectives did, and a police doctor. But it was taped and videoed. Quite a smart little thing, really. Bit too small for me, I like them taller, bigger tits, and as for that blue hair! But ... Where was I?'

'The medical.'

'Oh yes. Well, they found traces of saliva in her hair, Taylor's saliva. And in her pubic hair too. And that's not all. Taylor's semen, in her pubes and on her hair, and inside her as well. Pretty conclusive stuff, eh?'

I have to agree with him, even if I don't want to. That's

117

when I realise he's waiting for me to speak, an expectant puppy-dog. 'There's more?'

He almost jumps up and down with excitement. 'Taylor gave out some cameras at the party. We found his, definitely his, only his prints on it. And the photographs?' He wants to milk the moment.

'Go on.'

'Taylor and Peranski having sex. In his room. I mean, what more do you need?'

'What more indeed. Sounds like an open-and-shut case.' I hope he appreciates the cliché. I hold out my hand to him. 'Well done.'

'Yeah,' he says immodestly, takes my outstretched hand and shakes it in what he thinks is a firm, manly way, 'I suppose we all played our parts.' He looks around, his men are working efficiently. 'Jesus Christ, you stop for a minute and everything goes to pot.' He raises his voice. 'Come on, you lazy bastards, do I have to do everything myself?'

'See you around,' I tell him. 'Enjoy the rest of the weekend.'

'I will,' he cries, throwing the words over his shoulder.

I hurry away to join the small crowd of students clustered by the gate. They seem remarkably well behaved, silent and attentive as Arnison makes his statement and deflects the reporter's questions. I sidle up to Vicky. 'What's going on?' I whisper.

'It's taken him about ten minutes to say bugger all. They've arrested a suspect, it was a horrible murder, they've made rapid progress. He's started talking in police-speak as well, God knows why they do that. "I was approachin' the buildin' at approximately ten twenty-one and fifteen seconds when I 'eard a sound of laughter. On further investigation I discovered it was only a student expressin' 'er 'umour at my accent." They watch too many fifties police films on the night shift.'

'What's the reporter been asking, then? Anything to make Arnison nervous?'

'No, just what you'd expect from a local jock. Mundane stuff, nothing that might cause too much trembling. But just wait, something'll happen. Look, Belle's moving round. This should be good.'

'What do you mean?'

'Well, why do you think the reporter's here?'

I know it isn't a pointless question, I know that Belle's involved somehow, but I'd rather have Vicky confirm my suspicions. 'I would imagine she's here to interview Arnison, of course.'

'And how did she get to know about the murder?'

'Same as reporters always do. Either there's been a press release, or there's been a leak from the force, someone who knows someone has said . . .'

'Oh, someone knows someone all right.' She leans closer. 'The reporter's called Stacey Ellison. She's a graduate of this very university, one of the luminaries they wheel out for PR events. She does her bit for the old *alma mater*, she gets fed the occasional scoop. So if this is Stacey's exclusive, it'll be interesting to see what Belle gets in return.'

Kenny sidles up to join us, puts his arm round her. 'Wait for it, Vicks,' he says, 'this is her big moment.'

'What are you on about?' Vicky asks.

'Well, not her only big moment, but certainly one of them. She's going to persuade the big bad policeman to let her go ahead with the show.'

'She's what?' I can't hide my surprise.

'"The show must go on," and all that crap. Since the police appear to have their murderer, Belle's going to persuade the Inspector that she should be allowed into the cloisters and get the play going again.'

'But Anna had the main part,' Vicky says, her voice incredulous. 'How can we go on without her?'

'And there's just been a murder.' I add, 'Belle can't realise how that affects everyone connected to the play.'

'Well that's what she's going to do,' Kenny says. 'Silly

bitch. Lack of self-confidence was never one of her faults. She knows she can do it.'

'Come on,' I tell them, 'we need to get closer.' I lead them towards the gate where the interviewer is nodding vigorously in response to something Arnison's said. Belle's moving closer to them all the time.

'I understand, Inspector' the interviewer asks, 'that the cloisters in the university grounds where the body was found were actually set up for a play.'

Arnison recognises a double question when he hears one. 'The cloisters are undoubtedly set up for a play,' he replies, 'but I can't comment yet on where the body was found.'

'Why is that, Inspector? After all, if the body had been discovered on a piece of waste ground the public and the press would be able to see clearly the general area.'

'But this is not a public place, Miss Ellison, and we're still searching the area.'

'The play was to have been performed from Wednesday, Inspector. Is it likely to go ahead?'

'I'm afraid I can't answer that question, Miss Ellison, the producers of the play may be able to do so with more authority. But I feel it's highly unlikely that .. .'

The camera moves to one side and Stacey Ellison speaks directly to it. 'We have with us now the director of *Twelfth Night*, the play which was scheduled for performance in the university cloisters. Isabelle Hewitt, will the play go ahead?'

Belle steps forward into the gateway, right beside Arnison. She lowers her head a little, her expression is one of sorrow, yet touched with pride. 'May I say first of all how sad we all are at the death of our friend and mentor, Jonathan Taylor.' Her voice is rich and melodious, her eyes hypnotise the camera with a look that says 'believe me'. She pauses. 'Staging this play in the university cloisters was Jonathan's idea. He and many others have, over the past few months, devoted a large part of their time to making this performance one of the highest standard. It would be

120

easy to lose ourselves in mourning the loss of our teacher, but we feel, as a group, that this is not what Jonathan would have wished.'

Vicky is incensed. 'How can she say that?' she hisses, 'How can she say "we as a group" when she hasn't asked me, she probably hasn't asked Kirsty either. Has she asked you, Mr Oliphant? No she has not! How can she say we all want the show to go on if she hasn't asked us all?'

Belle continues, Vicky's comments unheard. 'We want to go ahead with our production as a memorial to Jonathan Taylor.' There's a murmur of approval from the crowd. 'We want to show that we can overcome adversity, that we can perform in a way that Jonathan would have been proud of that demonstrates how good a teacher Jonathan was.'

'I think I'm going to be sick,' Kenny says.

Stacey Ellison nods gravely. 'So when is the first night, Isabelle?'

'That's the problem,' Belle replies. 'As you've heard, the police won't give us access to our stage, to our auditorium. Our friend and colleague has been murdered, but they won't allow us to honour his memory by performing our play. They clearly have the necessary evidence to charge someone with the crime, I would have thought that access to the performing space could have been arranged by, let us say, this evening. Perhaps the Inspector would care to say why this is impossible.'

The camera swings towards Arnison. The microphone, safe and warm in its faux-fur coat, hovers above his head. For the first time he looks as if he's not in control.

'Would you answer the question, Inspector?' Stacey Ellison reminds him.

'As I've already said, the stage is the scene of a murder and . . .'

'But you've made an arrest. You already have the evidence to do this. Why can't you let these young people have their stage back again as soon as possible?'

Arnison sees an escape route. 'We will certainly return

the crime scene to the relevant authorities as soon as we've completed our investigation and exploration . . .'

'When will that be, Inspector Arnison?'

'I can't give an exact . . .'

'Why not, Inspector? You wouldn't want to be seen as the man who, having solved a crime so quickly, is then tardy in allowing these young people back into their theatre.'

Arnison is beginning to lose his temper. 'Now look here, young lady, in the first place I haven't solved a crime, it's up to a court to judge whether the suspect is guilty of the murder of Jonathan Taylor. And secondly, if I can get the place cleared by this evening I will certainly allow the actors to . . .'

'Oh, thank you so much Inspector!' Belle is clapping her hands with glee. She reaches out and pulls Arnison towards her, kisses him on the lips. 'Everyone will be so pleased!' She turns round to address her followers. 'The Inspector says we'll be able to get back into the cloisters later today,' she shouts. 'Rehearsals can go ahead. We have a show!' There's a cheer, the camera pans around the fresh, happy faces before returning to that of the reporter.

'Well,' she says, 'a day of high drama on the campus. Following the death of Jonathan Taylor, a lecturer in Drama and Theatre Studies, Detective Inspector Harry Arnison has informed us that a young woman has been charged with his murder. It was originally thought that open-air performances of Shakespeare's *Twelfth Night*, produced by Mr Taylor and scheduled to have begun on Wednesday, would have to be abandoned. After a plea by the play's director, Isabelle Hewitt, Detective Inspector Arnison agreed to withdraw his men from the performance area by this evening. The play will be performed as a tribute and memorial to Mr Taylor. This is Stacey Ellison, City University campus.' There's a pause of a few seconds during which Arnison looks as if he's going to throttle Belle, Ellison, the camera and sound men and anyone else

122

within reaching distance, but he's too much of a professional to show his anger on camera. 'Okay,' Stacey Ellison announces, 'that's a wrap.'

'What the hell was that?' Arnison explodes. 'What do you two think you're up to? I said nothing whatsoever about letting you back into the cloisters. It might take two or three days, it might take a week until we're finished. So you can take yourselves and your actors and your silly set-ups and, as far as I'm concerned, you can flush them all down the toilet. No one gets into a murder scene until I say so.'

I wonder what's going to happen next. Neither unstoppable nor immovable appears willing to give way, and I can't see Arnison letting established police procedure suffer because of Belle's whims. She, however, might have other ideas. I move closer still, I want to hear exactly what she says.

'Inspector Arnison, this means a lot to us.'

Surely, I tell myself, she can't intend appealing to his better nature; there's no evidence that he has one.

'For many of the performers,' she continues, 'this is the key to their future. Important people in the world of theatre, agents and producers and directors, will be coming to see the play.'

I note that she's moved from talking about 'we' and 'us' to 'their'. She's trying to suggest that she's motivated by altruism rather than selfishness, that she won't benefit from the play going ahead. Surely, if it does go ahead and is successful, then the plaudits will be hers. How can she fail to profit?

'Are you going to deny these young people their opportunity?' She fixes Arnison with her gaze.

'I'd love to help,' Arnison says, his voice sounds wheedling and evasive in comparison to Belle's, 'but my hands are tied by procedure, I have to ensure that ...'

'Utter bollocks,' Stacey Ellison interrupts, 'you've got your suspect, Inspector.' She waves at the vehicles being prepared for departure. 'The evidence must be pretty good

123

if you're dismantling this lot already. What harm would it do to let Belle and her group back into their theatre?'

'I'm not prepared to discuss the evidence with you, young lady.' Arnison's patience is being pushed to its limits here, he's no longer polite cop referring to his interviewer as 'Miss Ellison'. 'My men have been working damn hard to collect evidence and information and my enquiries have not yet been completed.' He's speaking louder now.

'What's happening, Dad?' Kirsty's reappeared at my side. 'Is it working? Are we going to get the play back on?'

'I don't think so,' I tell her. 'If I was in charge I'd want to take the stage to pieces. I'd have officers on their hands and knees working the cloisters backwards and forwards looking for evidence. I'd be doing the same in every room in the halls. But that's very labour-intensive. Now, Arnison's got a suspect and some evidence, some pretty conclusive evidence from what my sources tell me. He might be persuaded to go with that, it would save a significant amount of money.' I'm about to ask whether she actually wants the play to go on, but she slips quickly away and I see her whisper in Belle's ear. Belle looks back at me and nods, it could be a thank you.

I'm confused. Kirsty has obviously been enthused by Belle's speech, whereas Vicky had been almost antagonistic towards the director. She's still standing close to me, listening to Arnison's worthy repetition of police procedures in these circumstances. I lean towards her. 'What do you think, then? Should the show go on?'

'I don't know,' she says, 'I was ready to scream at her when she started talking, but now ... Now I'm almost beginning to believe in her. Quite how we could do it without Anna I don't know, but ...'

'I still think she's an arsehole,' Kenny adds, 'an eloquent arsehole, but an arsehole all the same.'

'How do you feel about going ahead with the production, then?'

Kenny turns to face me, his vulture nose aimed directly

between my eyes. 'I've just finished my course, Mr Oliphant. I've got a good result, a 2:1. I've applied to go on a post-grad course in design for the theatre, in London. The course supervisor was coming up on Saturday to see the play.' Kenny emphasises each point he makes by jerking his head at me. 'She is – was – a friend of Jonathan Taylor's. Getting on the course depended on the quality of my design. Now, I don't like Belle. We argue all the time. We wanted different things from this play, but we compromised, what we'll end up with is still going to be bloody good.' He stops. 'No, rewind. Insert past tense instead of future. What we *were* going to end up with *would* have been bloody good.'

'Future conditional tense,' Vicky corrects him, 'not past.' She grimaces at the frown he aims at her. 'Oops, sorry. I'll keep my mouth shut.'

'There are other people in the same position as me, the play would be a showcase for our work. I don't like the way Belle's doing this, I don't like what she's doing. She stands to gain as much as, probably more than, any other individual if the show does go on. But I have to be selfish. Yes, I want to go ahead with it.'

It's taken him a long time to get there, but at least I have a decision from him.

'But none of this crap about "for Jonathan Taylor's memory",' he goes on, 'that's just hypocrisy. Taylor was even more of a bullshitter than Belle.'

Vicky has her say again. 'The evil Taylor did lives after him, the good already appears to be six feet under.'

Kenny's vigorous 'Piss off, Vicks!' accompanies me as I move away. I haven't missed much. The discussion between Arnison and his harpies has become an argument. Belle has suggested that she organise a benefit performance in aid of some charity for police officers injured in the line of duty; Arnison has accused her of bribery. Stacey Ellison has pointed out that an edited version of the interview could put Arnison in a bad light; Arnison has accused her of blackmail.

125

Belle tries to change course, her voice still pleasant and even, though she knows she isn't being filmed. 'Inspector Arnison, we all know how much the police force is stretched these days, both for money and for manpower. I'm not saying that your ongoing enquiries should be less vigorous, but couldn't you focus them on letting us into the cloisters as quickly as possible?'

Arnison has right on his side, technically, though even I can see that a thorough search of the cloisters isn't really necessary given the evidence he appears to have against Anna. I am, however, the only person outside the police force who has that information. I begin to wonder how I can use that information for the greater good. It may mean that I have to alienate myself even further in Arnison's eyes, although I'm used to being disliked by powerful policemen. But if he already dislikes me – or dislikes my presence, which are two different things – why should he listen to what I have to say? I never could understand poker, but I know what it means to bluff.

Arnison looks as if he's about to withdraw from the conversation, so I have to act quickly. 'Inspector, Belle, I understand you're having a problem. Is there anything I can do to help?'

Arnison looks down his nose at me. 'I doubt it, Oliphant. We aren't having a problem for the simple reason that there's nothing else to talk about. I'm about to leave now and so, I would suggest, is everyone else, since there's no reason for them to stay.'

Stacey Ellison shakes her head. 'The publicity you and the police force receive will be far from good,' she warns him.

'Miss Ellison,' I say firmly, 'I don't think threats will help your cause.'

Arnison seems surprised that I appear to be supporting him.

'I used to be a police officer, so I know that the Inspector's in charge, what he says counts, and he assigns priorities to every case in his control. Isn't that right, Inspector?'

'It is indeed. Thank you for pointing that out, Mr Oliphant.'

I notice that the formality of my title has been added to my surname; if I keep this up he'll soon be calling me 'Bill' and inviting me round for a meal. I continue to pile on the butter. 'All investigations have to be followed through. The only reason for abandoning or reducing the scale of an enquiry would be if the evidence already gathered was so conclusive that it renders further investigation unnecessary. Is that right, Inspector?'

'I think you've got it there, Mr Oliphant.' He's looking worried, despite his speedy confirmation. He's on an unfamiliar road and he's beginning to believe I've stolen the signposts.

'But the Inspector can't let anyone know exactly what evidence he already has. After all, courts decide on guilt; all the police do is assemble evidence. And if evidence was released before a case came to court, the case might collapse.' This time I don't even ask Arnison's opinion, I simply smile at him. He nods to himself, he thinks he knows where I'm going, thinks he has a better hand than me.

'That depends to a certain extent on the evidence,' he says. 'In this case, for example, it's already common knowledge – though I wish it wasn't – that the deceased is Jonathan Taylor and that he was killed by a knife. I can't hide the identity of our suspect, and you, Mr Oliphant, were present when some evidence was found.' He doesn't refer directly to Anna's bloodstained T-shirt, but we both know that's what he's talking about. 'The release of information to the public on that particular piece of evidence wouldn't really be harmful to our case. There are many other people who might have seen the evidence, or heard about it.' He's referring to the way Anna was carried out, to the noise she was making, to those staying in the halls

127

who might have seen the T-shirt and talked to each other.

Belle already knows this. 'So something on the internet, the most public place there is, saying that Anna Peranski has been arrested and charged with the murder of Jonathan Taylor, wouldn't worry you?'

'Not unduly.' Arnison's feeling a little happier. He thinks he's in control again.

'And you wouldn't be unhappy if it was common knowledge that the blood on Anna's T-shirt, the T-shirt found in her room, was Taylor's?'

'It would be supposition, Miss Hewitt. I've made no statement to that effect.'

'No, but you've arrested Anna, and people heard her shouting about her T-shirt being stained with blood.'

'It would be an educated guess, nothing more. I wouldn't be worried.'

Belle is thinking clearly. 'But if the guess was right, then Taylor was probably killed with a knife or some other sharp instrument. Perhaps one of the stage swords or daggers? Would it worry you if that type of speculation became public?'

'I have no further comment to make, Miss Hewitt. Mr Oliphant, Miss Ellison, I think I'd better be going.'

Belle looks at me, stretches out her hands. She's done what she can, she's urging me to take up the fight. There'll be no help from Stacey Ellison, she's played her part. She shrugs at Belle, puts her arm round her shoulder, prepares to console her.

I'm no soft touch. I'm cold to pleading smiles, fluttering eyelashes do nothing to me. But there are exceptions. Jen has the ability to make me malleable and ductile, while Kirsty has always had that talent. It's Kirsty's face that captures me, a small circle of flesh standing out from the crowd of observers. Her eyes fix on mine, her mouth moves, and though I can't hear what she says, I can read the words 'Dad' and 'please'. What can a father do?

I march up to Arnison.

'Inspector,' I say, but he doesn't turn round, he increases his pace. His legs are longer than mine, I'm almost running to keep up. 'What would happen if the information posted on the internet says that the blood on Anna's T-shirt was Taylor's, and that traces of his semen were found in her pubic hair and in her vagina?' That stops him. That stops him so fast I bump into him. His face is twisted, his eyes wide, he's a Great White Shark and I have a feeling I'm his dinner.

'What did you say?'

'I asked a question, Inspector Arnison. It was, like Belle's questions before, supposition. "What if?"' I have his attention, I'm beginning to wish he'd chosen to ignore me. 'I asked what would happen if it was suggested – on the internet or elsewhere – that the evidence you have included blood matches, traces of Taylor's semen in Anna's pubic hair and in her vagina? And what would happen if it was suggested – and I'm choosing my words carefully, Inspector – that the evidence included saliva traces of both victim and suspect in each other's hair? What about DNA samples under each other's fingernails? And photographic evidence showing victim and suspect having sex, taken by the victim before he died? What if these suppositions, this guesswork, was published? Would it be embarrassing?'

Arnison wants to interrupt but I won't let him, not yet. I speak faster, more urgently. 'Or would it be more embarrassing if it was confirmed that this was indeed the evidence, the cast-iron, gold-plated copper-bottom evidence, yet the officer in charge of the case insisted that a group of university students shouldn't be allowed back into the murder scene because his "procedure" wouldn't allow it? How would the public feel if "procedure" prevented these kids from getting the chance they deserved? How would the police authority feel? How would the councillors on the authority feel? And, of course, how would the Crown Prosecution Service feel if all this confidential information was made public?' Now I'm silent. Now I wait for Arnison to speak.

'You bastard!' he hisses. 'How did you know?'

'I know nothing, Inspector. It's guesswork. But the fact that you referred to things I "know" might lead me to believe I actually do have some concrete knowledge. But for the moment it's probably better to stay in the realms of possibility. Let's stay with supposition.'

'I'll have you in front of a magistrate with a gagging order before you can say another word!'

'You won't. See, more than one word, and no magistrate. But you won't do it, Inspector. Why? Well, let's suppose, just suppose, that everything I've suggested does happen. That the guesses I've made are about to be published on the internet. Your gagging me will just prove I was right. Supposition becomes fact. It might not destroy your case, after all, you've got everything on your side. Evidence, motivation, opportunity, the lot. But it would probably destroy your career. On the other hand, all you need do is go back to Belle and say that you've thought about things carefully. You'll concentrate your efforts on examining the cloisters. You should be out by – let's be generous – tomorrow morning, nine am. And that should leave her enough time to get on with the rehearsals so the play can go ahead on schedule.'

'And why should I do that?'

'Because you're kind? Because you have the interests of these young people at heart? Because you know that, for many of them, this is make-or-break time? Come on, man, make up your own reason.'

He appears to consider everything I've said, but his next words surprise me. 'I could make your life very unpleasant, Mr Oliphant. You know this, despite your bravado. So why are you doing this?'

Motivation. Always a problem. What makes a person do something, either illegal or illogical? Some motivation is easy to understand. The mother who risks her life to save that of her child is driven by a biological need, a need to protect the specific genes she has passed down to that child.

No one becomes a fireman unless they're prepared to risk their lives for the benefit of others; their training prepares them for such events and they may, if such situations arise, act automatically. Yet the motivation driving them to such an action is complex. We may not approve of the motivation that drives an individual to, say, revenge, but we can understand it because we can imagine ourselves in that individual's place. Why should hundreds of thousands of people give up their time to work for the benefit of others? Why should the hard-pressed teacher, in her limited spare time, guide her students through the lengthy process of a school play? Why should the self-employed builder take time off work to raise money for charity? Why do volunteers help with meals-on-wheels or in charity shops? What makes people do good? Evil may be motivated by selfishness, or greed, but why do good when there's no reward? This is, of course, dangerous ground, because it means that my thoughts may be led towards a dependence on faith or religion, which I don't possess. So I return to Arnison's question. He could, undoubtedly, do me some harm, he could probably have me arrested. So why am I helping a group of university students – privileged, I suppose, by definition – when I know only one of them and she's my daughter? Is it because I believe Arnison's wrong to deny them the opportunity to perform their play? It can't be, I would do the same as he's done if I were in his position. Is it that I have some degree of sympathy with the students? Well, yes, to a certain extent; I haven't known them long yet I recognise that some of them are pleasant, and some of them are Kirsty's friends. But is that enough to make me risk angering Arnison?

'Well, Mr Oliphant? Do you have an answer?'

'Do you have any children?' I ask.

'What?'

'Children. Daughters in particular. Do you have any?'

His face wrinkles as if my question is accompanied by an especially bad odour, but he still manages a grunted 'No.'

131

I'd hoped to appeal to him as a parent, but that's not going to be possible. I can't think of an answer that would satisfy him, he's unlikely to want to hear my rambling thoughts on motivation. 'I think it would be the right thing to do,' I say.

'And would you benefit?'

Would I benefit? I haven't really thought about it from the point of view of the cynical policeman. 'Yes,' I say, 'I would benefit.'

'I knew it! Come on then, tell the truth. What would you get out of it?'

I don't have to think any more. 'I'd have to work hard, very hard, over the next few days to make sure my lighting and sound system was up to the standard of the performance. Because – believe me, Arnison, when I say this – they are good. So I get the benefit of having my pride bolstered by being part of something good. I suppose pride motivates me in other ways as well, I want to see my daughter performing when I know she's worked very hard, but I know I'll feel proud of her however well she does. So I suppose it's selfishness that's made me do this.'

'And you're expecting me to give way because you've threatened me?'

'No, Inspector, the threat was just to focus your attention. I expect you to give way because of that.' I point back the way we've just come. Belle is staring at us. Stacey Ellison is still standing with her protective arm draped over Belle's shoulders. The rest of the group is watching, silent.

Arnison breathes in, exhales noisily. 'Quite a theatrical situation you've placed us in.'

'We all play a part in life's drama.'

He appears to be thinking, then turns away, shaking his head. I have only one lever left – Anna's note. I should have mentioned it when Stephenson interviewed me, but he seemed more interested in impressing me with his friendliness than finding out what I knew. Now, given what I know about the police investigation, it might be considered overkill. But it could be important, and it's all I have. It'll

132

be embarrassing to mention it. 'I forgot to show you this.' I could be charged with attempting to subvert the cause of justice, hiding vital information. But what else can I do? 'Inspector,' I announce, my mind made up, 'I have something else ...'

'No, Mr Oliphant, I don't want to hear another word from you.' He begins to walk away again, but stops then beckons me after him. He inhales, sighs deeply. 'Tell them we'll be out by tomorrow evening. Six o'clock.'

I can't hide my pleasure. 'Inspector Arnison, thank you.'

'Don't bother, I'm sure I'll think of some way for you to repay me. In fact I already can. If you hear anything or see anything that might be of interest to me – and I know how good you are at seeing and hearing, Mr Oliphant, especially things you shouldn't – you get back in touch with me immediately. No silly little investigations of your own, not on my case. Do you understand?'

I can't tell him about the note now, he'd throw me into a cell without opening the door, forcing me bit by bit through the inspection panel. I bring my hand up to my head in a salute, 'Yes sir!'

'Don't make me regret this, Oliphant.'

'No,' I say, control my exuberance, 'I won't.'

He makes his way towards his car. I resist the temptation to wave goodbye, and I'm pleased I didn't tell him the other reason why I want the play to go ahead. It didn't occur to me while I was indulging myself with an exploration of motivation, but when I was speaking to Arnison a small thought forced itself to the front of my mind. I promptly sent it back to the darker recesses where it belonged, but now's the time for me to examine it more closely.

My argument with Arnison depended on Anna being guilty. If he didn't have sufficient evidence to prove that, then there was no way he'd consider allowing the troupe back into their makeshift theatre. If I have a suspicion that there's too much evidence, that it came too quickly, then I have to set it aside; the weight of the evidence there is, even without the note I still have hidden in my bag, is too great. But that suspicion is still present. Being allowed back into the cloisters, having access to all the other people who were there, will allow me to do a little exploring of my own, to find out whether my anxiety is anything more than an extension of my neurotic past. Perhaps that's my motivation.

'Dad!'

My reverie is interrupted by Kirsty's yell, I swing round. Everyone is standing where I left them. No one has moved.

'Well?' Kirsty shouts again.

'The man from Del Monte, he says "Yes",' I call back to her.

Everyone moves at once.

Chapter Six

It doesn't take me long to decide that I'll head home to spend the night with Jen. Everyone else is going to a meeting in the nearest pub that will end up with a prolonged celebration and wake combined, Kirsty tells me. They'll end up sleeping on an assortment of floors in an assortment of houses and be back on Sunday evening to begin again the process of getting the play ready. Although I'm invited – I am, after all, the hero of the day – I decline with no grace whatsoever. I tell the assembled horde that I have no intention spending the night with a group of belching, farting drunkards whose interest in alcohol is exceeded only by their desire for sex. I agree to meet them the next day.

It's after seven when I manage to call home. Jen isn't there and she doesn't answer her mobile. That can only mean she's tied up with some medical business, perhaps working for the GPs' cooperative. If so it won't be long until her shift is over. I leave a message saying I'm on my way back, tell her I'll have to leave again early next morning. I begin to explain what's been happening, and that's when I realise how complicated my story is; if I saw it on a stage I'd think it highly improbable. In the end I give up with the summary, promise simply to tell all when I get back.

The journey is pleasant. The windows are down and the breeze is blowing hot air through the cab. Saturday evening is heading towards night and the streets are once again filling with pleasure-seekers. My road takes me through the middle of town. Pavements outside pubs are filled with tables and chairs and it feels like the south of France, not the north of England. Music blares from doorways and windows and I move in my seat to the rhythms of rock and salsa, my hands hit the steering wheel in reasonable counterpoint to Irish folk and Jamaican reggae.

The traffic is light and slow-moving, tyres held back by viscous roads, drivers unused to the brightness of their city; everyone is wearing sunglasses and clothes in primary colours; even nightclub bouncers are out early and smiling. I know the road well. It leads to the dual carriageway which leads to the motorway which leads home. As I leave the city centre behind I fish for a tape, something summery, something that could be used to sell open-top sports cars and fabric softeners. I settle for a guitarist playing blues chords and growling about his baby leaving him.

It takes me a little under an hour to get home. The flat is north of the river, not far from where Jen previously rented. It's a sign of our commitment that we've moved in together, that she's wearing an engagement ring and that I have a ring-pull from a drinks can – the equivalent of a ring and of as much value to me – secure in my wallet. When she proposed to me I accepted on the condition that we should live together for a year first. I figured that, if she could stand that, then there might be a chance of my second marriage lasting longer than my first.

Parking is easier than normal now that the student population has gone home. I find somewhere just round the corner from the flat, note with pleasure that Jen's car is already in its usual place, half-on and half-off the kerb. I pause for a moment, consider ringing her to tell her I'm almost home and that she should start removing her clothes, but decide against it. I've had a long day and need to shower before I do anything else.

I open the door quietly. We have this silly game, we try

136

to surprise each other when we come in. It's not an unpleasant surprise, the intent is not to frighten; instead we sneak up and kiss each other on the back of the neck, or run a finger along a thigh. I'm not very good at it; either I forget when Jen's due in or I make too much noise. This time I think I'll win. She'll probably be catching the last rays of the sun in the back yard (no garden here), but even as I close the door behind me she's there, arms outstretched. I can only gasp 'How did you know . . ?' before her lips and tongue silence me.

'You left a message,' she reminds me as we separate to breathe, 'on the phone, remember? I was watching for you.'

'Right. Yes, I do remember.' We kiss again and my need for a shower is rapidly assuming a minor importance. Beneath her sloppy shirt and faded cotton trousers (which might have started life as pyjamas) Jen's body is warm and round and welcoming. I put my hands under the shirt at the back, then down so my hands are resting on the swell of her backside.

'You must have had a hard day,' Jen says, backing away from me a little. 'And much as I enjoy the manly smell of sweat, you do need a shower.' She takes my hand, leads me to the foot of the stairs and hands me a towel. 'You just trot upstairs, hose yourself down, by the time you finish, dinner will be ready. You can eat, then you can sit down and tell me what's been going on while I massage your feet. When you're thoroughly relaxed we can go to bed, you can give me several loud and energetic orgasms before it's your turn, and we can go to sleep happy. Any problems with that?'

'You seem to have everything organised to perfection.'

'That's probably why you love me. Oh, and there's also my sexy brown skin, my curvaceous body, my intellect, my curiosity in all relevant areas and . . . I think you can add the rest. Off you go, lover, ten minutes.'

Sometimes I do as I'm told, straightaway. This time I

wait, watch Jen move off down the hall to the kitchen, watch the happy sway of her hips, watch the way she reaches round to scratch the small of her back, see the cartoon character elastoplast on her heel where her new shoe chafes. I wonder if she would understand if I told her those were also reasons why I loved her. 'Yes,' I tell myself happily, 'she would understand.' I head upstairs for my shower.

The hot water slakes away the dirty snakeskin of the day. I begin to feel less tired, able to review the day's events with some objectivity now that a degree of separation has been made. It's disturbing to think that a murder has been committed so close to me, both in terms of physical proximity and in that I knew both victim and murderer. Then I remind myself that Anna hasn't yet been found guilty, although the evidence against her is overwhelming. Perhaps the most unusual thing is that the show is still going ahead. I know the old saw to that effect, but I hadn't understood – until I became involved with *this* show – how much time and effort people invested in these productions. It seems churlish to say so, but Taylor's role as a catalyst is no longer necessary. The chemical reaction has been started and is now capable of resolution without his presence. The critics and agents will still come to see the performance – indeed, the news of Taylor's death will probably prompt even more publicity – and some good may yet arise from the sorrow and horror of a murder. But I still feel as if I'm dancing on his grave.

'Billy!' Jen's voice, distant at the bottom of the stairs, disturbs my thoughts. 'Are you nearly finished?'

I turn the shower off. 'Just getting out now,' I call down to her.

'Five minutes to get ready,' she replies, 'or I feed it to the cat.'

It takes me a little longer than five minutes. I have to find a clean T-shirt, and the pair of patchwork cotton trousers I wear round the house, multi-coloured, elastic-waisted for Jen's easy access. My meal will be safe, however; we don't have a cat.

Our small dining table is in the kitchen. It's set out formally, plates sitting smartly on mats, glasses containing folded serviettes, knives and forks that match. There's a jug of orange juice with ice sitting centrally, flanked by tall candles in thin brass holders. Jen is dancing in front of the cooker and something smells good. Normally I do the cooking. My hours are more flexible than Jen's and I enjoy being able to do something for her, to please her. In assuming this domestic role I've also considered that, as Jen herself acknowledges, she isn't a naturally gifted cook. Her ideas and intentions are good, but she's often distracted by something more interesting and forgets that pans need fairly constant attention. When Jen cooks, the smell of burning food and hot metal sometimes provide an interesting aperitif. On this occasion, however, all seems well.

'Chicken gumbo,' she calls over her shoulder.

'Smells wonderful. What's in it?'

She turns, sticks out her tongue at me. It was the wrong question, she thinks I knew that the gumbo part came from a jar.

'Anything I can do?' I ask, desperate to make amends.

'It's ready now,' she answers, pours the contents of the pan into a dish and lays it on the table in front of me. She brings another dish of rice from the oven, then some warm bread.

'You're spoiling me,' I tell her.

'You deserve it. Now tell me what's been happening.'

I manage to eat, drink and talk at the same time. Jen frowns or raises her eyebrows at appropriate moments, shakes her head, says 'Poor you,' when necessary, asks how Kirsty's coping, does all the right things. She takes great interest when I describe the forensic evidence against Anna Peranski. 'Remember,' she warns, 'this is only the first stage. Police forensic evidence is usually checked by an independent analyst, just in case there's any bias, any alternative explanation. It'll probably be Professor Edmondson, he tends to get important murders.'

'Do you know him?'

'Do I know him? Billy, every medical student in the region knows him. He's a renowned expert on forensic medicine, you can learn a hell of a lot from him if you can put up with his political discourse.' She sips her orange. 'He's just a little left-wing, always keeps his eyes open for anyone he thinks might be tempted to the dark side.'

'The dark side?'

'Private medicine. Hates it and all practitioners of its evil arts. So I got on quite well with him, being a bit of a Trot in my younger days. And I made sure he knew I was learning from him.'

We continue to eat, and I tell her about the students I've met, their peculiarities. There isn't a great deal of room in the kitchen, we're almost able to bump knees beneath the table. At the meal's conclusion I feel Jen's bare foot move up my leg and rest in my groin. She moves it slowly from side to side. 'Oh my,' she exclaims, 'I do believe you've nothing on under those trousers!'

I try to keep my smile inscrutable, she knows that they're my equivalent of pyjama bottoms; although I usually sleep naked, I wear them round the house in case of surprise visitors or neighbours with binoculars.

'Ah, the strong silent type.' I can tell she's feeling playful, she begins to vary the pressure, then takes her foot away altogether. 'I vill break you, Mr Borned,' she announces, 'you vill not be able to resist.' She rises to her feet and moves around the table to stand behind me, begins to massage my shoulders. I sense her ducking down to kneel behind my chair and her hands slide down the sides of my arms and onto my stomach, then below the waistband of my trousers. I can feel her breath warming the fabric of my T-shirt just below my shoulder. I'm enjoying this. Then she stops, stands up and moves away from me. I prepare to join her but she pushes me gently back down.

'Oh no, Mr Oliphant, I think you need to earn your pleasure. I'm going to go upstairs and prepare myself, and you're going to wash the dishes.'

'But I'm ...'

'Yes, I can see that. But gratification deferred is always far more enjoyable.'

'Can't I just leave them to soak?'

'No, but you can leave them to drain.' I must look disappointed. 'And I'll let you choose the outfit. Red or black?'

I let the images fill my mind. 'Black.'

'Skimpies or basque?'

'Jen, this really is torture!'

'Answer the question. Skimpies or basque?'

'Basque.'

'I take it that means you want suspender belt and stockings as well?'

'Mm, fishnet.' I think I might be drooling.

'And the high-heel shoes?'

'Yes please.'

'You're a bad boy, Billy Oliphant. I think you might have to dry as well if you want all that.'

'Jen!'

'All right, I'm just joking. But just in case you get really involved with this washing up business, you know, hooked on it and can't tear yourself away, here's a preview of what's waiting.' She tilts her head on one side and lifts up her T-shirt to reveal her breasts, gently rubs her hand from one to the other. Then she pulls the shirt down quickly and giggles, 'Don't be too long!' I hear her running up the stairs, still laughing, as I turn to my duties.

It doesn't take me long to wash and rinse the dishes, stack them neatly in the rack. Knives and forks are assigned their own standing place in the plastic drainer. The pans are a little more difficult; the rice grains we ate have left some of their less fortunate companions blackened and charred, coating the aluminium pan. That, I decide with relief, my mind already striding the stairs, needs to be soaked

141

overnight. I fill it with warm soapy water, stand back to survey my work. In other, less happy times, I would have arranged and rearranged the tea-towels on their rails until they were symmetrical. I would have wiped all the surfaces and the table, if a speck of food had escaped to the floor I would have hunted it down with the vacuum cleaner. I note with pleasure all those conditional tenses explaining how I *would* have been; those times are past, I've almost overcome the obsessive-compulsive neurosis that made me behave like that. Yes, I'm prone to be too tidy, but I can tolerate Jen's untidiness because the alternative – that she isn't there – is unthinkable.

I close the door loudly behind me. 'Coming,' I shout loudly, 'ready or not!' and leap up the stairs. The door to our room is closed, I can hear soft music inside that resolves into a smooth sleaze of saxophone as I edge the door open. The room is filled with candles on every flat surface and, aided by the light creeping around the side of the curtains, I see Jen swaying to the music in the middle of the room. She's wearing as much and as little as she promised, her eyes are closed, and she looks beautiful. I pull my shirt over my head, discard my trousers and slide across to the bed, unable to take my eyes from her.

Sometimes I worry about our age difference, I worry that Jen's nearer Kirsty's age than mine. I worry that she'll find someone else, someone better-looking, richer, with fewer hang-ups and problems. I worry that I won't be able to satisfy her. I worry that she'll leave me. I wonder what she sees in me, a short, middle-aged man with a tendency to flabbiness. But on nights like this I simply rejoice that she seems to love me as much as I love her.

I sit on the edge of the bed and watch Jen drop to the ground. She crawls towards me on all fours, reaches me and slithers up my body, pushing me backwards onto the bed.

The phone rings on cue.

'Leave it,' Jen growls. I'm happy to comply, but the

142

phone is connected to an answering machine, not Telecom's 1571 system. We both know we'll hear someone's voice, so Jen pauses her crawl up my body, and I try to slow my heartbeat. We stare at each other, wait for the eight rings, the click, the whir of the tape. Jen's resting against me now, her body warm against mine. I can feel the stiff bones of her basque, the soft silken sheen of her briefs, the mesh of her stockings.

'This is Billy Oliphant,' my mechanised voice says, 'I can't get to the phone at present but if you leave a message I'll get back to you as soon as possible.'

'Hello, Dad, this is . . .'

Jen rolls off me, she's closer to the phone than me, she picks it up quickly. 'Hello, Kirsty,' she says, 'sorry about that.'

'I hope I didn't interrupt anything important,' Kirsty says.

Jen grimaces at me. 'No, love, we were just about to . . .'

I grab the phone from her. 'Kirsty, is everything all right?'

'I think so. Yes, I mean, everything's all right.' She sounds confused.

'What's the matter?'

'I hope I've done the right thing, Dad. I'm at the pub. It's been a peculiar sort of evening, I've had quite a bit to drink but I'm thinking quite clearly. I need to say that because what I'm going to say sounds daft. There's someone here wants to talk to you. I wouldn't give him your number, so he said I should ring you and ask if you'd speak to him. He wants to hire you to do some detective work.'

'How does he know about me?' I'm puzzled. If he knew my name, knew I was a detective, then he could just ring me and leave . . . a message, of course, that's why he needs Kirsty. If he left a message at work I wouldn't get it until I got into the office, if he tried at home I wouldn't answer.

'Dad, you already know him. He's in the play, I pointed

him out to you. Remember George? He plays Orsino. Well, he says Anna didn't kill Jonathan Taylor and he wants you to find out who did.'

I can't think what to say. Kirsty must have mentioned to almost everyone my occasional line in detective work, but why would George in particular think Anna was innocent? Those questions have to be measured against the evidence, the mountain of evidence stacked against Anna. Even if I believed she was innocent, which I don't, how can I compete with the might of the entire police force and its access to forensic information? I look across at Jen; she shrugs and strides to the window, walking like waves. She pulls the curtains wide; the candle flames shiver in the breeze.

'Talk,' she says, reaching for a dressing gown from the back of the door, 'listen to what he says.' She kicks off her shoes. 'I'll make us a cup of tea.'

'Put him on,' I tell Kirsty.

'Mr Oliphant, I'm sorry to disturb you.' I expected him, like Kirsty, to be drunk, but he seems in control of his voice and his emotions. 'I've just come back from the police station where Anna's being held. They've appointed a solicitor for her, but they wouldn't let me see her. But I managed to talk to the solicitor for a few minutes.'

'And how is Anna?'

There's a long pause. I can hear Kirsty's voice in the background saying some soothing words. Then George speaks again. 'We went to school together, Mr Oliphant. I always . . . I sort of looked after her. I've never told anyone else this, I thought it would make me out to be stupid, but I came here because I knew she was coming here. I thought she might need me.'

He's telling me, without actually saying so, that he was and probably still is infatuated with her. 'It's okay,' I tell him, 'I understand.'

'She's not well, Mr Oliphant. A few years ago she had a breakdown, at school, she was in with a bad crowd and

... Anyway, she came round with a little bit of help, went to college, got her "A" levels and went off to university. I was always worried what she was doing but ... You know how it is, Mr Oliphant, with girls. You have to let go some time.'

George loves Anna, that much is clear. I just can't imagine what she feels about him. Resentment that he's followed her to university? Fear that he might tell people about her earlier problems? Certainly her behaviour around him, the way she attempted to bed even me, suggests that she has no feelings at all for him. 'What did the solicitor say?' I ask him.

'Apparently she has all the old symptoms, she's retreating into herself, confused, she doesn't know what's happening. He had to really push her to get answers from her. But at the end she seemed to come round a little, she wrote a note, asked the solicitor to get me to give it to you. She didn't kill Jonathan Taylor, Mr Oliphant. Everyone will be allowed back into the buildings tomorrow. Evidence could be destroyed. I want you to find out who the murderer really is.'

I think carefully. I ask George a few questions. Then I tell him what to do.

I place the phone in its cradle and get dressed again, go downstairs. Jen's in the kitchen, still wrapped in her dressing gown, but a small pile of black clothing lies forlorn on the table. Through the kitchen window I can see the sky reddening.

'I couldn't tell him everything I knew,' I announce to the room, as if I'm pleading extenuating circumstances to a jury. 'How could I explain that every single shred of evidence points to Anna being guilty? After all, he's as good as admitted that she's prone to psychotic episodes. And she was angry with Taylor, she had the motive and the opportunity to kill him.'

Jen hands me a mug of weak tea. 'So what did you do?'

I shake my head. 'What else could I do? I'm sorry, Jen,

I asked him to come round here.' I hurry on so she can't show her annoyance. 'The only alternative was for me to go and see him, and I didn't want to do that, not at this time. He's . . . he sounded distraught. I can sympathise with him, his relationship with Anna is complex. She's a complicated kid. He had no one else to turn to.' I sit down on the chair, put my head in my hands. 'I'm sorry.'

Jen moves the mug away from me, lifts my head up to look into my eyes. 'If you'd done anything else I would have been disappointed in you,' she says, kisses me on the nose then stands back to stare at me. Her voice becomes inquisitorial. 'How long did it take you to get back earlier this evening?'

'An hour,' I tell her.

'And you knew the way. George doesn't, so he'll take a little longer. That's more than enough time for me. Do you want to come back to bed?'

'Do you?'

She takes my hand. 'Billy, sometimes you ask the most stupid questions.'

The doorbell summons me from sleep. I hadn't realised how tired I was, but when I roll over I find that Jen has already left the bed. I can hear her voice downstairs.

'Please, come in, I assure you there's no inconvenience at all. I'm Jen, Billy's fiancée. Now then, when did you last have something to eat?'

'I don't really feel hungry at all, thank you.' It's George, his heavy monotone climbs inexorably up to me as I struggle into more decent clothing than I was wearing earlier.

'Something to drink, then. Tea, coffee? Or perhaps something stronger?'

'Coffee would be very welcome.'

George is waiting for me when I enter the living room, He looks smaller than I remember him, thinner, paler, ill even. There are dark shadows beneath eyes that are constantly on the move.

146

'Sorry it took so long to get here,' he says. 'I got lost a couple of time. And the car's a bit of a banger. And thank you for giving up your time, I know you're very busy and you've got better things to do than talk to me.'

Jen interrupts his thanks and apologies by bringing in a tray with tea, coffee and biscuits. She's wearing jeans and a sweatshirt and curls herself into the sofa beside me.

'I need to ask you some questions and listen to you as well, George.'

'That's okay, I understand. There's more than I could tell you on the phone.'

'All right. Please, start at the beginning. What did Anna say to the solicitor? Did she suggest you contact me?'

'No, Mr Oliphant, not at first.' He smiles sadly at the memory. 'Apparently she called you several names, but that's not unusual. She does that to me all the time. Or at least she did do that, but I thought she'd calmed down quite a bit. Recently she'd got much worse, she always does when she's stressed. I put it down to the play. She was more quiet by the end of the conversation.'

'Please, start at the beginning then. And my name's Billy.'

'If you don't mind, I'd prefer "Mr Oliphant". Makes me feel more comfortable, somehow.'

I nod my assent; George continues.

'I wasn't sure what had happened this morning, bits of it seemed to get glued together as the day went on. When I figured out what had happened I went straight to the police station, but they wouldn't tell me anything. They said she was with a solicitor, I could wait to speak to him, so I did. I asked them to pass a message to her as well, just to tell her I was there and thinking of her.'

He takes a sip of coffee, his protestations that he wasn't hungry shown to be untrue by his systematic demolition of the plate of biscuits before him.

'Even if she'd wanted to see me she couldn't have, but I thought it was important for her to know someone was there. Even if that someone was me.' He reaches into his pocket and takes out a handkerchief, blows his nose.

It strikes me then how old-fashioned he is. How many people carry handkerchiefs these days? And his devotion to Anna, his willingness to be there for her, is a relic from the nineteenth century. Some, however, might consider the more modern interpretation, that he's a menacing stalker. 'It's clear you're fond of Anna. What does she think of you?'

George sucks his lips into his mouth. It's clearly something he's thought about a lot. 'I'm not really as slow as I seem,' he says. 'The rest of them say I'm thick, I know some of the nicknames they call me. I'm heading for a 2:1, even these days that's worth something. It shows I can think. And sometimes, I do just that. I lie awake, trying to imagine what Anna thinks of me. Like I said on the phone earlier, we were at school together, we became friends. It was more than that, I asked her out, she said yes. We were similar in those days.'

He pushes a hand through his hair, as if he's thinking of the best way to tell his story. He nods to himself, the narrative organised, and begins again. 'She's a very complicated person. Anna never knew her father. Her mother wasn't really interested in her, I think she was on the way to becoming an alcoholic. She once even came on to me! I haven't seen her for years, though. I think when Anna had her problems she said she wanted nothing to do with her daughter. Certainly Anna never talks about her.' His face is creased, but then he dispels the unpleasant thoughts and smiles instead at a long-distant, happier memory. 'You know, we'd even go to the library together, after school, to help each other out with our homework.' He lowers his head and his voice. 'When we had study leave, for our GCSEs, we'd go to each other's houses when we knew no one would be there and make love.'

Jen and I are both listening intently. The image I have of Anna is changing as George describes her, as he describes them together.

148

'She did well in her exams, far better than me. We chose different "A" levels, and we saw less of each other. She was very much into arty things, she began to go to galleries and the theatre and concerts, they didn't really interest me much. Then one day I saw her, I was on a bus – number 45, Polwarth Drive, top deck – and she had her arms round a boy. She started kissing him.' Even now the memory hurts him, his face crumples into a mask of incomprehension. 'I didn't mention it at first. We still saw each other, we still made love. She moved out, into a flat with some girls from the Art College. I went round to see her one evening, she wasn't there, even though we'd arranged a time, but I waited. I waited till two in the morning. When she came in she was drunk. She didn't apologise. I didn't accuse her of anything – I'm not much good at accusing – but my expression must have told her I was upset and angry. She told me she'd been seeing other boys, sleeping with them. She said she wanted to experiment. She told me "monogamy wasn't her thing". I didn't argue, I didn't want to lose her, but it didn't matter anyway. She stopped answering my calls, she didn't speak to me. She dropped out of school. People I knew told me she'd started drugs. I tried to contact her but she wouldn't see me.

'One night she turned up on the doorstep. At first my parents wouldn't let her in, she was dirty and obviously something was wrong with her, she was shaking, she could hardly speak. I persuaded them to help her.'

George is deeply conservative in his manners, his dress; his parents can only have been even more conformist; George's persuasive techniques must have been formidable.

'She lived with us for a few months. She had her own room. We managed to get her to see a doctor, she spent some time in hospital. She missed a year of school and my results that year were so bad I had to take the year again, so we had something in common. We talked a lot. We never slept together again, though the opportunity arose. When she was better – not entirely recovered, but better

149

than she was – she found another flat. She didn't come back to school, but she went to the local Arts College. We both got our "A" levels. That was when I did something very silly.'

George stops. He looks around the room, stands up, stretches. He rotates his neck one way and then the other, as if he's very tired. He inhales deeply. Then he begins to walk, as if movement is necessary to push the words from deep within him.

'It was more than silly. It was probably the single most stupid thing I've ever done in my entire life. Anna and I had become, almost by accident, like brother and sister, though that wasn't the way I wanted it to be. She told me the course she'd been accepted on and I waited and waited until results day, until I knew for certain where she was going, then I applied through clearing for the same university. It was a risk, but I got in. On our first day I registered early then I waited around by the Theatre Studies desk. She was surprised to see me. Surprised and not pleased, she made that quite clear. So I had to be honest with her, I wrote her a note. I left my address, my phone numbers. I told her I'd always be there for her. I told her I wouldn't try to contact her as long as she let me know, once a week, that she was okay. And then we both got on with our lives. Separately. I realised I'd become an obsessive. I didn't stalk her, I didn't need to see her every day. And she left me a message once a week to tell me she was okay.'

He stops pacing, resumes his seat. The most difficult part of his confession is over, he's acknowledged his obsession.

'This kept on for a year. Then she left a different message. She said she was in a play, would I like to go and see it. She told me where and when. I went along. At the end of the performance she came to find me, said how pleased she was to see me. We had a coffee together. That was the beginning of rebuilding our relationship, and it had come from her.' George beams at us. 'It was good enough for me. By then I'd got used to not being able to have her,

150

it was enough just to see her happy every now and then. We'd be able to laugh together, joke together. She started telling me about her boyfriends. She introduced me to a girl she said fancied me; I went out with her on a few dates. She was nice, but she wasn't Anna. I've even started chatting up other girls, like Lorna.' He taps the side of his nose, letting us in on a secret. 'I don't really fancy her, and I know she doesn't fancy me, but it gives the others something to talk about.'

I take his pause as a sign that I can ask a question. 'So how did you get involved with the acting? Didn't Anna think you were getting too close again, chasing her perhaps?'

'Good God, no! It was Anna invited me to come along! They were short of men, and you don't have to do that much if you're Orsino, just look handsome and mope about in a lovesick sort of way. Anna said I'd be good at that.' He reflects again. 'You know, that's probably a sign that I'm getting better. When she said that, I could see the compliment and the humour without feeling any pain. We both laughed.' He lapses into pleasant and private memories again.

'So things were on the mend?' Jen asks, determined to keep him talking.

'I thought so. But then they started going wrong. It wasn't me – at least I don't think it was – having an effect on her, though I did have to kiss her at the end of the play. She seemed distracted. The only time she came to life was on the stage. When I asked her if anything was wrong, she said no, there was nothing I could help with. I don't think she was doing drugs again. In the play we had to get close to each other and her breath was fine, she was taking care of herself. I even started looking at her arms to see if there were any marks, but there was nothing. Things got worse and worse and then ... Then Taylor was killed.'

'Keep going, George, tell us about the police station and the solicitor. And you mentioned a note Anna wrote?'

151

'Oh yes, I'm sorry, I'd forgotten about all that. There isn't much to say, really. Anna was in a bad state, the solicitor said he couldn't get her to see how serious the charges were. I told him just about the same story I told you, just to let him know how close we were. He went back in to talk to her.'

'You knew Anna when she had her first breakdown, if we can call it that. Do you think she's about to suffer this type of thing again?'

'She's definitely been under some type of stress. She didn't cope easily with things like that.'

'And she didn't say whether there was something in particular causing her problems?' Jen asks.

'Nothing at all,' George answers quickly, perhaps too quickly. I try to look him in the eye; he sees what I'm doing and smiles, glances down. When he looks back up again his face is set. 'That's not really true,' he says. 'She said she'd argued with Jonathan Taylor. She wouldn't – or couldn't – say why she argued. I wasn't actually sure if they'd had a disagreement or not, I didn't know if she was telling the truth or making things up.'

'I think we can assume they had some type of falling out,' I reassure him. 'They certainly didn't appear to be on the best of terms before the party began.'

'That's what I told the solicitor, before he went back in. When he came out for the second time he said Anna had calmed down a bit to start with, she wrote me a note, the one I told you about. She acknowledged that she.'d had a lot to drink and made a fool of herself. She'd got herself in a compromising position with Louis and then made a pass at you.'

'That's right,' I tell him. I feel Jen stiffen at my side. That's part of the story I'd forgotten to tell her. Or was it 'neglected'? No, I tell myself, I've nothing to feel guilty about.

'She said you turned her down in no uncertain terms.'

Jen relaxes again.

152

'That's when she called you lots of names. And then she went inside and started drinking even more. Taylor began to make advances towards her but you intervened, rescued her. Some friends helped her to bed. She fell asleep and woke up to find her room full of policemen accusing her of murder.'

'So she can't remember anything that happened between falling asleep and being woken up?'

'Not a thing.' George shifts uneasily in his seat. 'She got confused again after that. She said no one would ever be able to find out who killed Taylor because it was the other her who did it! She said the other Anna had killed him. She said there was too much evidence against both of them. And then she stopped talking. The solicitor's asked her to be referred for a psychiatric report. He had to go and then the police said I had to go. That was when I first looked at the note Anna sent out. Here it is.' He fishes in his pocket, hands me a folded piece of paper.

'Do you mind if Jen sees it? I ask. He shakes his head to give permission and I read it aloud:

Dear George, thank you for coming, I can always rely on you. I'm sorry I've caused you so many problems. They've told me what I'm meant to have done, and I suppose I could have done it because I can't remember not doing it. I'm confused. Please say sorry to Kirsty's dad. If he wants a good puzzle, he can always try to sort this one out. Come and see me some time. Love, Anna.

George fills in the silence quickly. 'I went back to the campus. I wanted to look for you but the only people there were police and they wouldn't let me in. I knew the rest of them would be in one of the local pubs. When I found them I spoke to Kirsty straightaway. You know the rest.'

He seems relieved that his role is over. What I have to say, however, won't please him. I have to tell him about the overwhelming evidence against Anna.

'George, I want you to listen carefully. What I'm about to say is confidential, I was told it earlier today by a policeman. He told me in error, but what he said was what the police consider to be the truth, and when I finish telling you, I want you to say honestly whether you think it's worth me investigating the case further.'

He nods eagerly, I feel sorry for him; he feels he knows Anna well, but I'm not sure he knows her well enough.

'You may not like to hear this, George, although you may know some of it already. I'm sorry if it upsets you. Jonathan Taylor was killed by a knife. The knife has Anna's fingerprints all over it. One of her T-shirts was found hidden in her room, it was covered with Taylor's blood. They'd had an argument and she was drunk, that's certainly enough motivation for murder. Taylor had a camera; on it there were photographs of Anna and Taylor having sex. Traces of Taylor's semen and saliva were found in Anna's hair and pubic hair, and in her vagina. Similar traces of Anna's saliva and body fluids were found on Taylor. She was seen during the night heading for his room. Evidence, motivation and opportunity point irrevocably to Anna having murdered Jonathan Taylor.'

George says nothing at first. I've sat in front of him and hit him hard, in the face and the body, one-two in the solar plexus, dirty below-the-belt punches, hooks and jabs and uppercuts. I've hit him with evidence, with information, and he's about to fall to the canvas and be counted out.

'And that's not all,' I tell him. 'I found a note in Taylor's room. Yes, I know I shouldn't have been there, I know I may have disturbed a crime scene. The reason I'm telling you this is that it was from Anna to Taylor. It seemed to be inviting him to have sex with her. It could therefore be used as evidence of entrapment, a wish to get him out of his room to a place where he could be killed. There was always the chance that someone else wrote it, but it seems to be in the same handwriting as the letter Anna gave you.

By itself, it doesn't mean a lot; add it to everything else we know, and it's pretty damning.' I'm even beginning to persuade myself that Anna's guilty.

'It sounds as if there's nothing you can do,' he says quietly, almost amazed that he can still speak. 'Even when Anna was babbling, when she said she couldn't remember anything but then said "the other her" killed Taylor, she must subconsciously have known she did it.' He turns to Jen, pleading. 'That's schizophrenia, isn't it, when the mind is split into multiple personalities? Perhaps we can plead insanity, perhaps she'll be put in a hospital instead of a prison. Perhaps they can help her there.'

'Hold on,' Jen says brusquely. 'She doesn't sound schizophrenic to me. Delusional, perhaps. Withdrawn? Depressed? Yes, I might agree with both those descriptions, but that's hardly surprising in the circumstances. Making a statement about "the other me" is hardly the sign of a schizophrenic.'

'But if she's not mentally ill,' George explains slowly, as if asking Jen to change her mind, 'then she's guilty of murder.'

'Bollocks!' Jen doesn't swear very often, but when she does, she does it with emphasis. I'm not sure who's most shocked by the outburst, me or George.

'But Jen,' I try explaining, 'the evidence is ...'

'The evidence is an indication, that's all. Christ, even I can see that. Just wait there.' She hurries away, thunders upstairs then back down, rushes past the door and into the kitchen, then skids back into our company again. She's carrying in one hand a tray, on it a bottle of tomato ketchup, a tube of toothpaste, a glass of water and two dinner plates; in her other hand is the briefcase in which she keeps what I refer to as her 'doctoring kit'; and under one arm is a roll of toilet paper. She kneels on the floor between George and me.

'Right, let me think how best to do this.' She stares into space for a short while, then tears off two sheets of the toilet roll and places them on the floor. She takes a felt-tip pen out of her case and writes, crudely, the letter 'A' on one of the sheets, 'T' on the other. She places each sheet on a plate, then on top of the sheet marked 'T' she positions the ketchup, the toothpaste and the water. 'Taylor's blood,' she explains, pointing at the ketchup, 'semen and saliva.' She squirts a small swirl of each on the sheet of kitchen roll marked 'T'. 'Now,' she explains, 'one way for the transfer of all of these from Taylor to Anna is for them to have sex.' She picks up the sheet and wipes it on the sheet marked 'A', holds it out for her audience to see. A substantial amount of the ketchup, toothpaste and water has been transferred from one sheet to the other.

'But let's look at it another way,' she continues. She throws the sheets of paper to one side and prepares two new ones exactly as she did before; I take the opportunity to pick up the sheets she's discarded and put them in the wastepaper bin. I notice her write a question mark on a third sheet, then again she marks the 'T' sheet with her materials. I can see what she's going to do. She wipes this on the question mark sheet, then takes that and wipes it on the 'A' sheet. The result is similar to the first time she did it.

'So you're suggesting,' I say, 'that someone, we don't know who, stole Anna's shirt and, dressed in it, had sex with Taylor.'

'And killed him while – no, not while having sex, he had to ejaculate. Afterwards, straight afterwards, killed him.'

'The result would have been blood all over the shirt. Semen in, I presume, a condom?'

'Exactly. Transfer it to a syringe, then it could go anywhere. Same with saliva, though you mentioned Taylor had been pawing Anna earlier on, so it's quite possible there was some saliva on her from then. Either way would do. And Anna's drunk, remember, so whoever killed Taylor can easily deposit the evidence.' She's in her medical mode now, speaking authoritatively but concerned less with the person than with the process she's going through. I suppose it's a way doctors cope with the personal tragedies they're involved with every day; they depersonalise them. A patient is no longer a woman facing the trauma of a mastectomy, it's an interesting case of breast cancer; a man with emphysema becomes an x-ray of scarred lung tissue. But with us, sharing Jen's explanations, is George who might find it difficult to imagine his friend, drunk and semi-comatose, having a dead man's body fluids inserted in her body.

'George,' I say hurriedly, 'there's no need for you to wait and listen to . . .'

'No, I think I ought to hear this all the way through.' He doesn't seem shocked by Jen's revelations. 'Look, I'm aware more than anyone of Anna's attitude to men, to sex, to alcohol, to drugs.' He faces Jen, holds out his hands as if blessing her. 'So I'd like you to continue with your explanation.'

Jen's enthusiastic search for the truth has been tempered by the interruption. Her voice is quieter, less triumphal than it was. 'The transfer of body fluids from Taylor to Anna is certainly a possibility. The reverse would be just as easy using a vaginal swab or, in its absence—' she searches for an alternative '—a baby bud, a toothbrush, a pencil with some cotton wool wrapped round the end.' She shrugs her apology. 'It's an alternative, that's all. I suppose a good defence lawyer would think of it straightaway.'

'Perhaps,' I say. 'But there are still other problems. You were right, you've given us an alternative. But there's other evidence as well. A knife with Taylor's blood on the blade and only Anna's fingerprints on the handle. A witness who saw her heading for Taylor's room. A photograph of them having sex. My letter. I'll have to tell the police about that. And when all this is compared to our alternatives, a jury wouldn't choose your explanation, Jen. Juries go for the obvious, and the total evidence against Anna is too great.

Unless you have any further explanations you've kept up your sleeve?'

Jen is silent. She gathers together her visual aids and places them on the tray. 'Sorry,' she says to George. 'I didn't mean to get your hopes up.'

'That's all right,' he answers, though his small voice tells the lie. 'Can I see the note you found? I'd like to see exactly what it said.'

I shake my head. 'It's definitely the same handwriting, I'm sure of that. I don't really think you need to make matters worse for yourself, George, but I can get it for you if you want to.'

George nods solemnly. I reply in a similar coin, go to bring the note from my bag. When I get back Jen and George are exactly where I left them. I suspect nothing has been said. I pick up George's message, compare the handwriting with that of the note from Taylor's room. It's identical. I hand both to George. He scans them quickly. At first his bland face shows no sign of emotion, then slowly it changes. He looks puzzled, he reads the notes again. I think he's going to burst into tears, but the contortions of his face become a smile, then he begins to laugh. 'Oh, my God,' he chortles, 'I don't believe it. I really don't believe it. And you thought . . ? But then you wouldn't know! My God!'

'Are you all right?' I ask. He's been through a lot today, he must have snapped, hysteria has taken control.

'Oh, Mr Oliphant, yes, I'm all right. I just wish the other evidence was as conclusive as this. Look.' He hands my note back to me, Jen shuffles across to read it aloud over my shoulder.

'I really want to screw you. I'd like to wrap myself round your _____, put your beautiful _____ in my _____ and we could _____ on the _____ for hours. Come and find me now, you can use the yellow stockings to tie me to the ____! You fill in the missing words! Your True Love (gagging for it!), a'

158

'I can't see why this is so funny,' I tell George.

'Hang on,' Jen says before he can reply, 'they're doing *Twelfth Night*, aren't they?'

George nods happily.

'Isn't there a plot device, doesn't someone leave a letter lying around to trick one of the characters into believing that another one loves him?'

George nods again. 'Maria tricks Malvolio, that's right. But that isn't the important bit. You see, when we first started rehearsing someone replaced the prop letter with a fake one, rather a rude one. It became a sort of tradition, we all made them up at some time. This is Anna's. It's not a real letter from her to Taylor, it's a joke letter!'

If I sound bad-tempered it's because I didn't recognise the note for what it was. I don't know the play well enough, I don't know any Shakespeare well enough. 'It has a large "a" at the bottom. That's why I thought it was from Anna.'

George snatches the note back. 'That's strange,' he says, 'normally we'd sign them "O", the letter was meant to be written by Maria in the hand of her mistress, Olivia. Let me see.' He looks at the note again, hands it back to me for my opinion. 'Doesn't that look like a letter "O" with a little tail added to make it look like an "a"?'

It doesn't take long to realise he's right.

Jen takes the paper from me, nods to show she agrees. 'So what does that mean?'

'It means I'll start the investigations as soon as I get back tomorrow,' I announce, and even as I say it regret the theatricality of the statement. Jen and George share a look of amazement.

'But I thought you said ...'

'Surely the evidence is too loaded against ...'

They start and stop at the same time. The silence becomes melodramatic.

'The note is an attempt to frame Anna,' I explain. 'It's a crack in the overall evidence. Put together with the

159

doubts Jen raised, it gives me something to work on. If someone else did kill Taylor, then that person must have had a motive. And if Anna didn't kill him, then whoever did went to a lot of trouble to pin the blame on her. So much effort demands a substantial reason, and quite a bit of time to actually do the work involved in framing Anna. That sort of thing leaves clues. All I have to do is find them.'

For a moment it looks as if George is going to throw himself to his knees and offer a prayer of thanks that someone is going to help him. My obvious hostility (the glare of an arch sceptic can be a terrible thing) prevents this. 'Mr Oliphant, thank you so much,' he says, grasping my hands in his, 'you have no idea the relief it brings, having someone share a belief in Anna's innocence.'

I push his hands away. 'Don't thank me yet, George. There's a chance Anna may have been framed. All I can promise is that I'll investigate.'

'That's a start, Mr Oliphant.'

'And it's a long way to the finish. I'll only have a few days. The odds aren't in Anna's favour, particularly when she can't offer anything to help me.'

'I'll go back to her solicitor,' he says with urgency. 'I'll tell him you're trying to help. Perhaps he can persuade Anna to talk a little more, he might be able to get her to remember something. I'm sure she'll be able to remember something.'

'No,' I tell him, 'don't mention this to the solicitor. They're strange creatures, they talk to each other. I don't want it known that I'm doing anything formal or official on this case.'

He sits back in his seat. 'Are you sure?'

'Not a word. If I hear you've mentioned it to anyone, I'm out.'

'Okay, then, if you're sure.' He checks his watch. 'I'd better be getting back. They say we're going to start rehearsing again tomorrow night. I don't know how we'll manage, but if we are, I'm going to need some sleep.' He stands up, shakes my hand, does the same to Jen with the addition of a small, barely noticeable bow. We go with him to the door, wave goodbye. When we come back in we collapse on the sofa.

'Interesting evening,' I say.

'Almost as interesting as the one I had planned.'

I reach across to her, let my hand rest on her thigh. 'Did you see his face when I said I'd accept the case?'

'Yes. He was pleased.'

'He was more than pleased. He was filled with joy. It was as if I was the knight on the white steed who would gallop to Anna's rescue, defeating the dragon in the process. That worries me.'

'Why? You gave him hope. What's wrong with that?'

'I'm what's wrong with that. I'm no knight in shining armour. I'm an ex-cop who installs security systems for a living, a job I can do reasonably well. Sometimes I solve crimes, though I feel it's more by accident than design. I can do a bit of surveillance, a bit of research, I can come up with the goods in divorce cases and petty crime. And I've had enough experience to know when I'm out of my depth.'

Jen seems to want to say something, but I'm determined to finish, I hold up my hands to silence her. 'Jen, despite what you said, what I said, the chances are Anna Peranski would be found guilty. You didn't meet her, I did. I'm in my mid-forties, I'm shorter and balder than I'd like to be, and God knows why you stay with me, but I'm thankful you do. She came on to me, Jen, and yes, she was drunk, yes, she was young, but I saw her when she was sober and she's a pretty peculiar person. It's possible – and the police think it's probable – that she could have killed Taylor, and no matter what I believe, I might not be able find any evidence to prove she's innocent. I'm a private investigator, not a superhero.'

161

'Are you quite finished feeling sorry for yourself?' Jen moves at last, comes towards me, stands in front of me. 'Look at me,' she says. I do so. 'Okay, George may be clutching at straws. Put yourself in his position, wouldn't you do the same if it was me or Kirsty?'

'Yes, but . . .'

'Be quiet, Billy, that was a rhetorical question. I haven't finished yet. You haven't ever taken on a job where you thought there was no chance of winning. You've always followed your instincts, and I refuse to believe you've changed. So there's a chance Anna Peranski's innocent. Now I know you're just protecting yourself and I know it's not because you're frightened of failing. But you are frightened of letting people down. Can't you see why I love you?'

'Was that a rhetorical question as well?'

'Billy, I swear I'll hit you!'

'Okay! If I'm being honest, no, there are times when I don't know why you love me. I'm just thankful you do.'

'Good. Well in that case it doesn't matter at all to George whether you find any evidence to prove Anna's innocent or whether you don't. What matters is that someone – you – has decided she's worth helping. The "why" is less important than the act itself. So have some confidence in yourself.' Jen kneels down in front of me, takes my hand. 'Billy, I love you because you care. I love you because you love me. I love you because you have doubts about yourself that are unfounded, but you overcome them. I love you because you're you.'

'I know. I'm sorry.'

She kisses me. 'And there's one other thing.'

'What's that?'

'I love you because you fuck me so well. Now can we please go to bed? I'm definitely a more-than-once-a-night woman, and you've never let me down in the past. Get yourself up those stairs!'

She hits me with a cushion. I could retaliate, but that

162

would delay the inevitable pleasure waiting for me.

'I always try to rise to the occasion,' I reply, standing and bowing. Before she can even aim the next blow I'm halfway out of the room.

Chapter Seven

The journey back to the university is interminable. Jen tempts me to stay later than I ought, so I catch heavy traffic on the central motorway, families heading out to the countryside to make the most of the fine weather before its late afternoon descent into thunderstorms. The sun fractures every glinting, golden windscreen; it hurtles the blue sky down into the river to make a jagged broken bottle of reflections. The only closed car windows and sunroofs shout 'air-conditioning' at other jealous road-users; flaring horns and blaring tempers fire the day into purgatory.

Once over the bridge the slime-sheened, slug-like pace increases marginally as we hit the dual carriageway. The journey south is never pleasant, there's always a feeling of descent – reflecting, no doubt, the geographical bias of a northerner – and the scenery is, for the first dozen miles, uninspiring. Dead factories and wide, dreary housing estates cluster for attention like needy children. Fields are flat and scorched, no birds sing in the dog-eared, rioting hawthorn hedgerows.

Once the hills begin to roll in, once the breeze begins to hit my back and arms, my discontent with my surrounding begins to disappear. It's replaced by worries about the next few days. I'm not exactly investigating a murder, I'm trying to find evidence that a specific person didn't commit the crime. I'm not used to that; police investigations, my

investigations, are normally concerned with proving something, with making one or more links between criminal and
victim. Here I'm supposed to snap the links that already
exist, and I'm not quite sure where I ought to begin. At
least, I tell myself, I'm not working alone. Jen's decided
she ought to be involved and is renewing her acquaintance
with her old tutor, Professor Edmundson. She's certain that
he'll be involved in overseeing the analysis of the forensic
samples taken from Taylor and from Anna, and she feels I
ought to have some accurate basic information to work
with. I asked her how she intended persuading him to
give her access to the necessary files; she replied that she
wouldn't give away trade secrets. I hope she hasn't picked
up this devious nature from me.

I'm giving myself plenty of time to look around, to talk
to people, to ask questions. The group won't be allowed
back into their buildings, they won't be allowed access to
their stage, until early evening. I've already arranged to
meet Kirsty late morning. There are some things I need to
discuss with her. She said she saw Anna going into Taylor's
room in the early hours of the morning, but I need more
detail from her. I also have to find out more about Taylor's
relationships with his other students, because if Anna didn't
kill him, someone else did and that person must have had a
motive. She – or he – must also have had a quick mind; the
evidence against Anna has been put in position with great
care.

I park well away from the patrol cars still clustered
round the honeypot of the dormitory and the cloisters. I use
my binoculars and find that one or two familiar faces are
on duty at the plastic ribbon. Arnison has probably put me
on the 'most unwanted' list as a result of my interventions
the day before, and I don't want to make my presence
known to him. I head off to the main reception area with
no specific purpose in mind other than curiosity. I'm
surprised it's open at all on a Sunday, but there are signs
outside showing that various conferences are taking place;

165

organisations with acronyms I don't recognise are keen, apparently, to use the university's facilities. It isn't too busy, however, most of the students have returned home to low-paid summer jobs in an attempt to stave off the debts howling at their door. I stroll up to the desk and beam at the older of the two receptionists. She looks like the type to gossip.

'Can I help you, sir?' she asks pleasantly.

'Oh, it's nothing important. I've come to collect my daughter. She's got a room in town, and I'm a little early. I thought I'd wait for a while in the cloisters, the last time I was here they were really beautiful, but I couldn't get in. All those policemen! I was just wondering what had happened.'

The receptionist leans her grey-haired coiffure towards me and looks around, as if she's going to tell me a secret. 'Well,' she says conspiratorially, once she's made sure there are no secret agents watching us, 'there was a murder here yesterday, in the early hours of the morning.'

'No!'

'Yes! One of our own tutors as well. And I've heard he was involved in an orgy, there's even been talk of some sort of ritual sacrifice.' She looks around again, I have to stop myself mimicking her.

'Surely not. Here?'

'Yes, right here. Well, in the cloisters actually, that's why they won't let anyone in. They're doing a search. But they've already arrested someone, and from what I hear it's definitely the right person. A student! A female student! What is the world coming to?'

'I wouldn't have believed it, murders and orgies, right here.' I can't resist it. I look to my right and to my left, quite slowly; I'm rewarded by my informant doing the same. Then I continue fishing. 'So who was the person killed?'

'Like I said, one of our tutors, Jonathan Taylor was his name, he lectured in Drama and Theatre Studies.' She turns

166

to her colleague. 'That reminds me, Mary, we must take his name off the staff list. And there's the brochure to look at, just in case he's in there. I think there's a photograph of him teaching a class, we'll have to get rid of that.'

'So what was he like, this Taylor bloke? Why would anyone want to kill him?'

Before the grey-haired woman can speak, her friend Mary offers a contribution. 'He was a bit of a philanderer,' she says slowly, her speech not slowing her flying fingers' dance over her keyboard.

I look at her. She's only a little younger than her associate and considerably broader. She doesn't look like Taylor's type.

'Was he, Mary? Oh, do tell, did he try it on with you?'

'No, Eleanor, he did not. If he had done, I'd have kept him locked up till I'd finished with him. He was quite a tasty one, was Mr Taylor.'

'Mary!'

'On the small side, perhaps, but good things come in little packages.' She carries on, blissfully unaware of the potential for double entendres she's just ignored. 'Alas, he never did approach me, Eleanor. But he did others.'

'Who? Go on, tell me who!'

'I don't think you know her. In fact I can't even remember her name, she'd just started in Human Resources, very young looking. I think he went for the young ones. Thing was, she'd just got married, but that didn't stop him. He made some improper suggestions, there was nobody else there, though, so she couldn't prove anything. It was Marilyn told me, and Marilyn said he'd done the same to others. But he was always careful not to do it in front of witnesses.'

I butt in. 'You don't think he tried it on with his students, do you? I mean, surely there's some rule against that.'

Mary replies on behalf of the coven of two. 'There are rules, but no one sticks to them. I mean, there are thousands of young people on site, and some of the lecturers are only post-grads themselves, not much older than their students. It's only natural, isn't it, if there's an attraction.'

'I suppose, in that case, there could be quite a lot of suspects. If this bloke Taylor had been going round chatting everyone up, there would have been a lot of jealousy. After all, you said he was good-looking.'

My last comment is aimed at Mary and she offers her considered reply. 'The exact word was, I believe, "tasty". But that would be tasty like a starter, not like a main course. Unless you had a small appetite. Like I said before, he wasn't a big man.'

I catch Eleanor's eyebrows rising at the possibility of an entirely different meaning to that Mary intends, but Mary chooses to forgo its pleasure.

'I suppose something like that,' I muse, scratching my head, 'regularly hitting on his students, would be noticed by his bosses. If there'd been any complaints, even if they hadn't been serious, they would have been put into his personal records. Human Resources and so on. That's what would happen in my job.'

Mary's left her typing now, she's determined to play her part to the full. 'Ah, but that relies on somebody regularly checking the file, and that wouldn't happen. Some over-worked secretary . . .'

'Like me,' Eleanor offers.

'Like us,' Mary corrects her. 'Some poor secretary would be asked to file the information. She'd find the folder and just put the complaint away, she wouldn't bother looking through the rest of the file.'

'Not even,' I suggest an alternative, 'if it was a complaint about sexual harassment? Perhaps, out of inter-est, curiosity, call it what you want, the secretary might read everything?'

'Yes,' Eleanor concedes, 'she probably would.' She goes on after only a moment's further thought. 'But then she'd just put the whole thing away. After all, it wouldn't be her

168

job to point out that he'd done the same thing before.'

Mary nods her agreement. 'Not her job,' she repeats, 'not her job.'

I let the discussion sink in. 'I wonder what's in this bloke Taylor's folder, then. I don't suppose we'll ever know.'

'Why's that?' my audience asks in one voice.

'Well, surely the police will have taken the file away?'

Mary shakes her head. 'No paper files here, this is an ultra-modern, state-of-the-art university. Everything's on computer.' There's a long pause 'Are you thinking what I'm thinking?' she asks Eleanor.

'No, we couldn't.'

'Why not? It wouldn't do anyone any harm.'

While they're talking I move far enough away so they feel unthreatened by my presence, near enough to hear what they say.

'Someone might find out,' Eleanor warns.

'Like who? There's no one else here.' They look around; I've become invisible, I'm part of the scenery now, a collaborator.

'Don't they keep tabs on who's looking at which bits of the network?'

'No. And if they do, we could just say it was an accident.' She's desperate to find out what Taylor's file contains. 'Anyway, we probably won't be able to get in, there's bound to be a password.'

'In that case,' Eleanor announces with a degree of finality that surprises me, 'I don't suppose there'd be any harm in trying.'

They cluster round the computer screen and I hear the tap of fingers on keys, the scrape of mouse on pad. 'Human resources icon,' Eleanor says.

'I know, I know.'

'Records,' Eleanor carries on regardless. 'Search by name or department?'

'Doesn't matter, you get the same result whatever you do.'

'Go for name then.' There's a short pause. 'Yes, you were right, Mary, password required. That's it then.'

'Excuse me,' I speak up, 'I think I might be able to help.'

'Pardon?' Mary seems to have taken the lead.

'I might be able to help you. Get past the password, that is. You see, I'm a computer technician and I have to do work on lots of computers, so I find out what the passwords are. I've done a sort of study on the type of passwords people use.' I get up and go towards them, not giving them time to object. 'It's like this, you see. Big organisations tend to have some sort of "house style" in their passwords, so if you know one you can work out the others.'

As I talk, I move round the counter to where Mary's still sitting in front of the computer terminal. 'So let's start at the beginning, when you log on at the start of the day you should have a username and a password. You have to decide on the username, but within certain criteria, like "at least six lower case letters and two digits".'

That's right,' Eleanor says, 'except it's four and four for us.'

'So what do you do? Most people choose their name, such as "Mary", or their name abbreviated to four letters, perhaps "Elli".' I spell out her name to make sure I have it right. Both Mary and Eleanor seem impressed by my skills, so I can assume I've guessed the first part of their respective usernames. I hurry on. 'Then they add either the year of their birth in full, 1980 for you, Mary ...'

Mary laughs. 'Flatterer! You'd have to take another twenty years at least off that.'

I smile back. 'Really? Surely you're not in your forties?'

'Forty-eight this September,' she says proudly.

I do the calculation, year of birth is 1959. That means her username is mary1959. 'I wouldn't have believed it. But where was I? Oh yes, the username. For the number it's either the whole year, or the month and year. You know, if you were born in May 1974, your number would be 0574.'

'That's amazing,' says Eleanor, 'that's the way I do it.'

'So when should I plan on buying a birthday card for you?'

'Oh, I'm younger than Mary by a huge amount. February '61.'

I'm feeling pleased with myself. I have two usernames, mary1959 and elli0261. I repeat them to myself, they may be useful; all I need now is the password. 'Right, Mary, what I need you to do is log out, then log back in. Don't let me see your username – you wouldn't want to breach security – but I have to know the password so I can guess the next level. It's not an abbreviated form of the university name, I hope, that would be too easy for hackers to get in.'

'No,' Mary says, 'it's "success".'

'Lower case?'

'Yes.'

'Okay, enter that and go to the location where the personnel files are kept.' I watch the screen to make sure that the path is the same as that I remember from earlier; it is. 'Now then, if general access is gained by using the word "success", what similar word might get you into the personnel records files?' I don't really mind whether the golden girls guess the second password or not, I can gain access to the network with the information I already possess. And someone, somewhere, will have written down the key to the next door. All I have to do is find it.

'If success gets you in,' Mary declares, 'perhaps failure takes you further.'

'Try it,' I suggest.

Mary types in the word. 'Access denied,' she tells me.

'It's just like the movies,' Eleanor says excitedly, 'thirty seconds to go until the bomb goes off!'

'Ellie, stop being silly. Now what?'

'Open the thesaurus and type in "success", see what it brings up. There we are. "Achievement" is too long, so is "accomplishment". Try "victory". No, same result.

171

"Triumph"? No luck again.' I know what I want to try next: what comes after success? The answer's probably 'reward', or a synonym of the word. But I'd rather test that in private.

'Now what do we do?' Mary asks.

'I think we'd better leave it,' I tell her, 'there might be a lock-out facility after three tries, and I wouldn't want you to get into trouble because of me. Sorry.' I look at my watch. 'My goodness, I'm late. I'll have to go now, my daughter'll be waiting for me. Bye.' I give the ladies no opportunity to complain at my speedy departure, I'm out from behind the counter and into the open air before a word is spoken.

I feel very pleased with myself. I've found a way into the university's computer network and, with a little luck, I should be able to access Jonathan Taylor's personnel files. They might tell me if there was anyone still on campus who had complained about him in any way; they might tell me what his employers felt about him; they might tell me ... nothing at all. Even that thought fails to remove my self-satisfaction, the psychological benefit of talking to Mary and Eleanor has been great.

Experience has taught me to enjoy such moments before their inevitable swift departure. I haven't even begun to savour the taste of my cleverness when a voice sours it to an acrid bitterness.

'Oliphant! I want a word with you!'

There's no point in running from such calls, unless the person approaching you is wielding a weapon of some sort, and Detective Sergeant Mike Stephenson is threatening me with nothing but his imposing bulk and the harshness of his speech.

'Sergeant Stephenson,' I say loudly, 'how can I help you?' Politeness and courtesy sometimes work, though not very often. The wide-eyed expression on Stephenson's face and the redness of his cheeks would alone suggest that being pleasant won't win his friendship. Add to that the

172

way he's hurrying towards me with such urgency that coffee is spilling from the plastic-lidded containers he's carrying, and my tactic seems doomed from the outset.

Stephenson, when launched from his traditional, sedate mode of travelling, into swift motion is, in all senses of the word, awful; his motion is both ugly and dreadful, yet it inspires reverence. I am overcome with awe.

I once saw a race between a long distance runner and a shot-putter over 200 metres. The former could easily manage lap after lap under sixty seconds and then finish the race with a sub-four minute mile; but the latter's explosive strength was phenomenal and, despite difficulty with the bend (his bulky legs weren't meant for such tight curves), he finished a second ahead of his rival. It then took him another lap to slow his bulk to a walk.

Perhaps that last statement is an exaggeration, but Stephenson does bring the image to mind. Where the shot-putter had height and muscle, Stephenson has width and fat; they certainly share a look of determination, and both – once moving – have the advantage of momentum. I feel like a suicide who, having placed himself in the path of a train, realises too late that he doesn't want to die, but the bulk and speed of the object bearing down make escape impossible; Stephenson's approach is inexorable.

'Oliphant, you bastard!' he yells as he begins his slow-down. His jacket billows behind him like a parachute; his arms stabilise his descent to the runway. Like a hero in a Hollywood action movie I stand my ground, wait for him to slew to a halt; he does so inches from my face. He smells of yesterday's sweat and doughnuts.

'There are people listening,' I tell him, pointing to both sides as the general public manoeuvre around us.

'I don't give a flying fuck about ...' A woman with a pushchair glares at him and he shows that he does indeed care about the tender ears of his wider audience. He reaches out with a fat, coffee-filled paw and nudges me off the path into the space between two cars. He tones down the volume to a viperish hiss. 'You, Mr Oliphant, have caused me a great deal of grief. Chief Inspector Arnison has been on my back most of last night and all of today because of what you said. He's blaming me!'

'That's probably because he thinks it's your fault.'

'But it's not! It's your fucking fault!'

'Oh! Really? Strange, I thought it was you blabbed the details of your case to a member of the general public – namely me – who was simply repeating what you said in the innocent belief that it was in the public domain. I must be wrong. Sorry about that.' I turn to walk away but he spins me around.

'Not yet, Oliphant. I haven't finished with you.'

'Are you arresting me?'

'Listen, smartarse, I've been around long enough to recognise dickheads like you. I know there's no point talking nice to you, so I'll be plain and honest. You've made a fool of me, and I don't like that. I bear grudges. And I get revenge. So watch out!'

'What you gonna do, fat boy? Sit on me?'

Stephenson is beginning to try my patience. He's the worst sort of policeman, he relies on bullying and threats, he's got where he is by being bad at everything else he's tried. Some old pal of a similar ilk has taken sympathy on him and promoted him so his pension will be maximised. Stephenson brings out the worst in me, my desire to fight back despite the consequences. I don't know people here, I can't rely on acquaintances like Kim Bryden to help me out if things go wrong; I should say nothing. I never could learn to be sensible. So I go on, while I've got the opportunity.

'Listen, lard-arse. I like you even less than you like me.' He seems surprised that I'm willing to continue the attack. 'I know the way you work. I was going to say, I know the way your mind works, but I honestly don't think you've got anything inside that skull of yours to do any thinking. I know you've probably got some contacts, some hard men

174

you think you can get to come and lean on me. But I've got friends as well, just as nasty as yours. And they'll be coming to find you if anything happens to me.' I lean closer. 'Just pray I don't slip and fall, Stephenson, in case you get the blame. Now get out of my way.'

I'm quite pleased with my own bravado, my own lies. They've made him even angrier than he was. I take my keys out of my pocket and wave them at him. 'If you've finished, I've got work to do, places to go, people to see.' I'm tempted to break into song, a singing detective made real, but that would be too silly. 'So let me past, please.'

'Posh car for a little shit like you,' he says, gesturing towards the Volvo on my right.

'Not mine, burger boy.'

He turns the other way. The Ford Ka convertible isn't new, but the paintwork's shiny, obviously well-kept. 'Yeah, this is more you. You want to be careful, Oliphant, vandalism's rife these days. And the police just don't seem to care about it.'

'Don't touch that car,' I warn him.

'I wouldn't think of it,' he smiles, 'might leave finger-prints. But accidents happen.' He takes off the lid off one of the coffees he's carrying. 'Hot liquids probably won't harm the roof that much,' he pours the coffee over the fabric of the foldback top. 'But you never know. And people are so clumsy these days.' With his heel he kicks hard against the plastic wheel trim; it shatters.

'I wouldn't do anything else if I were you,' I warn him.

'Me? Do anything? Oliphant, these are day-to-day things that happen in our crime-ridden world, and I'm a police-man, I'm paid to stop them happening. Why would I deliberately harm anything?' He's looking at me carefully to see if I'm likely to fly at him, attack him, hit him, punch him. When I don't he takes it as a sign that he can go further. He empties the second coffee over the car. Then he takes his own keys from his pocket. 'The things people do today, eh Oliphant?' He holds a key between his knuckles and jabs it at the wing-mirror; it cracks. He hits it again and shards of glass fall to the ground. I take a step back so I'm on the pavement again, and he takes the opportunity to slide the key along the wing. The gouge in the paintwork is deep.

'Why did you do that?' I ask innocently.

'Who, me? I didn't do anything. If I were you, I'd ring the police and say your car's been vandalised. They'll get someone out to see you in, oh, an hour or two. Perhaps a bit longer if you mention who you are.'

'It's all right, Stephenson, I'm not going to complain about my car being vandalised. Why should I? It's not my car.'

I walk away. I take twenty, thirty steps, that's all I can manage before the temptation is too great. I turn to see Stephenson standing where I left him, mouth open, brain short-circuited into inactivity. He looks in my direction and shouts my name.

'Don't forget to smile for the CCTV,' I call back, pointing at the mast where the camera is gazing straight at him. He shouts again. The words aren't recognisable but I assume they're some type of oath: 'I'll get you, Penelope Pitstop, if it's the last thing I do!' I manage a dog-like laugh in response then turn the corner on my way to meet Kirsty.

It's cool in the pub where she takes me. The doors are open and most of the lunchtime customers are in the beer garden at the rear. Kirsty would go there too, but I mutter 'Too hot,' and we head instead for two seats in the corner. The window's open and there's a pleasant murmur of noise from outside.

I refrain from comment as Kirsty orders a pint of bitter to accompany my orange juice. I can't understand why girls, women, who normally drink fluorescent, fruit-flavoured alcohol, go to university and choose instead pints of beer. After three years of drinking and occasional studying for exams they find jobs and their fingers never touch a pint glass again, their lips won't allow beer to pass beyond them. Perhaps it's a gesture of independence or equality. Perhaps it's a determination to find out what appeals to those other strange creatures that inhabit the planet, men. Perhaps it's a desire to get drunk as cheaply and quickly as possible. It's far more likely, I realise, that the problem lies with the perception than the perceived. My point of reference is my own youth, when working class lads didn't go to university and when pubs had bars where women didn't dare venture.

'What you thinking, Dad?' Kirsty's voice brings me back. Did I really live through those times? Surely I'm thinking of my father's youth, of steam engines and cloth caps, of men running in front of cars waving red flags, of airships and the instigation of the penny post. Didn't my father fight at Waterloo? And I'm sure his father thought up ideas for plays, sold them to that Billy Shakespeare who lived just down the road. He used to tell the story of his father as well who shared a fag with Gutenberg behind the bike sheds, gave him the idea for the printing press.

'I was thinking how old I feel sometimes,' I explain.

'That's all right, then. I thought you had trapped wind.'

'You're so kind.'

We sip from our glasses; the white head of froth leaves a faint line on Kirsty's upper lip and she licks it off like a child savouring the last stickiness of a summer ice-cream.

'Thanks for helping out,' Kirsty says, 'we all appreciate you chipping in like you did, taking our side against that Inspector bloke.'

'I wanted to see the play,' I tell her, 'I feel involved. But now there's something else come up.' I tell her about George's visit the previous night. She puffs her cheeks and exhales loudly. 'I tried to tell him that all the evidence points to Anna as the murderer, but he wouldn't listen. And Jen took his side. Give her credit, she was right: there are other possible explanations of some of the evidence; but not all of it.'

177

Kirsty ponders what I've just said. 'Does that mean you think Anna's guilty?'

'No, it means there's an element of doubt, more doubt than there was before, but the balance of probability still lies with Anna being the murderer. And she could have done it, couldn't she?'

'She was certainly bad-tempered enough. And Taylor did treat her badly, so ... Yes, she could have done it.'

'And you saw her in the corridor, going into Taylor's room?'

'Yes.' There's a finality to the statement, an awareness that – at some time in the future – Kirsty will be called to testify against Anna.

'Tell me again what you saw, tell me what you told the police.' That's the real reason I wanted to talk to her, to find out if her evidence could be read in any other way. She is, at the moment, the most accessible witness I have.

'There isn't that much to say, Dad. I woke up, Tom too, there must have been a noise. We lay there and we heard the noise again, like someone knocking or banging on the wall, opening and closing doors. There was laughing as well, really loud and wild. I thought it was somebody playing the fool so I got out of bed and opened the door, I was going to tell them politely to piss off. The only person there was Anna, down at the far end, near to where you were sleeping. She was trying to get into Jonathan Taylor's room, at least I think she was, but she was swaying from side to side. I said something like "Anna, please go to bed." She turned round when she saw me, sort of waved. Then she managed to get the door open and went inside. I went back to bed myself, I didn't think anything of it. I mean, I thought it was strange, Anna going to Taylor's room after what had happened earlier, but he'd said there was something between them. I just supposed she wanted to be his friend again.'

'Friend?'

'Friend, lover, sex object, whatever euphemism you

178

want. You couldn't guess anything about Anna, she was her own woman. She didn't care about anything or anyone else.'

'How did you know it was her?'

'Come on, Dad, I'd be able to recognise her a mile away.'

'Humour me, love. Imagine I'm her barrister and you're in court. How would you answer the question?'

'Okay, let me think.' She refreshes herself further then begins to speak. She doesn't look at me directly, she closes her eyes and opens them as she talks, slow motion blinking that must help her see again what she saw two nights ago. 'Well, first of all, obviously, there was the hair. It was Anna's hair, that silly bright blue.'

'Did you see her face?'

'Yes.'

'And you recognised her?'

'Yes.'

'At night? In a dimly lit corridor, from quite a distance away? You recognised her face? Could it be that the obvious thing, the blue hair, actually forced the recognition? Was it her face?'

Kirsty closes her eyes again. 'I suppose it could have been someone in a wig. It was quite dark.'

I change tack. 'What was she wearing?'

'What was she wearing? Oh, I don't know, a T-shirt of some sort.'

'Colour? Was there a pattern on it? A picture? Some words? Think.'

Kirsty closes her eyes again. 'I think it was yellow. Yes, it was a short yellow T-shirt or nightshirt.'

'How short?'

'Short enough to be decent, I suppose, most of the time. But only just. She was going from side to side across the hall, banging and laughing, and once she twisted and her shirt went up and ... Well, I could see she didn't have anything on underneath.'

'What did you see?'

'Pardon?'

'When she twisted. You said she had nothing on underneath, did you see her backside?'

'Dad!' She's a child again, embarrassed to find me showing her how to dance in the middle of a Saturday afternoon shopping centre.

I press the point, ask again. 'Front or back view, Kirsty?'

She capitulates. 'Front.'

'What colour was her pubic hair?'

'Dad!' This time the exclamation is louder.

'It's important, love.'

Once again her eyes close. She smiles. 'Blue! Yes, it was blue!' Her eyes snap open. 'Perhaps that's why I'm so convinced it was her, she'd died her pubes blue to match her head. And I think ... Yes, I'm sure she'd told me she'd done that. I think she was trying to shock me.'

'So you're certain it was Anna you saw?'

'Yes. Yes, I'm certain.'

'Okay then, go on.' I try to make my voice a little kinder, a little gentler. 'Tell me what else there was.'

'Nothing much. She was almost at the bottom of the corridor. She opened the door to Jonathan Taylor's room and waved at me, then she went in. I went back to bed, it was quiet after that. That's it.'

'Good. That's all I need to know.' I fish in my back pocket for my wallet and bring it out, inside is a small notebook and a pen. Most of the time it's used for measuring buildings, writing down the names and addresses of clients. Occasionally it serves other purposes. I write down the details of what Kirsty's told me and read it back to her; she agrees that it's accurate.

'So now what do you do?' she asks with what appears to be genuine interest.

'I don't know. Wait, I suppose. Jen's gone to see an old friend of hers, a Professor Edmondson who's an expert in forensic science. Even academics work on Sundays. She thinks he might be called in to verify the police findings on Taylor and Anna, and she's hoping she might be able to persuade him to give her some information. She said she'd call if she heard anything.'

Kirsty's fiddling with a menu. 'Are you hungry?' I ask.

'Yeah, but ...' Food is temporarily forgotten as she leans forward. 'Dad, shouldn't we be doing something pro-active? I mean, if Anna's innocent then someone else is guilty and they went to a lot of trouble to frame her. So there should be some clues. All we need to do is find them.'

Kirsty's said several things that require attention and I'm not sure this is the time or place to deal with them. But her enthusiasm reminds me of me when I was just a little older than her, and if I don't sort this matter out now then I may regret it later.

'Your English is wrong,' I say, looking her in the eyes.

'No it's not,' she bristles straightaway, 'it may be collo-quial at times, but it's generally accurate. And anyway, there's no such thing as right or wrong English, what counts is whether it's appropriate or not.'

'Yours is wrong,' I repeat, 'fundamentally incorrect. Do you want me to tell you why?'

She nods silently, a puzzled look on her face as if I've instigated some type of game. What I'm about to say is a remembered fragment of some bygone lesson; it's stayed with me (like John Keats' 'On First Looking Into Chapman's Homer', a poem set as a punishment that destroyed any chance of me ever enjoying poetry) over many years and is my sole claim to any knowledge of English grammar. There's no need to rehearse it, I know it word perfect.

'You mistakenly used the first person plural pronoun when you ought to have used the second person singular pronoun in the future conditional tense referring to possible actions. Do you wish me to repeat the statement?'

181

Kirsty's exasperated. 'No I do not "wish you to repeat the statement". But you can tell me in plain English what you're trying to say in ridiculously convoluted English. Honestly, Dad, there are times ...'

'When I really annoy you? Good, that's just what it's like having children, remember that. And as for what I said before, here it is in language even an undergraduate can understand. "We" don't do anything, because "we" implies more than one person, it implies that you're involved in this somehow. And you're not. No "we", just me.'

'But Dad ...'

'But me no buts, it's final. If Anna didn't kill Taylor, then the person who did is still loose and I don't want you annoying him, her, it or them. Understood?'

She's going to argue, just as I would have done, just – I'm horribly aware – as her mother would have done. With parents like us she stands no chance. I silence her before she can begin. 'I want your promise that you won't do any silly investigations of your own. No promise, then I go straight back home and I take with me my expertise, my cables and wiring and my goodwill. I'm sorry, Kirsty, but this is non-negotiable.'

Kirsty drains her glass. She's angry with me, but she won't be for long; her bad moods are quick to blow over. 'I don't have any choice,' she says, 'if I want the play to go ahead. I suppose the greater good of the greatest number of people is what counts. As John Stuart Mill would have said.'

'Good. Now let's get something to eat. As Billy Bunter would have said.'

By the time we finish our respective sandwiches Kirsty has forgotten to be annoyed with me. I'd like to think that this is due to her realising that, when she considers the facts carefully, I'm right in all I said; but I suspect it's because she knows that I do need some help from her. I've already had to ask her if she'll show me where Taylor's office is. We've agreed, after some wary bartering, that she'll take me there later in the afternoon, but we'll then leave so I can return in my own time to investigate further. We both know that's a euphemism for breaking in; we both know that I don't want her caught up in any illegality; and I know that, given the opportunity, she'll do everything she can to be involved in everything I do, whichever side of the law I'm operating on. I accept that I'll have to deal with her enthusiasm whenever it shows itself.

It's shortly after two when we leave the pub and head back to the university. I feel a great sense of pride when Kirsty links her arm in mine, guides me (at my request) away from the familiar accommodation block, still busy with police in blue and white, and leads me on a trek through a labyrinth of corridors. I try, without much success, to orientate myself in relation to the cloisters, but Kirsty's twisting, turning route confuses me.

'If I said I didn't think I'd be able to find my way back again,' I ask her, 'would you be disappointed?'

'Devastated,' she answers sardonically.

We pass through buildings old and new; some walls are panelled with dark wood and decorated with old water-colours of poor quality; others are bright and sunny, large-leaved plants grow out into airy pastel spaces that could be offices or waiting rooms or simply meeting places. We go up escalators and descend staircases, past two libraries, I even think I'm visiting the same rooms over and over again. I'm surprised that so many doors are open, that so many rooms are empty. Kirsty tells me it's the way the university has to run, they need money (so rooms stay open for visiting organisations) and they don't have enough staff to keep opening and closing doors. She warns me, however, that all we're doing is passing through corridors; the Theatre Studies department will be locked. I don't tell her that this won't be a problem.

When we're indoors I peer out of every window we pass, searching in vain for some familiar landmark; when we reach the open air I look for shadows to show where the sun is, for signposts so I can find my way again. It doesn't take long for me to realise I'm lost.

'The thing is,' Kirsty says, as if she's explaining something to a naughty child, 'the university's very old. And it didn't have separate colleges, if it had, then things would have been sort of gathered together. It did have lots of land, so there was no real need to build upwards, until about fifteen years ago. Instead, it just spread outwards.' She turns to look at me as she walks. 'You know, there's a race held every year through the corridors, it doesn't cover every building and it never crosses its own path. Guess how long it takes the winner to finish.'

'Three months.'

'Dad, don't be so grumpy. The race takes almost three quarters of an hour, that's nearly ten miles of corridor. So it's hardly surprising, is it, that it's taking us a few minutes to get to Taylor's rooms by the scenic route?'

'I suppose not.' I still feel there must be a shorter way.

'When we get there I'll show you the stair that leads to the door that leads to the corridor that leads to the cloisters. It's that easy. But you don't want to bump into a policeman, do you?'

'I'm sorry, love. I didn't mean to be bad-tempered with you.' Those are, of course, only words, and they aren't really true. I know that Kirsty's smart enough to see when I'm in a bad humour, and I'm smart enough to be able to hide my feelings if I want to. It's simply that I didn't want to. I couldn't bring myself to accuse her of taking me on a deliberately long and confusing journey; that would mean I felt she was sulking, it would mean I didn't trust her. But the truth was, I did think she was sulking and I wasn't sure I could trust her; retreating into a morose and taciturn mood was my way of showing that. Kirsty recognised that but, instead of accusing me, she simply explained what she was doing. My daughter is clearly more mature than I am. My apology is honest, a recognition of that fact; only the corollary, the denial that

184

I'd wished to show my poor humour, was misleading.

'That's okay, Dad,' she replies. She links her arm in mine, squeezes gently. 'You must be under a lot of pressure.'

Strangely enough, I feel under no pressure whatsoever. That could be because I'm still not sure that Anna Peranski is innocent, despite Jen's impassioned pleas on her behalf, despite the deliberate attempt to plant incriminating evidence. I just can't think of a reason why anyone else would want to kill Taylor.

Kirsty stops abruptly, holds me back. 'We're nearly there,' she says quietly. 'The door ahead of us leads into a courtyard, when you look through it you'll see a wall on the right; on the other side is the cloisters. Straight ahead is another door, it opens onto the Drama and Theatre Studies department. On the ground floor there's a rehearsal room, a performing space and a couple of teaching rooms. At the end of the corridor there are some stairs. If you go up them you'll find a tutorial room and two offices. The first was Taylor's, the second his secretary's. At the end there's another door leading onto some stairs, go down those and turn right and you'll get to the cloisters. But I imagine the police will be down there, or it'll be locked.'

'Thanks, love. If I ever need an assistant, I'll know where to come.'

'Keep it in the family, you mean? Somehow I don't think Mum would thank you for that. In fact, I don't think you'd thank you for that, would you? Your daughter as a private detective?'

'I'm not a private detective,' I protest. 'I install security systems.'

'Dad, you quack like a duck, you walk like a duck, you swim like a duck, you fly like a duck.'

'But that doesn't . . .'

'You've even got a label round your neck saying "I'm a duck." There's a girly chorus following you everywhere you go singing "Look at Billy Oliphant, he's a duck, even though he denies it."'

185

I'm about to speak again but Kirsty holds a finger to my lips. 'Face it, Dad,' she whispers, 'you're a private detective, always have been, always will be. It's in your blood.'

'As long as it's not in yours!' I hiss back at her.

She ignores the bait. 'What happens next?'

'We see what's happening.' We head for the door. It has glass panes top and bottom, it's easy to see that the court-yard is empty and the door opposite has no one guarding it.

'Want me to see if there's anyone on the other side?' Kirsty asks.

'No,' I say instinctively.

'Is that a no meaning no or a no meaning yes?'

I don't answer straightaway.

'Only, we've come all this way, there might be no one in the office, there might be no police because they've already searched the place. If that's the case, it would be a pity if you didn't take the opportunity to have a look round.'

'And?'

'There's no "and". But there's a "but".'

'Tell me the "but".'

'But suppose there's a policeman on duty somewhere over there. Suppose he's been told you're about and he's not to let you into the premises. Suppose he's been asked to let his bosses know if you appear, 'cos you're such a pain in the arse to them. Two possibilities, Dad. Fifty-fifty. If you go and have a look, and it's possibility two, there's a policeman there, you might get arrested. But if I go, it doesn't matter if there's anyone there or not. I just make an excuse. I've come to see if my last essay's been marked, something like that. So tell me, did your no mean no, or yes?'

'Kirsty, you're definitely my daughter.'

She laughs aloud, she obviously thinks this is a compliment of the highest order. 'The milkman'll be pleased, then. So I go take a look?'

'Just be careful,' I tell her.

186

There's no need for my advice, she doesn't get any further than the door leading into the drama department. She tries the handle, pushes and pulls at the door, but it won't open. She turns to look at me, shrugs a question. I wave her back.

'What's your excuse going to be for wanting to get in?' I ask urgently.

'I'm due an essay back? I wanted to see if Taylor had marked it before he died?'

'That'll do. Okay, go back and knock on the door. Knock loudly, if there's anyone inside I want them to come down to see what the noise is. If someone appears, you've got your excuse.'

Kirsty goes back to the door. Her banging disturbs no one, either inside or outside the building. She doesn't even feel it's necessary to come back to fetch me, after a decent interval she simply waves me across to join her. There's still no one in the courtyard, no secretary sunning herself, no clerk come out for a cigarette. There's only birdsong and empty benches, cool shadows and the smell of flowers, and Kirsty urging me to join her.

'No answer?' I whisper as I reach her side.

'No need to be quiet,' she says, 'there's not a soul about. I take it that you can actually open this door?'

I fish in my pocket for my skeleton keys. 'You keep a lookout. If anyone comes tap me on the shoulder.'

'If you're caught with those,' Kirsty asks innocently, 'does that count as going prepared for burglary?'

'Yes.' I look at the lock and choose my key.

'And you'd be arrested?'

'Yes.' The key turns a little, it engages with one of the levers in the lock. I choose another key, this one is a little better, I can feel the pressure on three levers.

'You'll have to teach me how to use them one day.'

'No chance.'

Kirsty bends down to watch me. 'It's okay,' she smiles, 'I'm a visual learner. I can see what you're doing. Find the type of key for the lock and pick one of the skeletons that looks as if it might fit. Then it's trial and error. Can you actually feel whether it's the right one?'

'Yes. Is there anyone coming?' The next skeleton should be the one. It doesn't take long to open a door if the lock has five or fewer levers and I can recognise the type.

Kirsty doesn't even look around. 'There's no one around, Dad, stop fussing. Are you there yet?'

I can feel the skeleton exerting pressure against the final lever, and the lock clicks.

Kirsty hears it, pushes the door open. 'Well done, aged parent. Come on.' She holds the door open for me and ushers me inside. 'I suppose the police have already looked around.'

I lock the door behind us. 'They'll definitely have done that. But it's not the scene of a crime, so there's not really any point in guarding it.' I move forward. 'Didn't I say you weren't allowed to do anything illegal?'

'You're the one who broke in.'

'And you're accompanying me. Aiding and abetting. That's a criminal activity.'

'I know! Isn't it exciting?'

I check as I lead the way forward. I can see no CCTV cameras, no motion or heat detectors, no red lights in the high corners of the corridor. Of course, there might be some of these in any of the other rooms we might enter, but it would be unusual. The basic premise of any detector system is that the detectors are placed in those rooms where there's an initial point of entry; a burglar will therefore set off the alarm as he enters a protected building, rather than when he enters the actual room where items of value are held. Perhaps the drama department had nothing of value within. Or, far more likely, any security system was built around the perimeter of the premises rather than rooms near the centre. Whatever the reason, it seems safe to move on.

Kirsty tells me the purpose of each room as we pass it. I find myself wishing she would be silent; I know there's no one around but I'm feeling nervous. I'm being irrational; the outside door was locked and the only other door leading out of the department will be locked as well. But I can't be too careful, and I should tell Kirsty to shut up. I refrain from doing so, but only as long as the gaps between Kirsty's pronouncements are longer than her utterances.

'Dad, tell me again why we're here? Apart from the thrill of doing something we're not meant to.'

I raise my finger to my lips and whisper a response. 'Motivation, love, we're looking for a reason why someone might have wanted to murder Taylor.' We're at the bottom of a staircase.

'But . . .'

I press my finger to Kirsty's lips. 'The other door might be open. Someone might be working in the office. Let's proceed as if someone is there. Perfect silence.' She nods and I lead the way up the stairs. At the top there are four doors, two on each side. Nameplates signal their purpose: Jonathan Taylor's office beside a tutorial room; his secretary's office beside a waiting room. There's no electric light switched on, no sound of activity. The air is still and hot, as if windows and doors have been closed for too long.

Beyond the short stretch of corridor a rail shows where another staircase descends. I motion to Kirsty that she's to stay, go down the stairs. At the bottom there's a solid door, no glass in it. I try the handle; it turns but the door's locked.

I hurry back up the stairs; my voice is louder now. 'It's okay, Kirsty, we're alone.'

'Good. The tension was beginning to get to me.' She coughs loudly. 'Bit dry and dusty, isn't it?'

'The place has been locked up. Hardly surprising, really. I doubt that the police will have spent much time up here. They've already got their suspect.' I try the handle to Taylor's office door. It's locked.

'Suspicious people round here, Dad. Come on, work your magic again.'

She steps back to give me room while I begin to play with my skeleton keys again. This is an old lock, the levers are worn, it's difficult to find a match. I can feel sweat beading on my forehead as key after key proves ineffective. Behind me Kirsty's trying the other doors but I need to concentrate, I hear her words but they don't mean anything, they're only sounds.

'Dad, I think you should . . .'

'Not now, Kirsty, this is just a little awkward.'

'But Dad, if you . . .'

'Please, Kirsty, just shut up!' At last I've found one skeleton that almost fits against one lever. I try its neighbour – gently, very gently – and there's a further click. The two skeletons together should do it, I merge them, place them in the lock, squeeze gently – and the lock gives way.

'Kirsty,' I call over my shoulder, 'we're in.'

'I know,' she says. She's already in the room, bending over the desk. She points to another door in the room, a door connected to the tutorial room. 'It was open, so was the one off the corridor. I tried to tell you but . . .'

'Don't touch anything,' I tell her, ignoring the triumphant tone in her voice, reasserting my authority. 'Put these on.' I hand her a pair of latex gloves, courtesy of Jen's trek through the nether regions of the NHS.

'Cool. No fingerprints.'

'Yeah, but you leave a thin trace of powder, so don't touch anything unless I ask you to. And if you do, put it back exactly where you found it.'

Kirsty salutes, 'Yes Sir, Captain Dad, Sir!'

'And less sarcasm, young lady, or I'll send you to stand in the corner.'

'I'll have a hard job. There's not a lot of corner left.'

She's right. The room is small anyway, and very cluttered. Opposite the door through which I entered is a tall sliding sash window looking out onto a brick wall. Its long lace curtains are greying. Below the window sits the desk, a computer squatting on top of it; to the right of the window is a wall calendar, variegated with stripes of different colours, stars and circles, scribbled appointments. To the left is a notice board with lists of names and telephone numbers, scraps of paper, all held in place with drawing pins. The rest of the wall space is taken up with bookcases, floor to ceiling, full and overflowing onto the floor. The only relief to this bibliomania is a Victorian fireplace, overlooked when the university's schedule for improvement was drawn up. Its iron mantelpiece has been over-painted many times, a variety of drab greens, reds and browns show through the chipped blue paint that is the primary colour. The mock Bewick tiles either side of the grate are, where original, cracked; some have been replaced with modern alternatives, colourful dancing cows and a sepia wine bottle and glasses. Sitting squat on the floor in front of the fireplace is a massive (in the sense that it appears to be very heavy) green safe.

'That looks the place to start,' Kirsty says. 'Come on, open it up.'

I don't even bother bending down. 'Easier said than done, love. It's not key operated, it works by turning the dial and moving the tumblers inside.'

'So? I've seen the old films, all you need is a stethoscope so you can hear the click.'

'No, what I need is someone to tell me the combination. I don't even know how many numbers are involved.'

'So we look for something else?'

'We look for something else.' The desk is the obvious place to start, but the bookcases catch my attention. 'Lots of plays,' I show Kirsty, 'and books on costume. Biographies of famous actors. In fact, everything to do with the theatre.'

'Nothing unusual, then.'

'Apart from these.' I point to one section, take out a thick volume. '*Plants of the Amazon rain forest*, not quite what I'd expect to find.'

'There's more. *The Theory and Practice of Biological Study*.'

'There's one here on how to take care of your lawn.'

'What?'

'Just joking. But it is rather unusual. Why all these books on biology?'

Kirsty's thinking. When she's sure she has my attention she strokes an imaginary beard. 'Now then, when I think about it, I'm sure someone told me that Taylor studied biology at university. That's it, he did! But he joined the drama club or something and got bitten, changed course, never finished his biology degree. But he must have been good. In those days they didn't let you into university unless you were good.' She's quiet for a while; I let her think. 'Do you think it's important?'

I shrug. 'If something is important, you can guarantee you find out it's important long after its importance has become important.'

'Oh. I see.'

'In other words, I don't know. But since it isn't hitting us on the head saying "I'm important, look at me," I'd suggest we look for something else.' I draw Kirsty's attention to a worn, blue-backed A4 book on the desk. It isn't thick enough to have a spine and there's no writing on the cover.

'It looks like a mark book,' she says. 'You know, the type you get at school. I didn't think university professors would use them, but I suppose they have to keep records of the work we do.'

'Handier than a computer. More portable than a laptop, and you don't have to keep switching it on and off. Doesn't need batteries. Requires no knowledge of software or operating systems. And you can customise the data retrieval system easily.' I open it at the first page. 'Not very secure, though. Anyone can understand it. Let me see, Oliphant, Kirsty. Here we are. Thirty doesn't seem a very good mark.'

Kirsty pushes me out of the way and sits down. 'Let me see! Where? That's ... That's my first module, it was

192

marked out of fifty, that's 2:1 schedule, Father.' She looks in more detail. 'No comments, only marks. I'm not doing too badly, though, keeping up with the rest of the class.' She flicks over a page. 'And here's Tom. He missed one assignment, that's not very good.'

'We're not here for nosiness, Kirsty, we're after information. See if you can find the page with Anna Peranski's marks.'

'Okay, okay. She's in her second year, she should be near the end. No, this is the present third year, there's Belle's grades. Look at that, she's heading for a first, easily. A few pages back then. And there's Anna. Not too good early on, but she seems to have pulled herself together just before Christmas and ... A 2:1's on the cards for her.'

'Would have been,' I remind her, 'as things stand she's not going to complete her course.'

'Mmm, poor thing.' Kirsty's sadness appears to be genuine. 'But it shows that, if you really try, you can get yourself together.'

'How's that?' I'm genuinely curious. The esoteric conventions of university mark schemes are beyond me, all I see are rows of numbers.

'Well, Anna didn't do any work. At least, that's what she told everyone. But secretly, she was handing in the assignments and getting good marks. At least, that's what it says here.'

I look over Kirsty's shoulder, follow her finger as it traces a set of marks across the page. There aren't many; Taylor clearly didn't believe in overstraining his marking hand. But the numbers show a gradual improvement, and following some of them – marked in red Roman numerals – there's an indication of the degree status that particular mark would bring. Anna's row has several gaps and, in one place, there's a large red zero. After that there are two 'III's, then several 'II:I's and even a 'I'.

'You're allowed to scrub the lowest mark,' Kirsty explains, 'that would be the zero for the missed assignment.'

'What about previous years? Don't you get credit for what you do in the first year of courses?'

'Usually the first year doesn't count towards the final degree grade, but you have to pass the assignments to get onto the second year. Then it depends on the course, with some you find it's weighted 70-30 or 60-40 in favour of year three. I'm not actually sure what it is with this course. But if Anna was improving this much, she'll have finished the year heading for a 2:1 or a 2:2. And of course, part of the assessment is based on practicals.'

'Are these all essay marks, then? No exams?'

'No exams. There's a final dissertation, of course, at the end of the third year.'

I look at the bookcase. On a shelf conveniently close, an arm's reach away, there are similar ledgers, though of different colours. I reach out for one of them, the nearest, and flick through the pages until I find one with the same familiar names as in Anna's class. I lay it on the desk in front of Kirsty. 'Interpretation, please?'

Kirsty looks at the pages. 'Not very good. Missed assignments, poor grades except for the practical. Look, see those two marks at the end, separate from the rest. I think they're the modules she had to do again because she failed them.' She sniffs. 'It's amazing she managed to even start her second year.'

'So we've got a student who's good at acting ...'

'*Very* good at acting!'

'Okay, very good at acting. But she doesn't do the work, she doesn't hand in essays on time, and when she does they're not very good. Then suddenly, since Christmas, her grades improve.'

Kirsty looks at me over her shoulder. 'Surely you don't think ...' She doesn't finish her sentence.

'Think what?' I prompt her.

'That Anna was, you know, doing something. For Taylor. With Taylor. In return for high grades.'

'Kirsty, if you're going to say something, say it in

language I can understand. You want to know if I think Anna Peranski was swapping sex for marks, yes?'

She nods, still not keen to confirm the accusation in words.

'The answer is, I don't know. If she was, why would she want to kill him?'

'He was going to confess? But then he'd suffer as well, he'd probably lose his job. Perhaps he wanted more from her.'

'More what?'

'I don't know, Dad, I've no idea. Money as well as sex. More sex, more often. Kinky sex. Perhaps he had a friend he wanted her to sleep with. But it still wouldn't make sense.'

'Why not?'

'What would he threaten her with? If he told anyone what she'd been doing, he'd implicate himself as well. I don't think he'd do that. He liked his job too much.'

I'm tempted to agree with my daughter. The opportunity for Taylor to blackmail Anna was so limited as to be non-existent. 'Okay, then, why else might she kill him?'

'Why would anyone want to kill anyone else? Perhaps she didn't like him.'

'That could be it. She didn't like him, didn't like what he'd forced her to do, decided to end it all. Killing him would be a way out.'

Kirsty seems exasperated. 'Rather an extreme way out. And, if she did do it, not very well planned.'

I'm looking through the contents of the bookcases again, not for anything specific, just for something that might stand out and give me a clue. 'Murder isn't necessarily well planned,' I tell Kirsty, 'sometimes the mind just snaps. Anna was drunk; Taylor had obviously upset her; killing him might suddenly have seemed a good idea. But there are other possibilities as well.'

Kirsty spins the chair round to look at me. 'Such as?'

'Revenge.'

195

'Revenge?'

'Yes, revenge. We've been working on the assumption that Anna didn't like Taylor.'

'But she didn't,' Kirsty interrupts, 'we know that, we saw the way they behaved the other night.'

'But was that typical? We've been assuming a long-term resentment. What if Anna and Taylor were lovers because they actually liked each other? What if Anna improved because she was in a stable relationship and she actually began to get her work in on time?'

'And then her *work* improved,' Kirsty adds enthusiastically, 'simply because she was trying. Or even because Taylor was giving her some extra tuition.'

'Or because he was marking her essays leniently, giving her good grades when she didn't deserve them.'

'So why would she kill him?'

I've found nothing of interest on the shelves, it's time to start searching through the desk drawers. But before I begin that I have to answer Kirsty's question. 'Taylor was a philanderer. You told me as much yourself. He started a relationship with Anna, then tired of it. He found someone else. Anna took revenge.'

Kirsty slumps back in her seat. 'I suppose it's possible.'

'It's possible that an alien took possession of Anna's body, killed Taylor, then left again. It's possible that Taylor's in suspended animation. It's possible that everyone else – apart from us – is an actor in a play, they're all just pretending. But the chances of any of these being what actually happened are non-existent. We have to deal with better odds of probability. So it *is* possible that Anna, in a fit of drunken revenge, killed Taylor.'

Kirsty nods to show she agrees that such a premise is possible. 'So is that the assumption you're going to work on?'

'No. That's one I've conjured out of nowhere. It would tie in with the evidence, it would allow some motivation for the murder. It might even be the theory the police are working on. But we should really be trying to find evidence suggesting that Anna didn't kill Tayor at all.'

Kirsty nods again, she's becoming one of those toys people place in the rear window of cars, locked in perpetual motion, agreeing with everything anyone says. 'So what next?'

'We look for evidence. Evidence to prove Anna didn't kill Taylor, evidence to prove someone else did, evidence to show that Anna wasn't sleeping with Taylor, evidence to show that she *was* sleeping with him, evidence to show ... Well, any type of evidence. No, not even evidence, Kirsty. Facts. Any facts, we really don't have many, all we have are lots of guesses. And the best place to start ...'

Kirsty's curiosity has often been her downfall. It was never enough that she was told there were eggs in a birds' nest, she was the one who had to climb the tree and see them herself. When recovering from the ensuing broken leg, she said at least she'd now know how it felt to have a broken limb. I was about to tell her something, then I stopped, and she's desperate to find out what I was about to say. The fact that I'm tilting my head from one side to another, trying to hear something, won't stop her inquisition. That's why I have to lean forward, put my fingers on her lips, hold her shoulder so she doesn't try to get up. When I'm sure I have her attention and I know she'll make no noise, I point at the door. I listen again, straining to catch any repetition of the faint sound I thought I'd heard a moment before, the click of a key turning in a lock. There is no recurrence; instead there's a distant heavy tread of feet on stairs.

Kirsty hears it too; a look of panic crosses her face. That's when I realise how silly I was to bring her with me, despite her desire to play an active role in the investigation. Whoever is coming up the stairs could be dangerous; even if that isn't the case, Kirsty and I have broken into an office. We could be charged with burglary. Both of us might suffer, but Kirsty could be thrown off the course, thrown out of the university. Hindsight is a curse.

The room has no hiding place. The room next door has chairs and a low coffee table, there's nothing to hide behind. There's nothing I can do but wait. I pull Kirsty softly out of her seat, propel her forward to the corner behind the door. I take my place beside her.

The footsteps are muffled but audible, then a voice speaks. The words are indistinguishable, but they aren't important; the mere presence of a voice is worrying. It's not someone singing or whistling, it doesn't have the timbre of someone talking to themselves. It's short, abrupt; it's an instruction. And that means at least two people.

I press my ear to the door; further footsteps come up the stairs, more hurried than the previous set, heavier. And there's a reply, this time I can hear the words. A voice grunts 'Coming, coming.'

Whoever the people are, they haven't come because they feared intruders; if that had been the case they would have made less noise. But they have a key. Could they be policemen? Are they looking for further information?

'I want you to look at the safe,' the first voice says. It isn't loud, but it's recognisable. Arnison. There's the sound of a key fumbling in the lock, it turns quickly one way and then the other, then back again; the owner is having a problem with the fact that I'd already unlocked the door. At least the delay gives me time. I pull Kirsty to her feet and into the side room, as I close one door with a too audible snick, the other opens. Kirsty's crouching down to make herself small, I'm not sure why; there's nowhere to hide, and even shrunk into her foetal position she's no less visible than when standing upright, and must be much less comfortable. I motion her to her feet, bring my mouth right up to her ear.

'Foot against door,' I whisper, 'like this.' I show her how my foot is jammed against the foot of the door, far away from the hinges, and my shoulder is leaning against it. If Arnison wants to come in he may think the door is locked; if he then tries the key, he'll find – or so the theory goes – that it doesn't work.

Kirsty moves, slowly, softly, to the outer door and copies my posture. My ear is close against the frame, I'm trying to hear what's happening but Arnison and his companion are being infuriatingly quiet.

'Combination,' announces the second voice, one I don't recognise, a woman's voice.

'Can you get in? Arnison asks.

'Course I can. But not here. Lock needs drilling out, I could bring the gear in, I suppose, but ... it's not that heavy. Stairs are awkward, but I've got a hydraulic lift. I'd rather work on it back at base. Are you in a hurry?'

'No, not really. We've got a cast-iron case already. But it's best to check everything.'

There's silence. I imagine the safe expert bending down to re-examine the reason she's been brought here; Arnison's footsteps move around the room, I think I can hear the slide of books being withdrawn from and replaced on shelves.

The expert speaks again. 'The easiest way of getting into a safe like this is to find the combination. Most people write it down somewhere, or use a familiar number. Have you tried his home telephone? Date of birth? Any other significant numbers? Anything from his diary or his address book?'

'We've been through them all,' Arnison answers, 'nothing works.'

'We take it away then,' the expert concludes. 'I can get it picked up tomorrow if you're in a hurry.'

'There's no rush.'

'In that case, Wednesday would be better.'

'Great. I'll still have a couple of men here, we're due to get an office down by reception.'

One pair of footsteps heads for the door; after a short delay (is the expert also looking at the shelves?) a second pair follows.

199

'What's this I hear,' the expert says, 'about you having a bit of a problem earlier on?' She hurries on, 'I mean, I know you've got a suspect and that the evidence is pretty good ...'

'Damn near conclusive,' Arnison corrects her.

'Yes, yes, of course, incontrovertible evidence. But you've had your men rushing through the cloisters like demented souls, when I saw them earlier on they were ... Well, they were ...'

'Not complaining, I hope?' Arnison's voice is threatening.

'Oh no, no no no. Not complaining. But they seemed rushed. They weren't used to working at such a speed. I'm sure I heard one of them say that, if there was any evidence to be found, they might miss it. With going so fast, that is.'

I swear I hear Arnison growl. 'It's that bastard Oliphant and that bloody woman Belle what's 'er name.'

'Who?'

'Oliphant, Billy Oliphant, some short-arse ex-cop who's helping out with the play Taylor's kids were doing. He overheard something – it certainly wasn't because he was doing any quality investigations – and told this stuck-up bitch of a student, Belle, and they set me up. In the middle of a prime-time interview on local TV, they somehow managed to get me to say their bloody show could go on.'

The expert obviously knows Arnison well, she voices her incredulity. 'Got you to do something you didn't want to do? Sounds a bit improbable to me. Sure you aren't just making it up? A good story to tell at the Masons? Set yourself up as an idiot before you get all the praise for solving the crime so fast?'

'No, I tell you, they set me up. Believe it or not, call it improbable, call it fiction, but I tell you, they managed to do it. And you know what? I'm still not sure how. He's a bastard, that Oliphant.'

'Can't you do him?'

'No, he's like a bloody kite, keeps on the windy side of

the law. You think you've got him then he flies away. Anyway he's small fry, we've got the case sewn up already. All I can say is, he'd better not cross me again.'

There's a sound of the door locking again.

Arnison seems to calm down quickly. 'Come on, I'll buy you a pint. There's a real ale pub round the corner, it's pretty good.'

'No, I have to get back. It's my daughter's birthday, I've to pick up the cakes for the party. But thanks anyway.'

As the odd couple move away I glide over to Kirsty's door, add my weight to hers just in case they decide to come in. One set of footsteps moves past, then another. I wait for two minutes, then wait another two minutes before motioning Kirsty to one side and opening the door. There's complete silence. 'It's okay,' I tell Kirsty.

'Thank God! I was so frightened I thought I'd pee my pants. I wanted to cough, I wanted to sneeze, and now they've gone I don't want to do either.' She slumps in one of the chairs. 'Did you hear anything?'

'It was Arnison and some police safe-cracker, a woman. They were talking about getting into the safe. They're coming to take it away on Wednesday, they can't get into it here.'

'So there's no chance of us getting in either.'

'Not unless we can guess the combination. But, according to what I heard, the police have tried the usual numbers. There's a standard procedure for these things, you know, certain numbers, like birthdays, your name translated into numbers. They'll have done all those, tried everything logical.'

Kirsty shrugs. 'In that case, we'll have to try the illogical. How many numbers did you say there were?'

'Six, I think. It looks like six.'

'So we start at the most illogical combination there is, "00-00-00", then "99-99-99", then "12-34-56".'

'Too late,' I tell her. 'I tried those while I was looking at the dial. None of them work.'

'So what do we do?'

'Well, it sounded as if Arnison's plods are just about finished. We could go down, see what's happening. Then we start thinking.'

'About getting into the safe?'

'I think your priority should be putting on a production. And remember, your leading actress is locked up in jail.'

Kirsty has the answer to that. 'From what she was saying last night, Belle should be able to do it, she knows the part well enough. In fact she knows the whole play well enough.'

'So you think you'll be able to do it? Put the play on despite what's happened?'

'Yeah. I mean, there's not a lot of enthusiasm amongst some people. But it's technically possible.'

I look back into Taylor's room, just in case we've missed something. It seems to offer up no clues at all, but on one shelf, stuffed into a corner, something black and animal-like catches my eye. I walk over, reach up and pull down a dusty short-haired wig. When I beat it against my hand it opens out to resemble a sleeping grey cat.

Kirsty's followed me in. 'It's not your colour, Dad, you'd look even older than you already do.'

'I shall ignore your pathetic attempts at humour. I just want a low-maintenance pet.' I crush the wig into my pocket. 'Should we go then?'

'Yes. I've had enough excitement for one day.'

I find myself agreeing with her, always a mistake; days are often far longer than they ought to be.

Chapter Eight

As soon as we step out into the normal world, the open space beyond the entrance where we won't be arrested for breaking and entering, Kirsty switches on her mobile phone and presses some buttons quickly.

'Hiya, Tom, you'll never guess what I've been doing!'

'Kirsty,' I hush her, 'people might be listening!'

She looks at me as if she can't understand my words, shakes her head in forgiveness. 'Never mind,' she continues, 'I'll tell you later. What's going on?' She listens attentively, nods occasionally. 'Okay, I'll tell Dad. Bye.'

'Tell me what?'

'Everyone's meeting in the common room in the block at six o'clock, that's just under two hours. Belle needs to speak to us all. Apparently the police are packing away, they've told Belle we can have everything back by this evening. Good, eh?'

'Sounds good.' It actually sounds as if I've a great deal of work to do. Instead of working with Taylor I'll be following Belle's instructions, and I'm a little nervous at the prospect. Taylor was almost *laissez-faire* in his attitude, he seemed willing to leave decisions to me; I've a feeling that Belle is going to be more autocratic. I reach into my own pocket for my mobile phone. I dislike them intensely; most of the time – to the annoyance of friends and colleagues – I have mine switched off, for use only in emergencies: my emergencies. But I want to find out what Jen's been up to, whether she's had any success in her day of investigations with Professor Edmondson.

As soon as I switch on the phone it begins to make distressed beeping noises. 'Help,' I say to Kirsty, 'what do I do?'

She takes the phone from me, glances at the screen. 'Someone's left you a text message,' she explains, presses a key. 'It's from Jen.' She holds the phone out in front of me. On the screen are three simple words, 'Ring me. Urgent.'

I may be a technophobe but I know how to contact Jen; she showed me. Her number's stored on the phone itself, I key in her name and press ring. She answers very quickly.

'Billy,' she says, 'about time. Where are you?'

'Where I'm meant to be, at the university, with Kirsty. I'm sorry . . .'

'Never mind being sorry, where are you in the university?'

I look around me. Most of the place seems like everywhere else, tall buildings with meaningless names like the one we're passing now, the 'Olive Stedman Centre'. But then I notice a familiar red, sandstone wall. 'We're at the back of the cloisters,' I say, 'heading round to the car park at the front. Why?'

'Because. Just keep walking. I'll speak to you later.'

'But . . . Jen, I want to know how you got on! What did . . .?' My voice splutters to silence. It's no good, the line is dead.

'What's up?' Kirsty asks.

'I don't know. She just hung up on me.' I shake the phone gently, as if it's at fault.

'Perhaps she's out of credit. Or the battery's running low. Happens to me all the time.'

'No, Jen's too efficient for that, she charges every night and she's on one of these billing things, not pay as you go.' We're almost at the end of the wall now, passing from its shade into bright sunlight. I hold out the phone to the sun, as if the warmth might bring it back to life.

'Ring her again,' Kirsty suggests as we reach the corner.

'No need for that,' says a familiar voice. Jen's waiting for us, sitting on a wooden bench beneath a twisting shelter of clematis leaves. 'You took your time.'

Kirsty's the first to react. A smile conquers her face without any resistance, she lunges towards Jen who rises quickly to her feet.

Sometimes it feels strange to see my daughter and my fiancée together. Only seven years separate them, while I'm almost fifteen years older than Jen. They're dressed similarly, in jeans and strappy cotton shirts, and they behave like close friends; I've overheard them talking, at speed and with enthusiasm, about fashion and film stars, make-up and movies. They haven't seen each other for almost two months and they're jumping up and down, squealing like twelve-year-olds. Just as I'm beginning to feel old they separate and Jen steps towards me. In that instant she transforms herself from girl to woman. She looks straight at me and holds out her arms, hugs me close, kisses me gently but manages to touch my lips apart with her tongue. When she pulls away there's promise and love in her eyes and I can't help grinning.

'Love you,' she mouths, takes my hand and leads me to the bench. 'You're a difficult man to contact,' she says. 'I've been trying for most of the afternoon.'

'We were ...' Kirsty begins, but my glare silences her.

'I was involved in a delicate matter that required silence,' I explain.

'I assumed that was the case. That's why I tried Kirsty's phone, and that was switched off as well. Now that *is* unusual. I don't suppose you were being delicately silent together?'

If it had been Kirsty's mother asking such a question I would have denied any such thing. Sara always was, always will be, over-protective so far as Kirsty's concerned. But Jen's different.

'We broke into an office,' Kirsty announces, reading my complaisance and unable to hide her excitement, 'and someone else came in, but he didn't find us. I was nearly shitting myself, but Dad was calm as anything.'

'And did you find what you wanted?'

I reply on Kirsty's behalf. 'A locked safe, and no one seems to know the combination. Apart from that, not much else. How about you? How was Professor Edmondson?'

'Pleased to see me at first. He thought it was lucky I'd found him at the labs, it being a Sunday. Then, when I told him I knew he'd be there and I knew what he'd be doing, he wasn't quite so pleased. He went on and on about confidentiality, how he couldn't talk to me. He even said he'd have a porter come to escort me off the premises. I had to point out that there were very few porters on duty, that I already knew my way out, and that I thought he was being a reactionary lackey of the privileged bourgeoisie. At least that made him laugh. And he told me that being a member of the bourgeoisie automatically conferred privilege, so what I was saying was actually tautology.'

I'm becoming impatient in my middle age. 'So you got on like you'd never been away. Did he tell you anything?'

'He mentioned his reputation. That's when I told him he didn't have a reputation. Or rather, he did, but it was the wrong type of reputation to have.'

'So did you have to apply some pressure?'

'No.' Jen seems surprised. 'But I did have to explain in some detail why I was involved, what you were doing. I even had to tell him about you; he made me promise to introduce you, so you could tell him how you got on. He was very impressed that you'd been thrown out of the police.'

'I wasn't thrown out,' I protest, 'I resigned as a matter of principle.'

'The principle being,' Jen continues, 'that they didn't want to employ you any more. Face up to it, Billy, to the left-wing intellectual you're a bit of genuine working-class

206

rough. That's why I love you. Now shut up and listen or I'll take the huff.'

'Go on then. Not a word shall pass my lips.'

'Good. So I told him all about you and Taylor and Anna, I told him our suspicions, and you know what? He asked me to help him with the autopsy, straight off.'

'So you saw Taylor's body?' Kirsty's not quite sure what to make of this. Jen is an enthusiastic doctor, and sometimes her descriptions can be a little too graphic for lesser mortals. She doesn't seem to be aware that tales of blood, gore, excreta and severed limbs often don't appeal to everyone.

'Saw it, poked it, prodded it, listened to Edmondson describe it, even pointed him in the direction of some unusual findings. And that's why I came down to see you. Some of the things I found out were bloody interesting. I just had to tell you in person. Billy, I know Anna Peranski didn't kill Taylor.'

'That's nothing new,' I reply, 'you haven't changed your opinion at all.'

'No, but now there's evidence. Listen to this. First of all, Taylor was drunk when he was killed. He had so much alcohol in his body, it's more than likely he was unconscious. What's more, he won't have gained consciousness, the blade went straight into his heart, killed him outright. And he wasn't killed on the stage either, there wasn't enough blood.'

'How on earth could Edmondson know that?' I'm beginning to get interested now, my squeamishness has been overcome by Jen's enthusiasm.

'He had photographs of the body and the surrounding area. Measurements of the size of the bloodstain. Analysis of the porosity of the wood on the stage. And striations on the back and buttocks suggest the body had been dragged a little way across the stage. He'd done all that before I got there.'

'And he told you everything?'

207

'Billy, he was *keen* to tell me, and there's a reason. You see, the police haven't found an alternative site for the murder, they just assumed it was the stage. Edmondson's figures seem to suggest that assumption is incorrect. He's dead against sloppy police work. Actually, I think he's just anti-police.'

Kirsty's shaking her head. 'But even if Jonathan Taylor was killed somewhere else, it could still have been Anna who killed him.'

'True,' I say, not particularly to Kirsty, more thinking aloud, 'but Anna's not big. She would have needed an extra person to help her carry or drag Taylor's body to the stage. And if she'd dragged it, there would have been signs of that on the grass, on the stage as well.'

'But they weren't looking in much detail,' Kirsty points out, 'they already had their suspect, they'd already decided Anna had killed Taylor on the stage.'

Jen leans across us both, arms outstretched. 'Children, children, please. Listen to all of teacher's story before you start your analysis. There's much not yet told.' We speedily subside into silence and she continues. 'Edmondson was already suspicious before I arrived on the scene, that's why he wasn't too bothered about telling me what he'd found. And there's more. The knife that killed Taylor wasn't the knife found in his body.'

Kirsty leaps to her feet. 'So someone else killed him, then put the knife with Anna's fingerprints on it into the wound. Come on, Dad, we'll have to tell the police. That definitely means Anna's innocent.'

I don't even have to contradict Kirsty, Jen does it for me. She pulls Kirsty back to her seat. 'It doesn't mean Anna's innocent, love. All it means is that Taylor wasn't killed with the knife that was in his body. The thing is, both knives were similar. The differences between them were small, Edmondson himself didn't notice, it was me who pointed them out. The knives were probably a pair.'

I reach across to take Kirsty's hand. 'Like the ones

Taylor and Anna were fighting with, on the stage, before the party. Can you remember what happened to them?'

Kirsty's brow furrows. 'I think Taylor took them away. He certainly brought them with him. But they're props, they should have been with Rachel, she's in charge of costume and props. I can't remember her saying anything about them not being there.'

'It's okay, we can ask her later. Go on, Jen, anything else?'

'Well, so far there's an indication that Taylor wasn't murdered where his body was found, and therefore the body must have been taken there by two or more people. The knife that killed him hasn't been found, though it's similar to the one with Anna's fingerprints on it that was still in Taylor's body. That doesn't prove Anna's innocent, but it is leading away from the presumption. It's looking more and more as if she's been framed.'

'There's another possibility,' I tell her. 'She did kill Taylor, and she's being clever. She's involved someone else, perhaps without them knowing. She could have told someone Taylor was drunk, got him or her to help them move the body ...' Kirsty and Jen are both preparing to interject, but I pre-empt them. 'All right, I admit it's not very likely, I just don't want to get anyone's hopes up.'

'Billy,' Jen says, 'there's more.'

'More to do with Taylor?'

'No, more to do with Anna. Edmondson's department has the contract to check all the police specimen analyses as well. They had Anna's tests there. He let me see the secondary analysis.'

'Jesus Christ! And he was talking about confidentiality! If you ever need information in different circumstances, you'd certainly have the right type of lever with Edmondson.'

'Except I wouldn't want to, Billy, would I? I couldn't, not after he's been so helpful. He doesn't believe Anna was guilty either.'

209

'No, you're right. Come on, then, what else is there?'

Jen turns to face Kirsty. 'The police employ their own forensic scientists, but when a case depends on forensic evidence being absolutely correct, they get someone else to look at it as well. These secondary tests are often more thorough than the primary ones, they go into far more detail.'

'And they have to be done quickly,' I add. 'All it takes is for someone to have a shower and evidence can, literally, be washed away.'

'So this is what they found.' Jen takes a notebook out of her handbag, reads from it. 'Firstly, Anna's blood alcohol was high. Allowing for her body mass, it's unlikely that she was capable of any coherent thought when Taylor was killed. She was probably as unconscious as he was. Secondly, there were skin cells under her fingernails, Taylor's cells. Large numbers of them; that puzzled Edmondson. He hadn't found any substantial contusions on his body, particularly his chest or his back, that looked as if they'd been caused by fingernails.' Jen looks at Kirsty again. 'Those are the two places where a woman's nails might be expected to gather skin cells from a partner if they were engaged in coitus, depending upon whether the male or female was in the superior position.'

Kirsty nods wisely. 'You mean, if I'm on top, I'll rake his chest; if he's on top, I'll gouge furrows in his back?'

'Isn't that what I said?' Jen looks puzzled, but hurries on. 'On closer examination there were some marks on Taylor's body, but they were partially obscured by the drag marks made by the stage floor. They were primarily on his buttocks and the inside of his thighs.'

Kirsty offers her opinion. 'Someone was giving Taylor rough head.'

It's my turn to look askance at Kirsty. It's not that I believe she shouldn't know about sex, or worry that she appears to be very familiar with terminology comparatively new even to me. No, it's the ease with which she speaks up that concerns me.

210

'What?' she says, and the single word accuses me and finds me guilty. 'I read widely,' she explains, 'I watch films.'

'The point is,' Jen continues, 'the scratches on Taylor's body and the skin cells beneath Anna's fingernails matched in type, but not in quantity and distribution.'

Jen holds out one hand, rests it against my chest. 'In the throws of orgasm, or even in an attempt to sexually arouse someone, the fingertips, and hence the nails, can be used against the skin. But they do so like this.' She pulls her hand gently down my chest. 'Skin cells would be gathered primarily at the tips of each nail. There would be more beneath the nails of the strongest fingers and less beneath the nails of the little finger. And look at my thumb, it's almost sideways on. There's little opportunity to gather any skin there. Yet Taylor's skin cells were packed under all Anna's nails, as if someone had put them there.'

'That means someone else had sex with Taylor,' I point out. 'Someone determined to frame Anna for Taylor's murder.'

'It gets better. See, I've got you persuaded even before the last piece of evidence.' Jen refers again to her notes. 'The police were very thorough, they took swabs from every possible part of Anna's body. Billy, you told me that traces of Anna's saliva and vaginal secretions had been found on Taylor's body, and his saliva and sperm had been found on hers. Is that right?'

'That's what Sergeant Stephenson let slip.'

'The primary lab reports confirm that to be the case. The secondary reports back that up.' She stops, letting the information sink in.

'So does that mean Anna and Taylor did have sex?' Kirsty asks.

'But everything else seems to indicate the opposite. I'm puzzled,' I admit. 'Taylor and Anna were both drunk. I suppose it's possible they did have sex, but . . .'

'Go on,' Jen encourages me.

211

'I keep on thinking back to your little demonstration with the ketchup and toothpaste and water, the suggestion that body secretions normally transmitted by sex don't have to be transmitted by sex.'

'Or they can be,' Kirsty says quietly. 'Someone else had sex with both of them, transmitted the body fluids in both directions.'

'Well done,' Jen compliments Kirsty, pats her on the back, 'that's just about it.'

'Go on then,' I interrupt, 'what's the evidence? If someone else was involved ...'

'Then they must have left some trace of their own body fluids. Not necessarily, Billy, and even if they did, in such small amounts that it would be difficult to trace. But there was something. The swab from Anna's vagina showed a significant amount of Taylor's semen, but also traces of anti-spermicide, the type found on condoms. What's more, there were actually two different condoms used; one standard, one with traces of strawberry flavouring.' Somehow Jen manages to keep her face straight when delivering the information.

'But why two condoms?' Kirsty asks.

'Think,' I tell her, as if it's natural for a father to be discussing multiple condom use with his teenage daughter. 'You're the one who said someone had sex with both of them. So imagine they're both drunk, though not completely out of it. Someone has sex with Taylor, using a condom. She takes the condom, ties it. She gets some sterile material as well, wipes his mouth, gets him to spit, anything like that. She then goes to Anna ...'

'Or even has her partner go to Anna,' Jen interrupts, 'remember, it takes two to move the body. So *she* gives the condom to *him*, he has sex with Anna ...'

'Using a different condom,' I continue, 'because he doesn't want any trace of his semen left on Anna. Now she's amenable but drunk, it might even be that she likes this guy.'

212

'Perhaps he fed her that date-rape drug in her drink?' Kirsty's thinking again.

'No trace in her bloodstream,' Jen points out, 'though it's possible it could have dispersed quickly.'

I reclaim the right to speak. 'No matter, he has sex with her. Then he smears the contents of the first condom on her body, in her vagina. He does the same with the saliva, then goes back to Taylor and reverses the process with swabs taken of Anna's fluids.'

'Tissues?' Jen suggests. 'I don't think anyone thought to test for small samples of paper, it's just something you expect to find when people have sex.'

'But it could be done,' I stress, 'we're all agreed on that. Anna's in her room, safely unconscious. All we have to figure out now is where our pair – let's assume there were two of them – took Taylor to kill him. And why there's been no trace of blood other than on the stage.'

'And why they'd want to kill him in the first place,' Jen points out, 'and why they tried to blame Anna.'

'And who they are,' Kirsty adds. 'Because they must have been here during the party. They must have been something to do with the play. And they're still out there.'

'We'll find them,' I reassure her. 'They still assume there's only one suspect and that the police case is sound. They'll make a mistake.'

We sit in silence for a moment. The day intrudes on our thoughts. While we've been talking, the sky has grown duller. The dash of white cumulus clouds that has provided occasional relief from the sun has become a high wash of dark grey. The heat has, if anything, grown more intense. All shadows have fled, taken refuge from some impending unpleasantness.

'The forecast said thunderstorms,' Jen tells us. 'Perhaps we should head indoors.'

'It looks as if the forecast was right.' I find I no longer have to squint, my eyes can open wide; they see colours that are more muted than they were a moment ago. The

213

scent of flowers is, if anything, heavier, more decadent. The air is denser.

'At least if we get the rain over now it should be all right for the performances.' Kirsty is, as always, optimistic.

'What performances are they?' I ask.

'Come on, Dad, keep up! The play, we're going to have a talk about how we go ahead, in about half an hour. Belle will sort things out, she's good at organising . . .' She trails to a halt. Realisation comes swiftly. 'We won't be able to go ahead, will we?'

'No, love, not now.'

'The police will come back. Now they know Anna didn't do it, they'll have to carry out more investigations. That'll mean closing the cloisters again, questioning the cast and crew.' She runs her hands over her head. 'Shit!'

'It sounds as if you're not pleased that Anna's innocent.'

'No, that's not true, you know that. But . . . There was so much hanging on this play, Dad, not especially for me, but some of the others were depending on it.'

'The police don't actually know Professor Edmondson's findings yet.' Jen's voice is quiet, authoritative. 'He's writing up his report now, but he won't finish it until late tonight. It's going to be mid-morning before the police see a copy.'

I can see where Jen's heading and I don't like the terrain ahead. 'I don't think it can be done,' I tell her. 'There are too many people, too many questions. And the people who killed Taylor thought things through, they won't be found easily.'

'What are you talking about?' Kirsty asks.

It's not that I ignore Kirsty, just that I need to speak. 'Not only that, they're dangerous. We don't know why they killed Taylor, but it was cold-blooded. And the likelihood is that they're still around, and if they find out that we know for certain that Anna's innocent, they may start to behave irrationally.'

'Will one of you tell me what's going on?' Kirsty's voice is becoming more demanding.

'Kirsty,' Jen begins to explain, 'the police won't know until tomorrow what we know now about Anna. It is, of course, unethical on Professor Edmondson's part to withhold information, and morally indefensible on our part to use that information. But to hell with that. It means that we have just over half a day – or a whole night – to find out who killed Jonathan Taylor. But your father thinks ...'

'Your father thinks,' I interrupt, 'that it's too dangerous to carry out an investigation like this. So my plan is that we say nothing ...'

'You've done more stupidly dangerous things than this in the past,' Jen points out.

'But not with you two around. I can't afford to be watching out for you two when some knife-wielding maniac comes looking for his next victim.'

'That "when" should be an "if", and you're more likely to make carefully considered decisions when we're around than if we weren't here. Besides, we might just be able to help; just like I've helped by bringing you this information.'

'Dramatic irony!' Kirsty's exclamation makes coherent thought impossible.

'What?' Jen and I chorus together.

'Dramatic irony. It's when the audience of a play knows something the characters don't. Like when Romeo kills himself because he thinks Juliet's dead, but the audience knows she's asleep. So we don't tell anyone else that we know Anna's innocent, that lets us watch a little more closely, see if anyone gives themselves away.'

'Does that mean we're the audience,' Jen asks, 'or are we in the play? Does the real audience, the one watching us, know something we don't? Is this double dramatic irony?'

I'm beginning to lose patience. 'No, it means nothing, because we aren't doing any investigating.'

'Well I think we should,' Kirsty says flatly.

'So do I,' Jen echoes. 'That's two to one, you're outvoted, Billy.'

'Except this isn't a democracy, it's a dictatorship, I'm the dictator and I say no.'

Jen and Kirsty exchange glances. I'm not sure which of them is the leader, it seems as if their move is choreographed so they both stand up together. 'We're going inside to the meeting,' Kirsty says. 'Are you coming?'

'No investigations,' I warn her.

'That's up to us,' Jen says. 'There's just been a revolution. If we want to ask questions, to look around – perhaps even in places we shouldn't be – that's up to us. We're both adults, you can't tell us what to do.'

'Or rather, you can *tell* us, Dad, but we don't have to do it. Unless we want to.'

Jen supports Kirsty. 'I couldn't have said it better myself. Are you coming, Billy?'

I can feel myself becoming angry now. 'No I'm not coming. I'm going to phone Arnison and tell him what we know. He'll be down here straightaway, the show most definitely won't go on, and there's a good chance Professor Edmondson will be charged with subverting the cause of justice.'

'Possibly,' Jen says softly. 'But in that case, I'll be struck off as well; after all, my behaviour hasn't actually been up to the standards expected of a doctor. And all for wanting to help people. For wanting to help Anna Peranski, for wanting to help Kirsty and her friends, for wanting to find a murderer and let this production go on. The last two aren't mutually exclusive, Billy.' She puts her warm hand in mine. Somewhere far away there's a grumble of thunder.

'We've got nothing to lose,' Kirsty adds from my other side. She puts an arm round my shoulder, quite easily, she's almost as tall as me now. 'If we should fail . . .'

Jen finishes the line. 'We fail! But screw your courage to the sticking-place, and we'll not fail.'

'Don't tell me,' I say wearily, 'more Shakespeare.'

'The Scottish play.' Kirsty seems pleased to demonstrate her knowledge. 'Lady Macbeth trying to encourage her

216

husband to murder King Duncan.'

'Great,' I tell her, 'we're talking about solving murders and you're quoting lines where one character's trying to get another to kill someone. And *Macbeth* is a tragedy, so far as I recall. Not quite a good omen.'

'You just said "we're talking about solving murders." Sounds as if we've won you over with our persuasive tongues,' Jen sniggers.

'You're witches, both of you.'

The thunder sounds again, closer, more urgent. My daughter and my lover take my arms and we hurry together along the wall. They seem in ridiculous good spirits given all that has occurred in the past few days. I know that, during my time with the police, I became hardened to the injustices I met. As a rookie I found it difficult to do anything except dwell on the horrors of the crimes and criminals I had to deal with. I couldn't understand why anyone would beat an old woman black and blue. I didn't comprehend the workings of a mind that thought it was acceptable to steal, often from those who had little to begin with. Those who made the lives of others miserable with anti-social behaviour were aliens to me. But after a while I came to care less and less for the victims, just as I became less tolerant of the criminals. The procedures of the justice system became too tortuous for me and, like some of my colleagues, I learned to distribute a rough justice of my own to those I felt deserved it. Victims and criminals alike were merely the inhabitants of my world, they were created to give me some satisfaction in solving, in an abstract way, the crimes in which they were involved. I became tainted by the very nature of my profession.

At the same time I mocked those who tried to capture the essence of crime in films and television, those who tended to glamorise, to parody or even to reflect my world. There was never any blood spilled in afternoon TV whodunits, amateur detectives lived in a perpetual middle class of chintz and mock antiques. Or, conversely, the police inhabited a netherworld somewhere beyond the doorway to hell where evil was part of every man's and woman's psyche. Their realities were all false, I felt, though I was too wrapped up in my own false reality to see that there could never be a 'truth' when it came to crime. The dividing line between freedom-fighter and terrorist, wide-boy and thief, kept woman and prostitute, high-spirited behaviour and vandalism, became too blurred, too narrow for me to see clearly. Only when I left the police force did my perception readjust itself, did I imagine becoming more tolerant towards all those involved with crime: victims, criminals, investigators and justices. But now Kirsty's and Jen's lightness of spirit forces me to question my tolerance. They seem unable to appreciate how unpleasant crime and criminals can be. They seem aware only of the sanitised version that accompanies their viewing and reading. And they seem to lack the insight to recognise my own concerns.

We pause outside the door to the cloisters. The first tremulous drops of rain are hissing on the stone pavement slabs.

'Do you think they'll have changed the code?' Kirsty asks.

'I doubt it,' I tell her. 'No one thinks of the mundane these days. Try it.'

Kirsty punches in the six-figure code I remember; the door buzzes and, when she presses against it, opens. She leads the way through.

'Hadn't you better tell me what the code is?' Jen complains. 'After all, I'm here for the night.' The words resonate inside me. The prospect of spending the night with Jen is balanced by the knowledge that we'll probably be too busy to even retire to our room.

'I'd better write it down,' I tell her, 'you know what you're like with remembering numbers.'

'Just tell me,' Jen says impatiently, 'I can store it on my mobile.'

'112358,' I say quickly, spitefully even, before she can switch the phone on.

'That's easy,' she replies, 'I don't even need to write it down, I can remember it. Who thought of it anyway?'

'Taylor himself. It's a temporary code, just until the play's over.' I try to control my curiosity; why would this number be easier to remember than any other?

'Was he a biologist?'

I think back to the books on his shelves. 'Yes, I think he started his university career doing a biology degree.' Kirsty nods her agreement. I continue, even I recognise that my voice is incredulous. 'How did you know that?'

'You're not the only detective around here, Billy Oliphant.' For a few brief moments I believe she's not going to tell me, and I'll have to plead with her. But then she takes pity on me. 'Basic biology, Billy, any life scientist would know. 112358 is the opening sequence of the Fibonacci series. Each number, when divided by the one to its right, gives a fraction that's related to the growth of plants and the relative position of leaves spiralling round the stem of a plant so each leaf gets the maximum amount of sunlight. Every plant has a Fibonacci fraction.'

We pass through the door. I should be showing her the stage, the place Taylor's body was found, but Jen just keeps talking. 'It's fascinating how wide the Fibonacci numbers extend. For instance take any three consecutive numbers; square the middle one; multiply the two outer ones together; take one product from the other and there'll always be a difference of one!'

'Wow.'

She ignores the sarcasm in my voice. 'So that's biology and maths. It occurs in art as well; imagine a long, thin rectangle, so thin it just doesn't seem right. Now squash the long sides together, lengthen the short sides until it just seems the right size to look good. The ratio between the sides is called the golden section, and the further out in the Fibonacci series you get, the closer it is to the golden section. Isn't that clever?'

'Yeah.'

If I haven't really been paying attention, Kirsty has. 'So Taylor based the pass code on this series of numbers because it's easy to remember?'

'Yes. Oh, I almost forgot. Each number is the sum of the previous two. So it starts off one-one, add them together and you get the third number ...'

'Two,' Kirsty fills in the gap, 'Add one and two to make three, three add two makes five ...'

'And so it goes on. Eight, thirteen, twenty-one and so on.'

I pause to look out at the arena, not really listening to my companions. There's no sign that any policeman has been here. The grass looks undisturbed, the stage is pristine (though rapidly turning piebald with the unwelcome arrival of even heavier drops of rain), all is as it was when I was last here, save for the empty space where Taylor's naked body was hunched. The thunder is louder now, it sounds more often, and a sudden harsh crack of lightning shows how dark the sky has become. As if waiting for that sign the rain begins to fall harder, it rebounds from stage and roof, its hiss and fizz silencing Jen and Kirsty.

'So this ratio, this series of numbers, is the key to life, the universe and everything,' I say to no one in particular. 'Come on, we'd better go inside or they'll start without us.'

Kirsty grabs my arm. 'Dad, hold on.'

'Now what?'

She can see I'm impatient but she won't let go. 'What did you just say? About the Fibonacci series?'

'I'm sorry, I was being sarcastic. I know I shouldn't have been, but we're at the spot where a man died and I couldn't quite get my head round the fact that you two are involved with ...'

'Dad, shut up! Now listen, what were your exact words? Not the emotion behind them, the words themselves!'

She thinks she's found something important so I ignore her apparent rudeness. 'I don't know. It was just some flippant remark about the numbers being the key to life, the universe and ...'

'Stop! Think, just for a minute.' Kirsty's urgent voice has even pulled Jen away from the torrential rain to listen. 'Taylor admitted he had a bad memory, he must have used the series as a sort of mnemonic to help him remember the pass code. Do you think he would use the same type of thing for other series of numbers? Like the combination to his safe?'

The lightning flashes again.

'I suppose it's possible. Or perhaps some other series.' I turn to Jen. 'Are there any other biological series of numbers Taylor might have used, numbers that were easily memorable?'

'Probably,' Jen admits, 'but none as well known or as easy to recall as this one.'

'Good, that gives me something to work on. I'll go back to Taylor's office later on and . . .'

'We'll go back,' Kirsty says. 'If it wasn't for me you wouldn't even have thought of this. I claim squatter's rights.'

'I wasn't planning on waiting till night, Kirsty, and you'll be busy with rehearsals this evening. You'd be missed if you came with me.' Kirsty looks disappointed.

'But I wouldn't be missed,' Jen buts in, 'and you might need someone to act as lookout. It wouldn't be the first time either.' She turns to Kirsty. 'I must tell you about it someday. Just think, he's introduced both of us to a life of crime.'

'Jesus Christ, save me from assertive women!'

Jen grabs my backside and murmurs huskily in my ear, 'You know you like it, lover.'

With that message still in my mind we enter the familiar hallway. There's nothing on the door of the room Taylor occupied to suggest that it shouldn't be used, but I suspect that no one will sleep there for a while.

'Don't mention anything,' I whisper to Kirsty and to Jen, 'not even to Tom.'

'But . . .'

221

'But me no buts, young lady, or the deal's off.' I expect Kirsty to remind me that there isn't actually a deal to cancel, that I haven't agreed to do anything specific. Still, as a general threat it serves its purpose.

I hold the door of the common room open to let Kirsty and Jen enter. Everyone else seems to be there already; faces look up, recognise Kirsty, wonder who Jen is. The mood appears to be appropriately sombre. Vicky's sitting on the sofa, when she sees us she elbows her fellow occupants and beckons us to take their places. Kirsty declines, she's already moving towards Tom, but Jen and I head towards her, pensioners summoned to the duly allocated bus seats.

Belle and Kenny, the set designer with whom she'd been arguing on the day I arrived, are standing beside a table on which are spread pieces of paper. Kenny's the one who speaks first.

'Uh, thank you for coming under such, uh, difficult circumstances.' His hands are dancing in front of him. 'As you know, Belle has managed to persuade our, uh, friends from the police force that we should be allowed to continue with our play. This does, however, present us with some difficulties.' His speech is hesitant, as if his words are coming in parcels of ten or twelve and he's unwrapping each parcel before moving on to the next.

'You will, I think, all be aware that Anna, our Viola, has, uh, been arrested and charged with murdering Jonathan Taylor.'

There are murmurs of 'Shame', and 'She didn't do it', but when I look across at Kirsty, she's draped around Tom and staring at me, saying nothing.

'The evidence, I'm afraid,' Kenny continues, 'appears to be pretty, uh, strong. From what we've heard, that is. Though it is, of course, unofficial.'

George is sitting, alone, in a corner. He looks tired and sullen, angry enough to say something in response to Kenny's comments. He catches my eyes, sees me

222

looking at him, and shakes his head slowly. But he says nothing.

Kenny raises his head and allows his glance to travel the room, as if counting heads. Satisfied, he begins to speak again. 'Everyone involved is here. What we, uh, need to do now is make a decision: does the show go on?'

There's a mutter of sound, words with no meaning. Belle steps forward and, without saying anything at all, she conjures silence again. Her voice is soft, her audience concentrates on what she has to say. 'Before we can make a decision, I think I ought to let you know certain facts. First of all, the university will leave the decision to us, I've checked with the vice-chancellor. Second, it is actually feasible that we can do the play. I can fill in as Viola, the parts I was doing were small and we can cut them or someone else can do them. Third, and this is the most important thing, we can only do it if everyone here takes part. We have no slack at all. One person saying no, refusing to do as they're meant to, will result in cancellation. So I have a proposal to make.' It's her turn to sweep the room with her eyes, to check that everyone is listening. 'I suggest that we discuss this, we take a vote, and we follow the majority's opinion. If there's a majority of one in favour, we go ahead; if there's a majority of one against, we stop, we pack up and go home. Does anyone disagree with this?'

It's not necessarily the only way of proceeding. Someone could demand that there be at least two thirds in favour, others might say that, since cooperation is required by everyone to make the play work, everyone must want to go ahead. But there are no dissenting voices to Belle's idea of democracy. She nods her thanks and retreats again.

Kenny takes his place in front of the table. 'Does anyone have anything to say?' he asks.

'We go ahead,' announces a spike-haired young man.

'He plays the jester,' I whisper to Jen; she replies with the character's name, 'Feste.'

'Go for it, Rad,' someone shouts from the back of the room.

'We should go ahead because it's what Jonathan would have wanted,' he continues. 'He spent a huge amount of time setting this up, and our performance would be a celebration of everything he stood for, everything he believed in, everything he enjoyed.'

'You mean,' says the red-haired girl, Rachel I think, 'we all stand there at the end, turn round and ask the audience to feel our arses? He enjoyed feeling arses.'

Laughter blooms but withers quickly under Rad's stare. 'He wasn't that bad,' he says, 'and all of us stand to benefit from the show going on.'

'Not quite all of us,' Rachel points out. She stands up and faces the room. 'I'll declare an interest,' she says softly, 'just as Rad ought to have done. Jonathan had arranged for someone to come up from the Central Design School in London to see my costumes. And I believe the casting director from Northern Drama was coming to see Rad perform. We both stand to gain from the show going on, but not everyone's in the same position. It's important that you know that. I believe we should go ahead; but I'm biased, I have a vested interest.'

'I don't have anyone coming to see me,' says goateed John.

'Don't tell me,' Jen whispers, 'Sir Toby. And the gangly scarecrow next to him is Sir Andrew?'

'Got it in one,' I commend her.

John's voice is as round as his body and face. 'Just because I'm not under the microscope – which I wouldn't be, since I'm studying astrophysics – doesn't mean that I don't want to go ahead. But I'm worried that the events of the past few days will have affected us all in some way. Are we actually up to performing? And if we do perform, will we be able to do ourselves and our colleagues justice?'

Vicky springs to her feet as a rumble of conversation begins. 'People,' she silences them, 'people, I don't feel up to anything except sleeping at the moment.' She pauses. 'And crying. Especially when I think of Anna. I just can't imagine that she could . . .'

Even as Vicky fails to complete her statement, there's a whisper spreads round the room. Comment? Disagreement? Support? The sibilance becomes louder, voices are raised, there's even a shout and a push.

'Please,' Kenny barks, 'can we discuss this with a little, uh, decorum.'

I can see that this may take some time, and I don't really want to hear the arguments, selfish or altruistic, honest or deceitful. Part of me feels I should stay, after all, if Anna didn't kill Taylor then it's likely that the real killer is in the room now; I should watch to see whether clues or real emotions are revealed. The other part of me wants me to go back into the cloisters, to have a good look round. The less gregarious me wins. 'I'm just nipping out,' I whisper to Jen, 'if it comes to a vote you have my proxy.'

'If you're back within the hour,' she hisses back, 'you can still vote yourself, this lot won't be making any decision quickly. Though it is fascinating watching the young of the species.'

I sidle out of the room, nodding at unremembered faces as I pass. I head down the corridor but am halted by my name being called. When I turn round I see Belle hurrying after me.

'Mr Oliphant,' she says, 'I thought you might be out here.'

'And you were right. What can I do for you?'

'I need to ask you a favour.'

'Ask, then. The worst that can happen is that I'll say no.'

She draws her lips into two parallel lines and nods as if she's considering the wisdom of what I've just said. 'I hope you'll say yes, but . . . We won't know until I say what it is.'

'So?'

225

'I want you to break into Jonathan Taylor's safe.'

I'm surprised at the request and curious about the motivation behind it. 'That's illegal.'

'I know. That's why I need you to do it. You're the only person I know who might be able to do it.'

'Great. My daughter's friends think I'm a criminal.'

'No, Mr Oliphant, it's not like that at all. It's precisely because I know you're honest that I'm asking you to do this, as you put it, illegal act. And you will admit that you have the ability to do it?'

I have to take care, no one except Kirsty and Jen know I've been anywhere near Taylor's office, let alone seen the safe. 'Until I know what type of lock it is . . .' I begin, but don't finish.

'It's a combination lock, six numbers.'

'And how do you know that?'

'I've been in Taylor's office before. I once commented on it to him and he told me it was a combination lock. He wouldn't tell me the numbers, though. That's why I'm approaching you, I can get you into his office . . .'

'How?' The interruption is abrupt.

'I've a key.' Belle decides further explanation is necessary. 'Mr Oliphant, I'm directing this play because I'm good at it. Jonathan Taylor knew I was good, Christ, I could do his job blindfold. And sometimes I did, I covered for him when he was "unavailable" for the day, led tutorials for him.'

'And do you know why he went missing?'

'Of course! Everybody knew. He was screwing someone.' She pushes her glasses back onto the bridge of her nose. 'Of course, I didn't know for certain who he was screwing. But I could guess. Usually the girl who suddenly started getting good marks.'

'And was he screwing Anna Peranski?'

Belle takes a deep breath. 'That's the big question, isn't it? If the police are right, then she did.'

'That's not what I meant. Did they have a relationship

226

prior to this weekend? Had she, perhaps, been sleeping with him in return for favours? Good marks, perhaps?'

'Mr Oliphant, I know that's what you meant. Like I said, I could usually guess who was his favourite at any given time. I didn't think Anna was his type. But she was having problems with her essays – her practical work was good, though – so I suppose they could have come to some arrangement.'

'You haven't answered the question.'

'That's because I don't know for certain. "I can say little more than I've studied, and that question's out of my part." But if you want my opinion – yes, she slept with him. She must have done. She was going round saying how good her marks were, how much they'd improved, and I know she wasn't that good.'

I remember how good Belle's grades were. 'Did you sleep with Taylor in return for good marks?'

'Are you trying to shock me, Mr Oliphant? You can't, you know. "I'm one of those gentle ones that will use the devil himself with courtesy." Act Four, Scene Two. I could make a living from it, a quotation for every situation. Look at me, Mr Oliphant, do I look like I'm Jonathan Taylor's type? And he certainly wasn't mine. Besides, I don't need to sleep with anyone to get good grades, and that isn't being big-headed, it's just stating a fact.'

'I apologise,' I say. There seems little else I can do under such a defence. She has this habit of saying things that could be her words, or Shakespeare's, or from some other playwright, and I can't tell which. Her acknowledgement of someone else's authorship might help me, it might sound pretentious, but at least it would let me know whose words she's speaking.

'Don't worry, I haven't taken offence,' she beams. 'And if I didn't answer your question, then you didn't answer mine. Would you be willing to break into Jonathan Taylor's safe for me?'

'So far as I remember, you didn't actually tell me why you had a key to his office.'

'Touché,' she ripostes, 'though I thought I'd implied it. I needed to gain access to the rehearsal rooms and even his own office at times when he wasn't around. So he gave me a key.'

'And why do you want me to break in? What's in his safe that's so valuable?'

'There's a list, Mr Oliphant, of names. They're the names of Jonathan's contacts, probably in an address book, the people he's invited to come to the play. The thing is, they'll probably have heard about the murder, they might think it isn't worth coming because the play's been cancelled. They might think not coming would show support or sympathy for Jonathan. For everyone's sake, I need to get in touch with them to make sure they all come. And I don't know who they are, or how to find them.'

There's some sense in what Belle's saying, and she wants a quick answer; she's glancing repeatedly towards the door.

'Do you know for certain that the list is there?'

'No. I just know it's not anywhere else. Believe me, I've searched.'

'Perhaps he had it at home.'

'No, Mr Oliphant, I've been to his home.' She sees the look on my face. 'And before you start jumping to conclusions, I went once, with a group from the department, for a glass of wine before going to see a play. We all arrived and left together. And I noticed that, in his one-bedroomed minimalist flat – when I went to the loo I peeped into the bedroom – he had no books at all. He kept everything at work.'

She's looking at the door again. 'Are you in a hurry?' I ask.

'I think they'll be finishing their discussion soon, I need to get back.'

'Why did you leave?'

She adopts a Pythonesque voice, '"No one expects the Spanish Inquisition!"' She's suddenly weary. 'Some of the others don't like me, Mr Oliphant. I think they suspect I'm doing this for my own gain, they think I'm the one who'll benefit most if the play goes ahead. But at the same time, they won't speak up and say that with me there.' She ponders that statement. 'Well, one or two of them might. Anyway, in the interests of free speech and full expression of concerns, I thought I'd better leave the room. But they're bound to be finished soon, and I need to get back. So what's your answer?'

'Even if I decide to do you the favour, if I say yes, I might not be able to open the safe.'

'It's better to try and fail than not to try at all.'

'Is that a quotation?'

'Probably. Though I can't remember where I stole it.'

She looks at the door again.

'Give me the key, then,' I tell her.

'You mean . . ? Thank you, thank you so much.' She looks as if she might throw her arms round me, I step away from her and she takes the hint. 'It's a great weight off my mind, to know that you're prepared to do that.'

'The key?' I remind her.

'But I thought we could go together. I need to show you the way. And if you get in, I'll know what the paperwork is. There might be lots there, I could find it quickly.'

'It's a list, Belle,' I remind her, 'or a diary, or an address book. I can recognise all those when I see them.'

'I still think I ought to come with you.'

'I go alone or not at all.'

'When? When are you going?'

'So you can follow me? Why are you so keen to come with me?'

Belle reconsiders her position. She can't win the argument. All she can do is fight the rearguard. 'I don't have it with me. I'll give it to you later on this evening, during rehearsals. Then you can decide yourself when you're going to go.'

I stop myself pointing out that the group's decision might not be in favour of going on, instead I just nod my head. 'That's all right with me.'

'Thanks,' she says again, heads back into the meeting. And that's when I decide to do the search myself, using my skeleton keys, before anyone else can offer to accompany me.

Chapter Nine

I see no one as I make my way back to Taylor's office. I take the short route, the one by which Kirsty and I returned an hour or so before. My keys are still a deadweight in my pocket, my hand reaches to caress them, though I tell myself it's simply to stop them jingling, making too much of a noise.

I walk past the door leading to the Theatre Studies department to make sure no one's following; there's no sound and no sight of any other person. I examine the lock, it looks similar to the one I've already got through earlier in the day, the one at the far end of the corridor I soon hope to enter. I find the same combination of picks, feel the same satisfaction as they mesh with and turn the simple mechanism within. The lock disengages, I turn the handle and the door opens smoothly.

'Hold it right there, Oliphant!' a deep, brusque voice commands. 'And don't turn round. Hands on the door frame, legs apart.'

I do as I'm told, try, unsuccessfully, to catch a glimpse of my captor. There's no point in trying to escape, I'm a slow runner and this person, whoever he is, knows who I am anyway. 'I'm not armed,' I say slowly.

There's no reply. Instead a firm hand pats at my ankles, inside and out, then works its way up to my knees and beyond. I've been searched before, but this is thorough.

231

The hand brushes over my buttocks, reaches to smooth over the front of my thigh, then lingers in the region of my fly. It rests there for a moment, I can feel its warmth and a slow increase in pressure, and I'm beginning to think that there's something wrong with this over-familiar exploration.

'Mm,' the voice says, suddenly an octave higher and very familiar, 'either you're packing a substantial weapon, or you're very pleased to see me.'

'Jen!' I hiss, and whirl around.

She straightens up. 'Of course, it could be both.' She has the good grace to look sheepish. I think she knows it's difficult for me to be angry with her when she looks like a little girl who's done something wrong. 'Sorry,' she apologises, 'it seemed too good an opportunity to miss.'

In the brief silence that follows I think I can hear footsteps. I grab Jen's wrist and pull her into the corridor beyond the door I've just opened.

'Oh, I do like an assertive man,' she murmurs as I try to find the skeletons to lock the door behind us.

'Be quiet and get back!' The concern in my voice must be apparent, Jen moves away from me, up to the top of the staircase. I can't find the right keys, instead I crouch down and lean heavily against the door. The footsteps approach then, without pause, fade into the distance. I fumble again for the right combination of skeletons, this time I find them quickly, and I lock the door. 'Don't do that again,' I tell her. 'What would have happened if I'd thought you were attacking me? I could have hurt you.' I try to keep my voice calm, but Jen knows me too well. She can sense how angry I am.

'I'm sorry, really I am. I didn't think ...'

'That's exactly the trouble, you didn't think. You're just like Kirsty, you think this is all a game, it's solve-a-puzzle time, it's an abstract sort of quiz.' I've hit form now, my self-righteous indignation is at its peak. 'But it's not like that at all. Jesus Christ, Jen, somebody's died. No,' I correct myself, 'that's too impersonal. Not "someone's died." Somewhere out there is a murderer. This murderer killed Jonathan Taylor. This murderer took a knife and pushed it firmly between Taylor's ribs and into his heart. This murderer then rigged up a complex web of evidence to get someone else blamed for the crime. This murderer is clever, and I don't have the faintest clue who he or she is.' I stop for maximum effect. Perhaps I'm learning from being around so many actors. 'And you're playing stupid jokes.'

Jen and I have argued before, but only when we've taken opposing views and both been certain we were right. But this isn't an argument. As I finish speaking I realise I'm taking out my frustration on Jen. I'm annoyed that I originally thought Anna was guilty, I'm annoyed that I've found nothing to suggest who actually did kill Taylor, I'm annoyed that I've let myself be drawn into this investigation in the first place. The target of my anger should be me, instead it's Jen. She knows this. She should point this out to me, she should tell me to stop being so juvenile, to snap out of this self-pity. Instead she stands in front of me, accepts my caustic comments. 'Sorry,' she says again, quietly.

'So am I,' I tell her, and mean it. 'Thank you for wanting to come with me. Thank you for putting up with me. Thank you for ...'

Her *femme-fatale* interruption silences me. 'Less of the lists, buddy-boy. Ain't you got a job to do?' Her grin is infectious.

'Yeah, sorry ...'

'You're as bad as me: keep this up and we'll both have to join Apologists Anonymous.' She leans against me and kisses me on the lips. I respond, we feed off each other until she pulls away. 'Is that a gun in your pocket?' She giggles. 'No, I've already done that line. Hadn't we better solve the crime first? After all, someone might catch us *in flagrante*, and you've got your reputation as an upstanding member of the community to think about.' She breathes in

233

my ear, her voice a husky whisper, 'Very upstanding.'

'Jen!' I scold her.

'Ooh! Quite the puritan now, eh? So stop tempting me!' She puts one hand on her hip, daring me to contradict her. 'Come on, then. Lead the way.'

I do as I'm told, pleased that the rift I caused has healed so quickly. She follows me up the stairs, through the waiting room and into Taylor's office. Nothing has changed since I broke in a few hours before. There are no signs that anyone else has been here.

Jen wanders the walls, taking in the books. She pauses before the small biology and botany section, pulls out a volume and opens it. She exchanges it for another, then another. 'Quite old,' she says, 'nothing younger than twenty years. Some of it even older. Pretty dated. But Fibonacci's older than all of these anyway.' She turns and crouches down in front of the safe. 'So this is the baby. Think old Fibonacci'll work his magic?'

'It's worth trying. Come on, move over.'

Jen lets me examine the safe again. It's a standard design, with a handle and a round knob with numbers round the outside. The handle will only turn and disengage the bolts when the numbered knob allows weighted tumblers to fall into place within the door. In the gangster films that informed my youth, safes like this could be opened using a stethoscope. It was possible, young criminals were lead to believe, to hear the tumblers – small pieces of metal – fall into place. Once one had fallen, the knob could then be turned to allow the second and subsequent tumblers fall. It was, of course, a fallacy. When at police training college I was allowed to attempt listening to and opening such a safe; I heard nothing. That's why the cracker brought in by Arnison said she would take the safe away to drill it open; if you don't know the combination then breaking is the only way to enter.

'Go on then,' Jen brings me back from my reverie, 'try it.'

'Tell me the numbers again.'

'One, one, two, three, five, eight. Do you want more?'

'No, six will do.' I turn the knob to the requisite numbers, then tug at the handle. It doesn't give. 'Shit!'

'If the door code was the first six numbers of the Fibonacci series,' Jen suggests, 'perhaps the safe code was the next six.'

'Which are?'

'Thirteen, twenty-one, forty-four ... let me see ... sixty-five, then ...'

'No, it can't be, each number has to be between zero and nine.'

'Perhaps the individual digits, then. Not thirteen, twenty-one, forty-four and so on, but one, three, two, one, four, four. Try it.'

I do as I'm told. Again, the handle won't turn. The door won't open. 'This is stupid,' I say, 'it's as bad as just guessing. We might as well pack in now.' I stand up, make for the door, but Jen stands in my way.

'One more,' she asks, 'I'm sure we can work it out.' Her brows furrow, the concentration is both comical and appealing; I have to give way.

'Come on then,' I relent, 'one more. What would you suggest?'

'Add the integers of each number together? Thirteen is one plus three, that's four? And so on?'

'You work them out, I'll enter them.'

'Okay, four to start with. Then twenty-one gives three. Forty-four is eight. Then sixty-five, that's eleven ... Shit! Now what? One add one?'

'Makes two. Keep going.'

'Sixty-five plus forty-four is 109, that's ten which makes one. I don't think this is going to work, Billy. It's not easy enough.'

'I agree, but there's nothing else to try. Keep going.'

'The next number is 174, that's twelve, gives us three.'

I enter the last number. The handle remains firm,

unmoving. I turn round, lean my back against the safe. It feels cool and strong, unyielding. I lift my shoulders in a shrug of helplessness. 'Any more ideas?'

'How about the first six letters of "Fibonacci" turned into numbers?' She begins to work them out. 'No, still no good. It means adding the integers of numbers bigger than nine, and that's too complicated.'

'Why?'

She looks puzzled. 'What do you mean, "why"?'

'Perhaps we're thinking of this the wrong way round. You just said a word-to-number sequence was too complicated, and it is, I agree with you. The first six numbers of the Fibonacci series are easy to remember as long as you know the code, perhaps that's why Taylor chose them. Not because they were Fibonacci numbers, but because they were easy to remember. So instead of thinking of connections to Fibonacci and to biology, let's just think of numbers that are easy to remember.'

'Okay,' Jen says without much enthusiasm. 'You go first.'

'I don't know,' I splutter, 'I was hopeless at maths. You're the scientist, you should know about numbers. You think of something.'

There's silence. It's as if the air has grown thick and won't allow words to move from mouth to ear, its very heaviness is threatening to suffocate us. Breathing seems more difficult, thinking is almost impossible. But I make the effort, I don't want to be found here in a thousand years' time, a dry husk of papery flesh, mummified because I was unable to speak.

'Come on, let's go back.' I rise to my feet.

'Yeah, you're right.' Jen, crouches down beside me, holds up her hand to be pulled up. 'Luck just wasn't on our side.'

'Even less so on Taylor's,' I remind her. I pull Jen into my arms. 'And to think, he wasn't superstitious, apart from his refusal to call the play *Macbeth* by its name.' Jen feels warm in my arms, she presses against me in all the right places. I kiss her on the nose. 'And his lucky number.' I'm about to move from her nose to her lips, but she pushes me away.

'Taylor had a lucky number?'

'Yes. He told me he was a seventh child of a seventh child. I'm pretty sure that was a joke, but seven was his lucky number.'

'Billy!' She spins me round. 'Try it! Try six sevens!'

'That's too easy,' I tell her, but she's forcing me to the ground in front of her. I turn the dial. I try the handle. It remains firmly, irresolutely in place. 'Obviously seven wasn't lucky enough.'

Jen smiles triumphantly. 'But seventh might be.'

'What?'

'Seventh. Not "seven", but a "seventh".'

'I've no idea what you're ...'

'No, listen. A seventh is a repeating cyclical decimalised fraction.' Jen can see the complete lack of comprehension on my face, she hurries on. 'I can remember it from school, I don't even have to work it out. In decimals, a seventh is 0.142857 recurring. And the reason I remember it is that two sevenths is 0.285714 recurring. It's the same digits in the same order, just a different starting place. And it works for every numerator with a denominator of seven. Three sevenths is 0.571428, four sevenths is ...'

'I believe you! But why would Taylor use it as a safe combination?'

'It's easy to remember. Good God, Billy, I can remember it and I haven't needed to use it since I was fifteen. Go on, try it.'

I enter the numbers at her prompting, one, four, two, eight, five, seven. The handle moves easily. I pull the door open.

'Yes!' Jen jumps up and down like a little girl, clapping her hands with joy. 'We did it, we did it.'

'You did it,' I remind her, 'your idea.'

237

She stops suddenly. 'Yes, it was, wasn't it. Thank you, Mr Bradshaw.'

'Mr Bradshaw?'

'My maths teacher.'

The safe isn't large. Inside is a cash box resting on a thick pile of papers. I pull them all out, look in the cashbox first. It isn't heavy, there are no coins within. There are, however, several wedges of twenty pound notes, each wrapped in a blue bank money wrapper. I flick through them; they feel about the right weight, there seems to be about the right number in each.

'How much?' Jen asks.

'Three times five hundred,' I tell her.

'Why would Taylor have fifteen hundred pounds in his safe?'

'I've no idea.' I think carefully. There are times when I have far larger amounts in my own safe, particularly when customers pay in cash thinking they're avoiding VAT – the tax is, of course, always included in the price. 'It's not actually a lot of money.'

'It is for a university lecturer,' Jen says.

'It is indeed,' says a new voice.

Jen and I spin round. We find ourselves facing a tall figure in a trench coat, a hat hiding his eyes and face. He might look comical if he wasn't holding a gun in his leather-gloved hand. He raises his head to reveal a Humphrey Bogart mask.

'I think you'd better lie down on the floor,' he says, his lisping American voice straight from every film noir you've ever seen.

I can't resist it. 'Of all the gin joints in all ...'

'Cut the crap, Oliphant.' His voice remains in role.

'Okay, okay. Some people have no sense of humour.' I lower myself to my knees. 'Jen, I normally find, when dealing with a person pointing a gun at you, that the best thing to do is usually exactly as you're told. On the floor?'

Jen joins me. We stretch ourselves out, in doing so we

take up most of the space between our Bogart and the safe.

'Hands on your heads,' he commands. We comply, but there's no sound of movement, no creep or creak of shoes coming closer.

'You're probably wondering,' I tell him, turning my head a little to one side so he can hear me, 'whether one of us will try to grab you if you come any closer, or perhaps try to kick you.' There's no reply, so I continue. 'Neither of us is brave enough to risk being shot. If you want us to move we will, we can go and lie down next door. But I can assure you, we'll do nothing to harm you.'

'Good. But your silence would be appreciated now.'

I want to keep him talking, in case his voice becomes recognisable. 'You do realise you're mad, don't you?'

'Midsummer madness?' he snorts.

I hate television detectives. 'There's too much of it around.'

The feet step gingerly forward, one step, then two. I sense, rather than hear, Bogart reach out for the cash-tin. 'I knew Taylor had this cash,' he announces, 'all I had to do was wait until you opened the safe for me. Thank you, losers.' If I want to knock him over, now is the time, when he's stretching, unbalanced. But I can't see him, I don't know where his gun's pointing. It's too risky.

'What would your parents think of you?' Jen asks suddenly.

'What?'

Bogart's surprise is almost as keen as my own, I can't imagine why Jen would be asking about his parents. I'm worried that she might antagonise him. 'It's okay,' I tell her, 'just be quiet and things will be okay.'

She ignores me, rephrases the question. 'Would your parents be proud of you?' There's no reply, so she goes on. 'What is your parentage?'

There's an exhalation of breath from Bogart, almost a snigger. 'Above my fortunes, yet my state is well.' This time there's definitely a laugh. 'I am a gentleman.' The

239

footsteps retreat. 'I may go now,' Bogart says. 'Or on the other hand, I may stay to see how long it takes you to become curious and turn your head to see if I'm still here. If you do that before I go, I might get annoyed and do something I shouldn't.'

'We're hardly likely to chase you,' I tell him, 'you have a gun.'

There's no reply. I turn my head a little to one side; there's no command asking me to be still. I twist my head a little further; there's no one else there. 'It's okay,' I tell Jen, 'he's gone. You can get up now.'

Even as she turns over and clambers to her feet Jen's talking. 'Did you hear what he said?' she demands. 'When you said he was mad he said it was midsummer madness, did you recognise the line?'

'It's that stupid television show where there's a murder every week in some middle-class rural 1950s backwater. I hate it, you know I hate it.'

Jen's getting excited, she grabs my hands. 'It's also a quotation from the play, from *Twelfth Night*. That's why I asked him about his parents, that's a line from the play as well. And he answered with the next line. Whoever he is, he knows the play well. And he doesn't mind us knowing that.'

'And his trainers are very old, dirty red, with the heels worn down more on the right inside than the left. That's why I kept talking, so he wouldn't mind me turning my head.'

'Trousers?'

'Inconclusive. Faded denim jeans. Too common.'

'If we hurry we might be able to catch him.' Jen's already pulling me after her, eager to hunt down our quarry.

'If he's one of our actors, we know where he'll be, back down in the cloisters. And I'd rather meet him again when he isn't flashing a gun in my direction. Let's just think before we act, before we forget. Impressions? What type of person is he?'

Jen's brow furrows. 'Not too clever? By quoting from the text he let us know he was involved with the play in some way.'

'Not necessarily, you knew it was a quotation and you're not involved. But I'll admit that stupidity is a possibility. Or it could be that he's arrogant. Feeding us clues because they're meant to mislead us.' It's very rare that any evidence is conclusive, and I seem to have a talent for seeing the other side of anything Jen offers.

'How would quoting the play mislead us?'

'It could focus us on an individual. Whose lines was he quoting?'

'Viola's. Or rather, Viola as Cesario.'

'And who plays the part?'

'I don't know, I've only just arrived.' Jen's beginning to lose patience.

'I know. It's the part Anna would have played.'

Jen sounds crestfallen. 'So it could have been anyone.'

'No, it was someone with a very good knowledge of the play. Not all the cast would know all the play. In fact, there's only one person who would know it all, according to Kirsty. And that's our director, Belle. She has a photographic memory, she's a talented actress, she can probably even do a reasonable impression of Humphrey Bogart.'

Jen shakes her head, 'No, that was never a girl.'

'How do you know?' I'm genuinely curious, Jen doesn't often make statements so firmly without some support.

'The trainers,' she replies triumphantly.

I think back. They weren't that close to me, but they were close enough for me to remember the colour and the fact that they were unevenly worn. I can't recall how big they were. Even then, some men have small feet, some women large. Jen's waiting for me to respond. 'Go on then.'

'He had to step close to me, and his trainers smelled. Not just sweaty, that could be anyone, but like some fungal infection. I've smelled it before, while I was training. And

I'm afraid it's mostly men who have chronic fungal infections.'

I'm curious. 'Why's that?'

'Because women are sensible enough to see their doctors for any type of thing like that. Men just don't seem to care. I think it's because women are conditioned to watch out for crevices in their bodies, especially warm moist places, like between their toes; they have so many of them. Whereas men are more exposed, more visible. Reasonable diagnosis?'

'Don't you think it may be a little too general?' I ask her. 'And what if it was a woman, let's say Belle, who had borrowed a man's shoes? But it's something to think about, another question to ask when we're nearer to our suspect.'

I turn to the desk behind me, the cash-box has disappeared but the thick pile of papers appears to be undisturbed. I pick up the first, it's a marked piece of writing. The others are similar. The title on all the papers is the same, a question about Brecht, epic theatre and the alienation effect. Jen's beside me, looking over my shoulder. I keep on looking through, not sure what I'm looking for. Each paper differs from the others only in the handwriting or the font, the number of red marks, and the mark at the end.

'That's unusual,' Jen says.

I haven't seen anything unusual at all, simply a number of essays on a subject I know nothing about. I humour Jen. 'What's that?'

'Why would Taylor keep essays in the safe?'

'He didn't want anyone to see them?'

'That's obvious. But why wouldn't he want anyone to see them? They've been written, they've been marked, he's probably noted the marks. All he has to do is give them back. Instead, he locks them away. Why?'

I try to find an answer. 'It's a handy place to keep them?'

'But he could have just left them on the desk, no one would be interested in them except the person they should have been returned to, the person who wrote the essay. It doesn't make sense.'

'You're right,' I agree, 'but it doesn't help us. It just means Taylor had a peculiar habit of locking essays away.'

Jen isn't about to give up so easily. 'Let's assume it's not a peculiar habit, let's say he had a good reason.' She takes the remaining essays from my hand and continues to look through them, but her frown tells me there's nothing there of note. 'Essays, that's all they are.' She tosses them onto the desk.

'I wonder how Kirsty did,' I say, picking them up again and flicking through once more.

'You can't do that,' Jen tells me, pulling the papers back, 'if she wants you to know she'll tell you when she gets the mark.'

'She's already finished her work,' I tell Jen, 'she's got all her marks. She said she had nothing outstanding. And I don't think one of hers was there anyway, I checked the names.'

'Then it must be another year group,' Jen explains. She begins to look through again. 'No, not a single year group, two groups. Look, Billy, look at the dates.' She holds out one paper to me, then another. 'These essays were submitted almost a year apart.' She flicks through them again, sorts them into two separate piles. Then she reaches into her pocket and flips open her mobile phone.

'Who are you ringing?' I ask. 'And why?' I can be abrupt when I don't know what's going on, even to Jen.

'I'm ringing Kirsty, which is what we should have done as soon as we stood up ten minutes ago. She could have told us if anyone was missing.' Her explanation is as curt as my question, and it clearly points the finger at me; I should have thought of phoning Kirsty, after all, I'm the expert investigator. Even if I had the words to excuse myself, the opportunity to speak is lost as Kirsty answers. 'Hello love,' Jen asks, 'what's happening? Have they made a decision yet?' She nods, looks at me. 'Okay, hold on a second.' She explains, 'They talked for a while but in the end a majority decided to go ahead. They're heading out into the cloisters now for a rehearsal.'

'Ask her if ...'

'Did you notice,' Jen needs no prompting, 'if anyone disappeared a little while ago? No? Yes, we know Belle came out, but did anyone else?' Jen shakes her head at me, whispers a summary of Kirsty's response. 'No one left, according to Kirsty. But she says she wasn't really watching for who wasn't there, so I suppose ...' She shrugs, returns her attention to my daughter. 'One more thing, love. When Taylor marked your essays, did he give them back to you or did he just tell you the mark you got?'

There's silence for a while. It's infuriating not being able to hear both sides of a conversation. I'm startled at how impatient I'm becoming. 'What does she say?'

'Right. Right. Okay, love, thanks, we'll be along soon.' Jen ends the call and closes the phone. 'He always gave them back,' she explains, 'but he told everyone that he kept photocopies. He said it was because sometimes people altered their essays after he gave them back, then complained that his marking was wrong.'

'I've never been to university, you have. Is that believable?'

Jen thinks for a while. 'I don't really know. I suppose so, if he's had an accusation like that before, then he'd want to make sure it never happened again. Or it could be for helping him teach, he could pull out the good points from all the essays.'

'But why mix the old essays and the new ones? Why these ones in particular?'

Jen picks up the pile again, flicks through them. 'We don't even know which year group they're from.'

'We can find out,' I say, reaching for the mark books on the shelf, 'there are lists here of ...'

'Of what?'

I checks several shelves, just in case I'm mistaken, but

the book I'm looking for isn't there. 'It's gone. The most recent mark book is gone. And the one before that.' I run my fingers along the shelves, pull the books out for two years before and three years before. 'Bogart must have taken them. But why?'

'Souvenirs? A memento of his theft, something to keep after he's spent the money? I don't know.'

'Maybe he didn't really come for the money. Maybe he came for the mark books.' I find myself clenching my fists, not a habit I'm aware of. Perhaps it helps me concentrate. 'But he could have taken those anytime, after all, he had a key. So it must have been something in the safe. That just leaves . . .'

Jen's looking at me expectantly, as if I'm capable of coming up with an idea from nowhere. She's like a midwife urging a mother to give birth to a reluctant baby; if that's the case then this one's breached and elephant-sized. But then, without the flash of light and the heavenly choir singing of revelations, it comes to me; not a birth, more the successful scratching of a persistent itch.

'The essays! He must have taken one of the essays. For some reason there was something in an essay that was important, something Bogart didn't want us to find. So he took it, and the money was a bonus, he didn't expect that to be there.'

'So why . . ? Jen begins to ask, but I'm ahead of her.

'He took the books because they were the last evidence, the last easily accessible evidence, of who was in each class. You see, with the books and the remaining essays, we could figure out which one was taken.'

'Clever,' Jen says.'

'Thank you, Watson.'

'No, Billy, not you, I expect you to be clever all the time. I mean Bogart. It was clever of him to think about that.'

Jen's comments force a rethink. 'Perhaps it was too clever. Might he have been leaving another false trail?'

245

'Billy Oliphant, stop double-thinking! You said the mark books were the last easily accessible evidence. What did you mean by that?'

Jen's getting too quick, she's anticipating my thoughts too easily, too often. She knows me too well.

'Bogart didn't realise,' I tell her proudly, 'that for once I was ahead of him. I spent part of the morning chatting to a couple of interesting ladies.' I switch on Taylor's computer. 'I think I might just be able to get the information I need from another source.'

Jen and I watch as the computer goes through its warm up, flexes muscles it hasn't used for a while. I follow its instructions politely when it asks me to do so, wishing it no malice despite its slowness.

'How will you get into the network?' Jen asks eagerly. 'There are bound to be passwords.'

'Not too long ago, I thought I'd change the business name from "Oliphant Security" to "Passwords 'R' Us", but it would have been too self-congratulatory.'

The computer is still taking its time, playing hard to get; but I know it'll come round, they always do. All you need is patience, charm, ingenuity and knowledge.

'Most passwords are easy these days, there are too many of them about.' I don't mean this to turn into a lecture, but the computer is particularly slow. 'You need a password to access your bank account, your credit card, your computer at home, your computer at work, the internet. So what do people do? They use the same password or code for every-thing. All you have to do is a little psycho-analysis.'

At last the screen is asking me to log in.

'Now what?' Jen asks. 'More playing around with Fibonacci?'

'We don't need to be Taylor. The type of information we want isn't restricted to his department. All we need to do first is get in. Watch.' I type in one of the usernames I found out from the secretaries 'elli0261', and the generic password for the university, 'success'. The screen flickers, then I'm in; the university's network is open to me.

'How did you do that?' Jen asks, her voice tinged with equal measures of incredulity and jealousy.

'Talent,' I tell her. 'And a little forethought. Oh, and I had the help of two gullible women.'

'Billy!' She hits me on the back of the neck.

'Okay, okay! I persuaded some secretaries to give me their usernames, the password is a default and they hadn't been bothered to change it. It's nothing startling.'

'No,' says Jen, and her voice is kind again, 'but it does show how persuasive you can be.'

'Yeah, I had them eating out of my hands. Now then, we need to get into students records. Let me see.' My fingers hover over the keyboard, but Jen's ahead of me.

'Go to "start", then to "my computer".' She looms over my shoulder; I take my hands away, slide sideways out of the seat. I know my limitations with technology and Jen is faster than me at a range of tasks, from programming a video recorder to fathoming the inner workings of a mobile phone. She takes my place without comment.

'There are several choices,' she says, 'different servers. Of course, the usernames you acquired—' there's a hint of sarcasm in her voice '—may have limited access to certain files.'

'In my experience secretaries have access to anything and everything. Let me see, what are the server titles?'

Jen reads them off for me. 'There's human resources, student support, shared files, tutor files. Probably folders and sub-folders within each.'

'I'll have student support please, Carol.'

'Students support it is. And ... Yep, you need another password. Ideas?'

'Let's assume a default that hasn't been over-ruled. It's a university, the first gate was "success", let's work on the same principle. I think we should work on what follows success, at least in a university. How about "reward"?'

Jen switches on the computer's thesaurus. 'You might as

well go for a synonym of success, like . . .' she waits for it to churn out alternatives, '. . . yes, like "victory" or "triumph". Or even alternatives to reward. We have "prize", "payment" and many others. But none of them are right.'

'Oh yes? And how do you know?'

'Simple. I perceive where others only see. I engage with a problem where others only think about it. I . . .'

I place my hand gently over Jen's mouth. 'You're a smartarse of the first order, a trait I usually find endearing, but under present circumstances a swift, accurate and brief response would be very much appreciated. Am I understood?'

Jen nods, my hand can't hide her smile; she's pleased she's been able to annoy me, pleased at the way I'm dealing with it. She always says my sense of humour appeals to her. I hope she never finds out that I sometimes mean the things other people think are jests.

'I'll take my hand away now. Please start your explanation immediately.'

'The first screen,' she says quickly, 'after the password. It had the university shield on it.'

'I remember. Ugly looking thing with unicorns and lions.'

'It also had a Latin motto at the bottom. *Succedere est laborare*. A literal translation is "to succeed is to work". Less literal might be "success comes through hard work". And if the first password is "success" then the second is likely to be "work". What do you think?'

'Try it.'

Jen enters the four letters, w-o-r-k. The screen goes blank for a second. Then it comes to life again with a screen full of files, each with the name of a department. 'I am a genius,' Jen declares.

'I love you and want to have your babies,' I reply, without recalling the television programme I stole the line from.

248

'The feeling is mutual.'

The silence reflects the enormity of the statement. I could take Jen's throwaway line as a repetition of the humour I intended, but I don't think it was really meant in that light. It was a response, a quick response, but I suspect it came from the heart. We intend getting married, she did, after all, propose to me, and I accepted. We've talked about dates and places, who should be invited, whether I should wear white and she should be in a morning suit. It's been that light-hearted. But this is something different, this is more than I can cope with at the moment, and I think it's more than Jen wants to consider as well. She hurries on, as if the words she spoke had little meaning, stares at the folders on the screen in front of us. 'Drama, I take it?'

I want to tell her it is, certainly, drama of the highest order, but that isn't what she means. 'Drama department seems to be the people's choice,' I tell her. She opens the folder. Inside are other folders and documents, without me saying anything she opens the folder names 'class lists'. Once again there are options, but they're easy. Tables appear to be listed according to the year in which the course commenced, and they go back for quite a while; 'first year 2000' obviously finished the three-year course in 2003.

Jen holds the cursor over the present first year. 'This one?' she asks.

'No, that's Kirsty's year. They didn't do that essay. Try the previous year.'

Jen does as she's asked; a list of names appears, in alphabetical order, with dates of birth, headings show essays and exams and their dates, scores and marks in both numbers and letters. Jen and I had, by accident rather than design, sorted the essays into their two year groups. I pick up the most recent, check off the name; it's on the list.

'Hold on,' Jen says, 'let's be methodical. I'll just create another column here.' She plays with the mouse and the keyboard and an extra column appears at her conjuration. 'you read the names, I'll put an "X" in the column beside

249

the name. That way we'll see who's missing.'

I read out the names, a column of crosses appears. Soon there's only one gap, beside Anna's name; hers is the only essay missing. Jen moves the cursor across the columns from left to right. A heading appears, 'Brecht essay', and a date which precedes that on most of the essays by about a fortnight. In the column below, alongside Anna's name, there's a number, 92.

'It looks as if she did the essay, then,' I say, seeking corroboration.

'And she did it bloody well. That's easily first-class honours grade.' Jen looks at the marks to both sides. 'She didn't do too well in her first year, but after that she was really flying.'

The thought occurs to both of us. A sudden improvement in marks could be due to Anna working harder, but it could also be due to her buying good marks from Taylor with the only coin she possessed, sex.

'It doesn't prove anything, then,' Jen pronounces, delivers her verdict to the court.

'But Bogart stole her essay for a reason. Why?'

'In case it was a crap essay, not worth the marks it was given. And that's why he took the mark book as well. So it couldn't be checked.'

I can't think of any other reason why both essay and mark book should be stolen, but that would suggest that Anna had a reason to kill Taylor, and both Jen and I know that she didn't do that. Jen's mind has been working in the same direction. 'That's illogical, it supports the theory that Anna had a motive for killing Taylor. So, if it's illogical, the first premise is incorrect. It wasn't a poor essay. Bogart took the essay and the mark book for a different reason.'

'That's all right, then. All we have to do is think of the reason.'

We both lapse into silence again. The room feels dustily warm. It smells of academia, of afternoon tea and crosswords, of tweed jackets and digestive biscuits. It seems impossible that, only a day or so before, a man should have been killed not far from here. There's little of Taylor in the room, no photographs of him – nor of anyone else – on a stage. There are no certificates, no ornaments, no little personal belongings. It's an empty husk of an office, its life was the man who inhabited it.

'Do you want me to close down?' Jen asks.

'There must be something else.' The pile of essays is mocking me. 'And I still don't know what the alienation effect is, or what it had to do with Brecht.'

'It was one of Brecht's pet theories,' Jen explains. 'The idea was that the audience shouldn't become involved with the play, they shouldn't be sympathetic. They should realise that what they were watching was unreal, that it had another purpose. In Brecht's plays, that purpose was largely political.' Lecture over, she asks the question again. 'Do you want me to close down?'

Something is annoying me, an itch demanding to be scratched. And then, after the scratch, it wants to be bathed, then anointed with soothing creams; it's that persistent. 'Let's be Brechtian,' I suggest. 'Let's step back. Let's detach ourselves from the little play we've been in, let's separate the drama from the purpose. Why did Bogart come here?'

'Because he knew we were here. Because he wanted the contents of the safe, which could well have been money. But he also wanted Anna's essay.'

'And the mark book.'

'And the mark book, so we wouldn't know that Anna's paper had been taken.'

'Okay. Why make us lie down?'

'So we wouldn't attack him? So we'd concentrate on his feet, a misleading clue? I don't know, it could be anything.'

Jen's missed the obvious. 'So we wouldn't see him taking the essay and the mark book.'

'Mark books,' Jen reminds me. 'There were two mark books missing.'

251

The itch returns with renewed vigour, but this time I know exactly where to scratch. 'Plural,' I say.

'Yeah, books, not book.'

'Then why not essays instead of essay?'

It doesn't take Jen long to figure it out. 'But we've already checked and Anna's was the only one missing ... Shit! The other year group!'

I don't have to tell her. She opens the class list for the year before Anna's, inserts a column again. 'Go on then,' she says, 'read them out.'

I do. When I finish there's one name with no mark next to it. Isabelle Hewitt. Belle for short.

'Now we close down,' I say. 'I think we need to ask some questions.'

'Hold on,' Jen announces, 'we're not finished yet.' She scans along the row. 'Wow! Belle must be good, look at these marks! Christ, she's got 100 for one of them, I thought that was impossible. Transfer them into grades, no matter what weight you put on them, and this is a first. Hang on a sec, let's see ... Here we are. Brecht essay. Mark? 93.'

'One more than Anna. Is that significant?'

'It's almost identical. An almost identical mark. Perhaps the essays were almost identical.'

'Fuck!'

'Later, Billy. After you've solved the crime.'

'No! I mean, yes, but ... We have to find some proof. I mean, it could have been her, couldn't it? She's an actress, for Christ's sake, she could do a Bogart voice. And she knows the play. We could check on her shoes, see if she has any trainers like the ones I saw. And you could sniff them ...' I realise, too late, what I've said. The image of Jen going round sniffing shoes is more than I can bear. I start to laugh and Jen, appreciating the humour of the notion, does the same.

'I think,' she says between laughs, between snorts, 'that the technical term is hysteria. Caused by stress.'

252

I take her in my arms, hold her tight. If there's anyone I want to share my hysteria with, it's Jen. Slowly we calm down. That's when I notice that Jen isn't laughing any more. The noises she's making are different. I hold her away from me a little, see the tears in her eyes and on her cheeks. Her nose is red, she sniffs back drops of salty water from its tip.

'Hey, love, hey. What's the matter?'

'Oh, Billy, I was frightened, I was so frightened when he, or she, or whoever was underneath the mask, when they had a gun. I thought she was going to kill us. And you were so easy, so much in control, at first I thought you didn't care. Then I thought you were trying to distract him, draw his attention away from me to you. Then I thought . . . I didn't know, I didn't know what to think. I thought he was going to shoot you, then I thought he was going to shoot both of us. And when he left, or when she left, if it was Belle, you were calm, as if nothing had happened, and that made me feel so strong. And now . . .'

'Now you feel there's nothing left, no strength left at all.' I hold her close, try to reassure her. 'It's okay, Jen, I'm here, I'll take care of you. I won't let anything happen to you.'

Jen looks up at me. 'I know, Billy. I know you'll protect me. But one day you might not be there.'

'I'll always be there, love. I'll always be there for you.' Sometimes I say things I don't mean. Sometimes I mean things I don't say. Often, like Alice faced with the mad Hatter and the March Hare, I'm not sure what I'm saying or what I mean. But this time I know that what I'm saying is what I mean, and that it's the truth. 'I'll never let anything happen to you. I love you.'

Jen's arms tighten around me. Eventually, after the earth orbits the sun a few times, she lets me go. 'I'll hold you to that,' she says, and smiles. 'Come on, we've got work to do.' She exits the various screens, closes down the computer. I put the essays back in the safe and lock the door. We retreat to the door and look back; it's as if we haven't been there. I lead Jen down the stairs, lock the door behind me.

The evening's fresh and clean, the rain has only washed away the dust from the day, leaving a palette of bright, vibrant colours. Flowers are seeking the last rays of the sun, swifts screech their racetracks high above, an occasional stuttering in their flight showing where they've braked to scoop up a high-flying insect. A silent jet, wings swept back like the birds it imitates, draws a line across an azure sky. A distant bee-like hum of traffic reinforces the atmosphere of summer. All I need now is the click of cricket ball on bat, the rise and fall of polite applause, and I could be in a time and place I've never experienced, a stereotype of conservative contentment and Englishness. Instead, I try to think ahead, think of what I must do next, think how I can identify the real murderer of Jonathan Taylor. And that person looks more and more like Belle.

With Jen on my arm I feel confident. 'I need to get some things straight in my mind,' I tell her, 'and I need to say them out loud so you can tell me if I'm wrong.' I don't tell her that I've been wrong so often over the past few days, I'm almost expecting her to point out further errors in my thinking.

'Go on, then. But you'd better be quick, we'll be back at the cloisters soon.'

'Okay, here goes. Whoever murdered Taylor tried to frame Anna. They did quite a good job of it as well, and the police will soon find that out. But at the moment, we're the only ones who know that Anna's innocent. Assuming that person did all the swapping of body fluids and so on, they also mocked up the photographs of Anna in Taylor's room. Yes?'

'Seems good so far.'

'We need two things: motivation and opportunity. The opportunity could be accidental, but I think it's more likely to have been planned. The photographs of Anna and Taylor having sex, Kirsty seeing Anna in the corridor; could they have been someone else? Could they have been Belle, perhaps, in a wig and wearing Anna's T-shirt?'

'Can't see anything wrong with that.'

'Good. Let's move on to motivation, the ...'

'Hold on.' Jen does exactly that, holds onto my arm but also stops, spinning me round to face her. 'You've established opportunity, but not method. We know how Taylor was killed, but not where. It certainly wasn't on the stage, there wasn't enough blood. But, so far as I know, no one has found any blood anywhere else.'

'Let's come back to that,' I suggest, 'that's the most difficult bit. Do you agree that the missing essay questions might be motivation for Belle killing Taylor?'

Jen shakes her head. 'No. At least, not yet. Explain.'

'Belle's an A-grade student. She sells her essay to Anna, or lets Anna borrow it. Anna isn't an A-grade student, so Taylor reckons something's wrong. He checks back and finds Belle's original essay, Anna's is almost identical – it would have to be for her to get such a good mark – so Taylor's going to blow the whistle. Belle finds out, she knows that her degree, her whole career, is at risk. So she does something about it. She kills Taylor, thinking she'll be able to destroy the evidence. When she can't find it, she figures it's in the safe, hence the gentle persuasion aimed in my direction and the whole Bogart thing. Possible?'

'Possible. Or it might be that Taylor was blackmailing her, that's why there was so much money in the safe. She could have run out of cash to pay him off. But either way, it's worthless without proof. You need the essays.'

'What would you do if you'd just stolen them?'

'Destroy them?'

'Agreed. And the quickest, most thorough way of doing that?'

'The quickest way of destroying a few pieces of paper? Burn them.'

'In?'

'I don't know. Not just on the ground, they might blow away or be difficult to set fire to. In a waste-bin?'

If Bogart and Belle were the same person, then the quickest route back to the cloisters would have been the one Jen and I are following right now. We're still inside the university grounds. It's a Sunday evening. Few people will have used this route, and there aren't many waste-bins about. There's one ahead of us, just at the door to the cloisters. We hurry on, peer inside. It's almost empty, but in the bottom are some ashes and an empty plastic water bottle. The ashes have been soaked through and the bottle has been used to stir them into a sodden mass.

'Coincidence?' Jen asks. She doesn't mean it, she knows the chances of such a find are minimal; she's mentioning it to give me the chance to voice my thoughts, to counter her argument, but there's no need. 'So we've lost the evidence,' she adds. 'No chance of pinning it on Belle now.'

I push open the door to the cloisters. To my surprise there's a performance underway. The sound system is clear and true, even as we stand furthest from the stage we can hear the nuances of Belle's persuasive voice, thanking the ensemble for deciding to go ahead with the production. Moths are dancing in the spotlights, the cast are a series of hunched shapes on the seats nearest to the stage.

I pull Jen into one of the benches close to the door. 'Do you still have your essays from university?'

'Yes, of course, you never know when ...' She comes to a halt. 'Belle would keep her essays as well, the copies Taylor handed back. She wouldn't destroy her copy of this essay, why should she? In the lack of Taylor's evidence, no one's going to start searching her old papers.'

I feel quite smug. 'I bet she keeps them filed neatly and labelled. I just hope Anna kept hers as well, we need both.'

In the background Belle has left the stage and George has taken up her position, moping into an empty wine glass. 'If music be the food of love,' he says softly, 'play on, give me excess of it, that, surfeiting, the appetite may sicken, and so die.'

'It's the beginning,' Jen explains.

'A full rehearsal. That gives me the chance to borrow some keys for a little housebreaking.'

'Make that an "us", partner. Two houses to search, little time – so we take one each.'

'No chance, you said how you felt before, completely washed out. And anyway, this is illegal. You could be struck off if you were caught.'

'No, lover-boy, you're going to do the illegal stuff. First of all you're going to get Belle's keys from wherever she keeps them, probably in a handbag lying around somewhere. Then I'm going to her flat to collect some stuff she left there, but, of course, she's too busy to get it herself. I'll be completely above board. Honest Jen, they call me. You're the one who's going to break into Anna's flat, wherever it is. So my normally worried little mind isn't worried at all now, because I can justify my actions. Many hands, Billy. You know it makes sense.'

I do, and that makes it even more annoying. It's only then, while I'm coming to terms with the fact that Jen is increasingly becoming as vital to this investigation as she is to my whole life, that I realise how this course of action might end. If Belle killed Taylor – if I can find evidence of that, rather than just supposition – then the play won't go on. Belle's the one holding it together, and she'll be arrested. So despite my efforts to help Kirsty, I could be the agent of her – and her friends' – disappointment. I hope they'll understand.

257

Chapter Ten

The rehearsal is underway, all involved are focused on the stage. Belle is standing in the aisle between the two front rows, arms crossed, staring at the action on the stage, her face unreadable. In the dim light I can see she's wearing doublet and breeches. If I didn't know it was her I would swear she was a long-haired boy. Other members of the cast – most in costume as well – are scattered around the auditorium, also watching intently. The stage is lit, the sound system is working, the stage is occupied, the performance is in progress; I'm fascinated.

I sit down close to Belle, but she doesn't notice me, so intent is she on the stage. A handbag occupies the seat nearest to her, but there's no way I can get hold of it without her seeing me do so. Further back, Jen has drawn Kirsty to one side. She's scribbling down the addresses Kirsty's giving her, those of Belle and of Anna. I know that Kirsty will be curious, but I've told Jen to offer no explanation; it's bad enough having one of the two women I love involved in suspicious activities.

Jen has told me it won't be long until Belle's up on the stage, the role she's playing – Viola and her alter-ego disguise, Cesario – are involved throughout the play. She's right; the two characters Sir Toby and Sir Andrew are in conversation on the stage, John and Louis playing their parts with great physicality, Belle nodding her approval.

The costume mistress, red-haired Rachel, materialises at Belle's side, pushes her away to the side of the stage. Belle allows herself to be moved in this way, her entrance must be close.

There's no point in searching her bag in semi-darkness, I pick it up as if it's my own and head to the side of the cloisters. Jen's waiting for me, we go through the door into the dormitory. It's silent; no one is around.

'Got the addresses?' I ask, already looking through the bag as we head through into the car park.

'Of course. Though I had to resort to bribery and black-mail to persuade Kirsty to come up with the goods. And I could have saved you a job as well.'

'Good, honest, investigative techniques,' I tell her. 'The police use them all the time.' Despite my comments, I'm not really listening to what Jen's saying. Belle's bag contains too many compartments, and I have to investigate each of these to find the usual mixture of cosmetics and medicines, tampons, several condoms, two mobile phones, a purse containing little money. But no keys.

'Yeah,' Jen continues, noticing my abstraction, 'I threat-ened I'd tell you about her four-in-a-bed lesbian encounters. When that didn't work I told her you'd buy her a new car.'

'Good. Now where the hell are those keys?' I'm resort-ing to feeling the bag now, in case the keys have slipped into the lining somewhere.

'She also told me Belle's moved into one of the rooms here for the duration of the play, and she'd asked Kirsty to get her some things from the room. She gave Kirsty the keys. Kirsty still had them. She gave them to me. Here they are.' She dangles the keys in front of my nose. 'There's one that's obviously for her room here; I assume the others are for her house. Front door, back door, perhaps her bedroom door.' She looks more closely. 'There's one that could be for a bicycle lock, another might be for one of those kid's diaries or a jewellery box, you know, made of tin foil. Oh, and there's one labelled "drama" that would have saved us a few minutes getting into Taylor's office. Of course, if we'd had it then Belle wouldn't have been able to steal the money and the exam papers.'

'You could have told me,' I say, snatching them from her.

'You could have listened,' she replies. She hands me a slip of paper with two addresses on it. 'Belle lives quite close, her flat's just across the car park, walking distance. Anna's flat's a bit further away.'

'Sure you want to do this?' I ask.

'Sorry? I thought for a moment you said "Thank you Jen, well done, the addresses and the keys, what more could I want?" But perhaps I was mistaken.'

She isn't angry with me; Jen's simply reminding me of something I already know, that when my mind is focused on something, I tend to exclude all else from my thoughts. That includes good manners. 'Sorry,' I tell her, and mean it, 'thank you for everything.'

Jen knows that my words go beyond the acquisition of keys and addresses. She leans forward and kisses me. 'The answer is yes,' she whispers, her nose touching mine, 'I'm ready to go breaking and entering.'

'We'd better get a move on, then. Belle might want the keys back from Kirsty, I don't want to involve her any more than she is already.'

'I told her to say she'd put the keys back in the bag. You can always hide the bag somewhere, a place it'll eventually be found but only after a lot of searching.' Jen's face looks innocent, youthful; it's what attracted me to her in the first place. When I first met her I couldn't believe that someone who looked so young could be on the point of qualifying to be a doctor.

'You really are devious,' I tell her.

'You say the nicest things.'

After placing Belle's bag under a seat at the rear of the cloisters, I join Jen and together we search Belle's room in the dormitory. There's a small suitcase on the bed, the flimsiest key on the ring opens it, and it's clear that Belle hasn't begun unpacking yet. I run my hands through the contents, searching for anything that isn't fabric or cloth.

'Just don't start enjoying this,' Jen warns me, her voice soft and low in my ear. 'You're not old enough or dirty enough to start feeling young girls' knickers for kicks.'

I have to make an effort not to laugh; being a private detective shouldn't be this much fun. 'There's nothing there,' I whisper, making sure the top layer of clothes is as neat as when I found them. I lock the case. We look quickly round the room, but there's nothing untoward. I press my ear against the door, listen carefully and, when I hear nothing, open the door a fraction of an inch to confirm that no one's there. We hurry out into the car park and I give Jen the keys.

'You know the story,' I tell her, 'if anyone asks you why you're there ...'

'Billy, I'm a doctor. Not only do people trust me, but my profession makes me an expert at telling lies.'

'That doesn't reassure me. Got your mobile?'

Jen nods.

'Okay, keep it on, but set to vibrate. Open your address book to my mobile. If there's any trouble, all you need do is press the call button. If I answer and you don't say anything, I'll come running. Got it?'

'Loud and clear.'

'Let's go then. I'll drop you off at the door.'

'No, drop me off at the end of the road, it'll be less noticeable if anyone's watching.'

I have to admit that everything Jen says makes sense.

When Jen gets out of the van I have to make a real effort to drive away, even with her signalling that I should go. On occasions I've put friends like Norm and Sly – sometimes as employees, more often as willing volunteers – in potential danger. It's never been intentional, and they've always been aware of the risks of working for me and with me, but they have been in some precarious situations. Why, then, do I feel differently about Jen doing something comparatively straightforward? The answer is simple: Jen could have told me herself because it's something she'll already have considered. Someone killed Jonathan Taylor. That person is still on the loose. If it was Belle then she is, for the moment, tied up with other business. But it needed two people to move Taylor's body to the stage from wherever he was murdered, and the extra person could be watching Jen or me or even both of us. We could be in danger.

I persuade myself that two teenagers lounging on the street corner are just waiting for me to drive away before going to attack Jen. I force the thought from my mind, but it's replaced by the assumption that the driver of the car in front of me, suddenly braking and pulling into a parking space, has only one thing on his mind, and that is harming Jen. My brain feels divided in two, one half is urging me, logically, to get on with my part of the job, breaking into and searching Anna's flat; the other half is tormenting me with visions of what might happen – no, what is surely already happening – to Jen. I fish in my pocket, check that my phone is switched on; the glow is at least reassuring. Then my logical part begins its sweet-talking, sugar-tongued persuasion. The sooner I do my bit, it tells me, the sooner I'll be able to go back and help Jen. I shouldn't be thinking of going back; on the contrary, I should be urging myself forward, because speed is of the essence. I am, after all, more familiar than Jen with the art of searching rooms, I know how to do it, I know the shortcuts, I know what I can get away with. Calm descends. I begin to feel more purposeful, in control. That's when I turn the corner into the street where Anna's flat is situated.

Like most other streets in the area, it's dominated by student accommodation. The terraced flats have small courtyards at the front, these are occupied by dustbins and black plastic bags overflowing with beer bottles. The cars are old and shabby, several are clamped. Broken windows are boarded rather than repaired, through them I can see, where bright ceiling lights without lampshades permit it, postered walls and cluttered rooms. It's sultry weather, the heavy rain has dispersed and some of the low walls are decorated with young people drinking and smoking. It could be any student street in any student area in any university town anywhere in the country. But it isn't. Only here are all eyes turned in one direction. Because only here, near the top of the street, just where I figure Anna's flat ought to be, are a police car and van, lights flashing.

I could drive away. No one would notice. I could go and find Jen, help her, after all, I've been looking for excuses to do so. But I'm pig-headed, I've managed to redirect my resolve and the police's presence only serves as an extra motivator. Theirs must be a random search whereas mine is focused, I know what I'm looking for. They have no right to be there, while I'm about to find clues that will help me solve a crime. They're probably stomping around with their huge policeman feet, muddying the waters; I, on the other hand, will be able to tread lightly and softly in my deft and delicate search for evidence.

Both police vehicles are marked, the van is forensic, the car probably belongs to a door-stopper. None of the plods I've talked to, not even Arnison or Stephenson, is likely to be there. This is routine, humdrum work, it's been passed down the line and these poor devils have been hauled out on overtime to give the place the once-over. In times like this stealth can be invaluable. It is, however, a commodity I've never possessed, so I'll have to rely instead on brazen cheek.

I pull the van up beside the police car, take a clipboard from the dashboard and push Anna's address under the fastener; I also push a battery-powered movement sensor into my pocket. Even as I climb out, the plod in front of the door is moving towards me.

'I'm sorry, sir,' he says, 'you can't leave your van . . .'

'Look, sunshine, less of your fake politeness with me. I'm not in the best of moods, I was comfy in bed with the missus, early night and all that, when I get a call to come out here.' I flash the board at him, just long enough for him to catch a glimpse of the address. 'I don't know how you've managed it, you being experts and all, but you've set off the burglar alarm of one Anna Peranski.'

'We're busy searching the property . . .'

'I can see what you're doing, sunshine, but my boss's message board is flashing like St Mary's Island lighthouse. Now every time one of my boss's alarms goes off, your boss,' I pretend to examine the clipboard again, 'Sergeant Stephenson, raises bloody hell with him. "It's a nuisance," he says. "It's disturbing the peace," he says. "Get somebody round to switch the bloody thing off!" No matter that some glue-sniffing little yob's tried to break in, might even still be inside the building, it's "Switch the fucker off!"'

'I don't see what this has to do with . . .'

'I'll tell you what it is to do with the price of parsnips! This time, it's your fault. You've set the bloody alarm off, my boss has already been in touch with this Stephenson *and* with his boss, what's his name, Arnison, and my instructions are to get round here and switch the bloody thing off. Now!'

The plod's not sure what to do. 'Do you have any form of identification?' he asks.

'Identification? Look at the sodding van, sunshine, it's got "Oliphant Security Services" written all over it! I've got my driving licence with the same name on it, that should be proof enough. But if it's too much for you to understand, I'll go away. My boss will ring the chairman of the police authority – who's probably also in bed, where I ought to be, with his rather attractive young wife – and complain. And whose head will be on the block? Yours.'

The plod is nothing more than a gate-keeper. It's not his job to field awkward, antagonistic men who threaten him with the names of people he recognises and who would be annoyed if he didn't do the 'right thing'. The trouble is, his training hasn't told him what the right thing is in these circumstances. So he does what any good policeman does; he passes the buck.

'Hello,' he says, pressing the button on his radio, 'I've a security man down here who says you've set off one of his alarms. He wants to come in and switch it off.' He waits for a response. 'They say they haven't heard any alarm.'

By this time the plod has backed himself to the open door. Inside there's a corridor, I can see no one inside.

'Of course they haven't heard an alarm,' I tell him, 'it's meant to be ...' Inside I can see a figure in a white suit. I raise my voice to a shout. 'Of course you haven't heard an alarm, it's meant to be silent. That way the burglars don't get away!'

The figure inside walks toward the door and peers out at me. He's a tired-looking young man with stubble on his chin to match the shorn hair on his head. He's small, shrunken, only the luxurious growth of his eyebrows suggests any vibrancy about him. He sees the sign-written van. He scratches his head, this is something new for him. He's on the dog-shift, obviously inexperienced; he knows this isn't a crime scene, he's just on a routine search. He considers the options. 'Okay,' he motions wearily to the plod, 'would you mind getting him some overalls and slippers.' He looks at me. 'You can come in. You find the sensor, you switch it off, then you leave. Got it?'

'I don't want to stay any longer than I have to,' I tell him. 'Anyway, what're you looking for? Somebody lost their keys?'

He closes his eyes as if he's trying to keep his temper, opens them again to stare at me. I offer some conciliation. 'Seriously. I mean, it's not as if you've got the road blocked and the sub-machine guns out, there's no sniffer dogs, just you and the doorman. Is it something important?'

The forensic officer relaxes a little, stretches and yawns. 'Wish I knew,' he says, shaking his head in an attempt to disperse his lethargy. 'Somebody's up on a murder charge, the evidence is fairly conclusive, they tell me. This is insurance. Look through the suspect's house, see if there's anything to strengthen the case.'

I take the white suit from the plod and step into it, pull it up, over and on, zip it up. 'What, you mean like a pool of blood in the middle of the carpet? Body parts in the freezer?'

'Subtlety isn't actually one of your strengths, is it? Put the slippers on over your shoes, I don't think a hat'll be necessary.' He inspects me and nods his approval. 'Right, don't touch anything unless I say you can.'

'You been through all the rooms?' I ask.

'No, we only arrived fifteen minutes ago, time for a look round, nothing more. But I don't think there'll be anything. If they really wanted the place turning over they'd have sent a whole team. Anyway, you get a sort of feel for these things. There's no bad vibe here.' He holds open the door to what must be Anna's room and ushers me in.

'Bad vibe?' I query. 'What's a bad vibe?'

'Oh, just a feeling.' Forensic's warming to his task now, he's not really searching the flat, he's explaining his holistic theory of investigation. 'You know how some places feel bad? Evil? I mean, I was once wandering round an abbey – well, the ruins of an abbey, to be precise – and I had this feeling, a sort of uneasiness.'

'Bad vibes?'

'Exactly. I said as much to my girlfriend. She had the guidebook with her, she was reading it and a few minutes later she said the place where I felt the bad vibes was where a monk was walled up, alive, back in the fifteenth century.'

'Wow. So do you get that feeling with your work as well?' While Forensic's expounding his theories and experiences I'm looking around. The room's a mess. The floor is covered with a haphazard mixture of clothes, books, CDs and newspapers. The bed in the corner is untidy, unmade. In an alcove beside the fireplace a desk is occupied by a large, squat, old-fashioned computer and printer; they're disappearing beneath a detritus of crumpled paper, it's as if a stationery tree has deposited its entire autumn of white A4 leaves over the desk top. There are books and files fighting for space on the shelves above. Candles in various degrees of decay occupy other flat surfaces, mugs half-filled with skin-topped tea or coffee are guarding the floor. Empty beer and spirit bottles lurch drunkenly against each other. There's a smell of unwashed bodies, nothing too serious, nothing that couldn't be cured by opening the windows for a few hours.

'... and as soon as I came in here I knew nothing unpleasant had happened. Anyway, like I said, I'm just the insurance; I'm to give it a quick once-over, a look-round.' He points to the bed. 'I'll probably end up bagging the quilt and the sheets, take them away to examine them for blood or semen stains.' He seems pleased to have an audience. 'Two main types of bottle, beer ...' He bends down and tenderly picks up a bottle. 'Expensive import, high alcohol content, not normally a girly drink. And alcopops, some vodka and gin. Might suggest she's been entertaining a man or men, so I'll take all the bottles and test for fingerprints, saliva on the rim might give us some DNA.'

Despite his youth and his somewhat unusual empathic approach to his job, Forensic isn't going to be an easy touch. It's going to be difficult to inspect or remove anything while he's there, and there's so much paper lying around. If I was Anna, where would I put my marked essays?

'So where's the sensor?' Forensic asks. 'Don't you normally put them up in the corner of the room?'

'First of all,' I say, playing for time, 'is this the right room? There are probably a few students sharing, is this definitely Anna Peranski's room?'

Forensic nods. 'I checked, her name's on some of the folders on the shelves, and there's a pile of unopened bills in the corner. It's her room all right. So where's the sensor?'

'Unfortunately I didn't install it,' I explain. 'I don't even know the type. But we've got some new ones came on the market about six months ago, that's when her contract began. They work on average ambient temperature increase, and they don't have to be placed on a wall. In fact, the manufacturers recommend they be placed low down on the floor.' I let my eyes skim the room. 'This one could be anywhere.'

'No cable?'

'Battery powered. And the signal is radio boosted. It's the future of intruder detection.'

'Ah, but do they work?' Forensic asks. He too is looking round the room, searching for any piece of plastic that could be masquerading as a sensor.

'They work,' I tell him. 'After all, I'm here as a result of this one working.'

Forensic can't contradict the obvious. 'So now what?'

'I find the sensor and reset it, or remove it. It must be somewhere in the room. Can I move things?'

Forensic looks doubtful. 'How big is it? What does it look like?'

'It's just like the normal type of sensor, white plastic, flashing red light, you know the sort of thing. You'd recognise it if you saw it.' Forensic still isn't sure whether he should allow me to move anything. He needs a little persuasion. 'You said yourself the place had no bad vibes, and I can see what you mean.'

'You can?' He seems surprised.

'Yeah. Well, not so much see as feel. Nothing unpleasant happened here. It's just some kid's dirty room. Could belong to anyone. It's ordinary.'

'That's just the way I feel. I'm glad you can sense it as well, everybody else I talk to thinks ...' He tails off.

'They're narrow-minded, that's their problem. Unwilling to listen to anyone who's a little different.'

'Exactly!' Even his eyebrows seem to cheer up, rise a little up his forehead.

'I'll tell you what,' I say, determined to keep him on my side, 'I know you don't want to be here longer than necessary. There must be a kitchen and a common room you need to check out as well. I'll work round the perimeter here, you can sort through the other rooms. I'll just pick stuff up then put it back till I find what I want.'

He wants to trust me. He wants to do the minimum amount of work necessary then get away. All it needs is that little bit of extra subliminal influence on my part. 'This is not the 'droid you seek,' I want to whisper, 'you can allow him to search the room without you being present.' My Jedi abilities are, alas, under-developed. After careful thought Forensic comes to a compromise. 'Many hands,' he announces. 'We'll start here, by the door, one goes clockwise, the other anti-clockwise. If either of us finds anything interesting, we call the other across. That way we both benefit.'

'Sounds fair,' I reply, 'but check shelves and ledges as well. This little beaut isn't big.' I bend down to look along the wall leading to the desk, that's the most likely place for Anna to have left her essays and I want to be the one heading in that direction. Forensic tosses me a pair of gloves, cautious to the end, he doesn't want any extra fingerprints on anything. Then he turns his attention to the mess on his side of the room.

We work silently, though I move more quickly then my new friend. I have the advantage of having, in my pocket, the device we're meant to be searching for; and I know exactly what I'm really looking for. I sift quickly through discarded underwear and girls' magazines, junk-mail, an occasional text book (I check within in case my essay is hidden in the pages), even a dirty plate with hardened gravy and the emaciated petrified crust of a pie. Soon I'm at the desk and standing upright; Forensic, still at floor level, looks jealously over his shoulder but says nothing.

'Is it okay to look behind some of these files?' I ask. 'The sensor could be on one of the shelves.'

269

'As long as everything goes back where it was,' comes the reply, 'it's okay with me.'

The first folder contains notes in a scrawling, untidy hand. The ink is in a variety of colours, there are few headings or sub-headings. The whole points to a lack of organisation which seems likely to make this task even more difficult than I'd anticipated. There's the added problem that Forensic might, at this very moment, be looking at and discarding the very piece of paper I need. I put the thought away, press on.

The second file contains bills, demands for payment, threats of court action. The third is a box file with the heading 'essays', but even as I lift it triumphantly from the shelf I know it's too light; inspection confirms that it's empty.

'The art lies,' Forensic tells me, 'in maintaining a detached interest. You don't really want to look at everything in detail, you don't want to read every piece of paper, but you need to be aware of what it is you have in your hands.' He's clearly warming to his task and to me, his new best friend. 'I like to describe it as an intellectual squint. Remember those 3D pictures that were so fashionable about ten years ago, where you had to train your eyes to see beyond the surface? That's what this type of search is like. I mean, yes, we know we're looking for something specific. But we have to watch out for something new as well, something that could be a vital piece of evidence.'

'I know exactly what you mean.' The next folder contains what looks like a play, or a part of a play, the title page announces that it's 'The Seductress, by Anna Peranski'. I replace it without reading any of it.

The shelves above seem to contain only books, both novels and works of reference. I ignore them, turn my attention to the desk top. On moving an old newspaper aside I find an ashtray; I bend down to sniff it. 'This any use to you?' I ask. 'Smells like a particularly aromatic tobacco.'

270

Forensic comes across. 'Cannabis,' he says. 'Doesn't really mean anything. In fact, I would have been surprised if we hadn't found any. Still, might as well bag it. Ordinary fags as well, filters with lipstick on the butts, and some non-filters without.' He takes some clear plastic bags from his pockets and, using a pair of tweezers, sorts the contents of the ashtray into three bags. 'It's arbitrary, of course. There could have been six or seven people contributing to this. But it'll keep the lab boys busy.' He adds the ashtray itself to a larger bag and labels them, places them all in a red bin bag and puts it outside the door. 'Well spotted. Keep your eyes open.' With that praise we return to our respective searches.

I find nothing else of interest on the desk top, nor in the drawers beneath. I have no option but to head for the bedside table, and Forensic is already running his hand beneath the bed. Perhaps Anna didn't keep her essays. Perhaps she saved them all up then ceremoniously burnt them at the end of each year. Then the word hits me. 'Saved.' Perhaps she just saved them on her computer.

It's something I have to pursue, but how? I've no reason for wanting to turn on the computer, let alone search the files, and Forensic is unlikely to allow me to remain in the room without him also being there. Then I have an idea. It's ridiculous, far-fetched, but I can't think of anything better.

I bend down, take the sensor from my pocket and place it on the floor beside the desk, under a pair of faded and torn jeans. I move them aside. 'There you are, you little bugger,' I say, stand up, still holding the jeans, and motion for Forensic to come across.

'Is that it?' he asks, unimpressed by the small plastic box, red light flashing a semaphore of welcome.

'That's it. The user has an electronic key that switches it on and off, but I should be able to over-ride it. Do you mind?'

'Be my guest,' he says, curious to see what's involved.

I take a screwdriver from my pocket and, with a few deft turns, am able to remove the cover. Inside there's a jumble of wires and circuitry; it means nothing to me.

'That's the most important part,' I say, pointing to a transistor attached to a small circuit board, 'that's the temperature monitor. It measures and records the changes in temperature and, if there's anything different to what's stored in its memory, it switches on the alarm. Someone coming into a room, for example, has a different temperature gradient signature to central heating switching itself on, or even a television being left on.'

'I see,' Forensic says knowingly.

'Now if I just close this circuit here,' I bridge the gap between two pieces of exposed wiring, 'the signal should be switched off.' I turn my attention to the red light which, I'm pleased to see, is still alive and flashing despite my playing with the sensor's intestines. 'Except it's not. It's still transmitting.'

'Why's that?'

'I don't know. At least, not for certain. But I've seen something similar in the past where the triggering system has been altered by some piece of electrical equipment close at hand. The only thing I can think of is this.' I point in the general direction of the computer. 'Do you mind if I try it out?' Without waiting for an answer I switch it on.

'I don't suppose there'll be a problem . . .'

'Good. Now then, if you watch the red light, you might see its pattern change when the computer gets into gear.'

We both stare at the light; it keeps on sending the same regular emission every few seconds.

'The only other thing it can be,' I announce, 'is the connection to the printer. Here, you hold that, tell me straightaway if there's any change.' I hand the sensor to Forensic and face the screen. The operating system is, I'm pleased to see, as ancient as the computer itself. There's no need for a password, the machine is little more than a word processor; a list of folders appears on the screen in front of

272

me. I click on the one called 'essays', a further list appears. They're numbered from one to nine but not named. I try to remember the approximate dates of the missing essays, they were late in the year but not at the end; and the subject matter was Brecht and the alienation effect. I open number nine, it's about Stanislavski. 'Any change?' I ask.

Forensic is still staring at the light. 'Looks the same to me.'

'I'll have to print something out, something about the right length. Here, give me back the sensor, can you put some paper in the printer and switch it on?' While Forensic does exactly as he's asked, I open file eight; it seems to be about *A Midsummer Night's Dream*. I close it, head for file seven. It flicks open. My eyes catch the magic words 'Brecht' and 'alienation effect'.

'Sorted,' Forensic announces. I give the appropriate instruction and the printer drones into action. Forensic's attention is drawn to the machine and the text; I take the opportunity to flick the battery out of the sensor and into my hand.

'Yes,' I hiss triumphantly, 'look!' I hold up the sensor to Forensic's gaze; the red light is no longer flashing.

'So what does that mean?' he asks.

'The sensor was working all right, that's why it detected your presence. But the radio switch had been affected by the printer signal, that's why I couldn't switch it off manually. Still, it's sorted now.' I begin to put the sensor away in my pocket, then stop. 'You don't need this as evidence, do you?'

Forensic shakes his head. 'I don't think it'll be material to the case. But then, I don't think anything much here will be.'

All I need now is the essay, resting tantalisingly close in the printer's tray. 'Thank you for your help,' I say ingratiatingly, 'I don't know how I would have managed without you. It's not very often you meet someone in public service who's so sympathetic.'

When Forensic smiles, his eyebrows perform a little excited shiver of joy. 'Glad to have been of service.' I'm just about to reach across him when he anticipates my move, picks up the essay and begins to read it. 'Seems quite a clever lass, does our Anna. This little lot doesn't mean a thing to me. The alienation effect. Is that something to do with Sigourney Weaver?'

'I've no idea,' I answer, feigning a lack of interest.

Forensic folds the essay in two and reaches into his pocket. I think he's going to put the essay into a plastic bag, instead he brings out a handkerchief and blows his nose. 'Sorry,' he apologises, 'bit of a cold coming on.' He puts the handkerchief away, looks again at the folded essay in his hands.

'Want me to get rid of that?' I ask.

'Would you mind?' He hands me the paper.

'No problem,' I say, trying not to show how relieved I am, how pleased I am to receive this gift. 'Is there anything I can do to help you?'

'No, it's okay, thanks. What would my bosses say, letting amateurs onto the scene? No, I'll just bag up some more key pieces. I've already videoed the place as back-up, so I'll make my report then be away.'

He guides me to the door and even allows me to keep the white overalls 'as a souvenir'. As I drive away he's waving. It's like saying goodbye to an eccentric relative. My emerging smile is stillborn as I feel the vibration of the phone in my pocket. I struggle to get it out, press the answer button.

'Jen? Are you okay?'

'I'm all right, Billy, calm down. But I think you'd better get round here. There's something you might want to see.'

It takes five minutes to get to Belle's flat. I can't park outside, there's no space, and much of that time is taken up with walking quickly, breathlessly, the few hundred yards to the door. I push it gently, it opens to reveal Jen

274

standing behind. She holds up her finger to her lips, leads me up some stairs. I can hear a television behind one of the doors we pass, the next door is open and Jen pulls me inside. When the door is closed she switches on the light.

'This is Belle's room,' she announces.

The contrast with Anna's room couldn't be greater. There's the same amount of furniture, even a similar layout, but everything is tidy, clean, ordered and efficient. The posters on the walls are of plays from a wide range of theatres. On top of a chest of drawers there are several framed photographs of family and friends. On the bed (the quilt cover is neatly arranged, its trailing edge parallel to the floor) a well-mannered Winnie-the-Pooh pyjama case stares at me, as if to tell me that no one of my gender is ever welcome in *his* bed.

'Did you find the essay?' I whisper.

Jen nods. 'In the folder marked "essays", in date order. It took me about three minutes. And you?'

'It took me a bit longer.' I pull out the crumpled sheets from my pocket while Jen hands me three unfolded pieces of paper. Belle prefers her own handwriting to the mechanical labouring of a printer, but her letters are pristine and legible. I compare the first sentences; they're identical. As are the second and the third.

Jen has been looking over my shoulder, she reads faster than me. 'It looks like the same essay to me.'

I check the endings. 'I agree.'

'So what does it mean?'

'Anna copied from Belle. Plagiarism disqualifies the plagiarist from a degree, but it can also do the same for the plagiarised if it's with her consent. We know Anna didn't kill Taylor. Taylor had the essays in his safe, he must have considered them valuable for some reason. He wouldn't have wanted to jeopardise the production, so he was going to reveal the truth later. Belle tried to blackmail him – hence the money in the safe – and when she found out he wasn't going to bite, she killed him. It all fits.'

'That's not all that fits. I might have the missing piece of your jigsaw.' Jen switches off the light and opens the curtains. Belle's room is at the rear of the building and, although it's now dark outside, there's a lamp in the lane at the rear of the house. It shines into a yard and, in that yard, squeezed beside two brick-built stores that were originally an outside toilet and a coalhouse, is a rusty old Ford Escort van. Jen closes the curtains again. 'I had some spare time,' she says, 'and there were several more keys than I needed to get in. I went exploring. Come on.' She takes me to the rear of the house, past another bedroom and a toilet-cum-bathroom, through a communal kitchen and down some stairs. At the bottom a door leads into the yard.

'It was just curiosity,' she explains, 'but look what I found.' She takes me round to the rear of the van. 'Look at the rust,' she says. The wheel arches are indeed rusty, bubbles of red oxide penetrating the white paint. The doors are just as rusty, and trails of red lead down over the paint-work at the bottom corners and middle of the doors where they meet, just behind the rear bumper.

'It was still light when I came down before,' Jen explains. 'It looked different then, it looked wrong. So I brought this.' She brings a small torch from her pocket, shines it straight at the marks.

'It doesn't look like rust,' I say, bending down to examine the marks more closely, 'it's the wrong colour, and it's just lying on the surface.'

'It's not rust,' Jen says. 'It's blood.'

I raise myself, my knees complain with a cracking sound. 'Are you sure?'

'I've seen quite a bit of blood in my time, Billy. It's diluted, but it's blood.'

My mind's jumping ahead. Jen's already had time to think this through. I let her continue, any questions I have can wait until later.

'That's not all,' she says. 'Look behind you.' She turns to one of the two outhouses, it has a padlock on it. 'One of

276

the keys opens that lock. Again, I was curious. I had some spare time.' She fiddles with a key, opens the lock and removes it from the staple, swings back the hasp, opens the door. 'I didn't want to bring this out in case it might be used as evidence, what do you think?' She shines the torch on an old mattress; it's stained with red; even I can see that it's blood.

'It's damp,' Jen says, 'the whole mattress is damp. It's as if someone's tried to clean it but hasn't succeeded and has given up.'

'Shit!'

'Yeah, that's what I thought. Belle, or Belle and her friend, entice Taylor into the back of the van. They kill him, but there's blood everywhere. They hose him down, can't do anything with the mattress so they hide it, try to clean the van.'

I decide to add my own thoughts. 'But there are lots of little nooks and crannies in a van. It takes a while for the diluted blood to appear, and when it does there's no one to see it, no one to wipe it away.'

We stand in silence. A moth flutters around the street-lamp, the beat of its wings overpowering the gentle buzz of electricity. The faint smell of honeysuckle, perhaps from a pot in a neighbouring yard, dances in front of us.

'I don't suppose,' I ask, 'that one of the keys on the ring would open the door?'

'It doesn't look like it,' Jen says, examining the keys in her hand. 'None of them is a car key.'

'I'll have to resort to other techniques, then,' I tell her. First of all I try the doors, there's a faint possibility that one of them will be open, but examination proves that the odds were too long.

'Coat-hanger?' Jen asks.

'You've been watching too many crime films. I don't suppose you have one hidden about your person?'

'No, but there's one here.' She bends down and reaches below the car, produces a long piece of metal that might

277

once have been a coat-hanger. 'I tried the locks before you arrived, then I thought I might be able to get in myself. I went back inside and brought this. I didn't have any luck, though.'

I take the metal coat-hanger from her. 'It's not just luck,' I tell her, 'it's practice and experience. Watch.' I move to the driver's door, that's always used most on any car and the seal between door and frame is most likely to be worn and pliable. I twist the end of the coat-hanger into a hook that's almost an oval then push it between the door and the rubber seal; it passes through easily. I manoeuvre the hook down towards the lock button and pull it back so it captures the button itself. A sharp pull back locks it into position; a similar pull up and the lock's disengaged. I open the door.

'Wow,' Jen says, 'I'm impressed. That took about thirty seconds.'

'It's a good job the van's old, more modern vehicles don't have this type of lock. But if you've got the right sets of master keys, you can get into most cars, even the top range ones.' I put on a pair of rubber gloves, pull open the door and climb into the driver's seat, look around. It's easy to see onto the floor, the seat's pulled right back, but there's nothing there. I lean across to the passenger's seat, open the door and Jen climbs in; she too has put on a pair of gloves. She opens the glove box.

'Nothing there,' she says. 'But the smell from the back is typical – dried blood, I'd recognise it anywhere.' We both turn to look behind us. I'd normally expect to find the rear of any van boarded out with plywood, but this one has had the boards removed. The light from Jen's torch shows the corrugated floor of the van is white, too white.

I kneel on the seat and examine the floor further; there's no dust, none of the rubbish that should be there. 'It looks as if it's been cleaned, probably with a hose.'

'But not cleaned well enough.' Jen points to the wheel arches where the ribs of the floor end. There's a thin film of brown there, it looks almost like diluted paint. 'Whoever hosed the van down probably did it at night, they must have missed this patch.'

'Is it blood?' I ask, wanting to be convinced.

'I don't have my testing kit with me, Billy. But it looks like blood to me. And the smell, the smell's definitely blood. It's probably pooled in one of the cavities under the floor. What else is it likely to be?'

There's a metallic odour in the air, a scent of decay familiar to me. I decide Jen's right.

'Okay, so this is what happened. Someone – and it looks as if that someone's Belle – enticed Taylor into the van . . .'

'Hold on,' Jen protests, 'how do you entice someone into the back of a van? "Come into my van, have sex!" How would Belle get Taylor into the van?'

'Jen, he was a man with a high sex drive. "Come and have kinky sex on a mattress in the back of a van" is probably the line that would appeal to him most. Especially if he'd had too much to drink.'

'Go on then.'

'She gets him into the van, wherever it is, probably parked outside the university.' I think back to arriving and then moving my own van, but I can't remember seeing this old Escort. 'Perhaps she's decided to kill him because she knows he's found the similarity between her essay and Anna's. Perhaps he's blackmailing her, that's why he's got money in his safe. Whatever the reason, she kills him. With some help . . .'

Jen can't help interrupting, 'Whose help?'

'I don't know yet. But whoever it was, helped her put the body on the stage, then drove the van away and cleaned it while Belle began to frame Anna. Any problems with that?'

Jen's thinking, and I don't interrupt her. 'It might work. There are questions of timing, working out who the other person is, but . . . It hangs together well enough. So what do we do now?'

'I think we have to involve the police. But . . . This is strong evidence, but there are still too many unknowns.

279

There's not actually any evidence linking Belle to the murder, just a series of coincidences. Perhaps ...'

'Perhaps what?'

'You said you found the essay easily, then you found the van and looked at it. You didn't search Belle's room, did you?'

'No,' Jen shakes her head, 'it wasn't part of my instructions.'

'I'm not criticising you,' I say, in case it appears that I am, 'you've done well to get this stuff. I don't think I would have found the van and, if I had, I wouldn't have been able to identify the blood. But we might be able to find some more specific evidence if we look upstairs. Then we ring the police.'

'You're the expert, Sherlock,' Jen concedes. 'I'm just your humble Dr Watson.'

'Let's go, then.' We climb out of the van. Close the doors as quietly as possible (though the only room directly overlooking the yard is Belle's) and head back into the house. We're just at the foot of the stairs when the front door opens and noisy voices proclaim the arrival of some of the house's other occupants. There's not enough time for us to hide, we'd be seen running upstairs; there's only one further option. I'll have to say that we're friends of Belle's, we've come to pick up something for the play that she left behind. That's it, we'll brazen it out with a lie. I don't have time, however, to put my plan into operation. Jen pushes me against the wall and kisses me. She pulls my hands onto her buttocks and begins to move against me, her hair's hiding my face and she's making sounds that show she's enjoying herself. The voices cease, but the footsteps continue.

'Sorry to interrupt,' says a girl's voice.

'Yeah, don't mind us,' adds another.

'Enjoy yourselves,' suggests a third, deeper, a male voice. The owners of the commentary shuffle past us and into the kitchen. Jen waits for the door to shut then separates herself from me.

'What . . ?'

'Upstairs, Billy, before they come back.'

I head upwards, protesting as I go. 'What was that all about? I had things under control, I knew what I was going to do.'

'You've never been a student, Billy, I have.' Jen's following close behind. 'Students might be worried by a strange couple in their house, if they weren't they'd certainly remember us, no matter what your excuse.'

'Yeah, I suppose so.'

'But a couple having sex on the stairs? That's reasonably commonplace, and the reaction's to look away or to look closely. But the one thing they won't have seen is our faces.'

We arrive in front of Belle's door. 'Yes,' I say, 'I suppose you're right.'

'And anyway, it was more enjoyable than listening to you making a feeble excuse. Should we go inside?' She opens the door.

'Where do we start, then? What are we looking for?' Jen seems keen to begin the search.

'Clues, evidence, anything that might link Belle to the murder.'

'Or that might link her to the cover-up, or even to blaming Anna.'

'Quite.'

We both move at the same time, Jen heads for the wardrobe while I go to the dressing table and its drawers. Either of us stands an equal chance of success. I begin at the bottom where T-shirts are folded neatly, ironed to perfection, on one side; several pullovers and sweatshirts occupy the other half of the drawer. There's a fragrant scent of artificial flowers, Belle obviously uses fabric softener. I run my fingers around and between each piece of clothing, not wishing to disturb them but making sure there's nothing hidden. The next drawer contains bras and briefs (nothing outrageous, a sea of sensible white save for two or three islands of black lace), coloured socks adding some character, tights in conservative tan. The top drawer reveals perfume and deodorant, some necklaces and other jewellery, tampons and paracetamols, contraceptive pills. 'I'm having no luck,' I tell Jen, 'how about you?'

'Nothing yet. Boring middle-aged clothing, long items on the left, short on the right, some coats, jackets and blouses. Shoes on the bottom, a few boxes with, let me see, ornaments, official documents – do you want me to check them through?'

'Might as well, there might be something important in there.'

'Here you are then, since you've finished the drawers.' She hands me a cardboard box, I take the lid off and place it on the bed.

'There's a plastic bag here,' Jen continues, 'bet there's nothing interesting in it.'

I'm leafing my way through photographs of Belle and her friends, Belle and her family, Belle on the stage, no one I recognise save for Belle herself. Beneath those there's a small bundle of letters in their envelopes, no more than three or four, tied with a red ribbon. I'm examining the knot, making sure that, when I untie it, I'll be able to tie it again in the same manner. I don't get that far.

'Billy,' Jen says, her voice taut, 'I think you'd better look at this.'

I put down the letters. Jen's holding out the bag to me, whatever's inside must be heavy, the bag is weighed down. I peer into it. There's a mess of electric blue.

'Good evidence?' Jen whispers.

I say nothing. I'm still wearing my rubber gloves, I reach into the bag and take out a blue wig. 'Looks convincing to me,' I smile back at Jen.

Jen's still holding the bag out to me. 'There's more,' she says.

I take the bag from her, remove another piece of fabric, again woven with blue threads of what appears to be nylon,

282

though shorter than that of the wig. I hold it up. 'What on earth is that for?' There are two pieces of elastic holding it all together and I tease them open. The material is a simple triangle, the fibres are coarse and curled and died a similar colour to those in the other wig; there are two loops of thin elastic, flesh coloured, each running from an upper corner to the lower point.

Jen stares, then her eyes open wide and she begins to giggle.

'What is it?' I ask. 'What's the matter?'

Jen raises her hands to her mouth. 'I don't believe it,' she says, 'I think it's . . .'

'What? What is it?'

'I think it's a merkin.' She begins to laugh again, then checks herself. 'I'm sorry, I shouldn't laugh, this is serious.'

I'm becoming impatient. 'So tell me, what's a merkin?'

Jen calms herself down. 'It's a wig,' she explains, 'but not for the head. It's for people – normally women – to wear between their legs. It's a pubic wig.'

'But why . . ?'

'They were common in the seventeenth century, women, especially prostitutes, wore them. They were for ornamentation, they would be made in fancy colours, but they could also hide disease or even deformity.' Jen pokes it gingerly. 'Looks bloody uncomfortable to me,' she announces, 'it's obviously been made by an amateur, that elastic would dig into your thighs.'

'I don't think it was designed for comfort,' I tell her, 'it's purely for disguise; someone wanted to be mistaken for Anna.'

'I can see that, but it's not something you throw together on the off chance that you might use it. If Belle wanted to frame Anna then she must have planned the whole thing in advance. And that includes killing Taylor.'

That makes things more awkward. Premeditation means that Belle is even more dangerous than I suspected, and even as Jen and I are searching her room, she's at large with, amongst others, my daughter. I feel an urge to be away from here, to confront her, to make sure she's locked up so that everyone else is safe. But there's more to be done.

The bag still contains a piece of wood or metal, it's certainly quite heavy. I reach inside and reveal what lies within: a knife. It's a similar size to that found in Taylor's body, but its shape is entirely different. Its handle as well as its blade is made of steel, there's no embellishment, no decoration. I bend closer to examine it in greater detail. 'Shine your torch on it,' I say to Jen, 'look at it closely. Can you see any blood on it?'

We bend almost double, subject the weapon to the closest possible inspection. Jen's the first to surrender. 'I can't see any blood,' she says, 'I can't see any marks at all.'

'It looks as if it's been wiped clean,' I acknowledge, 'but it's been well looked after in the first place. There's no dirt or grime, no blemish. And it's an unusual design, I haven't seen anything like it before.'

'It's a knife, Billy. They're used for cutting things or for sticking in things, it could be a fisherman's knife or a hunter's knife, it could be for skinning animals. Its design isn't really important, its purpose isn't important, could it have been used to kill Jonathan Taylor?'

I look more closely still. The edges and point of the blade have the scuff marks I associate with sharpening and honing, they seem functionally sharp, razored. 'Yes,' I say, surprised at how weary my voice sounds, 'I think this knife could be used to kill.'

'Is this enough evidence? Do we have enough motivation?' Jen sounds tired as well.

'I think so.'

'So what happens now?'

'We tell the police what we've found. I can't think what else we can do. We have to let them know.'

Jen's already reaching for her mobile. 'I'd better ring

284

them, since I'm the one who found the van.'

'No.' I take the phone from her hand. 'No, first we make sure there's no trace of you being here. Are you sure no one saw you coming in?'

'No, apart from when we were on the stairs, but ...'

'No buts, Jen, I'm in charge now and you do as I say. You've had nothing to do with this. I'm a former police-man, I've a PI licence, I'm already involved in this. That gives me a reason for taking investigations further, even if I've been warned off. There's not a lot the police can do, apart from stamp their feet and yell. But you have a lot more to lose. So you do as you're told.'

'Okay.' Jen's accession is too easy, too quick.

'Promise!'

'I promise. Don't you trust me?'

'In everything but this, I trust you.'

'You have no choice but to take my word.'

She's right, as usual. 'In that case, I trust you.'

'So do you ring them from here?'

'I suppose so. They'd probably be annoyed if I told them I'd found all this wonderful evidence, then mentioned that I'd actually found it hours before and was only telling them after I'd left the scene. They might charge me with subvert-ing the cause of justice. But I do think you ought to leave. I want you away from here, back at the cloisters, before I ring. Do you think they'll be finished their rehearsals yet?'

Jen looks at her watch. 'It's after eleven. I suppose it depends on how much of a slave-driver Belle is.'

'If that's the deciding factor, they'll still be at it. Come on, I'll drop you off then come back.' My wish to return Jen to the university isn't purely due to my kind nature, and we both know that. Jen's stubborn, despite her promise that she wouldn't get involved once the police arrive, she wants to make sure that I'll be okay; returning her to the univer-sity won't guarantee that she'll stay there, but it'll help. And if I can't get Kirsty away from what might be a dangerous situation, having Jen there to look after my

285

daughter helps alleviate my fears.

I put everything back where it was and check the room to make sure there's no sign we've been there. Then we leave. It's raining steadily, another excuse to drive Jen back to the university; we walk back to the van with our arms round each other.

'It looks as if it'll soon be over,' Jen says, pulling me closer.

'What, the rain?'

'No, the rain's set in. And anyway, it always rains somewhere, every day. Someone always gets wet.'

I think she's talking metaphors now. I try to make my own contribution. 'But it's amazing how often some people, usually the same people, manage to stay dry, and some people are guaranteed to get wet.'

'Perhaps the dry people have a monopoly on umbrellas. Or they might have stolen the wet people's umbrellas.'

'Or they could be sheltering behind the wet people, or under the wet people's coats. Using them.'

It's raining even more heavily now. Neither of us have coats. The road is becoming an oily reflection of amber street-lights, the water's dribbling down my nose and the back of my neck. When I look at Jen I can see that even her curls are becoming flattened, sticking to her face. She burrows into me for warmth.

'I don't think I want to be a dry person,' Jen says. 'I'd rather be wet. Facing up to what's thrown at me. I don't want to use other people to shelter me. I'm a wet person at heart.'

The imagery is beginning to get too complicated for me, I'm more concerned with practicalities. 'You'll be even wetter by the time we get to the van. I think we'd better run.' We break into an ungainly trot, arms still round each other, as the rain rebounds from the hissing pavement. As soon as we climb into the van the windows begin to mist up, when I switch the engine on, put the fan onto full, the blown air slowly forces a curve of clarity onto the windscreen.

286

'I think the rehearsal will be over,' I tell Jen.

'It'll be over for good in a few hours.' She begins to sing. '"With a hey-ho, the wind and the rain; but that's all one, our play is done." Sad, so sad.' She subsides into her own reflections as I drive the short distance back to the university.

Chapter Eleven

I park the van in its allotted space and accompany Jen into the halls, curious to find out what's going on before I return to Belle's flat and phone the police. The cloisters are, as we suspected they would be, empty; but the rehearsals aren't over. The entire cast and crew are in the common room. We take turns to peer through the glass in the door; we see the chairs moved back to the walls, the floor taped to reflect the dimensions of the stage. The actors are still in costume. Even as we watch, Rad – in role as Feste – is riding his unicycle and juggling with three balls at the same time. John, corpulent Sir Toby even when he isn't acting, is staggering drunkenly at the far reaches of the room clutching a wicker basket. With unerring accuracy Rad lobs the balls, one at a time and in time, into the basket. There's a round of laughter and applause.

'It seems a pity to spoil their fun,' Jen says.

I'm looking for Belle. She's standing in a corner, arms folded, watching the action with unadulterated pleasure. I can sympathise with Jen's feelings. I have to picture Belle, a knife in her hand, Taylor drunk on the mattress before her, to remind myself how dangerous she might be.

'I'm soaking,' Jen announces, 'I'm going to get changed. Have you got the key?'

I hand her the keys from my pocket, it's hardly worth me joining her and changing into drier clothes, I'll shortly have to go out again. I notice Kirsty close to the door, push it open and whisper her name. She seems surprised to see me but sidles out of the room.

'Dad, where on earth have you been? It's a good job we're going over bits of the play again, I thought Belle would want her keys back before now. Did you find anything?'

I ignore the question. 'Is everything all right?'

'Yeah, the rehearsal's gone well, everyone's up for it. But what did you find? Why did you want Belle's keys? She's not involved, is she? Surely you can't think that she . . .'

'Billy?' Jen's voice interrupts Kirsty with her urgency. 'I think you'd better come and have a look here.' Jen is down the corridor, not outside my room but standing beside Belle's.

'What's the matter?'

'Come and have a look.'

I hurry towards her, Kirsty trailing after me.

'I thought I'd look in Belle's room again, just to check we hadn't missed anything. I just had a feeling something wasn't quite right, the play was going so well, and when you tell the police it'll all come to a halt.' She holds the door open for me and I glance inside.

'What have you found?' Kirsty asks, her question could be aimed at me or at Jen. 'What do you mean, "It'll all come to a halt"?'

'Be quiet,' I tell her, 'go back to the common room door, stand outside it and if anyone tries to come through, stop them. I don't care how, just hold on to the handle. And whistle, yell, let us know somehow. Got it?'

The urgency in my voice dissolves all Kirsty's questions. 'Got it,' she replies, strides back to the common room, grabs hold of the door handle then puts her thumb up for me.

Jen and I go into Belle's room. On the bed is a pale grey double-breasted full-length coat. On top of it lies a mask of

Humphrey Bogart and a dark trilby hat with a black band around it. 'More evidence?' Jen asks.

Once again I find myself reaching into my pocket for rubber gloves. I gingerly turn the hat over, there are no marks inside, no identification at all. The mask is the same. I gently search the pockets of the coat, they're empty save for a pair of thin leather gloves.

'Well?' Jen prompts.

'If Belle wore these there should be plenty of forensic evidence attached to them. Hair, skin cells, sweat, saliva, you name it. There'll be something here.'

'You said "if". Is there any doubt?'

'We had the key, love. There's no way Belle could have got in.'

It doesn't take long for Jen to realise what this means. 'So someone else . . .'

'I don't know if I can do this again, love. Someone's trying to aim our suspicions at Belle. Someone's thinking ahead of us, and we're doing exactly as they want. They know what we're doing; they know what we're going to do. We fell into the trap with Anna and now we're doing the same again with Belle. I think we have to tell the police straightaway, I think we have to let them take on the responsibility of sorting things out, of doing the investigations properly. We've lost, Jen, we've got nowhere to go.'

'There must be a second key, Billy. And if there is, anyone could have it, including Belle. This doesn't rule her out at all.'

She's right; I'm not thinking straight. 'Okay, it could be her, but it could also be someone else. Could it also be someone else who's planting other evidence? I feel lost, Jen, I don't know what's happening.'

'Neither do I. But let's think. If Belle used these, then she wouldn't just leave them here. At the very least she'd put them away or hide them. Let's assume someone's trying to incriminate her. Who could it be? And why would they be doing it?'

290

My mind won't work. There are too many possibilities, too many things to think about at the same time. I'm on overload.

'Billy!' Jen puts her hands on my cheeks, turns my head, forces me to look at her. 'Billy, if someone else is doing this, it's to put us off the scent. It's because we're almost there. This someone is worried. We probably already know who he or she is, we just haven't clicked the information into place. All we need do is think.'

'All we need do,' I tell her, pulling her face away, 'is tell the police. Let them think, they get paid for thinking.'

'But they're not very good at it.'

'And we are? Jen, so far I've been a complete failure in this. I've been going round in circles. I've run out of ideas.'

'So you give up? Is that what happens when something goes wrong?'

I'm beginning to feel annoyed now. Jen seems determined to annoy me, to aggravate me, to force me to do something I don't want to do. All it needs is a call, one call, and the police will take the whole burden of the investigation on again. It'll take a lot of explaining, and it's inevitable that Jen will be involved; how else can I explain my knowledge of Professor Edmondson's findings? But they'll know all about them in the morning, they'll be like dogs at a lamp-post, and when they start asking questions, I'll be the first in line. They'll want to know why I didn't get in touch with them earlier, they'll want to know why I interfered at all. Even now my mind can't focus. It should be easy, there's a limited number of people who had the opportunity or the wish to kill Taylor, and that number should be reduced further by those who could have tried to blame Anna or Belle. Why, then, can't I work out who it was? Who's been pulling my strings? I sink down onto the bed, my head in my hands.

'Billy, what do you want me to do?' Jen's voice is conciliatory now, she's worried in case I'm being pushed closer to an edge I've already fallen from in the past. She kneels down in front of me. 'Just tell me,' she says, 'I don't want to ...'

'Just be quiet,' I tell her. 'I should never have got involved in this, I'm out of my depth. I don't even understand the play. Stupid bloody Shakespeare. Stupid bloody *Twelfth Night*. It's got nothing to do with Christmas, why the hell call it that anyway?'

I recall something Kirsty said to me, about Twelfth Night being the time of year when the accepted order of things was turned upside down, when a household would be taken over by the Lord of Misrule who would confuse everyone with jokes and tricks and disguises. 'There's certainly been a Lord of Misrule operating here, he's the only one who knows what's been going on.' I'm aware that I'm rambling, that my disjointed words will mean nothing to Jen, but it doesn't matter any more. 'Words mean nothing,' I mumble, 'somebody said that to me, somebody says that in the play, and it's right, they're right, words do mean nothing.'

'Billy, you don't need to say ...'

'And people mean nothing. Girls dressed as boys, but they aren't girls because in Shakespeare's time girls didn't act so they were really boys anyway, so they're boys dressed as girls dressed as boys. Everything's false, everything's pretence, everything's make-believe. Everything's a joke.'

This time Jen does manage to speak, but only by putting a finger to my lips to keep me quiet. 'It's all right, Billy, it doesn't matter. The only thing that matters is you. I don't care about anyone else, I only care about you. Yes, everything's upside down; don't worry about it.' Her voice is calming, it sooths the chatter of voices in my head, and she seems to realise this; she keeps talking. 'It's the way things are, it's the way things happen, in plays and in life.' The words themselves are unimportant, it's the tone, the gentleness, the love that I'm listening to. 'People do things we don't expect them to, they pretend to be what they aren't.

292

Sometimes it's to protect themselves, sometimes it's to protect others, sometimes it's so they can do unpleasant things. But we allow for that in plays, we suspend our disbelief because we want to believe what we see and what we hear. It's when people tell lies in real life that we suffer, and some of us are very good at telling lies.' She searches for the easiest examples she can find, dwells naturally on the play. 'There's no way anyone could see Viola dressed as a man and fail to see she was a woman. Perhaps it was easier in Shakespeare's day, when boys in make-up did play women's roles, but it doesn't work these days.' She giggles. 'I mean, can you imagine me dressed in a man's clothes? I'm the wrong shape, everyone would know I'm a woman. Perhaps that's why drag artists are popular, because it's easy for men to dress as women; after all, they're adding something – boobs and hips – rather than trying to hide it. Having said that, it would be difficult for you to dress up as a woman, unless it was very dark and you just jumped out from round a corner then disappeared.'

I have to smile at the thought. Jen sees the relaxation in my face, the slight upward curl of my lips, and continues.

'We're all acting, Billy, we're in our own tragedies and comedies, we're serious or we're clowns. I mean, look at the clowns around here. Kirsty was telling me about Vicky, then there's the young man playing Feste. Playing the joker, getting money from Olivia and from Viola and from Orsino, having a licence to entertain but being forced to do exactly that. And why? Because he can do it. Because he can do funny voices and ride a unicycle and juggle, because he can act funny. He probably wants to play Hamlet or Henry V. He probably wants to play a romantic lead. He probably wants to get the girl.'

'Perhaps he did,' I interrupt. 'Tom seemed to think he'd got off with Belle on Friday night.'

'But that's real life,' Jen puts me right. 'He's condemned to play the fool in the play.' She kisses me gently on the lips, pleased I'm responding to her. 'Come on, let's ring

293

the police. We might as well get it over with.'

'I think I'd better talk direct to Arnison.'

'Yeah. How do you think he'll respond?'

'He'll be angry with me. He'll be angry with himself as well, but he'll take it out on me. He'll think of some way to charge me with something, even if it doesn't stick. If he finds the real murderer quickly he might let me off with hard labour or deportation to the colonies.'

Jen grins, pulls me to my feet. If I can make jokes about my predicament then she can worry about me less. 'Do you want to use my phone?' she asks.

'No, I think . . .'

She waits a while until the silence becomes abnormal, until it stretches to breaking point. When she speaks, her voice and her face are worried; all she can offer is a prompt, a single word disguised as a question, 'Billy?'

'I think . . . I think I need to speak to Tom.'

'Tom? Why . . ?' The question remains unasked because there's no one to answer it. I move – I have to, before the moment passes and my train of thought is disturbed – back into the corridor and head for the common room.

Kirsty's still at the door, watching what's going on inside, turning at the sound of my footsteps. 'Dad, what's going on?'

'I'll tell you later. I need to speak to Tom.'

'He's inside. I was just coming to get you anyway, they've finished rehearsing.' There's a ripple of applause from within.

'Are you all right, Billy?' Jen has hurried up behind me.

'As all right as I'll ever be. Did you close the door behind you?'

'Of course.'

'Good.' I look inside, outbreaks of hugs and back-slapping are evident amongst cast and crew, and Belle's beaming her blessing and approval over the ensemble. There's no time to waste, I push the door open and head straight for Tom. He sees me coming. 'Mr O, did you see that? I mean, no stage, no lighting, but it was so good. When we do it ...'

'Tom, I need to ask you some questions.'

He isn't taken aback by my lack of manners. 'Yeah, sure. Ask away.'

I put my arm around his shoulder, guide him away to a corner where we won't be overheard. 'Remember when we were talking by the gate, on Saturday, and you were telling me who was who?'

Tom looks puzzled. Kirsty and Jen arrive, both shrug at his raised eyebrows, none of them know what I'm thinking; even I'm not sure what direction my thoughts will take me.

'Yes,' Tom says, 'I can remember.'

'Good, think back. Can you recall who we were talking about?'

'Nearly everyone, I think, I was ...'

'No!' My voice is raised, people around us look at me. I try to control myself, force my voice to become a whisper again. 'Think, Tom, you mentioned lots of people but we talked about one in particular who was on the wrong side of the fence, someone who was arriving late.'

'Oh, yes, I remember now. Rad.'

'And what did you say about him?'

Tom looks puzzled. 'I think I just filled in some background information. Told you a bit about him.'

'And you didn't mention why he was on the other side of the fence? Didn't he have a room in the halls?'

Realisation dawns. 'Of course!' He lowers his voice, looks around to make sure that the subject of his revelation isn't within hearing distance, then begins to explain, more to Kirsty and Jen than to me. 'I was surprised to see Rad wasn't with the rest of us because I knew he'd booked a room. The only other person who stayed away was Belle, and I suggested it might be because he managed to get off with her. I mentioned that to Mr O, I got the feeling he sort of doubted it, but I couldn't think of any other reason why Rad would give up a free room and free booze.'

295

The next question – or rather, the answer Tom gives – is the most important. 'You said you were going to ask him where he'd been; the exact words were, I think, "I'll have to give him the old cross-examination myself." Did you ask him?'

'As a matter of fact, I did.'

'Well?' Kirsty breaks in, the subject of who has been sleeping with whom is obviously of great importance to her.

'He told me to mind my own fucking business.'

That isn't the answer I want, and my face clearly shows it.

'That's not Rad,' Kirsty says, 'Rad would have boasted about it. Think what he was like with that first year at the Freshers' Ball, he was telling everybody he'd had her even before the disco started.'

'I didn't say that was all he said,' Tom continues, affronted.

'Well?' I can't hide the hope in my voice.

'He said he'd been seeing her for a few weeks. I asked him what she was like; he said she was a bit of a goer.'

'Tom, why didn't you tell me?' It's Kirsty's turn to sound annoyed.

'There were other things happening, it slipped my mind.'

It's coming back to me now, things are no longer falling apart, they're falling into place. There's something else Tom said, something important, my subconscious knows that but my conscious mind can't dredge it to the surface.

'I don't know what she sees in him,' I hear Kirsty saying in some distant place, the words barely registering, 'she must have no sense of smell.'

'Why's that?' Jen asks.

'Haven't you noticed? He's got a problem, he smells.'

'You mean he doesn't wash?' Surely Jen can't be trying to make a medical diagnosis.

'No,' Tom explains, 'he does! I shared a room with him once. He's got some type of Athlete's Foot, but it's really

296

nasty, when it's at its worst it makes his feet smell.'

'A fungal infection!' Jen says triumphantly. 'Does he have a pair of red trainers?'

'I think he must have a few,' Kirsty answers, 'he goes for bright colours.' She looks around. 'Yeah, he's got some on tonight.'

My colleagues are silent. Kirsty and Tom want information, Jen's waiting to find out what happens next. I can say nothing, my mind's racing. 'What does Rad study?' I ask.

'Something to do with computers,' Kirsty says.

'Software development,' Tom adds, 'website design, so far as I remember it's quite a wide-ranging course. He's definitely into computers, though, in fact I'm sure I told you ...'

'... that you had him figured as a computer nerd! Yes, I can recall now.'

'Mr Oliphant,' a commanding voice joins us, 'we seem to have suffered a slight setback due to the rain, but your lighting and sound system worked exactly as we'd hoped. Thank you so much.' Belle holds out her hand to me and I shake it; her grip is firm.

'You're welcome,' I tell her a little abruptly, I don't need to be diverted from my thoughts. Rad's hovering close behind her.

'I was wondering, though, if we might discuss one or two changes. There are some parts of Act Three where I feel ...'

'Belle, you're a workaholic and a pain in the arse.' George's deep voice puts an end to her deliberations in a way that's comic yet final. 'Mr Oliphant has had a busy day doing far more than any of us can appreciate. Whatever you want to talk about can wait until tomorrow – or rather, later on today, since it's past midnight.' Bear-like, he drapes his paw over her shoulder. 'I, however, need to speak to you about some of my lines.' He pulls her away from me, his spare arm captures Rad; 'You might be able to help as well, Rad.' As he passes me by he winks at me.

'I need access to a computer,' I announce, 'one that can connect to the internet.'

'At this time of night? There's nowhere open.' Kirsty's stating the obvious. 'All my stuff's packed away.'

'Mine too,' Tom says.

'Will the university server be working?' I ask.

'I would imagine so,' Tom answers.

Jen knows me too well, she's already anticipating my thoughts. 'No joy, Billy, you'd need to put some lights on to be able to use the terminal in Taylor's office, even with the place half closed down, you might be seen. You can't go creeping around the university at night.'

I suggest an alternative, 'Belle's flat?'

'Why do you need to . . ?' Kirsty begins to ask, but she knows I won't answer.

'Come on, then.' Jen's already ahead of me, trying not to look as if she's hurrying.

'You two get to bed,' I tell Tom and Kirsty, 'lock the door behind you, don't open it for anyone except me.' It sounds melodramatic, but I can think of no other way of forcing my daughter to do as I tell her without a long explanation. Explanations, if required, can come later. 'Get some sleep. I don't know how long I'll be. I'll wake you up when I get back.' I leave no time for an argument or a response, I'm already at the door, following Jen down the corridor. She pauses at the exit, it's still raining heavily.

'Run between the drops,' I tell her, 'there'll be nowhere to park anyway.'

'Have you still got the keys?' she asks me as she dives into the cool night rain.

'Yes.' Although I try to avoid the puddles my shoes and feet are already wet.

'She'll know, then, when she tries to get into her room.'

'She'll think she's lost them.' We aren't running too fast, but I'm praying that Jen will stop talking, stop asking questions. I'm already out of breath, I need to concentrate on the mirrored pavement and tarmac beneath my feet, and the rain is forcing me to half-close my eyes. There's little traffic and we cross the road without breaking stride then run up the middle of Belle's street. When we get to the door it takes me a little while to get the keys out of my pocket, long enough for me to realise that this time I made no objections to Jen accompanying me. She's far better than me and far faster than me when it comes to using computers, and anyway, I'd rather have her with me where I can watch her; I'm not sure she appreciates how dangerous hunting for a murderer can be.

We enter as quietly as we can, but there's no sound from within. The stairs are silent, there's no clichéd squeak or creak, and the door to Belle's room opens easily. We step inside and I close the door, slip across the room to pull the curtains closed. As I flick the light switch Jen's already powering up the computer, lowering herself into the seat in front of it. Its screen flickers into life.

'Passwords?' she asks.

'They won't be a problem,' I tell her confidently.

'Reason?'

I open the top drawer in her dressing table, take out a piece of paper. 'She's the efficient type who always writes things down; I noticed these earlier.' I hand her a list that contains Belle's university access password, her AOL password, her online bank password and username and her credit card access code.

'What more does a girl need? Except to know what you want me to do once we're in.'

'Pick a search engine, any search engine.'

Jen presses keys and enters passwords, soon the familiar Google logo appears. 'Now what, oh lord and master?'

'Somehow you say that as if you don't mean it.'

'Good, I don't. But tell me what I'm searching for.'

'I need you to use your imagination. I need to find out whether my idea's right or even possible. You're Anna. You need to improve your essay grades, your acting's good, you know that, but not your essays. So what do you do?'

Jen knows what I want her to say, but she decides to play devil's advocate. 'I go to my course tutor and ask for help, I explain ...'

'Bollocks! Your tutor's a lecherous sexist who seems to take a particular interest in feeling you up whenever he can get you alone. Are you really going to approach him?'

'So I ask my friends for help.'

'Which friends?'

'I don't know, any friends, friends on the course who can help me.'

'You don't have any. You're a loner, you seem to have a habit of making people dislike you. There's no one you can turn to.'

Jen gives way. 'Okay, so I see if I can get help from somewhere else ...'

'Help? Come on, Jen, you don't want help. You want a high-quality essay as quickly as possible. Where do you go? What do you do?'

She gives way. 'All right, you've got me. I look on the internet for an essay, a ready-made essay if possible, if not, one that I can easily adapt.'

'So do it,' I say triumphantly, 'you're Anna, do it. What do you look for? What are the key words?'

Jen closes her eye, lets her fingers rest on the keyboard. '"Brecht", I suppose. And then "essay".'

'Try it.'

She does as I say, whistles when the first screen appears. 'That's a lot of sites to visit,' she admits, 'over 100,000. I wouldn't know where to begin.'

'How do you narrow it down, then?'

'Be more specific. Limit the search to UK websites for a start. Add more detail. Key words from the essay title?'

'Go on then.' I try not to sound impatient, but it's proving difficult. I want to get this sorted out, I want to do it now. Jen dots the 'pages from UK' box, adds the words 'theatre studies' and 'alienation effect'. The result is helpful, we're down to just over 300 websites.

'Is that a small enough number?' Jen asks.

'Not if you can think of anything else to narrow it down.'

Jen inhales, I can almost hear the electricity zinging round the circuits in her brain. 'Let's say exactly what we want, then.' She types again, reads out the words as she does so. '"A grade brecht university theatre studies essay alienation effect." Beyond typing in the essay question itself, that's as narrow a search as I can make it.' She presses the return button; we're given thirty-two websites to choose from. 'I think that's enough,' she says, 'allowing for the obvious duplicates and university websites. But how does that help?'

'Let's see what we're left with when you filter out the sites that are no good. Anything with an "ac.uk" address is out, you're right there, no university's going to condone cheating.' I lean forward to look over her shoulder. 'That one goes,' she says, 'and that one, both universities. That one looks a bit gonzo, then there are more universities. That leaves ... four websites in total, Billy.'

'Open the first one,' I say.

She manoeuvres the cursor and we enter a website called 'youruniessay.co.uk'. The page highlights the general subject matter of the essay and suggests previewing 'an A grade response'; Jen looks at me, I nod. She presses the keys and there, in front of us, the opening paragraph of Belle's essay appears.

Jen leans back in her chair, looks up at me. 'Okay, you're a clever shit and our children will be bountifully blessed. Now would you mind telling me how you knew this would happen?'

'I didn't,' I tell her, 'it was a guess.'

'So how did you guess?'

'I haven't finished guessing yet. I'd guess that the person responsible for this website is Rad. He stole Belle's essay, probably all of the rest as well, and put them on his website. He's selling essays. I reckon Anna found the site by accident, paid her money, downloaded Belle's essay.

301

That wouldn't normally be a problem for any of Rad's customers, except that Anna and Belle were on the same course – albeit a year apart – and had the same tutor. And Taylor noticed.'

'But then what happened?' Jen's genuinely puzzled, and I'm certain I won't know the answer to the next question she's going to ask.

'Taylor found out about Rad.'

'How?'

That's the question. I don't know the answer, and Taylor isn't around to ask. 'I've no idea,' I admit.

'Leave that for the moment,' Jen suggests. 'You think Rad killed Taylor because he was going to go public?'

'That's the way it looks to me.'

'But how did Rad find out?'

Jen's getting too good at asking awkward questions. 'Again,' I have to say, 'I don't know.'

Jen turns the seat round so she's facing me. 'We don't have anything, then, nothing to connect Rad with Taylor. We've got the website, but that's all, and there's no way of linking that to Rad.'

'I'm slipping up,' I tell her, 'There's the van, I bet that isn't registered to Belle, but I should have checked it.'

'Can you do that?' Jen asks.

'I can't, but I know someone who can. There are some advantages to being an ex-cop.'

'Go on then, ring him.'

'It's not a he, it's a she; Kim Bryden.' I check my watch. 'And it's nearly two in the morning. Kim won't be pleased if I ring her now.'

Jen knows Chief Inspector Kim Bryden, she's aware of the mutual distrust we have in each other though she says it's due to the fact that we respect each other. I'm not so sure.

'Kim would ring you in the middle of the night if she needed you to help her.'

'There's nothing I could do for Kim that would be of

302

such use to her that she'd ring me up at this time of the night.'

'Billy, it doesn't matter. You'd ring Rak if you wanted information you could only get from computers, you'd contact Norm if there was something to do with cars, you'd get in touch with Sly if you wanted ...' She crawls to a halt; Sly is big and strong, a hard man and a hard worker. He looks fierce, though his wife and children might disagree with that statement. 'You'd ask for Sly's help if you wanted to intimidate someone,' Jen continues. 'That's what people do if they need help, they ask others with expertise.'

'Say that again.' I reach forward, take Jen's arms, pull her to her feet.

'What?'

'Say it again. What you just said, say it again!'

Her face twists, my grip must be too tight. 'Billy!'

'I'm sorry, it's important.' I let her arms go. 'What did you just say?'

Jen rubs her arms. 'If you need help,' she repeats, 'you ask someone with expertise. That's all.'

I dance up and down on the spot. 'Yes! Yes, you've got it. Jen, if you need help, you ask someone who knows. Tom knew Rad was good with computers, he told us, that's why we're here now. Surely Taylor would know that as well. So he gets Anna's essay, it's way too good, he remembers Belle's essay, he compares them and finds they're almost identical. But he knows Belle wouldn't condone that type of cheating, so he does what we've just done, he checks some websites. He finds Belle's essay there. What does he do then? He needs to know who owns the website, who runs the website, so he asks for help. He asks the one person he knows with expertise. He asks Rad. That's how Rad knew of Taylor's suspicions. And that's why he killed Taylor!'

'It fits,' Jen acknowledges. 'And if Taylor told Rad a few days ago, it would give Rad time to plan what he was going to do. So what do we do now?'

'The van. I'll check the registration number, ring Kim – I don't care what she's doing, this is important – and ask her to check the ownership. If it ties in, I let Arnison know. Immediately.'

Jen's already on her feet. 'I'll get the number,' she says, takes a pen and a piece of paper from the desk. 'Why don't you look around, see if there's anything else here points towards Rad. I mean, first he tried to blame Anna, then he tried to blame Belle; he must have left other clues here, and we weren't really looking for them before.'

I nod my assent. Without Jen I'd be nowhere with this case, her thinking's clear, full of common sense, whereas mine has been fuddled, muddied by my own carthorse, dancing, gum-booted feet. While she's gone I sit at the computer, type in a few words, press a few buttons. I'm so absorbed in what I'm doing, what I'm trying to do, that I don't even look up when I hear Jen return.

Except it's not Jen.

'Take your hands away from the keyboard, Mr Oliphant.'

I don't turn round, there's no need; I do, however, exactly as I'm told.

'Thank you. Now turn the chair round, keep your backside firmly glued to it, until you're facing me.'

I place my hands under the seat, turn it round slowly, until I'm facing Rad. 'No gun this time?' I ask.

'So you've figured that out?'

'Your feet smell, even if your Bogart accent is good.'

'Yeah, I must get some more of that cream the doctor prescribed. And the gun was a fake. From the props cupboard.'

'I thought it might be. But you can't take a chance.'

Rad nods. He's wearing a parka, stained dark from the rain, the hood pulled down. In his right hand is a knife; in his left, two more.

'Of course,' I tell him. 'I missed that. Juggling, the

304

unicycle, fire-breathing, the whole street-theatre-circus thing. I should have recognised the knife, the one inside the wig. It's a throwing knife, isn't it? Like the ones you're carrying at the moment.'

'I'm quite good with them as well,' Rad says. 'And these ones are specially sharpened.'

'Like the one you used to kill Taylor?'

'Fraid so.'

'He was on the trail of your website, wasn't he?'

Rad glances at his watch. 'You've been doing some homework, I see. And a little guesswork, of course.'

'I've also phoned the police to tell them what I know.'

Rad shakes his head. 'I don't think so, Mr Oliphant. You've held off and you've held off, you wouldn't ring them now, at two in the morning.'

'That's a risk you'll have to take, then, if you don't believe me.'

'Life is full of calculated risks. I think I'm quite safe in my belief this time.' He checks his watch again.

'Expecting someone?'

'Your killer, Mr Oliphant.'

'And who might that be?'

'Come on, Mr O, surely you can guess.'

He's weighing the knife in his right hand. If it's anything like the throwing knives I've seen it'll be well balanced and, given his admission of expertise and the distance between us, I have no doubt that he'd be able to hit me. Rushing him is out of the question. I can only hope to keep him talking until Jen comes back. Jen! Does he realise she's here? Will he have thought of that? And who is he expecting?

'I've no idea who's coming. My killer? It looks as if you're pretty well set up for the job yourself.'

'Yes, that's obvious. But who's going to get the blame?'

I shrug. 'Humphrey Bogart?'

'Whose flat is this? Who's all the evidence pointing at?' He's losing his patience, he even looks a little nervous.

305

'Belle, of course. She's coming back here, you see.' He relaxes a little, his throwing arm seems less tense. 'I'm like a fisherman, Mr O, and you're the fish. I've been tempting you, luring you, playing with you for so long, there was never any chance you would escape. I saw you take her keys, I guessed you'd be coming back here – the odds were good, you see, I measured the odds – and I told her. I made sure there was no one else about, of course. She went to get her coat, I was ready. I ran, she's been walking. She should be here any minute now. So first I kill you, I can hit you in the chest from here. Belle arrives to find you dead or dying, I kill her in the same way. I make it look like you killed each other, the knives will have the relevant prints on them. Then I leave the police to find the bodies.'

'What went wrong the first time?'

Rad's forehead furrows. 'What do you mean? Nothing's gone wrong.'

'You're trying to blame Belle; why bother with Anna in the first place?'

'Ah, yes. A stroke of bad luck, that, not quite an error, more a misjudgement. But it's turned out to be good luck as well, it'll make the little sub-plot of you and Belle even more believable.' He spins the knife in the air and catches it, makes as if to flick it at me. I have to keep him talking.

'The police will know you've been here,' I tell him, 'you'll have left something behind, fabrics from your coat, something from your shoes.'

'Don't you see, Mr Oliphant, that's the beauty of this little charade. I'm meant to have been here. I've been screwing Belle for the past month, that's how I got her essays. If only Anna hadn't found the bloody website, if only she'd had the sense to change the words a little.' He shakes his head. 'There's a disclaimer, you know. "These essays are for guidance only, copying is plagiarism, it's illegal, don't do it." A worthless statement, of course, but good advice.' He rotates his shoulders as if preparing for

306

action, does a little jog on the spot. 'There's no reason to prolong this,' he says, 'I'm sorry it's come down to this. I didn't mean to kill Taylor, just to frighten him. It was an accident. I'm sorry.'

Rad lifts his right arm quickly. I register that he's about to throw, dive to one side. As I do so I see the door being hurled open. I see Jen with a bread-knife charging at Rad, screaming, I feel something strike me in the chest, then I hit the floor. I struggle quickly to my feet, Jen's the only other person in the room. Wide-eyed, she's still clutching the bread-knife; there's blood on the blade.

'He threw the knife,' she manages to say, 'I saw it hit you.'

I look down at my chest. I can feel the pain where something has struck me, I open my shirt, but there's no bleeding. I'm close to hysteria. 'The hilt, it must have been the hilt. You distracted him enough for him to throw it unevenly.' I step towards her, put my arms round her. 'Where did he go?'

She's trembling. 'I hit him with the knife. In the arm, I think. He ran away.'

There's the sound of a door slamming, footsteps on the stair. I roughly push Jen behind the door, grab the knife from her hand. The door crashes back against the wall. 'What the hell are you doing here?' Belle shouts.

I grab her. 'Rad! Did you see him?'

'I think I'm the one who should be asking the questions, what . . .'

'Shut up, you silly cow! Rad killed Taylor, he was going to kill you, have you seen him?'

Jen surfaces from behind the bed. 'It's true,' she whispers.

Belle's voice is suddenly a whisper. 'He ran past me, in the street. Heading back to the uni.'

'Right. Take care of Jen, she's had a shock. Ring the police.' I turn to Jen. 'Try to tell them what happened. I'm going after him.'

307

I don't wait for any response, I hurtle down the stairs and out into the night. The gutters are swollen with water, it's lying in oily sheets on road and pavement, but the rain has stopped. I run down the street, arms pumping. Rad's panicking, he'll be caught wherever he goes, but at the moment he's heading back towards the university, towards my daughter. And he's still armed.

At the end of the road I see him, he's far ahead of me. 'Rad!' I shout. 'It's no good running. Everyone knows! Give yourself up!'

I see him look back, and as he does so his foot catches on a kerbstone and he falls headlong, water cascading into the air around him. That drives me on, arms pumping, but he climbs quickly to his feet again. It occurs to me that Jen might have wounded him seriously, that he could be losing blood. If so, then the rate of loss will be increasing as he puts more effort into his bid for freedom. He isn't limping, however, he isn't holding his arm, so I can't assume that he's weakened in any way.

He's heading straight for the university, straight for the halls where the rest of the cast should be sleeping. Perhaps he has something hidden there, money or weapons, perhaps he hopes to get into the university itself and hide in the maze of corridors. I can't try to understand what he's doing, I can only run after him, my lungs desperate for air, my legs kicking up the spray. On the edge of my consciousness I can hear the distant wail of a police siren; if I can hear it, then Rad can hear it as well, but it does nothing to slow him. I see him reach the door to the halls, he has to stop and key in the entrance code and I think I just might manage to catch him in those few seconds before he can gain entry. I overestimate my speed, however, underestimate the agility of his mind and fingers. He's inside while I still have fifty metres of ground to cover, the door closed behind him, and it's my turn to fumble with the key pad. I hurl the door open and then stop. Rad still has knives, he

308

could be waiting for me just inside.

'You might as well ... give up ... now, Rad,' I gasp into the corridor, uncertain whether there's anyone there to hear me. I listen in vain for the sound of his breathing, instead my own heartbeat and rasping lungs conspire to fill my ears. I consider the odds: he wouldn't come all the way here just to set a trap for me, there's some other purpose to his apparent madness. I risk a peep into the corridor, up and down; there's no one there.

Which way would he have gone? To my right is the common room, a dead end. The bedrooms off the corridor are the same, they could only be used as a hiding place. He must have gone to my left, down the corridor and into the cloisters. I make my way slowly in that direction, there is, after all, a possibility that he could spring out at me from one of the rooms. When one of the doors opens behind me I whirl, fists raised to strike at ... a sleepy-looking George, clad in T-shirt and boxer shorts.

'What's going on?' he asks.

'Go back to bed,' I tell him, 'keep the door locked.'

'I heard someone running,' he says, 'into the cloisters, a few seconds ago. What's been happening?' He steps back to look at me. 'Why are you so wet?'

'It's raining,' I hiss at him, 'now go back to bed, it might be dangerous out here.' I make my way down the corridor, when I look back George is still there. 'On second thoughts, keep your eyes open for the police, they're on their way. Tell them I've followed Rad into the cloisters, God knows where we'll be. Tell them he's armed, with throwing knives. Got that?'

He nods, ducks back into his room.

I pull the cloisters door open, this time I dive through and roll into the passageway beyond; again, there's no one there. It's dark, only the emergency lights are on and they glow feebly. I try to recall whether the only other door to the cloisters is locked. I passed through it only a few hours ago and can't recall. Then it comes back to me, the equipment's still there, the door was locked for security reasons. That means there's no way out for Rad, unless he has a key. Does he have a key? Surely he must have a key, how else would he have followed me to Taylor's office? I hug the wall and the angles, try to stay in the darkness and shadows, head for the door. Even as I move I'm listening, listening for anything that might give me a clue to Rad's presence.

The door creeps closer to me, too slowly. I stop when I think I hear a noise close by, above me, but it isn't repeated. I move again. When I get to the door I turn the handle; it's locked. Has Rad already passed through it, locked it behind him? Perhaps he doesn't have his key with him. Perhaps I'm wrong, perhaps he never had a key, he could have got into Taylor's office through the university buildings. Again there's a noise! I turn my head, trying to catch it once more, trying to determine its direction. Surely he can't be trying to lure me into the open where he can pick me off more easily. I decide it's time to fight back.

A few metres away from me is Tom's control panel, safe under the roof of the cloisters, covered with a black tarpaulin. I pull the waterproof cloth away, trace the mains cable back to its socket, flick the switch. The control panel lights up with a glimmer of red and green. I crawl back towards it, Rad may be close at hand, watching, I don't want him to see my silhouette. I reach up and over the panel, feel for the master slider, move it up; the cloisters are filled with light.

I stand up, there's no chance that Rad can see me now, even though he knows where I am. There's another noise, again from above, this time more sustained. Two of the spotlights are motor-driven, I use the manual override to turn them, point them upwards, and see a figure scurrying and sliding along the roof of the cloisters, heading for the tall red sandstone abbey wall. It's Rad.

'Come down!' I yell. 'Don't be stupid, you can't escape!'

310

He must be able to hear me, but he doesn't turn. He reaches the end of the cloisters roof and begins to climb the wall. It's only a few metres to the top, the sandstone is old and crumbling, but there are many handholds. If he finds a way to the top and then down the other side, he'll escape into the night.

The door to the cloisters opens and George appears. He points to me, looks up and sees Rad, points to him as well. Behind him is a uniformed police officer who runs quickly towards me. With a mixture of relief and trepidation I see that it's one of the plods I met only the day before.

'The guy on the wall killed Jonathan Taylor. He tried to kill me as well. He's got some throwing knives with him. I'd suggest you ring for back-up.'

'Already done,' he answers, 'but I'd suggest *you* think of a good explanation for Inspector Arnison; he won't be pleased when he gets here.'

Rad is making his way up the wall, his agility obvious. I'm just about to complain that he'll get away when George steps out into the cloisters, walks to the middle of the stage where he can clearly be seen. 'Rad,' he shouts in his best, enunciated Orsino voice, 'it's George here, there's no need for this. Come on down, you'll hurt yourself.'

Rad keeps climbing, though he seems to be making slower progress than before.

'If you don't come down, I'll have to come up after you.'

'He wouldn't do that, would he?' asks the plod.

'I'm afraid so,' I tell him, but there's no need for an explanation, George has already vaulted onto the railing and hauled himself onto the cloisters roof close to where Rad is climbing. At least, I tell myself, Rad's so busy holding on he can't throw a knife.

'One of us will have to go after him,' I tell the plod.

'I'm scared of heights,' he answers.

'Why did I know you'd say that?'

311

I leave him, follow the cloisters round (I still don't want to let Rad have a clear shot at me) then follow George up onto the roof. He appears to have found an easier way up to the top of the wall, he's already higher than Rad. The roof is slippery with rain, I crawl up it until I'm at the junction where the grey angled slates meet the broad stones of the wall. At least the wall is drier, I can feel the possibility of handholds there. I ease myself into a standing position to find that George has already reached the top of the wall and is crawling along it towards Rad. Rad, on seeing this, changes direction. He's already at the angle where the abbey wall is at its tallest, he abandons his upward climb and makes his way sideways instead, across the angle, and then up the tallest face of rock. He seems more confident now, he's moving easily.

'Mr Oliphant,' George calls to me, 'I'll go across the top of the wall, I'll try to stay above him. You follow him round and up. He'll be caught between us.' The logic of his plan is faultless; it makes no allowances, however, for my age, my lack of fitness, the weakness of my arms, my weight or my fear of Rad throwing a knife at me. Since I can see no alternative, however, I gingerly make my way along the wall, my feet searching for a firm grip on the slates of the cloisters roof. I can feel, rather than see, people below me, the spotlights are too bright. One of them swings round, follows Rad up the wall where, spider-like, he's nearing the top. George, however, has an easier time. The wall he climbed has a flat top and, where it turns at a right angle to meet the gable end of the abbey, the stones have collapsed or eroded into something like a staircase. I can see him using this to reach a position above Rad.

I can see no point in following Rad further, George is going to catch him. 'Watch out,' I shout, 'he's got a knife.' I'm close enough to see George nod, my attention is so focused on them both that I miss my footing. I feel myself fall and slide, hands scrabbling for a hold, then my feet jar against the gutter. I'm lying there on my back, legs braced to stop me from falling, spread-eagled like a starfish, staring upwards. Rad looks down at me, then up at George. He holds out his left hand and George, lying flat on his stomach close to the apex of the gable, takes it, wraps his second hand around Rad's arm so he can haul him up. A voice somewhere whispers familiar, barely heard words that disappear from my mind as soon as they arrive, forced to flee by what I see before me. Rad looks down again. He braces his feet against the wall and reaches into his pocket, takes out his knife. He aims at me.

I can't move, I'm a target again, and he can't miss. But he doesn't throw. Instead he looks up at George. He drops his knife, it rattles against the wall then thuds to the ground below. He reaches up with his right hand instead, twists in a desperate attempt to grab George but fails. He screams as he falls, turns in the air. There's a tall lavatera bush at the base of the wall, I'm sure he tries to aim for it, to break his fall. There isn't enough time. I hear the crack as his head hits a projecting piece of stone, then he hits the ground.

'I couldn't hold him,' George yells down. 'Is he dead?'

I look across at his body. 'He's dead,' I tell myself, 'he's very, very dead.' I turn round, feeling the evening's cuts and bruises for the first time, lower myself gently down from the roof onto the ground. Almost immediately I'm surrounded by people. Jen and Kirsty throw themselves, crying, into my arms, Tom's eager 'Mr O, Mr O, I got it all!' accompanies their tears, the rest of the cast are providing a Greek chorus of wails. Only the stentorian bellow of Detective Inspector Arnison silences them.

'I hope, Mr Oliphant, you have some sort of explanation to offer for this unfortunate series of incidents.'

I turn to face him, wet, knees and knuckles scraped bare and bleeding. 'No,' I say to Arnison, 'I don't have an explanation. All I have is a knot made of different threads

313

of supposition and guesswork. I can show you the knot, but you'll have to untie it. It's too hard a knot for me to untie. I've had enough.'

Chapter Twelve

Arnison evacuates the cloisters and the halls. Within minutes police are accompanying us into waiting buses, each of us with our own escort to make sure we don't talk to each other. Everything's done by the book. The first round of questions doesn't seek opinions, all we're required to do is state facts. I tell Arnison what I did, when I did it, why I did it. Sometimes his impatience comes to the fore; without him saying so, he's obviously wondering why I didn't contact him, tell him what I was thinking.

I assume the others are being subjected to the same rigorous questioning, but I don't have a chance to find out; when Arnison has finished with me I'm put in a box-room away from the others. It isn't a cell, the door isn't locked, but the police officer in the corridor outside makes it clear, when I open the door, that I should stay where I am. He even accompanies me to the toilet.

There's an armchair and a desk, some magazines (celebrity goings-on for women, cars for men), but that's it. I manage to persuade my tired body that the armchair's comfortable and fall asleep to dream of falling.

Round about noon the second round of interviews begins. This is rougher, there's more of Arnison threatening me. When I feel brave enough to ask him how he's managing to piece together his information, his evidence, he plays the grand inquisitor and leans back with an enigmatic smile on his face; it's left to Mike Stephenson to play nasty, to do the face-up-close, saliva-spitting Rottweiler act. It doesn't last long, everyone present realises it's nothing more than badly-acted melodrama. But I get no feedback. I'm out of the loop.

By mid-morning I'm released into the general reception area where I find Jen and Kirsty, Tom, Belle and George, Vicky and the rest. They're in sombre mood, conversation is limited to whispers. I sit beside Jen, hold her hand. Every few minutes one of us is summoned into Arnison's presence to answer further questions or to clarify what has already been said.

Shortly after noon a trolley with tea and sandwiches is wheeled in, but few of us feel like eating.

It's a time for reflection. I try to make sense of what I know. Rad was running a website selling essays to students. He begged, borrowed, bought or, so far as Belle was concerned, stole these; he must have had a network of suppliers at universities throughout the country. Anna needed to improve her essays, she bought Belle's essay, but Taylor spotted this. He may have told Anna, blackmailed her into having sex with him – I'm not sure of this – or simply deduced that she found her essay on the net. A simple search led him to Rad's website. His mistake wasn't wanting to know who was running the site, it was asking Rad (the only person Taylor knew who was into computers) for help.

From then on it's conjecture. When Rad saw Taylor pawing Anna he thought it would be a good opportunity to get rid of Taylor. He killed him, put the blame on Anna. Only when it became clear that the evidence wouldn't stick did he rethink his plan and try to incriminate Belle. It holds together, sort of, but I'm sure there are gaps. The trouble is, I'm so tired I couldn't see the holes in a colander, I can't think straight. But it's out of my hands, the police can finish things off. All I want to do is go home and sleep.

Jen's asleep, leaning on me, when a young policeman

comes in and stands in front of me. 'Mr Oliphant,' he tells me, 'your solicitor has left a message for you.' He hands me an envelope.

'Which solicitor was it?' I ask. 'There are several in the firm I deal with.'

'She didn't give a name, sir.'

'Would you mind describing her?'

'She was ... She didn't really look like a solicitor. She was untidy. And ...'

'Fat? Greasy hair? Looked as if she was wearing a sack?'

'I wouldn't use those exact words, sir, but that is a reasonable description.'

'Thank you.'

It's Rak. Rak's no solicitor, though she probably could have been if she'd wanted to be. Rak is a sort of white witch, she lives in the arcane world of computers, she conjures up meaning from binary codes. She speaks magic words to computers, to systems, to networks, and they give up their secrets to her. Last night, in Belle's flat, she was the one I was contacting. Even as Rad burst in I'd just finished sending her an email. This must be the response. I open the envelope slowly, trying not to disturb Jen. I read its contents, then put the slip of paper back in my pocket. Something still has to be sorted out.

Tom's sitting on the other side of me, half-dozing, sheltering Kirsty in his arms. I nudge him gently and he opens his eyes. 'Mr O? Did you want something?'

'Last night,' I say softly, 'in all the hysteria, I swear I can remember you saying something to me. Something like "I got it all". Am I imagining that?'

Tom replies quietly. 'No, I did say that. I had my camera set up. You know, the one I was going to use to film the play. When the first police car arrived its siren woke me up. I was in the cloisters when you and Rad and George were climbing the walls. I started filming you. I only stopped when Rad fell.'

'Where's the film?'

317

'The police took it. Then they had to go back to the cloisters to get my editing desk, it records on special tape and they didn't have a player here. I played it back for them. I think they were pleased I recorded it. I don't think they're going to blame you for Rad's fall, it was obviously an accident.'

The thought that others might believe I caused Rad's death had never occurred to me. I was hardly involved in the chase itself. 'Did they give you the tape back?'

'No. They said they would, but they want to make a copy.'

I shake Jen gently, she opens her eyes wide, sits up straight and stretches. 'Have I missed anything?' she asks.

'Not yet.' If the reply is cryptic she makes no comment, but doesn't seem surprised when I get up and walk over to the reception desk. 'I'd like to speak to Inspector Arnison,' I tell the policeman. 'I don't think this case is quite over yet.'

'Mr Oliphant, this had better be good.' Arnison's standing, waiting for me as I'm ushered into his presence, two other officers flanking him. This is a proper interview room, the tape machine is ready, as is – at my request – Tom's video editing machinery. 'I should tell you, we've already looked at the video and found nothing untoward on it. Mr Radcliffe's death was an accident, though our investigations suggest that he did kill Jonathan Taylor and also attempted to incriminate Anna Peranski. Once it became clear that the evidence he planted wouldn't hold up in court,' he has the good grace to sound embarrassed as he says that, 'then he made a similar attempt to incriminate Isabelle Hewitt. Your action prevented that and has saved us time and expense, for which we are grateful.' He doesn't sound grateful, he sounds as if he wants me as far away as possible.

'It would, however, have been better,' he continues, 'if you had informed us of your suspicions when they arose. There is no place for a detective to work outside the police

318

force on criminal, as opposed to civil, investigations, as I'm sure you're aware.'

He's finished his little speech. He's told me off, firmly but politely. Now all he needs is for me to say whatever I want to and leave, it can't be that important; after all, for the second time in two days he's found his murderer.

'There are still some loose ends to tie up,' he tells me, 'and I'm sure you and your family and friends would like to leave as soon as possible. So if you don't mind . . .' He holds out his hands, keen for me to say my part. I nod to him and he switches on the tape player. 'This is a statement by Mr William Oliphant who is still under oath. The time is . . .'

His voice drones the formalities; when it pauses, I begin.

'You said there were some loose ends, Mr Arnison; there are, I believe, more than you think. I should have recognised this earlier, but I was too tired. Why did Rad try to move the blame from Anna to Belle? Only a few people knew that the evidence Rad had planted wouldn't stand up. They were Professor Edmondson, Jen, me and George.'

'Are you suggesting that . . ?'

I'm determined to go on. 'I have a friend, a good friend, who can get into virtually any computer system. When Rad came to Belle's flat and attacked me, I'd just sent her an email. I gave her details of Rad's website, and I asked her to find out who was the beneficiary when someone bought an essay there. She did some investigating while we were chasing around on roofs last night, she came up with some interesting information. The cash was transferred to a company called "Illyria and Elysium". The partners in that company were James Radcliffe and George Prentice. Rad and George.'

'How does your friend get information like that?' Arnison seems less concerned with Rak's findings than with her method of discovery. 'Only the police are permitted access to bank account and credit card information.'

'I think she uses a secret police access code,' I tell him.

319

It isn't true, but it will certainly waste some of his time over the next few days trying to find out whether what I've said is true. I'm surprised, however, that he isn't more enthusiastic about the information I've just given him.

He seems to read my thoughts. 'Just because they set up a company together doesn't mean they were involved in a crime together.'

'My friend also found out that the account was emptied last night. The funds, in excess of £300,000, were transferred to a Venezuelan branch of a Swiss bank. There was one other transaction. A ticket was bought for a flight to Caracas. Tomorrow. Doesn't that worry you?'

This time there is a reaction. Arnison leans forward and takes the piece of paper from my hand.

'You can do your own checking,' I tell him. 'I'm sure you'll come up with the same results. You'll probably be quite quick as well.'

Arnison hands the paper to one of his subordinates with a nod.

'There's more,' I tell him, 'some of it supposition, but I think you'll find it fits rather well. You see, if Rad and George were partners, then both of them will have been worried when they found out Taylor was investigating their company. If Rad couldn't give Taylor any information, Taylor would probably turn elsewhere, probably to the university's own computer experts, and they'd put matters in the hands of the police. So Rad and George had to act. Have you looked at the van in Belle's yard?'

'Yes.' Arnison seems reluctant to give me any information.

'And?' I prompt him.

'The van's owner was James Radcliffe. There were traces of blood that match Taylor's, though attempts had been made to clean the van. There were no prints that match yours and your fiancée's, Mr Oliphant, though someone had been in the van wearing gloves. We're confident that we'll find matches of clothing thread, though.'

320

'And anything to connect the van to George?'

'One or two prints that matched Mr Prentice's. He says he borrowed the van last week.'

'Only one or two? That suggests they were cleaned away, doesn't it?'

'But we're assuming that Radcliffe tried to clean the van after killing Taylor in the back.'

I'm beginning to lose my patience. 'Come on, Arnison, you're making excuses. How did Rad get Taylor into the van? Where was the van? What happened in the van? Surely you've got some idea.'

'Of course I have,' he answers.

'So tell me. I can't help you if you won't help me.'

He appears to deliberate the matter, to discuss it with his conscience. Both of us are aware that he doesn't have to say anything, but I've already provided him with some vital information that could alter his approach; there could be more.

'We asked Miss Hewitt about her relationship with Mr Radcliffe. It would appear that his semi-public revelations about that relationship weren't quite accurate. Miss Hewitt informed us that they were friends, their relationship was platonic. There were two reasons for this, and this information is confidential, Mr Oliphant. Miss Hewitt prefers and Mr Radcliffe preferred sexual intercourse with their own sex. She is, and he was, gay.'

If Arnison expects this revelation to surprise or deter me, he's mistaken; if anything it provides me with the impetus to go on. 'What about Taylor?'

'What about Taylor, Mr Oliphant?'

'Have you done any digging into his sexual preferences?'

Arnison grins, nods his head. 'I can see where you're going. He was unmarried. You already know that he was somewhat predatory when it came to his female students. We've found one other relationship with a man, rumours of others. He appears, in modern parlance, to have been swinging in two directions. Personally, I can't see why that might be important. However, all I'm doing is letting you know what I know.'

'Let's keep going then. Have you matched the knife, the one in Belle's room hidden in the wig, with Taylor's wound?'

'It matches. That knife – or one very similar – was the murder weapon. What's more, it's a particular type of knife, a throwing knife manufactured in the USA, not many are made. These were bought on the internet, paid for by credit card. Definitely Radcliffe's knife, modified by him, sharpened. But no fingerprints on it.'

'So this is what happened. Rad and George would rather deal with Taylor direct before he informs anyone else, so they try to buy him off, hence the money in the safe.'

'We found that,' Arnison adds, 'in Radcliffe's room.'

'Let's assume Taylor wants more. He asks for it, Rad and George don't want to pay it. They see the way Anna reacts to him, they decide to act. They lure him into the van, perhaps just to scare him, who knows. Rad gives Taylor a hand job or a blow job, it doesn't really matter, he uses a condom. Perhaps the knife is part of the games Rad plays while he's having sex, perhaps Taylor likes it. We can probably only imagine what happened; a threat, an accident, a deliberate killing, it doesn't matter. The result is that Taylor was killed.'

'I can agree that what you're saying so far is a possibility. Go on.'

'I'm not sure about this next bit. Somehow, in the early hours of the morning, Rad and George deposit Taylor's body on the stage. George takes the van to Belle's house, presumably he's got the keys from Rad ...'

Arnison nods, adds some information of his own. 'Belle's been taking sleeping pills, the stress of directing the play was telling on her. There was no chance of her waking up.'

I'm keen to continue. 'So George drives the van to Belle's house, cleans it up, deposits the mattress in the lock-up. That takes him quite a time. While he's doing that Rad's back at the university. Now, I'm not sure where he got the idea of blaming Anna, but he does all the swapping of body fluids, then he goes further. He gets the blue wigs from somewhere, I'm not sure where.'

Arnison's working with me now. 'I think Radcliffe already had them. There are traces of Taylor's blood on them, I suspect he was wearing them in the back of the van. Taylor's sexual preferences were definitely unusual, he may even have provided Radcliffe with the wigs. Please go on.'

'They're probably too good a prop for him not to use. He puts them on, then makes a noise in the corridor, he wants to make sure he's seen going into Taylor's room. And then he goes back to wherever he spent the night.'

'He spent the rest of the night at Belle's house. She told us that when she woke up in the morning he was there on the floor. Apparently he was welcome to do that, his own flat is quite a distance out of town.'

Between us we're a good act, though I have a feeling Arnison already knows what I'm going to say. He's providing back-up to my ideas, but he isn't offering that information until it's justified by my suggestions. 'It's beginning to make sense, then.'

'It might be.'

'What do you know about George's background?'

Arnison consults some paperwork on the desk in front of him. 'He said he was a close friend of Anna Peranski. Her statement confirms that.'

It's my turn to help Arnison. 'He was besotted with her. Knew her at school, was her lover for a while, followed her to university. I think it was Rad's idea, trying to incriminate Anna. I think George really did want to help her when he came to see me.'

'Or it could be that he wanted to find out exactly what you knew. Or what we knew, since at that stage they were the same thing.'

323

'It doesn't matter.' I pick up the thread. 'He found out that the evidence suggesting Anna was the murderer wouldn't stick and that you'd have to start the investigation again. So he and Rad had to find someone else to take the blame. And Belle was the obvious person.'

Arnison leans back in his seat. 'Unfortunately, you were involved by then.'

'Would they have got away with it if I hadn't been?'

Arnison considers his response. 'If the amount of money they were earning from their website was so great, then I suppose it's quite possible that they could have left the evidence and then fled the country. By the time we sifted everything – and I'm sure we would have found out in the end that Belle was innocent – they would have been away. It's difficult to trace people, particularly young people, in some parts of the world. But you're off the track, you're trying to convince me of George Prentice's deep involvement in the case. Continue.'

'Things begin to go wrong. Rad escapes from Belle's house and heads for the university. I knew that was stupid, like deliberately running into a cul-de-sac. I couldn't figure out why he would do that. I think he was relying on George to get him out of the mess he was in, I think he went straight to George's room and woke him up. By that time George would already have moved the money, bought the airline ticket. So what does he do?'

'You tell me, Mr Oliphant.'

'He tells Rad to go into the cloisters, thinking that I'll follow, then they'll be able to gang up on me. I don't know his exact instructions, probably something about leading me onto the roof and the walls so I'd make an easy target.'

'That isn't what happened.'

'That's what George *said* would happen. What actually happened was what George planned. It was an ideal way of getting rid of his partner who had become a liability.'

Arnison's elbows are resting on the table, he's looking straight at me. 'My officer's statement says Rad's death was an accident. The video your daughter's boyfriend provided ...'

'Tom.'

'Yes, quite, that's in close up, but it still looks like an accident.'

'But what does it sound like?'

'I beg your pardon.'

'Have you listened to the sound?'

'Should I?'

'I think we both should. Just in case there's something important there.'

Arnison waves his hand at his remaining lackey. Tom's videotape is already loaded into his machine, it's connected to a monitor, and the officer switches it on. Arnison and I cluster round the screen.

'Turn the sound right up,' I tell the officer, 'the camera had an unidirectional microphone fitted to it, it might have picked something up.'

The screen shows a figure, me, clumsily edging along the roof of the cloisters. As the camera closes in, as I grow larger, the laboured sound of my breathing becomes apparent. Tom pans across to focus on Rad and the sound becomes that of foot scraping on stone; he pulls back and I can see George above Rad, I can hear the mutter of voices, a sharp intake of breath from someone watching. There's a sudden jerk of movement and the camera turns its uneven attention to me where I've slipped. I can hear Kirsty's voice. 'Is he all right?' she asks. Someone else says, 'Yes, but look over there!' The camera moves back to concentrate on Rad and George. George takes Rad's left hand in both his, holds on to him. There's a murmur of something but I can't tell what it is. Rad takes a knife from his pocket. Then he drops it, clutches at George, and falls.

'Rewind,' I instruct the officer controlling the machine, 'to the point where he reaches up, then play it again, louder. It's the sound I'm interested in.'

'It's already at maximum volume,' the officer says. I

325

ignore him, close my eyes as the scene rolls again, but my ears still can't resolve the sound into meaning.

'Shit!' I storm out of the interview room and through a door into the reception area. 'Tom,' I shout, 'get yourself in here. We need someone who knows how to work this bloody machine.'

Tom moves quickly, within a minute he's at the controls, headphones jammed on his head, explaining what he's doing. 'First we isolate the sound track, in case there's any interference. Then we slow it down, like this.' He plays back the portion of tape, it's a slow, meaningless rumble. 'It's easier to filter it when it plays slowly,' Tom explains. 'The software automatically takes out the background noise and anything that doesn't belong there, anything that isn't human voice. Then we play back at normal speed but boost the signal at its highest amplitude, the lower notes don't really matter.' He's playing with his toy, he knows exactly what he's doing, and Arnison looks on with balanced neutrality. Only if this works, will he show his approval.

'The sound's digital,' Tom explains, 'so I can amplify it artificially by playing with the wave-form rather than simply turning the volume up.' He adjusts some dials and sliders, the screen in front of us becomes a flickering cardiograph of green light. 'That should do it,' he says. His unfocused eyes show he's listening to the result. 'Wow. I think you ought to hear this.' He curls the earphones round his neck and flicks a switch; the speakers hiss into life.

'Here, take my hand,' George's voice says. Then there's a grunt. 'Got you. I'll hold onto you with my other hand as well. Get your knife out.' There's a slight pause. 'Let him have it!'

That's the phrase I can remember, those are the words emblazoned in my subconscious, words every policeman recognises. But there's more, one more sentence. It's George's voice again. 'Sorry, Rad. You've become a liability.'

'Fuck,' Arnison says. 'Can you play that in time with the images?'

Tom nods, presses some buttons. We watch and listen as George looks down on Rad. 'Here,' he says, 'take my hand.' Rad holds out his left hand, George grabs it, holds it firmly. 'Got you,' he says. 'I'll hold onto you with my other hand as well.' He reaches down with his left hand to hold Rad's arm even more tightly. 'Get your knife out. Let him have it!'

Rad reaches into his pocket with his right hand to produce his knife. He raises it to throw at me. But George speaks again. 'Sorry, Rad. You've become a liability.'

The words explain the look on Rad's face. He drops his knife, looks up at George. His right hand clutches for George's, but George has already let go. Rad falls.

'My God,' Arnison says, and his words are almost prayer-like. Tom switches off his machine. None of us dares break the silence until Arnison speaks again. 'I think it's up to me now,' he says, leads us out of the room. 'I may need you to play that again in front of Mr Prentice,' he says to Tom. 'Better still, you can show Gerry here how to do it, the less you're directly involved the better. You too, Mr Oliphant.'

We're back in the reception area. I'm surprised to find Anna, blue-haired as ever, looking tired but happy, talking to Belle and Kirsty. As we enter she turns to follow the communal gaze.

'Mr Oliphant!' she cries, runs towards me, throws herself at me. 'Thank you,' she says, 'thank you so much.' Her tears make her mascara run.

'Dad,' Kirsty's jumping up and down beside me, yelling in my ear, stating the obvious, 'Anna's free, Belle's going to play Feste, we can still do the play!'

Arnison holds up his hands. 'Ladies and gentlemen, this soap opera hasn't quite finished yet.' He stands in front of George. I notice that two large policemen have moved to stand behind him. Arnison's voice is weary. 'George

327

Prentice, I'm arresting you on suspicion of murdering James Radcliffe, of conspiring to murder Jonathan Taylor and of conspiring to murder William Oliphant. Anything you say . . .'

His words are lost as George springs to his feet. The two policemen behind him lean on him, not too gently, push him back to his seat. Then they raise him, pull him towards the interview room we've just left.

George can barely move. As he reaches the door, however, he manages to turn his head. 'Fuck the play!' he yells.

Chapter Thirteen

I don't like speaking in public. I know my limitations. Jen normally understands me, sympathises with me when it comes to situations like this. But not this time. She's standing beside me, telling me I can do it, telling me I've practised often enough, that I know what I have to say. I feel sick. I've already been to the toilet four times, and my innards feel as if they've had a prolonged and vigorous colonic irrigation.

'I can't do it,' I tell her.

'Yes you can, if you set your mind to it.'

'No I can't.'

'You can. And anyway, you've no choice now. The house lights are dimming.'

I'm standing by the side of the stage, the stage I helped build. My lights are about to start shining. The volume on the overhead microphones is about to be turned up. I look down, my costume fits perfectly. Hose and doublet, sword tucked neatly into belt, cloak swirling behind me, I have it all. I also have a wig and a false moustache, a hat as well; I look every inch the part.

The lights go up. Angie walks past me playing her violin, she winks, takes up her place on the stage.

'I can't remember what to do,' I hiss at Jen, 'I can't remember what to say.'

'Billy, we've been through it dozens of times. I've told

you, focus on something else. Don't even think of what you're going to do.'

'I can't think of anything else,' I tell her, 'I can't think of anything at all, I can't think where to go or what to do, I can't remember my lines at all. I can't do it!'

Jen smiles at me. She takes my shaking hands in hers. 'I'll give you something else to think about,' she says. 'Billy Oliphant, I love you. And I'm pregnant.'

She kisses me on the nose, turns me round gently (I can't protest) and aims me at the stage. And I find myself walking into the light. Angie sees me coming, she brings her music to a halt. And I begin to speak.

'If music be the food of love, play on.' I pause, look back into the wings where Jen's standing, giving me the thumbs up. 'Give me excess of it, that, surfeiting, the appetite may sicken, and so die.' I turn back to the audience. 'That strain again! It had a dying fall. Oh, it came o'er my ear like the sweet sound that breathes upon a bank of violets, stealing and giving odour.' I'm no actor. I'm no Orsino. But I know a little about love.

Moths hunt the night air, borne on the scent of honeysuckle. I feel calm, content, tranquil. The Lord of Misrule has been banished, order has been returned. Life is beautiful. The girls, especially Jen and Kirsty, are beautiful. Even the orchestra is beautiful.

But I always did prefer *Cabaret* to Shakespeare.

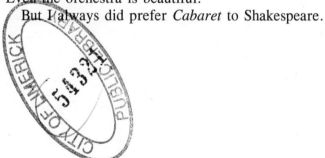